Sweet Caroline

Kelda Laing Poynot

DEDICATION

In loving memory of my parents.

ACKNOWLEDGMENTS

To God be the glory for His infinite wisdom, especially Proverbs.

Always, to my beloved.

Of course, Sarah.

This time, Joey, Madison, and Paige.

Cover art by Chelsea Guidry Poynot

CHAPTER 1

FOR RENT
Furnished Studio
Near campus
All Elec; UTIL Paid
Kitchenette
Laundry Access
$450/mo + $200 dep
Call ###-####

"Hello?" I asked hastily. I was in an awkward position to be answering the phone.

"Hello, I am calling about the room for rent," an accented, male voice said. "Is it still available?"

"Um, yes. Yes, it is." I struggled to hold the phone and the groceries and open the door at the same time.

Our last tenant, Marjorie told us she was planning on relocating, but we never guessed that she'd be arrested and taken away suddenly. Apparently, she and her boyfriend were running from the law. They thought separate addresses would help keep them out of jail, but they tracked his cellphone bill to this address.

"Crap!" I exclaimed when I dropped the phone. "Hang on!" I hollered down toward the phone. I pushed it through the door with my shoe and it slid harder than I expected and hit the pantry door. "Just a second!" I hollered again. I put the groceries on the counter and bent down to pick up the phone. "Hello?" I asked. "Are you still there?"

"Yes. Is this not a good time?" the voice asked politely, almost formally.

"I was just trying to get in the door. My hands were full." I hung the keys on the hook. "Okay, let's try again," I exhaled. "When would you like to come see it?"

"I can come tomorrow morning. I will be there at ten. Is that convenient?"

3

"Sure."

"What is the address?" he asked.

"214 South Elm Street, but don't come down Parkway because there's construction. You'll have to come down Eleventh and then swing around past the fire station."

"Whom should I ask for?"

"Oh, I'm Caroline. I'll be home. Just ring the bell. The apartment is attached to the carport. You'll see it from the road."

"Thank you. I will see you tomorrow."

"Okay, Bye."

I crossed my fingers, hoping this would be a good renter. I needed the money, desperately. Marjorie's arrest had cut her lease short by two months. I put away the groceries and started cooking dinner. Billy would be home tonight and probably starving. I enjoyed our evenings together since we moved Momma to the center, but the house was so quiet when he was at the station. Daddy hadn't been dead quite three years; I still missed him all the time.

Momma was diagnosed with dementia just after he passed. When Billy returned from his most recent deployment, he knew I wasn't equipped to handle her anymore. Hell, I was barely seventeen when Daddy passed suddenly. Momma's condition deteriorated rapidly. I graduated early and started college right away. Thanks to my dual enrollment in high school, I managed to graduate in a little over two years. I was a semester into graduate school at twenty, but even with my job at the center, I barely made ends meet.

"Hey, Little Sis," Billy said as he entered the side door. He kissed my cheek and pulled a piece of meat from the chicken I'd just taken from the oven.

"It's hot," I warned.

"I play with fire every day," Billy joked.

"Wash up; I'm pulling the potatoes out, now."

We sat together at the small kitchen table and Billy bowed his head. I asked God to bless the food. I thanked Him for bringing Billy home safely and asked for Momma to sleep well tonight.

"She's still not sleeping well?" he asked.

"No. The dietician is eliminating her caffeine, but I know she'll find a way to get a Coke. She can't remember her name or either one of us, but she can find a Coke."

"Can't they just give her something to sleep and let her have what she wants?"

I shrugged. I'd been working at The Center for Aging since high school. When Aunt June came to live with us when we were kids, I became fascinated by the elderly: their wrinkled skin and their gray hair, the way their dentures clicked sometimes, and the sparkle of mischief their eyes held, even when they were unable to speak.

My undergraduate studies were in general psychology, but my graduate program specialized in geriatrics. I worked as much as I could at the center, now. It gave me access to Momma's care and it paid better than any other part-time job a college student could find. I'd worked there longer than most of the employees and knew all of the residents. It also helped that I was desperately in need of money to cover my tuition and save for a new car, so I was willing to cover whatever shifts they'd allow.

"Hey, I'm showing the apartment tomorrow."

"What time? I'll be leaving for drill early in the morning."

"Ten. I'm fine. I can handle it."

He frowned slightly. "Who?"

"I didn't catch his name."

"*His* name?" he asked suspiciously.

"I don't think he said, or maybe I missed it. My hands were full when he called. He has an accent. He definitely doesn't sound like he's from around here. He's probably a student."

"Be careful. I don't feel comfortable you showing the apartment alone with a strange man."

"Okay, I will." I smiled reassuringly. "Don't worry. I've managed pretty well without you."

"I know, but that doesn't mean I like it."

We were loading the dishes into the dishwasher when my phone rang. It was the nurse's station. "Caroline, can you come in tonight? We're shorthanded."

"Sure. Give me fifteen minutes. I'll be on my way."

"Do you really have to go in?" Billy asked.

"Yes. Without the rent, I'm short on my tuition, and the final payment is due tomorrow. I hate using my car savings every semester. That piece-of-crap in the driveway isn't going to last much longer and I won't have any transportation."

As it was, it took ten minutes to get my car started. I had to hold the steering wheel just so and pray that whatever connectors held it together would do their magic and start the engine. I sighed in relief when I heard the engine finally turn over.

***

What a night! Momma had been in rare form. She was singing show tunes until after midnight. I couldn't help but sing along. Together with her roommate, the three of us made quite the trio. My replacement was late, so I didn't get in until after three in the morning.

I crashed on the sofa and didn't even bother to change out of my scrubs. The doorbell rang. I rolled over into the back of the sofa. The doorbell rang, again. Then the knocking started, insistent and commanding.

I tried to ignore it, but it was no use. I stumbled toward the door. The light was bright coming around the curtains. I opened the door and squinched up my face in the light.

"Hello, my name is Hashim Emir. I am here to see the apartment. I called yesterday." His tone was courteous, yet to the point and a bit impatient.

I rubbed my eyes, sleepily and recalled our previous discussion. "Oh shit, yes! Sorry, I worked an extra shift yesterday. I'm sorry. I overslept."

"No apology is necessary. Is this a bad time? I can come back later."

"No, it's fine. Give me a second, I'll grab the key." On the way into the kitchen, I caught my appearance in the hallway mirror. I even frightened myself. I went to the bathroom and looked full at my reflection. I grabbed a clip and put my hair up in a twist. I brushed my teeth quickly and covered my lips with a swipe of gloss. I took a deep breath and walked out onto the driveway in my sock feet. The sun was extremely bright as I left the dimly lit house. I blinked back the sun and shielded my eyes with the back of my hand. "I'm sorry, again. Hi, I'm Caroline Sweet. It's very nice to meet you." I put out my hand to shake his.

He moved in front of me, blocking the sun when he took my hand. At that moment I saw him, I really saw him. God! He was absolutely beautiful. He was possibly the most beautiful man I'd ever seen. His rich caramel features were smooth and refined. His dark hair was neatly trimmed and parted to one side. His beard was also trimmed neatly and defined his chin and jawline flawlessly.

I blinked and shook my head. I must still be dreaming. God! He was beautiful. Wait, I needed to move past that thought. His dark eyes were piercing. They were a rich, chocolate brown, like in a milk chocolate commercial when the melted chocolate is poured over something delicious and you're left craving and salivating. I swallowed. I'd lost my voice.

"Are you alright?" he asked and released my hand. His beautiful eyes looked concerned through his long, dark lashes.

I shook my head and tried not to be distracted by this man who was standing in front of me. I cleared my throat. "Yes, I'm fine. Here, let me show you the apartment." I fumbled with the keys in my hand and turned toward the apartment's separate entrance. I unlocked the door and stepped aside. Billy's words to be cautious came to mind. "The light switch is on the wall to your left."

He turned on the light and looked around at the room. It was an open space that had been the original garage. Daddy and his buddies had enclosed it before Aunt June came to live with us, but he had intended it to hold his pool table. He added the kitchenette and bathroom later. The cabinets and closet were built-in. He was a quality craftsman and had painstakingly paid attention to the details.

There was a sink and a small fridge along the wall. On the counter was a small convection oven and a two-burner cooktop with an above microwave. At the far-end of the room was a queen-size bed and a nightstand with a lamp. Aunt June's old loveseat and Lazyboy recliner were placed across an area rug from one another. There was also a drop-leaf table with two chairs on the opposite wall near the kitchenette.

He walked into the small three-quarter bath and then walked out just as quickly. I leaned against the doorframe, exhausted. I desperately needed a cup of coffee and my stomach growled. He pressed on the mattress and then sat down. He nodded approvingly.

I couldn't remember his name. Really? I felt so stupid. I felt the need to fill the silence. "We have Wi-Fi and the laundry room is under the carport. You can pick a day and we'll work around it. How long a lease are you looking for?"

"I am here for the semester. Beyond that, I cannot be sure. I am prepared to pay for three months plus the deposit. I will know my plans at the beginning of December and then I will pay you for another month or more."

He looked up, then, and his lips went up on the edge like he was trying to mask a grin. I followed his gaze up toward the ceiling. I exhaled. *The lamp.* Daddy's lamp that we couldn't find it in our hearts to replace. As soon as possible, Daddy had hung this god-awful fixture. It was red, white, and blue stained glass with a huge Budweiser logo on either side of it. Aunt June thought it matched her loveseat perfectly and had insisted it stay. Momma couldn't argue with her logic, so it stayed. Honestly, now that I'd thought about it, Aunt June probably thought she was living in a saloon.

"Very patriotic," he said wryly.

"Would you mind repeating your name? I didn't quite catch it the first time."

He stood and walked toward me. He put out his hand again as though we'd never met. "I am Hashim Rana Emir." *Hashim. Hashim. Hashim.* I repeated in my mind. "You are Caroline Sweet." I liked the way he said my name and it made me smile and feel a little tingly inside, or maybe that was hunger. My stomach growled again.

"So, are you interested?" I asked and stepped back to shut and lock the door behind him.

"Yes, I am interested. When may I move in?"

"Immediately. As you can tell, it's vacant."

"I will take it. I can move in today?"

"Sure. Would you like a cup of coffee? I have the paperwork inside."

"Yes, thank you."

I led him through the carport door into the kitchen. I went directly to the coffee pot and focused on the task at hand. The sound of the water swishing around in the glass carafe as I rinsed it and the aroma of the ground beans when I opened the coffee bag were settling and familiar. This was the way a body should wake up. I pushed the button on the coffee maker and heard the familiar click as it began to perform its magic on the beans. I closed my eyes and inhaled.

I turned to face Hashim. He stood silently at the door watching me. I felt warmth in my cheeks as he looked at me, but his face was impassive. *Shit!* I just let a complete stranger into our home. Billy wouldn't approve, but I didn't sense any threat from Hashim. Billy would argue that that's when you are the most vulnerable, when you don't sense any threat at all. I ignored his warning.

Remembering my manners, I said, "Please come in. Have a seat and wait here. I'll get the paperwork."

When I returned, he was seated exactly where I'd instructed him to sit at the counter. He looked incredibly out of place on the kitchen bar stool. He was wearing khakis and a white button-down. I could tell it was fresh from the cleaners by the crisp lines pressed into the sleeves. I suspected that he wouldn't need a laundry day. He sat perfectly still with his hands clasped together on the counter in front of him.

"Are you a student?" I asked. He looked about the right age, early to mid-twenties.

"I will be attending courses at the university this semester. I also work, but mostly from the apartment."

"What kind of work do you do?" I asked curious.

"I work with different agencies, computers and technology. I run programs."

"Sounds interesting." I walked toward the cabinet and pulled out a couple of mugs. I then grabbed some spoons from the drawer and the sugar. "Milk or half-and-half?" I asked.

"Half-and-half."

"Anything else? I don't have sweetener."

"Do you have cinnamon?" he asked.

"Sure," I said, taken by surprise.

I poured him a cup and watched as he delicately stirred the sprinkles of cinnamon into his coffee. I hastily put a heaping spoonful of sugar in my mug and poured the hot coffee over it. He added the sugar precisely and finally poured in a bit of cream. The color of his coffee was nearly the same color as his hands. The smell of warm cinnamon was a nice addition to my little kitchen.

I leaned against the counter and took in a long sip, savoring the warmth and caffeine as it radiated through my entire body. I could feel my brain finally awaken. My stomach growled again. He looked at me and tilted his head. I smiled a bit embarrassed.

"Are you in a big hurry? Do you mind if I make some breakfast? I'm starving."

"Go ahead. I am not in a hurry now that I know I have a place to live."

"Are you hungry? I'm going to scramble some eggs."

"I could eat. Let me step out while I make a phone call. I will return in a moment."

I punched down some bread in the toaster and scrambled enough eggs for two. I was plating them up when Hashim knocked on the carport door. "Come in," I said.

He entered and followed me to the kitchen table. We sat and he hesitated, almost expectant. I bowed my head and returned thanks, silently, thanking God for a tenant.

When I looked up, he was watching me. "You pray?" he asked.

"Yes."

"To God?"

"Yes." I felt a little self-conscious.

"The God of Abraham?"

"Yes. I'm not aware of any others," I said a bit sarcastically. He grinned, but I'd yet to see his teeth when he smiled.

I noticed he didn't touch his fork until I took mine and lifted it with my first bite. "Where are you from?"

"D.C.," he said plainly.

I chuckled. "I mean, originally, not where you lived last."

He nodded once. "I was born in Pakistan, but I have not lived there since I was five. It's not my home, just my birthplace."

I felt considerably more human now that I'd had breakfast. "Here's the paperwork. It's a standard lease, from what I understand. You can read over it while I wash the dishes. Here's a pen. Just fill out the information in the blanks."

He sat quietly reading over the two-page document. It felt and sounded so Great Depression to have a boarder, but I supposed that's what you called it when your parents both die and leave their children to fend for themselves. Okay, Momma wasn't technically dead but she surely wasn't among the living as we watched dementia slowly eat away at her brain. Hashim signed the contract and pulled out $1600 from his wallet.

"Thank you," I said sincerely, "but I don't any have change."

"Consider it payment for breakfast and for your hospitality." He bowed his head slightly. "Besides, you need shoes." He gestured toward my feet and smiled, a real smile, the kind that goes all the way into a person's eyes. He shook my hand again. "I look forward to being neighbors."

"Let me know if you need anything. I'll be home until four." I handed him the keys to the apartment and the laundry room and watched as he walked toward his car that was parked on the other side of mine. I shut the door and hugged the wad of cash close to my chest. "Thank you, God!" I exclaimed. Prayers answered.

CHAPTER 2

I took a shower and went back to bed. When I woke again, I felt normal. I made myself a sandwich and checked my phone. I texted my friend, Krissa. She and I would be in two geropsychology classes together this semester.

Rented apartment

Cool. A Hottie?

Yes

My type?

No

Why not?

He's employed

LOL

I didn't see or hear from Hashim for the rest of the day. I dressed for work and headed out. Billy wouldn't be back from drill until Sunday night. Before I got into my car, I noticed Hashim's car for the first time. It was a Subaru BRZ. I sighed as my hand stroked along the edge of the beautiful vehicle. Longing and lust filled me.

I cupped my hands and peered into the tinted glass window. Leather interior. Six-speed manual. I sighed again. Why did he have to drive one of my top five cars? Why did *this* car have to be parked in my driveway? I could imagine the purr of the engine as it started without hesitation. Hashim was a beautiful man with a beautiful car. Weakness!

I turned back to my piece of crap, but thankfully, I had a piece of crap to drive. I slid into the faded cloth interior and checked my mirrors. I turned the key. Nothing. "I'm sorry for calling you a piece of crap." Second try, grinding gears and struggling engine noises. "Please start. I don't want to be late," I said aloud to the car. Same as before. "I promise I'll put you out of your misery as soon as I can afford it. I'll have you hauled to a nice junk yard and nice people will let you rust in the sun." Pulling on the steering wheel, futile efforts. Hashim opened the apartment door and looked curiously at me. He took a step toward the car.

My face flushed from embarrassment. "Please!" I exclaimed, begging my car to start. Finally, the engine turned over and the car came to life. "Thank you," I sighed in relief. I looked up at Hashim and grinned sheepishly and gave a thumbs-up. I put the car in gear and pulled out of the driveway, completely mortified.

***

My shift wasn't particularly interesting. Friday nights were easy with movies in the lobby. It always reminded me of a wheel-chair, drive-in theater. We popped popcorn and once we even wore roller skates like car hops. The residents liked movie night and for the most part, so did I. I sat between Momma and her roommate. We always liked movies; so Friday nights when she was managed, we sat together and watched movies.

I took care to check on everyone on my wing. All was settled and easy which gave my mind time to wander. When Billy returned from his last deployment, we decided to pay down the mortgage with Daddy's life insurance. We transferred the house into my name and signed about a million papers to have Momma removed from all responsibility. Thankfully she was compliant and understanding as she signed over her entire life to her children.

Billy agreed to let me have whatever we made from the apartment to help with school. He paid the mortgage and utilities. He was in better shape financially on paper, but he had child support to pay for Zinnia. He and her mom, Jen, had been high school sweethearts. He left for boot camp. He came back for ten days before he went to tech school. He came back again for three days before his unit was deployed the first time. Jen didn't know she was pregnant until he'd been gone a couple of months.

They'd broken up and she'd begun dating someone else. It was a mess. I remember leaving middle school and going to the hospital and seeing Zinnia for the first time. I held her and nuzzled her. She was so tiny and precious. Momma and Daddy loved that little girl so much. Now, we only got her one weekend a month, but Billy spent afternoons with her when he wasn't at the station.

I later learned that it was too late for Billy and Jen. Jen married about six months after Zinnia was born. Billy was thankful for Zin's step-dad. He couldn't provide that kind of stability for his daughter with his work and drill. He was content to be on the periphery of her life and love her as much as he could when he had her.

I thought about classes starting this week. I considered adding a third class for the semester. Would that be too much? I surely had the cash, now. Thinking about the cash made me think about Hashim. Thinking about Hashim was pleasant but felt dangerous.

I'd never had a serious boyfriend. I had plenty of friends who were guys, but I never felt any attachment. I was focused on school and taking care of Momma. There wasn't much time to think about the opposite sex. That's a lie. There was plenty of time to *think* about the opposite sex, but not any time to act upon those thoughts.

I went out with one of Billy's buddies for a while. Cooper was also a firefighter and in the reserves with Billy. He was nice enough and seemed genuinely interested, but I wasn't prepared for his sexual advances and became exhausted at having to fight them back every time we were alone. He wasn't very interested in conversation or getting to know one another. I liked his attention, but I never felt like he saw me or had any desire to get to know me.

I went by Momma's room again before I clocked out. She was sleeping peacefully. I kissed her head and tucked her in. God, I missed her so much sometimes. She gave a little hum in her sleep. When she did that I imagined she was singing my song and it made me smile.

I pulled into the driveway just after midnight and sighed again, looking longingly at the BRZ. *One day*, I thought, *one day*. Saturday mornings were reserved for chores. I started laundry and swept under the carport before it got too hot. I weeded the flower bed and washed my car.

CHAPTER 2.5

A generous person will prosper;

whoever refreshes others will be refreshed.

– Proverbs 11:25

I had looked at three apartments already: too crowded, too noisy, too many undergrads, thin walls, and cheap furnishings. I hoped my appointment at ten would be more promising.

I drove into the older neighborhood. It was quiet and well-established. Large trees grew in the small yards, offering shade and peaceful surroundings. The lawns were tended and many of the homes had flower beds and vegetable gardens, a good sign.

I parked in the driveway next to an older Mercury. It had to be twenty years old. The sun was shining brightly as I approached the door. I rang the bell. No answer. I rang it again, but then considered that it may not be working. I checked my watch and knocked on the door, more loudly and insistently than was necessary.

A young brunette answered the door. I examined her closely. I had awakened her; she was wearing scrubs and polka-dotted socks and her facial features were indiscernible as she avoided the glare of the sun. She apologized too much for my liking but seemed kind-hearted and extremely southern.

Once she had given me the address, I reverse-searched the property and found that it was in the name of Caroline Sweet. I continued my search and found pictures of her with friends. She was twenty years old, a graduate of the university, pictured also on the staff page at The Center for Aging's website, and named in her father's obituary.

Her brother, William Sweet, Jr., also resided at this address. He was obviously military and was pictured only a few times on social media with a female child and his truck. I wasn't threatened by potential military paranoia, but I was concerned there may be undue prejudice. He may be unnecessarily observant as well. I would have to be careful.

The room was clean and well-ordered. The table would do for a desk. I could manage there well-enough this semester and it was most convenient to the university. Caroline was distracted by my presence. She seemed disorganized and embarrassed that I had awakened her. She was attracted to me, but I could not help that. Women were attracted to me; they always had been. My mother's Turkish beauty and my father's height and jawline had created me. By conventional standards, I was far above average in both looks and intelligence. I was accustomed to the response I received from American women. They masked nothing. Middle-Eastern women were better at disguising their attraction. It made the pursuit of them more interesting.

She had allowed me to follow her into her home without any hesitation. I agreed to the cup of coffee she offered because it was the polite thing to do. I stood at the door waiting. She was either terribly naïve or stupid. Could she be that trusting of a complete stranger? I had heard her stomach growl. She was obviously hungry, too.

Where was her brother? Why wasn't he seeing to his sister? Why was she so exhausted and ill-kempt? In her father's absence, her brother should be the one making the arrangements for another person living so near their home. A sense of protection flooded me. I scoffed at the feeling. I prided myself on modern and independent thinking, but I still reverted to the archaic social norms I had fought so hard to overcome.

Besides, she was small and wide-eyed and trusting. I reasoned that she may need protecting. Her hands were neither soft nor delicate; they were accustomed to work. She was not a beauty, either. She was plain and simple, but her smile was friendly and she had a gentleness about her. She made me feel perfectly at ease.

No one had cooked for me like this since I left my parents' house for good at sixteen, and even then, we had servants. Eggs and toast were so homey and normal. Normal felt good. I looked around at her kitchen and the outdated appliances, nothing modern, nothing of any consequence, and yet she was perfectly at ease.

It was proper to wait for the hostess to lift her fork first, before partaking of the meal. She hesitated and prayed, though. I should not have been surprised; she met the demographic. She made no sign of the cross before she bowed her head, so protestant for sure.

She seemed relieved to accept the rent money. I could have easily given her double what she asked, but she would not have understood that. Money accumulated and multiplied in banks all over the world. I supposed that, for one who had it, it was of little consequence in contrast to those who had meager means. It would mean the world to her.

I removed the two duffel bags from the trunk of my car. I spent an hour unpacking and organizing my belongings. I went to the grocery store and purchased a few items and then went for a run. The hot southern sun felt good and it gave me an excuse to see the neighborhood from a different perspective.

As I was getting out of the shower, I heard the struggle of an engine in the carport. Caroline's car was not only old, it had serious maintenance issues. Again, where was her brother and why did he not see to his sister's need for reliable transportation? I couldn't take the grating engine noises. I had to see if there was something I could do to be of assistance.

She smiled and gave the thumbs-up, as though it was the most natural thing for cars to start in such a manner. I shook my head and returned to my work. I planned to work until midnight at least.

Just after midnight, I powered down my laptop and stretched. The bed looked very inviting. It was then that I heard the loud engine pull into the driveway. She obviously needed a new muffler, the belts needed to be replaced, and she possibly had some steering connection issues. I had also considered replacing the starter or battery. There had to be corrosion. Why was I even thinking about fixing her car?

CHAPTER 3

Music played loudly on the small speaker in the kitchen. I chopped vegetables and allowed the chicken to come to a boil in the pot. It was really too hot to make soup, but I didn't care. It was what I was craving and I wouldn't be satisfied with anything else. Besides, it would be good for a few days and give me a jump-start on meals when I returned to class Monday night.

Krissa was at work. She couldn't come over. I had a huge pot of soup and the aromas wafted throughout the house. I'm sure Hashim could smell it through the walls. I decided to knock on his door and offer him some. It was the neighborly thing to do.

He answered his door wearing a blue, V-neck t-shirt and khaki shorts. Dark wisps of hair poked out from the top of the shirt. I shouldn't have been surprised to know he had chest hair, but it only added to his beauty. He looked down at me and smiled. Even in casual clothes, he looked like something out of a magazine.

"Yes?" he asked.

I took a deep breath and mustered up the courage to speak directly to him. "Hey, I made a pot of soup and I know you're just getting settled, so would you like to join me for supper? I made plenty and really hate to eat alone." He looked at me, but I couldn't read his thoughts. I wondered if I'd interrupted him or offended him in some way. I smiled, awkwardly, waiting on his reply. "It'll be ready in a couple of hours. Just knock if you want to come over. I need to take a shower and finish cleaning the bathrooms. It'll be ready by six." I stepped back, trying to escape the intensity of his stare.

He cleared his throat before he spoke. "Thank you. I appreciate the invitation."

I thought for sure he was going to add a *but* at the end of his statement, but he didn't. He just smiled and asked if he could bring anything. I shook my head. "Just yourself."

He knocked on the kitchen door precisely at six p.m. I opened the door and invited him in. He was wearing a starched shirt, again, but this time his sleeves were rolled up to his forearms. The dark hair on his arms looked smooth and masculine on his warm-colored skin, contrasting perfectly with the crisp, white shirt.

"Come in; it's nearly ready."

"Are you baking bread?" he asked.

"Yes. I was just taking it out of the oven. I know it's not really soup weather, but I turned down the a/c so it feels colder than it really is." I laughed at myself. He chuckled low. I hadn't heard him laugh. It was nice. "Take a seat; make yourself comfortable."

He did as he was instructed, but still looked formal and ill-at-ease at the small kitchen table. I could feel his eyes on me as I pulled the fresh-baked loaf from the oven. I nearly burned myself in my impatience to slice it, so I just pulled at the ends of the loaf and managed to peel apart pieces that were jagged but edible and placed them in a towel-lined basket.

I ladled the soup into bowls and walked toward the table. He stood and took one of the bowls from my hand and waited until I was seated before he sat. He waited politely before he picked up his spoon. I offered him a paper towel from the roll and he placed it neatly in his lap. I looked at him and smiled.

"Aren't you going to try it?" I asked.

"I expected you to pray," he said.

"Do you pray?" I asked.

He shook his head. "No."

"Not even to Allah?" I asked.

He bowed his head and laughed over his bowl of soup. I couldn't help but laugh with him. It was genuine and hearty. When he lifted his eyes back to mine, they were bright and amused. "I am not Muslim," he confessed.

"I'm sorry, I shouldn't have profiled you like that."

"It is easy to assume, given my ethnicity, but I declare myself to no god, and if I did, it would not be for Allah."

"Do you mind if I pray aloud? I don't want to offend anyone."

"Caroline, this is your home. If you cannot pray aloud in your own home, then offending me is the least of your concerns." I liked the way he said my name and I liked the way he'd validated me in one statement.

I smiled and bowed my head and thanked God for the food before us and Billy at drill and Momma to sleep well again tonight.

He lifted the spoon to his mouth and blew the liquid before he took a sip of the hot broth. "This is good," he said, changing the subject. "Who taught you to cook?

"My mom and Aunt June."

"Your mother's sister?"

"No," I laughed, "Aunt June was my grandmother. Her name was actually Glenda, but she insisted we call her Aunt June. She was crazy. Not like Momma crazy with dementia, just crazy, you know?" I shrugged.

"No, I cannot say that I do." He lifted the bowl of soup to his mouth and took another sip of the broth. He then proceeded to eat the meat and vegetables from the bowl with his spoon.

I watched his hands, his mouth, his lips. He even ate with confidence and refinement. He licked his bottom lip before a drop could roll onto his beard. My heartbeat quickened and warmth radiated from my chest. I took in a short breath, drawing me back to reality. *Holy moly, give me strength. For Christ's sake, the man is just eating soup. Get a grip, C.* Blink, blink, breathe in, exhale. I distracted myself with a piece of bread and pinched at the crust before I dipped it into the broth. My hand was shaking. I shook my head and tried to think of some other topic of conversation.

"So, what do you do? Other than the classes you're taking at the university."

"I will not divulge secrets, even for a soup as good as yours," he said with a playful smile.

Blush. *Focus on your soup, C. Be cool. He knows you're watching him. He's just playing with you.* "A man named Esau sold his birthright for a bowl of soup. It's possible." I was pleased I hadn't completely lost my ability to reason in his presence.

"I know Esau. He was a weak man. Impatient. I am neither." He set his spoon down gently next to his bowl and tilted the bowl back against his lips. He drained the bowl without even slurping and rested it back onto the table.

"Would you like some more?" I offered.

"I can get it, myself." He returned to the table and I asked him how long he'd been in D.C. before he arrived here. "I lived in D.C. for two years."

"What's it like there?"

"Crowded. Fast-paced and lively. I like Virginia, better."

"Sounds nice."

"May I ask you a few questions?" His eyes were sincere again.

"Sure."

"Do you live here, alone?"

"Oh, I forgot to tell you. My brother, Billy, lives here too. He's at drill this weekend. He'll be back tomorrow night. He's a firefighter at the station around the corner. You probably won't meet him until Monday at the earliest. He gets in pretty late on Sunday."

I thought for a moment that I should have said he would come home tonight, rather than tomorrow. I didn't like to lie, but for safety, perhaps it was okay to lie.

"What is wrong with your car?"

"About a hundred different things." I sighed. "It's old and needs repairs I can't afford, so I'm making due. Sorry about the ruckus earlier. I forget that those sounds aren't normal. My car and I have lost our love. He knows I lust after others. He was expressing his jealousy for me admiring your car."

"If he has no love for you, why is he jealous?" he asked, playing along with my reasoning.

I laughed. "I have no idea, but he knows I'm saving every penny I have to replace him. I promise him that he'll have a happy retirement, rusting in the sun."

"Did you make this bread?" he asked after he pulled a piece from what little remained of the loaf?

I nodded, proudly. "It's sort of a hobby. When Momma was diagnosed with dementia, I was stuck at home a lot with her. Before that, I sat with Aunt June every afternoon after school. There wasn't much else to do, so I took to baking. Do you like bread?"

"Who does not like bread?" He gathered his spoon and napkin and stood and then stacked my bowl and spoon on top of his.

"I can get that," I said.

"No, I can clean up after myself." He walked past me and washed the bowls in the sink and set the dishes and spoons in the dish drainer. I leaned against the counter, watching his hands move the soap around the bowls. When he was finished, he dried his hands on the dishcloth next to the sink. He turned to me and looked into my eyes.

"Thank you for the soup. It was delicious."

"You're welcome. Thanks for eating with me. It gets lonely sometimes, you know?" I was attracted to his dark eyes and stern facade, but his smile was more captivating than any other part of him. "I like your smile and your laugh" I added quickly.

He smiled, acknowledging my compliment. "I like yours, too."

"You seem like a serious guy. What do you do for fun?" I asked.

He shrugged, noncommittally. "What do *you* do for fun?" He returned the question.

"I watch movies, listen to music, go out with my friends, sometimes. I work a lot, so working is fun, too."

"Working is *fun* for me as well. Thank you, again, for the soup. Are you this friendly with all of your tenants?"

"Yes, mostly. What is your class schedule?"

"I will have class three nights a week: Mondays, Tuesdays, and Thursdays."

"Me, too. Well, Tuesdays and Thursdays for sure. I'm still considering adding a third. It's a lot for me to carry a load like that and work full-time. I'll have to cut my hours if I add it. I don't know what I should do. The more hours I take in a semester, the faster I'll be done." I sounded so hopeful when I said it out loud.

"What are you studying?" he asked.

"I'm getting a masters in geropsychology." He smirked and looked down at his watch. We'd been eating and talking for well over an hour. He was probably growing bored with me. "You can go whenever you're ready. You don't have to hang out if you don't want to." He didn't seem like a hangout kind of guy.

"I am fine; I have a phone call at eight o'clock."

"I'm going in for ten tonight, so I hope my leaving doesn't wake you."

"Would it be alright with you, if I took a look at your car tomorrow?"

"You know cars?" I asked skeptically. He definitely didn't look like a car guy, either. Cooper had looked at it a couple of times, but said it was too big of a commitment for him. Had I given in to his advances, perhaps he would have been more willing.

"I am not an expert, but I am sure I can assess the situation. It is the least I can do, and honestly, I cannot tolerate the noise. Consider it payment for another meal."

"Thanks, really, that's thoughtful. I'll probably be up by noon."

"Why not leave the keys in the console, and I will look at it while you sleep."

I blinked slowly, unable to conceal my surprise. No guy, besides my daddy, had ever offered to fix anything for me. Even Billy, as great as he was, rarely ever felt the need to do anything for me. I was typically the giver, so it felt odd to be the receiver.

<u>CHAPTER 3.5</u>

A bowl of vegetables with someone you love
is better than a steak with someone you hate.

– Proverbs 15:17

My phone vibrated in my pocket. I looked down at the number. I had no contacts listed by name in my phone, but I recognized his number. I told him I would be available at eight. It was only seven-fifty-nine. I nodded to Caroline and smiled, gesturing to the phone. She smiled understandingly and I silently excused myself from the kitchen.

I was not looking forward to this call. I stepped outside and directly into my apartment. He began speaking as soon as I answered the phone. "Hey, Emir, it's Marshall. Long time, no see."

"Marshall," I said flatly, acknowledging him by name.

"Where are you?" he asked in a friendly tone.

"Somewhere."

"Come on, man, you know it's only a matter of time before I find you, again. We need you. We want you to come on full-time. We'll make it worth your while. We always do." His tone was persuasive. I reflexively rolled my eyes.

"I have no interest. I have enough to keep me busy for now. Call me again in six months. I may be ready to make a deal by then, or you can just send me a proposal next month and I will see what I can do for you."

"You have serious commitment issues, man. You know you won't beat anything we can offer you."

Freedom, I thought to myself. He definitely could not top that, nor could he ensure it. I was content freelancing; he would have to suck it up to his bosses and make due.

"Just meet me, man. We can talk about it over a steak dinner and a few cold brews. You know if you put me off for too long, I'll have to come looking for you."

"Thank you, Marshall, but I need to focus on my current project. I will get back with you, soon."

"Yeah, well the sooner the better." His tone this time was biting and defensive, all pretense and friendliness dissolved.

I hit the end button and squeezed my phone in my palm, wishing for the briefest of moments that it was Marshall's neck in my hand. How pleasant it would be to crush his windpipe with my bare hands. I wished I was assigned a different handler. It was infuriating that this little man was able to push my buttons so easily.

I took a deep breath and calmed myself, and then a smile spread across my face as my thoughts returned to Caroline and soup and fresh-baked bread and two hours of ease with a relative stranger. My offer to look at her car had taken her completely off guard. The surprise in her eyes, her vulnerability, her appreciation and kindness. I was mistaken of my first assessment of her. She was still plain and unassuming, but I was just beginning to see her true beauty within.

I returned to my work. An hour or so later, I was distracted by the sound of her kitchen door closing, or maybe I felt it. I pulled my headphones from my ears and heard the jingle of her keys as she locked the deadbolt. I cringed when the loud, obnoxious cranking of her engine grated and grated. Once, twice, three times it struggled but failed to start. The fourth time, it did not even grind or crank. I heard a light click with each turn of the key. The starter, it was definitely the starter. I leaned back and rubbed my eyes and stretched. I placed my headphones next to my computer and moved from the make-shift desk toward the door. Just before my hand turned the knob, I heard the light tapping.

CHAPTER 4

"Crap! Crap! Crap!" I exclaimed. Why did this have to happen tonight? Billy and Cooper were both at drill. I looked next door. No lights. I could see the lights were still on in the apartment. Maybe Hashim wasn't asleep. I sighed, defeated, and walked to his door.

I was surprised that he opened it as soon as I knocked. "Oh! Hey, could you give me a jump? It won't start." My voice was breathy and my words came out in a rush. I hated to be an inconvenience.

"A jump may get you there, but what will you do in the morning?"

"I can get one of the maintenance guys to jump it at the end of my shift."

He frowned at that. He put his hand to the back of his neck considering. "May I drive you? I will sleep better knowing you did not break down."

"Okay, sure, but I feel bad asking you to get out this late."

"It is of no consequence." His eyes were so sincere when he spoke that way. His dark lashes framed his eyes when he blinked. "I will get my keys."

I grabbed my purse and waited by his car. He beeped the key fob. I put my hand out to open the door, but his was there before I could get to it. I jumped slightly. I hadn't heard him come up beside me. I looked at him again with surprise and jerked my hand back. I was afraid he didn't want me to touch his car.

He looked at me with the oddest expression, and I giggled. I covered my mouth. Oh, my goodness, he was opening the door for me. Wow! He was actually opening the door for *me*. I stood to the side and then lowered myself into the soft, leather, bucket seat. He shut the door behind me. I closed my eyes as I buckled myself into the dark car and took in the smell and the feel of the leather around me.

This is what a car should feel like, welcoming and ready. My eyes were still closed when Hashim got into the driver's side. I sighed when the engine started smoothly and flawlessly. The purr and the feel of the car's eagerness to respond made my pulse quicken. Hashim was looking at me when I opened my eyes and turned to face him, wondering why he hadn't put the car into gear. I smiled.

"This is nice," I said.

"You like cars?" he asked.

"I like *this* car, especially." I confessed, still smiling. "It's in my top five, for sure." He put the car into reverse and eased down the driveway. He put the car in gear and headed out of the neighborhood. "How fast have you gotten it to?" I asked.

"Speed?" I nodded. "107."

"How did it handle?"

"Felt like I was going seventy-five or eighty. No pull or drag at all."

"What? That's awesome! The next time you feel the need, may I go, too?"

He cut his eyes at me disconcertedly. "I hope you are not with me the next time I drive at that speed. It was not a time I wish to repeat under the same circumstances."

"Okay, so maybe you could find different circumstances, and I could be with you." I probably sounded like a complete whack-job, but maybe, just maybe, he'd be willing to take it out sometime. "It would be so much fun!" I exclaimed. He laughed and shifted gears. I smiled again, enjoying every bit of my ride to work.

"What other cars make your list?" he asked.

"Porsche, Audi, BMW, and I'm a sucker for most any Jaguar, but I can see myself in a BRZ because it's the most affordable."

"That is interesting."

"But I can't afford to be picky. I'd settle for any reasonably priced car that's more dependable than the one I currently possess." I laughed.

We were less than a block away from the center when I realized that I hadn't told him where to go. I felt a little uneasy that he was new to this town and already knew where I worked.

"How did you know where to bring me?"

"Your uniform and your badge."

I put my hand over my chest and looked down. The center's logo was plastered all over me. "How did you know where it was?"

"I noticed it as I drove to the store yesterday."

"Oh," was all I said, but I couldn't help but detect something knowing in his voice.

"What time do you get off?" he asked.

"Six. I'll get one of the nurses to bring me home at the end of my shift."

"There is no need. I will be here."

"You've already done enough, really, it's not a big deal."

"I will be here," he repeated, and I didn't argue.

"Thanks. I'll see you in the morning." I got out and stepped back from the car. I watched it longingly as he pulled out smoothly onto the road. I exhaled. He was a beautiful man with a beautiful car.

"Who's the fancy ride?" I heard Krissa's flirty voice say behind me.

I jumped and turned from my thoughts back to reality. "Billy's at drill so my tenant offered to give me a ride. My car won't start at all." I said dismissing the entire event.

"The hottie?" she asked, leadingly. I scowled. "What? You said he was hot."

"No, I didn't. You did. He seems really nice, okay?" I was surprised at how defensive I sounded. I didn't like the way Krissa objectified him. She didn't even know him.

"Whoa!" She raised her perfectly manicured hands in surrender.

"I didn't know you were working tonight," I said.

"I'm not. I forgot my shoes in my locker. I'm dancing at Pete's tonight."

I rolled my eyes. "I wish you didn't do that. It sounds so low-rent."

"What? Dancing? I'm only working here for my internship. I make four times as much at Pete's. Besides, he put me in charge of scheduling and I gave myself a raise. You should try it, sometime." She stepped away like she was in a hurry to get back to her car. I turned to go into the center. "Hey," she hollered back, "when'll Billy be home?"

"Tomorrow. Late. Don't waste your time." I heard her laugh as she got into her car.

Tonight, I wasn't on Momma's wing, so I had to contend with the older gentlemen. Fortunately, the night shifts were mostly quiet when lights out was at ten. I could read and catch up on homework and still get plenty of sleep before class at six the following night. I wasn't naturally a night-owl, but this schedule had worked pretty well last semester, so I was going to stick to it.

Krissa complained that my work schedule conflicted with a social life. She said that I was missing out on all the fun. Her life didn't look that fun to me, but I wasn't anything like her. She was drop-dead gorgeous. She had big blue eyes and long, blond hair. She was curvy in all the right places. I never saw her without makeup or her hair done. Who knew all those dance lessons and dance team practices would lead her right into an exotic dancing career, well, if one would call pole dancing exotic.

It had been a quiet night. I went by Momma's room on my way out. She was still sleeping. She smiled sweetly when I kissed her on the cheek. I wanted to think that sometimes she still knew me, somehow. From all my studies in geriatrics and dementia, I knew it wasn't likely, but I still hoped that she knew I was looking out for her.

I stepped out of the center at 6:07. Hashim was leaning casually on the side of his car. I smiled when I saw him. He was wearing khaki cargo shorts, an olive-green t-shirt, and river sandals. His hair was wet and combed back like he'd just had a shower. He looked incredibly rugged and masculine. "Are you tired?" he asked as I approached the car.

I shrugged. "Not particularly, why?"

"Want to drive?"

My smile broadened. "Are you serious?" I hesitated; I didn't want to appear too eager. He was actually offering me a chance to drive his car. Even if I had been tired, this opportunity would have awakened me for sure!

"Can you drive a manual?"

"Yeah, I can." He opened the door for me. *What a gentleman.*

I slid into the driver's seat and tried to act cool, like I did this all the time. My excitement won out, though, and I giggled. I adjusted the seat and mirrors. Hashim's legs were much longer than mine. I placed my hand on the gear shift and made sure it was in neutral.

He got into the passenger's seat and closed the door. I was instantly assaulted by his scent. He smelled clean and fresh and nothing like old people. *Oh, my God, why are you doing this to me?* Were his looks not distracting enough? Why couldn't he smell like old fry grease or onions? But heck, he'd probably make those smell good, too.

I started the car and put it in first. I eased off the clutch and got a feel for the gears. I put on my blinker as if to head back to the house. "Go the other way," Hashim instructed. I looked at him, confused. "Do you really want to go the quickest way home?" His eyes were telling.

He pulled out his phone and typed in directions. The automated voice began instructing me toward the outskirts of town. They were building sub-divisions out that direction.

"This is where I learned to drive. Used to be all farmland." I laughed remembering something from high school.

"Why is that funny?"

"It's not. I was just thinking about something else that happened out here." I was able to steadily increase the speed and the car took the curves beautifully. I thrilled at the exhilaration of going over fifty in a future residential area and pushing seventy on the straightaways. Hashim was laughing with me and seemed pleased when I let loose with a few squeals of delight.

I slowed as I approached the end of the vacant land. I hadn't had this feeling in a while, pure joy and adrenaline. "Are you hungry?" Hashim asked.

"I could definitely eat. I've got eggs back at the house."

"May I take you to breakfast?" he asked.

"Sure, but I warn you that I'll crash by nine, so we need to go, now. It's not pretty when I have to be carried from the booth."

"You speak from experience."

"It's not what you're thinking. I wasn't drunk or anything. I'd worked nights for a week and it was finals and it was my last undergrad semester and I was carrying twenty-two hours. Krissa's boyfriend was pissed when he had to carry me to her car."

He checked his phone and keyed in the directions. The voice came through, again. I pulled into the parking lot of one of the nicest breakfast places in town. I looked down at my scrubs and shook my head. "I'm sorry, I'm not going in there."

"Why not?"

"I'm not dressed for it, and they aren't going to let me in." I slipped the car into neutral and crossed my arms.

"Very well, then, where do you recommend we go?"

"The coffee shop around the corner from the house is good. You will not be disappointed, I promise."

The smell of fresh-ground coffee and waffles and cinnamon rolls and hash browns wafted out into the parking lot. I was salivating and my stomach was rumbling louder than normal from the rush of energy I'd exerted during the drive. We were seated immediately. I asked the waitress for two coffees, juice, water, and a shaker of cinnamon. Hashim's mouth went up in a grin.

After the waitress brought our coffee and juice, I thanked Hashim for letting me drive his car. "You drive well. How did you learn to do that?" he asked as he sprinkled cinnamon into his coffee.

"Daddy and Billy mostly, and I was always the designated driver in high school. Guys are stupid when they drink and they'd just give me their keys and let me go wherever I wanted as long as I got them home safely."

"I am curious. What memory amused you there?"

I looked up at the waitress and thanked her for bringing our plates. I caught Hashim's curious eyes and blush rose to my ears. I looked down humbly and closed my eyes. I was actually praying, but it wasn't for blessing over the food, it was for strength and control over my mouth. I hadn't been able to shut up in his presence. He would now know nearly every embarrassing thing about me in the course of one morning.

Lord, give me strength. Amen. I lifted my eyes again to his and he smiled encouragingly. I took a bite of food and lifted my fork to my mouth; he did the same. His omelet looked delicious. I had ordered eggs and bacon and hash browns with a cinnamon roll on the side. I took several bites before I answered him.

"Good, huh?" I asked, thinking that could change the subject.

"Yes. It is delicious, but I am still curious." He waited patiently for me to reply to his question.

"You aren't going to let it rest, are you?" He shook his head and flashed his teeth. *Damn.* "Okay, but you have to swear that you will never mention it again and that you won't judge me based on this one story." More blush on my cheeks.

"Agreed."

"Okay, so I was fifteen and my first boyfriend drove me out there to see the stars. We were studying astronomy that nine weeks and he told me it was the perfect place to do my project. I believed him. The night was clear and the stars were so bright away from the city. He'd brought his dad's truck and put a blanket in the bed so we could lie down and see the stars. It was amazing. Breathtaking. I didn't even mind it when he started kissing my neck. I've always been a pretty serious student, so I didn't think anything about it. I'd never been taught what boys expected in the bed of a truck in the middle of nowhere. We kissed for a while, but I got annoyed when he kept on putting his hands up my shirt and started groping me. I finally drew the line when he started unbuttoning my jeans and said he couldn't stop once he got started. When he rolled on top of me, I knew I needed to get the hell away from him. I kept pushing myself further into the back of the truck." Hashim looked concerned.

"I know that seems counter-intuitive, but I knew if I could get in the cab of the truck, I'd be safe. He'd left the back window open so we could hear the music. The keys were still in the ignition. I knew I could fit through the window. He wouldn't be able to. So, I kicked him away and told him to wait. I wasn't ready and he needed to give me a minute. I crawled in the window and he thought I was going to make myself ready in the backseat of the cab. He gave me this huge, shit-eating grin like he was about to get lucky. He got really pissed though when I locked the doors and started the engine. He was hanging on for dear life when I drove about seventy down that same road. I didn't slow down much when I got into town and was pulled over by a state trooper on the highway. He eyed my soon-to-be-ex-boyfriend in the bed, fuming. 'Would you care to explain why you were going sixty in a forty-five?' 'Yes, officer,' I said. 'I was avoiding a date rape scenario.'" He raised his eyebrow and eyed the boy in the bed of the truck. The officer asked if I were alright and then commented that I was making a serious accusation against this young man. I explained that I was pretty serious when it came to my virginity.

"'We were just kissing, sir. I wasn't going to rape her.' my ex-boyfriend interjected. The officer disregarded him completely. 'Want me to follow you home?' the officer asked. 'Yes, thank you, sir. That would be very nice of you.' He then made the guy get in the patrol car with him and they followed me home. I didn't tell a soul, but the gossip was all over school by Monday. You're the first person I've told in five years. Several people had seen us stopped on the side of the road. I didn't talk to boys again until after I graduated. I got an A on the project, though, so I guess it was worth it in the long run."

Hashim was shaking his head and laughing at the end of my story. I liked watching him laugh. I was full and getting sleepier by the second. "You'd better drive home. I'm having a hard time keeping my eyes open." He motioned for the waitress and looked at the ticket. He reached for his wallet and pulled out cash and left it on the table. He rose and took my hand as he led me through the café tables toward the door. My stomach tightened and I looked down at our hands. *What the hell is that supposed to mean?* He walked me to the passenger's side and opened the door for me. I relaxed instantly in the comfortable bucket seat. The quiet purr of the engine relaxed me even more. Through the dark, tinted windows, I was having a hard time keeping my eyes open in the bright sunlight. I warned him.

"Caroline, you are home." I nodded. "Where are your keys?"

"In my purse," I mumbled. I knew he'd opened my car door and had unbuckled me. I let him guide my body like a zombie toward the door. He found my keys and opened the kitchen door for me.

"Can you manage it from here?" he asked. I nodded again.

"Thank you for breakfast and for letting me drive your car," I mumbled, but I'm not sure what it sounded like to him.

"I enjoyed it, too," he said and shut the door.

CHAPTER 4.5

Wisdom reposes in the heart of the discerning
and even among fools she lets herself be known.

– Proverbs 14:33

Vulnerable and trusting, yet strong and unmoving. *Caroline*. I had awakened before five and ran eight miles through the empty neighborhood in plenty of time to shower before I needed to pick her up from work. *Caroline*. I had known her all of two days and already her name felt pleasant in my mouth and even more pleasant in my mind. It was easy to be with her. I could not remember being this at ease in anyone's home, ever. I was not even that comfortable in my own home. I never remembered meeting someone and instantly forming any sort of attachment. I was too busy for meaningful relationships and too self-absorbed to think about anyone else. I viewed women like I viewed most everything in my life: a necessary component for function, need, or pleasure.

I liked watching her. Her expressions were easy to read, so why was I surprised at the things she said? She liked cars. She liked *this* car. I had bought it the day I left D.C. for good. It drove well and was less presuming than my others. It made me blend in, if that were possible. I wondered what she would think if I flew her to the house and let her drive the ones in the garage. I think she would choose the Porsche for sure. I was being a fool for even thinking such thoughts. I berated myself for the brief thought of seeing her standing among my cars, giddy and delighted and unassuming, her bright eyes open, eager and excited. I shook the thought away and refocused my thoughts. I refused to allow fantasy to enter into the equation of the day.

After hearing her story about her ex-boyfriend, I would be more careful and not assume she needed to be taken care of simply because she was small and meek. I found myself hopeful that she would add the Monday class to her schedule. I could see myself spending three evenings a week with her, studying with her, eating meals with her. I had not yet mentioned what classes I was taking this semester. She had not asked, directly, nor had she offered her information. I shook the hope away. The geropsychology program was a small one. There were only three classes being offered this semester, so I knew we would be in class together. I should have guessed with her job at The Center for Aging that she would be pursuing a career in that area.

When I walked her to the door, I felt certain she could manage herself. I popped the hood to her car and took a look around. The battery connections were corroded; everything was corroded. The belts were obviously worn. I unplugged the battery and took it to the auto parts store. I also detached the starter and alternator to be tested. I would not confess to having any real mechanic's skills, but I spent time enough around engines to know the basics.

Her car was running again before she awakened several hours later. YouTube videos were informative, but I was relieved no one was there watching me. There were tools on the shelf in the laundry room, but I had to buy a wrench. It was nice to use my hands and mind for something other than listening and interpreting. It also gave me an afternoon to allow my ideas to work in the background. Running often afforded me the best thinking time, but everything today had given my mind a much-needed respite from the tedium of my work.

The day was hot and humid. When I was satisfied that I had done everything I could do and her car was starting consistently, I went inside to take another shower. At six, I heard her come to my door.

"Hey," she said sweetly. "I came to get my keys. Did you have any luck with figuring out what was going on?"

Her bright eyes were hopeful and expectant. She looked well-rested, wearing a pair of faded jeans and a fire department t-shirt. Her hair was still damp from the shower. Again, she was barefoot. Why on earth did I find that so amusing?

<u>CHAPTER 5</u>

He looked incredibly confident when he answered his door wearing another pair of khaki shorts and a dark green shirt that brought out his eyes. He was too gorgeous to be living here. Surely, he could afford nicer digs if he didn't spend so much money on his clothes. I was getting used to his looks, but my initial response to him was a pleasant surprise each time.

"Yes. It should not have any trouble starting, but you need to get your belts replaced immediately."

"Really? You got it to start?" I asked excitedly. Hashim returned my smile. "What do I owe you?"

He shrugged and looked like he was totaling up an amount in his mind. I hoped it wasn't more than a couple of hundred bucks at the most. If not, then I definitely couldn't add the Monday class.

"Fifty dollars."

"Really? That's it?" I asked, skeptically.

"Indeed." He smiled reassuringly. "You just needed a starter. The part was not that expensive and I had to buy a wrench."

"Wow! Okay, I thought more was going on than that. Thank you," I said sincerely. When he handed me the keys, he did something with the shape of his mouth. It wasn't quite a smile. There was a tightening just at the edge of his eyes. I tilted my head and really looked at him.

"Hashim, thank you for fixing my car, but I don't feel like you're telling me everything. I can't afford much, but I can afford to pay you back for whatever you spent. Really. Please be honest with me. Did you spend more than that on my car?"

He looked away and then grinned. "Yes, I spent more than fifty dollars on your car, but it is of no consequence and you owe me no more than fifty dollars."

His response was so matter-of-fact that I didn't want to argue with him. "Billy won't be back until late. May I at least offer you some supper? I put a tot casserole in the oven when I woke up. It will be ready in half an hour." He smiled, genuinely this time, and agreed to join me for supper.

I was pulling the casserole from the oven when he knocked. "Come in," I answered with my hands full. I walked the casserole to the table and placed it carefully onto the trivets in the center of the table. I turned and removed the oven mitts. Hashim took the dishes that I'd already taken from the cabinet to the table. I grabbed the silverware and a serving spoon and shut the drawer with my hip.

I poured myself a glass of iced tea. "Would you like a beer?" I asked.

"No, thank you. I will have whatever you are having." He gestured toward my glass of iced tea.

"Since you have no affiliation with God or Allah, is there another reason you don't drink?" I asked coyly, referring back to my earlier profiling.

He laughed. "I *drink* when the occasion warrants, but I have yet to acquire a taste for American beer. The commercials make it look appetizing, but my taste buds do not agree. As far as a religious preference, your god appreciates good wine and its benefits; he may have a better understanding of men's hearts than Allah. Go ahead, if you'd like one."

I laughed. "I hate the stuff. I can't afford anything good, but I've had a few drinks before that I liked. It's Billy's. He and his buddies drink it on their nights off. I'm looking forward to introducing you."

Steam rose from the dish as soon as I inserted the spoon to serve our plates. Ground meat, cream of mushroom soup, tots, and cheese were one of my favorite combinations. It smelled pretty good.

"What is a tot?" Hashim asked looking at his plate.

I laughed. "It's a Tator Tot. It's like a hash brown that's been formed into a little cylinder. They're pretty tasty. Have you ever eaten at Sonic?"

He shook his head. "Cannot say that I have."

"Well, I'll have to take you sometime. Chili cheese tots are one of the best things, ever!"

I handed Hashim a paper towel and then bowed my head and prayed. I don't know if he closed his eyes, but he lowered his gaze to his plate until I said, "Amen."

"Have you decided if you are adding the other class?" he asked before taking the first bite. It was still steaming hot on our forks.

"I think I am." I took a bite of the steaming casserole and sucked in a cool breath.

"What will you be studying this semester?" he asked, taking a bite. I watched for his response. I guessed he'd probably never eaten a casserole by his first examination of the pile of cheesy mush I'd placed before him. He leaned in slightly and sniffed. He didn't seem to be offended by the smell.

"I'll be taking Health Care Economics, Psychology of Aging, and Social/Cultural Aspects of Aging." I said between bites.

"Interesting," he said, but I didn't know if he was referring to the food or my schedule.

"Do you like it?" I asked eagerly.

"Yes, it tastes good, very filling."

"I could take that as a side-ways compliment. It's filling, so I don't need any more because I don't really like it, or oh, my gosh it tastes good and your country carb food will make me fat."

He didn't say anything else and focused on his food. He seemed to like it alright. He liked the soup better, though. Hashim didn't look like a meat and potatoes man. He was definitely a vegetable eater. He couldn't have that body and not eat plenty of vegetables. I should have made a salad or opened a can of green beans.

I caught myself imagining him without a shirt, eating green beans. I reprimanded myself for being such a hypocrite. I'd gotten all defensive with Krissa for objectifying Hashim and there I was doing the same. "What classes are you taking this semester?" I asked changing the subject in my mind. I was also making efforts to allow this stranger to do more of the talking since I monopolized our conversations so far.

"The same as you," he said.

"Yeah, I know you have class the same nights, but what are you taking?"

"The same classes. We will be in the same classes this semester."

I was confused. Didn't he say he did something with technology and computers? "Why are you taking graduate classes in geriatrics?" I asked cautiously. "It doesn't seem related to your current field."

He took a sip of tea before he answered. "I have a broad interest in developmental psychology. It helps me to understand people. I have studied early childhood development, adolescent behaviors, schizophrenia and neuroses, obsessive-compulsive disorders, and now the aging. I am especially looking forward to the social/cultural aspects of aging."

It was the most words he'd spoken in a row since we met. "So, you just travel around taking random classes at random universities?" I asked.

"Random? No, not random. Do you know that you are attending one of the top-rated programs in geriatric psychology in the south?" I nodded. I did know that and felt fortunate that I didn't have to move or accrue student loans in order to pursue my degree. "My training and expertise are in technology, but my interests are varied. Ultimately, the more I know about human behavior and interpersonal relationships the better I am able to perform my job. It also gives my mind new challenges unrelated to my field. It creates balance."

I liked that. I didn't have much balance in my life. It had all been for one purpose since forever. Krissa said I lacked a social life. I disregarded her opinion because I didn't agree with her idea of a social life. I had work and I had school. This weekend, I'd had meals with a handsome, intelligent stranger who also fixed my car. That had surprisingly grounded me more than anything else I'd done in the past few years. Okay, so driving his car was pretty awesome, too.

"Do you work tonight?" Hashim asked.

"No, I have tonight off. I'll have class until nine and work the ten-to-six shift five nights a week: Mondays, Tuesdays, Thursdays, Fridays and Saturdays. Sundays and Wednesdays off. It gives me a chance to do writing assignments and run errands in the middle of the week and catch up on sleep.

"Do you have plans this evening?" he asked. I shook my head. I had nothing. "Besides driving insanely fast, what else do you do for fun?"

"I like movies and music. I thought I'd watch a movie tonight, if you want to hang out."

"Hang out," he repeated.

"Or I might start a new series on Netflix. Do you like murder mysteries?"

"Indeed."

Hashim rinsed the dishes while I loaded the dishwasher. He also wiped down the counter and the table meticulously. I covered the nine-by-thirteen dish and placed it in the fridge. I wouldn't have time to cook for the rest of the week.

We walked into the living room and I found the remote. There was no need to afford cable anymore. Billy watched games at the sports bar, at the station, or with friends. I wasn't home enough to need it. I read the newspaper at the center, aloud to the residents mostly, which kept me up with current events and the weather and my daily horoscope.

Hashim sat in Daddy's recliner. I sat on the sofa and curled my feet under me. I turned on the tv and glanced over at the recliner. "You know that goes back."

He pressed the arms and propped up his feet. He then placed his hands across his lap in a formal gesture. I turned out the lamp when the show started. The shades were closed, so even with the setting sun, the room was pretty dark.

We had watched two episodes of the series when Hashim returned the recliner to its upright position. It was a good show, and I would definitely continue watching it when I had time. He turned toward me. The house was completely dark, except for the nightlight in the hall bathroom and the television. I turned on the lamp next to me and Hashim stood. He looked so tall and dark standing over me. He put out his hand toward me, not like he wanted to shake it, but like he wanted to help me up from the sofa. I took his hand and stood. He looked down at my feet and smiled.

"Would you kindly see me to the door?" he asked not releasing my hand. It wasn't that long of a walk, but I liked holding his hand so I nodded and allowed him to lead me to the door. "Thank you, again, for another meal. I look forward to spending more time with you this semester."

I smiled. "Ditto," I said. "I'll see you tomorrow evening, then." He squeezed my hand gently before he released it to open the door. "You'll probably hear Billy's truck around midnight. I warn you. It's loud. Oh, here. Thank you, again," I said handing him an envelope with the fifty bucks I owed him.

He took it and gave a brief nod and then turned back toward me. "Lock the door," he said sternly.

"You sound just like my brother," I said.

"I am most definitely *not* your brother," he said before he entered the apartment. Nope, he definitely was not. I shut the door and bolted it. My stomach gave a little lurch.

CHAPTER 5.5

The words of King Lemuel. An oracle that his mother taught him:
What are you doing, my son?
What are you doing, son of my womb?
What are you doing, son of my vows?
Do not give your strength to women, your ways to those who destroy kings.

– Proverbs 31:1-3

My parents' home was a compound, heavily guarded, and impenetrable, or was I describing myself? My mother scoffed at my desire to live among the *commoners* as she called them. "You, my son, are descended from princes. Why must you continuously perform this laborious, social experiment. You do not belong among them. You will return, one day for good." She held my chin in her long fingers and peered into my eyes when she spoke these words.

My mother was one of the most beautiful women I had ever seen. She may have been in her mid-fifties, but she was graceful, and elegant and well-preserved. She barely looked forty, much less fifty. She preferred the climate of south Florida over their Canadian home. My father was more understanding and had recognized my need for exclusion in order to work. He never judged my random disappearances, nor did he expect me to settle down until I was well into my thirties, if then.

They moved from Pakistan shortly after I was born and lived a variety of places throughout Europe and the Middle East with a brief stint when I was seven in China. I wish we had stayed longer; it would have given me a stronger grasp of the language. Leaving D.C. had been too fast, too abrupt. That was not my style. I preferred to have a plan, a very thorough plan. It would not happen

47

that way again. A plan would be formulated before Marshall could find me. Already the change of pace here had given me too much time for introspection. My exit strategy would be my next priority.

It was ridiculous, but I refused to tell Caroline what it actually cost to repair her car. I had spent over seven hundred dollars today, but she would only pay me fifty. I recognized that her pride would not allow her to be indebted to me, nor should a young woman ever be indebted to a man. She knew I was lying but was too polite to call me a liar. She read my expressions well. I was unsure how I felt about that. Either, I was losing my edge or she was insightful. I would consider it the latter.

<u>CHAPTER 6</u>

Not two seconds after I bolted the door behind Hashim, my phone dinged. It was Krissa.

What's up?

Nothing.

Coming over. Hungry.

He won't be home til midnight.

So? I know you have food.

I'm going to bed to read.

Please. Stay up til he gets home.

Not a good idea. Too combustible.

For me or for him?

My house is flammable.

LOL. Be there in ten.

Krissa was my only graduate school friend. She was a little older than me, but she had worldly experiences with men and relationships far beyond my comprehension. Her father owned three nursing homes among other service companies for the elderly and had promised her the lot of them when she completed her master's degree. He was ready to retire. She would be worth a small fortune and she knew it.

Her father paid for the basics and covered her tuition, but her style and affinity for partying required that she work for the non-essentials. Her father kept her on a tight budget. She wasn't a tight-budget sort of girl, so she danced and supported herself in the way she thought she deserved. If Pete wasn't careful, she'd own his place before she graduated, too.

She had a great head for business but had little patience for the elderly. She didn't much like women and children, either. She liked men. She liked men, a lot, and they seemed to appreciate her just as much. She currently liked Billy, but Billy didn't reciprocate the way she desired. He posed a challenge. *Game on.* Honestly, I think she intimated him. He wasn't used to forward women. He definitely wasn't prepared for Krissa. I'd known her for a couple of years, and I still wasn't prepared for her. When she arrived, I let her in and offered her leftovers. She chose the casserole and a huge glass of milk.

"How's your car?" she asked.

"Good. I need to get the belts replaced. Hashim was able to replace the starter."

"Hashim?" she asked, making his name sound alluring and exotic.

"Yes, Hashim."

"Where's he from?"

"D.C.," I said flatly, closing the subject.

She took her plate from the microwave and sat at the counter. She ate like she really was hungry. "Girl, you sure do know your way around the kitchen. Maybe you should have gone into food service."

I shook my head and smiled. "You just say that because you're starving and you have no food at home."

"You're right. I don't have any food at home, not food like this, and I haven't eaten all day, so it tastes especially good."

I listened while she described her weekend. I laughed with her, but I didn't tell her anything about Hashim, even when she asked directly. She and I would be in the same classes with him, but I didn't want to give her anything to look forward to. I'd just have to introduce them tomorrow night in class.

Billy arrived home before midnight. He was starving, too. They were eating up all of my week's meal prep. I'd be cooking Wednesday, for sure. I thought about chicken salad for some reason. Billy seemed surprisingly pleasant when he greeted me and Krissa in the kitchen. He offered her a beer and she accepted. I felt like a third wheel, but then I realized I was more like a voyeur, watching them. Their interactions were entertaining but made me curious. I could learn a great deal from Krissa, but some of what she knew, I had no desire to know. I loaded the dishwasher with their dishes and excused myself, leaving them to their own company. Krissa got up and gave me a brief hug and then opened the fridge to retrieve a couple more beers. She had no intention of leaving.

The next morning, I woke up at ten when I heard the shower running. When Momma moved to the center, Billy insisted that I take the master. We used my old room for Zinnia when she visited. I got up and found he'd already started coffee. I was standing at the counter savoring the mug of hot deliciousness, when he came into the kitchen, carrying an armload of dirty laundry from drill and his bag for the station.

"I'm going to start these; do you mind rotating them?" I nodded. He smiled. "I'll see you Thursday. We have Zinnia Friday night, too," he said in a rush. He kissed my cheek. "See ya, Sis. Have a good one."

I put my hand to my cheek. There was something strange about him this morning. I took a shower and went out in my bathrobe to rotate his laundry. Hashim's car wasn't in the driveway. I went back into the house and made myself a cheese omelet for breakfast. I grabbed the salsa from the fridge.

"Did you make enough for two?"

I jumped and screamed, "What the hell!"

Krissa was standing in front of me. "Good morning," she said, "Sorry, I didn't mean to scare you." She looked hungry again and eager and way too happy.

"You stayed the night?" She nodded and smiled her bright smile. "With Billy?" I asked accusingly.

She shook her head. "No, in your old room." I sighed in relief. "Don't act so pleased. You're so damn judgmental. I'm not *that* slutty," she said in her own defense.

"I wasn't implying that. Billy doesn't need this right now. He's probably going to be deployed again before Christmas."

51

"That's all the more reason; it gives us both a possible out." She lifted her perfectly arched brow, knowingly. "He's a man; he has needs. I'm a woman; I have needs. I find that mutually beneficial."

I rolled my eyes and cut my omelet in half and handed her a fork. "I disapprove."

"I'll keep than in mind."

Krissa left and I folded Billy's laundry and stripped Zinnia's bed to get it ready for the weekend. Hashim's car still wasn't in the driveway. I prepared chicken salad and made myself a sandwich before I headed to the university. I packed a container of soup and some granola bars for the night. I packed my backpack and took the cash Hashim had given me.

Class didn't start until six, but I needed to see my advisor and go by the comptroller's office to pay for the class I was adding. My advisor gave me the necessary paperwork to show the professor. I also went by the traffic office to pick up my parking sticker for the semester.

I still had an hour before class started. I pulled out a granola bar and sat on a bench outside the building. It was a warm evening, but not terribly unpleasant and the mosquitos weren't unbearable, either. I closed my eyes and listened to the birds in the trees. The campus was quiet at this hour.

"Good evening, Miss Sweet," a familiar voice said.

"Good evening, Dr. Watts." I replied without opening my eyes. I could hear the smile in his voice. He was my favorite professor, ever, and I was thankful to have him twice this semester.

"I'd like to introduce you to Mr. Emir. He's new to the university. I thought you might make him feel welcomed."

I opened my eyes and Mr. Emir was looking at me with a pleasant smile. He was wearing a button-down shirt and a tailored linen suit. He was way better dressed than our professor.

"Hello, Hashim," I said, returning his smile.

"You already know each other?" Dr. Watts asked, pleasantly.

"Yes, sir. We've met," I confessed.

"Good, Miss Sweet can help you if you need directions or need to know anything regarding the university. She's been with us since high school."

"Thank you, Dr. Watts," Hashim said and shook his hand. "We will see you in class."

Hashim sat down on the edge of the bench next to me. "You weren't home today," I said.

He shook his head. "I was here most of the day, finalizing my admission paperwork. I've spent the better part of the past two hours with Dr. Watts. He's an interesting man."

"He'd probably say the same about you."

"Ready?" he asked, looking down at my backpack and the half-eaten granola bar in my hand.

I rolled up the bar in the wrapper and stuck the rest down in my bag. I led Hashim toward the psych building; his hand was on the door before I could open it myself. I should have known he would beat me to it. We walked upstairs toward our classroom. "I'll meet you in there. I need to go to the bathroom before class."

He gestured to take my backpack for me. "No, thanks, I'll be needing that."

"Oh," he said and lowered his hand. "May I save you a seat?"

"Sure. I like to sit towards the front on the teacher's right." I smiled, again. I was getting used to that, the smiling part. He'd just asked to sit with me. Wow!

I went into the stall to pee. Krissa's clicky, shoes echoed on the tile floor. "C," she demanded, "who is that guy you were just talking to?"

I flushed the toilet to delay answering her and then opened the stall door. "Hi, it's great to see you again, too. Thanks again, for breakfast and for letting me drink your brother's beer and crash at your house."

"Whatever. He's incredibly fine. Who is he? You were smiling at him. No one ever makes you smile."

I walked past her and washed my hands. I glanced up into the mirror and into her curious eyes. They were burning to know more. I could feel my ears turning pink. "He's new to the program."

"Oh my God, he's beautiful. I wonder if he's that color all over," she said dreamily.

"He's really nice, okay?"

Krissa stepped back and realization dawned on her face. "Is that who dropped you off the other night? That's your tenant? What's his name? Ha-something?" she asked accusingly.

"Hashim," I corrected. "His name is Hashim." I picked up my backpack and slung it over my shoulder and turned before the blush covered my entire body.

Krissa grabbed my elbow and swung me around to face her. "You like him." Her face was glowing with gossip and scandal. "Oh, my God! You really like him!"

"It's not like that. Please don't make it a big deal. He's here for a semester. That's it."

Krissa's eyes softened only slightly. "Introduce me," she said in a tone that felt threatening and controlling and had *or I'll tell Billy* written all over it. She checked herself in the mirror and seemed pleased enough with her appearance to be introduced. I seethed as I followed her into class.

Hashim looked up expectantly when he saw me coming into class, but soon changed his expression when he read mine. Thankfully he didn't smile at me. Krissa walked directly toward Hashim, stopped, and waited to be introduced. He stood as I approached.

"Krissa, this is Hashim. Hashim, this is Krissa."

"A pleasure," Hashim said putting out his hand toward Krissa.

He could sense the tension between us, but he was pleasant towards her. Krissa smiled flirtatiously and held his hand longer than was necessary. Hashim stepped away and protectively pulled out a chair for me. Dr. Watts entered the classroom at that moment and I sighed in relief as I sat down in the chair next to Hashim. Krissa sat two chairs over from me, watching every move I made. I opened my backpack at the same time Hashim opened his soft, leather briefcase. I pulled out a pen and a notebook and wrote the date at the top of the first page: *August 17 Social and Cultural Aspects of Aging Dr. Watts*

As soon as Dr. Watts began lecturing, Krissa disappeared. I didn't think about her or our conversation in the bathroom again until Dr. Watts called for a break. I reached around and brought my backpack into my lap. I found what remained of my granola bar and a bottle of water. Hashim rose and stretched his long legs. "I am going to find a vending machine. Would you like anything?" he asked. I shook my head and focused on my granola bar refusing to allow Krissa the satisfaction of watching me watch him.

As soon as he walked out of the room, Krissa moved over into the empty chair between us. "O my God! You are the worst friend ever! I can't believe you've been holding out on me all weekend!" she said in an exclamatory whisper. "You suck! You absolutely suck!"

I hoped she didn't really expect me to reply to her tirade. I turned to face her but I didn't smile or give her the satisfaction of a response. "Are you finished?" I asked. She shrugged and leaned back into her seat when Hashim returned.

Hashim and I made small talk and commented on Dr. Watt's teaching style and the syllabus. We still had about five minutes left in the break when Krissa leaned forward and began speaking directly to Hashim.

"So, how are you liking it here? Is Caroline helping you feel welcomed?" I hated the lace of implication she alluded to in her questions.

"I like it here, thank you. I look forward to the semester."

"Where are you from?" she asked with curious eyes and briefly glanced at me.

I crossed my arms and faded into the background. Hashim's face didn't change but his eyes caught mine for the briefest of moments and they were smiling. "D.C.," he said plainly. I smiled. He could read Krissa clearly, and I felt relieved he wasn't so easily drawn into her feminine wiles.

After class, I walked with them toward the parking lot. Krissa followed me; she had more to say before she'd let me go. Hashim walked me to my car. "It was nice meeting you," Hashim said and shook Krissa's hand formally. "Enjoy your shift. I will see you tomorrow," he said to me. Our eyes met and he tilted his head slightly in my direction, but he didn't touch me or offer to shake my hand. I smiled and I felt warm all over.

"Goodnight," I said and watched him walk across the street to another parking area.

"Tsk. Tsk. Tsk. Tsk. Tsk. Shame, for shame," Krissa sang teasingly and put her arm around my shoulder affectionately. "Be careful my sweet Caroline, or he'll be mopping you up with a hand towel before he discards you."

I turned, anger rising. "Give it a rest, Krissa. I'm not playing." I pulled out from under her arm. She continued to look at me with amusement. "I don't have any designs on him, so lay off. Can't you just let me be his friend?"

"He's not the sort of man to have *friends*; he has conquests."

"Goodnight, Krissa. I'll see you in class tomorrow."

CHAPTER 6.5

The heart of a man plans his way, but the Lord establishes his steps.

– Proverbs 16:9

After class, I went straight into the apartment and put away my briefcase. I hung up my suit and decided to run for a while before I worked. I was certain of two things: this geriatric program was going to be a good challenge for me and I did not like Caroline's friend, Krissa.

I had worked very little for the past two days so my mind was ready for the challenges at hand. I was on the verge of a breakthrough with my program. The countless hours that I had spent recording words and phrases were finally paying off. The next several days would be spent tweaking the program. Rarely did I ever feel any excitement in my line of work, but anticipation of success was familiar to me.

I was not surprised that my last thoughts before I fell asleep had drifted toward Caroline. That was easy because I had spent the evening with her. But I was a little concerned when my first thoughts were of her when I awoke. I had the same feeling of anticipation with my program as I did with my thoughts of her.

It was barely five in the morning, I would run and clear my head. I had a full day's work ahead of me. I pushed myself to run nine miles. I was stretching under the carport when I heard her car pull into the driveway. I looked up and could not help but return her smile. Even after being up all night, her smile was unwavering.

"Good morning," she said cheerfully. "I'm going to make some breakfast; would you like to join me?"

"Yes, thank you. May I shower first?"

"Absolutely, I plan to do the same."

I had not intended to share another meal with her. I had not intended for her to cook and serve me again, but her ease and her contentment were hard to refuse. I could easily see this becoming a habit for me.

There were three messages on my phone when I returned. One from Marshall, one from my mother, and one from the organization with whom I was currently contracting. I only had time for a shower and one call; the other two would have to wait.

CHAPTER 7

Why had I invited him to breakfast, again? I was thinking how tired I was the entire drive home. I was thinking about Momma and how crazy she had been until nearly two o'clock this morning. The night nurse finally agreed to inject her with a mild sedative. The oral meds were obviously not working. She probably wouldn't be awake again until after eight, but I would more than likely be with her again tonight.

What was I supposed to do? Didn't he look hungry after his run? Didn't his smile say, *Hi there, Caroline, I would really love for you to scramble me some eggs*. Okay, I was reading way too much into that smile, but he did smile and he did say, *yes*.

Tuesday was much the same as Monday. Krissa, Hashim, and I attended class together. When I arrived home Wednesday morning, Hashim had just returned from his run again. The day was hot and muggy even at that hour. It felt like it could start raining at any moment. I was happy not to have any errands to run today. I had done most of my reading assignments the past two nights at work.

"Good morning," Hashim said as I got out of my car.

"Good morning, yourself. Looks like rain today." He nodded. I didn't invite him to breakfast this morning, but I really wanted to.

"When do you plan to get your car looked at?" he asked. I honestly hadn't thought about it again since he told me to get the belts checked. I rolled my eyes and sighed. I should probably do that today. So much for a day off.

"I guess I shouldn't put it off, huh?" He nodded solemnly, knowing it was the responsible thing to do.

"Would you like me to follow you to the mechanic and give you a ride home so that you can sleep?" I thought about it for a moment and then agreed with him.

"Let me get a shower and find some food, and then I'll be ready. I don't think they open until 7:30."

I felt a little down knowing that I was about to drop another wad of cash on my piece-of-crap car, which prolonged its life but delayed my ability to purchase something new, well newer. I needed to focus on today and not keep wishing for something different.

Hashim waited for me in his car while I went in to speak with the mechanic's receptionist. She took my information and my car key and assured me she would call once the mechanic gave her a price. I told her to go ahead and fix anything that cost less than $500 as I was going to sleep for a good portion of the day.

"Let me know when your car is ready, and I will take you to pick it up. I will be working at home today," Hashim offered as we pulled into the driveway.

"Thanks, again. I really appreciate your helping me out so much with my car. I don't typically need this much assistance. I'll let you know when I wake up."

"Safe and reliable transportation is important, especially for a young woman driving alone."

"You're right, but I hope it doesn't cost me more than $500. I'll see you later," I said sleepily and yawned. I was suddenly feeling exhausted. I climbed into bed and adjusted my sleep mask and played white noise in my headphones.

It was early afternoon when I awoke. The house felt cool and dark. I was confused because it felt really late. I checked my phone but it was just after one o'clock in the afternoon. There were no missed calls, but a text that said they wouldn't get to my car until after three and depending on what it needed, would have to stay the night. The light coming in from the bathroom window showed me why it felt so late in the day. The sky was heavy with rain clouds and there was a steady drizzle outside.

I was a little hungry, so I made myself a sandwich. I sat at the kitchen table and watched the rain while I ate. It was peaceful but it was also a little lonely, and I suddenly felt the longing for regular human contact. I missed my parents more than I liked to admit. Our home and our family had been everything to me growing up. I missed Billy like crazy when he joined the Marines. One by one, they were all taken from me: Billy, Aunt June, Daddy, and finally Momma. Billy's presence was temporary, so I refused to rely on it. Our time apart had altered us both. We weren't that close anymore. No other person had yet to fill that void. I managed my grief pretty well most of the time, but grief was sneaky and caught me off guard sometimes, like today, sitting alone in the dark, watching it rain.

I jumped when I heard a knock on the door. "Hang on," I called and wiped my eyes and face. I'd been crying for a while. My shirt was a little damp from the tears that had flowed down my cheeks. I was so embarrassed to be caught crying in the middle of the day for no apparent reason. I peeked through the gap in the curtain. I opened the door, smiling. "Hey," I said, but Hashim didn't return my smile. He instantly looked concerned and then looked past me into the kitchen to see the cause of my tears. He almost looked angry like he could fight whomever or whatever was upsetting me.

"Are you alright?" he asked, returning his eyes to mine. I stepped back from the intensity; he was a little frightening. He took my hands in his and examined me carefully. "Are you hurt?"

"No, I'm fine. Really, I was just sitting here crying. I promise. I'm fine."

"Why are you crying? What made you sad?"

I shrugged and tried to pull my hands away. He wasn't allowing it, so I let him sit me down on a bar stool. He pushed the door closed behind him with his foot. "It's so embarrassing. It's really silly. The rain, the quiet house, being here alone a lot, eating chicken salad?" I laughed self-consciously. I rolled my eyes and tried to look away. I could feel the tears flowing again with my confession.

He released my left hand and reached into his pocket. He dabbed my cheek with a soft cloth. "Here," he said offering me a crisp, clean handkerchief.

"Are you for real?" I laughed a bit hysterically and covered my mouth with my free hand, unable to accept his gesture. "My pawpaw used to carry handkerchiefs. No one ever carries a handkerchief, anymore." The memory of Pawpaw made me cry even more. *What the hell, C; get a grip!*

Hashim didn't waver. He could tell I was having a hard time getting ahold of myself between brief, inappropriate chuckles that sounded like sobs, and more tears flowed. He stepped forward and put his hands on my shoulders and then pulled me into a protective embrace. His tender touch and genuine concern only made matters worse. The dam holding back my grief burst and he just held me while I cried. I wasn't strong enough to hold it together anymore. He scooped me up into his arms and walked me to the sofa. He sat down and held me in his lap. He gently stroked my hair and let the tears just fall onto his tailored shirt. I could feel his heartbeat and his steady breaths. He tilted his head into mine and I felt his beard against my temple. How could a stranger's touch feel so naturally welcoming?

I hadn't cried like that in a long time, not since Daddy died. When I was all cried out, I took a deep breath. What would be the most graceful way to extricate myself from his comforting arms? "Hashim," I whispered into his chest. "I don't make a habit of crying on other people's shoulders, but I'm really thankful for you right now." I breathed in his scent and exhaled slowly making sure I wasn't going to lose it again.

He pushed me back, gently, and looked into my eyes. His eyes were kind and understanding. He didn't seem impatient with me at all. Our faces were so close. He cradled my cheek in the palm of his hand and gently traced my lips with his thumb.

I swallowed nervously and I felt my eyes widen. I couldn't blink or move. My heartbeat quickened. This beautiful man was touching me; he was looking at me. No, he was admiring me. I lowered my eyes and blushed. How had I allowed myself to get in this vulnerable position?

Hashim tilted my chin up slightly, willing me to look into his eyes again. The blush intensified. He smiled, still admiringly, and put his thumb over my lips like he was considering something. Was he considering kissing me? Surely not; he was just making sure I wasn't going to burst into tears again. I couldn't read his expression.

The blush was moving throughout my entire body now. I was melting from the inside out. *Breathe. Blink. Exhale.* I put my hand on his chest, thinking that if I touched him, it would ground me somehow and bring me back to reality, but instead it made all the dominoes fall.

He moistened his lips and gently moved his hand to the back of my neck and pulled me in closer. "Oh, shit," I gasped in a whisper before our lips met. I moved my hands around his neck and turned my face to better receive his lips. In a matter of seconds, my mind completely emptied like white noise and a blank canvas.

I wasn't exactly sure how much time passed before Hashim released me, but it wasn't long enough for me to collect myself entirely. I had been kissed a few times by boys I liked, but never like this. I had been kissed by a couple of men, but never like this. Cooper had been the last guy to kiss me, but this was the first time I'd been kissed and not felt an unspoken expectation. Hashim kissed me like he was attracted to *me* and not for purely selfish reasons.

I honestly didn't know what to do or say. My heart was racing, but thankfully, my breaths were steady. I tilted my head and examined his face cautiously. He didn't look disgusted, but he wasn't smiling, either. He seemed to be waiting on a response from me. How could I reassure him?

"I wasn't expecting that," I said smiling, "but it was a nice surprise." I hoped my eyes showed the sincerity of my words.

He blinked slowly and his long, dark lashes encircled his beautiful eyes. Then he smiled, really smiled, and showed his teeth and everything. There was no denying he liked kissing me, too.

"Are you hungry?" he asked. I shook my head. "Thirsty?" I nodded. He moved to help me to my feet. "Me, too."

He held my hand and led me to the kitchen. I released his hand and took down two glasses. I poured us each a glass of tea from the fridge. I stepped back and leaned against the counter across from him. I took a sip and felt the silence in the room grow awkward.

"So, why did you come over?"

"I wanted news of your car and if you had any plans this evening, but is that really the question first on your mind?"

I shook my head and looked down at my glass. I lifted my eyes to his again before I spoke. "No, but I'm not prepared for the answer, so I think I'll hold it for now, if you don't mind."

"What of my other two inquiries?" he asked.

"Car won't be ready before tomorrow, and I have nothing going on tonight, why? I thought I might watch more of the series we started on Sunday."

He looked down at my bare feet and grinned. "Do you own shoes other than the ones you wear to work?"

"Yeah, what kind of question is that?"

"I would like to take you to dinner, to a nice restaurant that would require shoes complementing a skirt or dress. Please take no offense, but I have yet to see you in anything other than scrubs and jeans and sneakers."

I laughed at his awkwardness. He didn't want to offend me. How adorable. "Are you asking me on a date, or are we going out as friends who happened to share a kiss?"

He cocked his head to one side, considering. "That depends on how the friend liked the kiss." Warmth flowed through me again, melting me from the inside. Charming. Handsome. Witty. *Irresistible.*

I took another sip of cold sweet tea but it did nothing to cool me down. "What time should I be ready?"

"Six-thirty. We have reservations for seven."

CHAPTER 7.5

Many are the plans in the mind of a man,
But it is the purpose of the Lord that will stand.

— Proverbs 19:21

Honestly, I had no intentions of kissing her. I had yet to decide if it was attraction I was feeling or curiosity. I already knew about her car, but she needed to be the one to tell me. Why did she have to be crying when she answered the door? She looked like a small, timid animal, frail and meek. Her vulnerability brought out my protective side.

Everything she did and said stirred me into action. My intention was to ask her to dinner, get to know her, and enjoy the distraction she provided. She was fun and I had *fun* when I was with her. She was smart and compassionate, friendly and adventurous, strong and… my thoughts ended there. She was still plain, but as I held her, crying in my arms, I could feel everything she was feeling.

She thanked me for being there with her. She appreciated me. I had never felt that before, genuine *appreciation*. It was different from admiration. It was different from attraction. It was different from adoration. I had not given her anything, and yet my presence and concern for her were treasured. I thought of everything that I could give her, every worldly possession, but that was neither what she wanted nor needed.

When I looked into her light, hazel eyes and felt her soft lips under my touch, I knew she needed to be kissed, really kissed. My instincts were correct; with regards to women, they most often were. She knew what I was considering, but I had not decided to act upon it until she touched me. She blushed and felt

65

warm in my arms, but when she laid her hand on my chest, it was no longer a consideration. At that moment, *I* needed to kiss her.

She encouraged me when she sensed my apprehension at her response. She reserved her question as to why I had kissed her. She had accepted my invitation to dinner. This afternoon's choice to kiss her did nothing to solidify my thoughts and feelings for her, but it did make me want to kiss her again.

CHAPTER 8

It didn't happen very often, but at this moment, I was thankful for my friendship with Krissa. Over the past year or so, she had given me several dresses and a few pairs of shoes that I would have never bought for myself. I chose a dress with tiny purple and blue flowers. The neckline scooped just past my collarbones and the sleeves went nearly to my elbows. The skirt was gathered at the waist, and had I still been seven, I would have been fascinated at the way it lifted and spun when I twirled around. Okay, so I was still a little fascinated. I chose a pair of cream-colored, wedge sandals that matched the dress perfectly. I took the time to paint my toenails with soft pink polish.

By Krissa's standards, I looked prudish, but I believed that modesty was more feminine than cleavage and exposing my thighs. Neither were my best feature. I pulled my hair up in a twist and curled the loose wisps of hair that naturally fell around my face. Momma liked to fix my hair. She had patiently curled and lovingly placed each tendril for special occasions.

I picked a simple pair of small, gold hoop earrings from Momma's jewelry box. I didn't have a lot of jewelry, so mostly I wore a long gold chain that held several rings. I smiled and slipped it over my head. I needed a little concealer under my eyes from crying so hard earlier. I powdered my nose and lined my lips with tinted gloss. My light-brown lashes looked better with mascara, so I made the extra effort. I stood and checked myself in the mirror and was pleased with the final result.

There was no need to ask Hashim if he approved. His eyes didn't lie. I think that he was genuinely surprised; he underestimated my abilities. He came to the door wearing dark gray slacks and a white dress shirt under a dark blue blazer. The woven pattern in the jacket subtly caught the light.

I stood patiently while he opened the car door for me. He played music low as he drove downtown toward the nicer restaurants and hotels. He pulled into the parking area and the valet helped me out of the car. Hashim put his hand on the small of my back and guided me into the restaurant. He smiled proudly as we walked together. He was proud to be with *me*.

We were shown to a small table in a private area of the restaurant. The area was surrounded by thick curtains that would give us complete privacy. The soft lighting was reflected by the crystal and mirrored fixtures. I don't know what he was going for, but it was terribly romantic.

The waiter arrived immediately and welcomed us in French and then in English. Hashim replied in fluent French. The waiter smiled at being spoken to in his native tongue. They laughed instantly like old friends. The waiter looked at me and spoke words that I didn't understand, but still made me blush because I knew he was complementing me. Hashim looked at me and interpreted. "He's from a province I visited a few years ago. He also approves of the lady." Hashim cocked his head to one side. "I trust his judgement; he has good taste." I thanked the waiter. "Would you like to see a menu or may I order for you?" Hashim asked.

"Please, go right ahead." I probably wouldn't be able to read it, anyway.

"Any food allergies?" I shook my head. "Any aversions?" I shook my head, again.

The two of them spoke for several minutes. Our waiter approved of Hashim's choices but seemed to talk him into his personal favorites. It was the most expressive I'd seen Hashim speak with another person. His French was fluent and relaxed; his English was formal and definitely not southern.

The waiter left us. Music played low in the small space. I tucked a loose curl behind my ear. "I'm impressed. How many languages do you speak?" I asked.

"Eight distinct languages, twelve dialects, and I'm still mastering Chinese and Vulcan."

"Like *Star Trek* Vulcan? Vulcan isn't a real language," I scoffed.

"No, but I need to know it."

I laughed. "I thought I was doing good learning baby signs with my niece when she was a year old. I barely made it out of Spanish in high school. Thankfully that was one of my dual classes, so I only had to take them once to count for college."

"We have that in common. I graduated early, also. I was sixteen when I went to university. How old were you?"

"Seventeen."

"How old are you, Caroline Sweet?" His eyes were so beautiful in the flickering light.

"Twenty." He nodded like he already suspected that I was younger than most graduate students. "And you?"

"Twenty-seven."

"That's Billy's age."

Our waiter brought our first course, then, and poured us each a glass of wine. Everything smelled so good. My stomach growled low. Hashim said something to him in French and he bowed his head politely and excused himself. Hashim then opened his hand toward me, offering me the opportunity to take it. "Here, give thanks to your god." I put my hand in his and prayed.

The food was delicious and the wine was better than anything I'd ever tasted. Hashim told me about France and a little about what he remembered in Pakistan while we ate through each course. When our waiter offered me a third glass of wine, I shook my head. "No thank you." I was feeling a bit giddy and way too relaxed. I was beyond my limit.

Over dessert and coffee, Hashim took my hand again. "If tonight has pleased you, would you consider it again?"

"Like a date?" I asked looking down at the contrast in our coloring.

Hashim smiled. "Or as friends who kiss."

I tucked my hair behind my ear and lowered my chin; I smiled broadly understanding his meaning perfectly. I also liked that *kiss* was in the present tense. I took a deep breath, mustering my courage, because I needed to say something important. I swallowed and cleared my throat and lifted my chin, looking him straight in the eyes.

"Hashim, I've had a wonderful time tonight, thank you, but I would like to make something perfectly clear." He could sense the seriousness and sat up straighter in his chair. "I very much liked kissing you today, and I like spending time with you, but I have no intention of having sex until I'm married. I hope that doesn't offend you or disappoint your expectations. It tends to offend some guys, when they are refused, and so I like to put it out there at the beginning. I'm not looking to get married, but I'm also not looking to get pregnant, or complicate my life in that way. School is my priority for now." I lowered my gaze when I felt the blush creeping up my neck and spoke my next words to the tablecloth because I wasn't sure I could look him in the eye. "You are an incredibly attractive man, and I would appreciate it if you wouldn't use that power against me."

I was too much of a coward to look at him directly. I felt my hand getting sweaty and I wasn't sure if it was nerves or the wine. He was probably thinking how to get this child home and not bother with me ever again, but he continued to hold my hand. I finally looked up when he chuckled. He was smiling wryly and didn't look disappointed in me at all.

"Interesting." He gave my hand a playful squeeze. "So, when did you decide this for yourself?"

"When I was twelve. When Billy got his girlfriend pregnant."

He nodded, considering my answer. "I see. Well, I'm glad you told me and it honestly clears the air. So that we are both clear, these are my intentions: I will kiss you and touch you in appropriate, non-tempting ways, I will take you out to restaurants and introduce you to food that does not contain *tots*, and I will be honored to protect your virtue." I trusted his words. They were spoken as a promise.

"I don't know any guys that talk like you. You sound like the protagonist in an Austen novel," I giggled. The wine was definitely getting to me.

70

"That is the most significant difference between a guy and a man." He winked.

"Agreed. I don't know very many men, for sure, at least not men like you."

Our waiter wished us a good night and hoped we would return again, soon. He kissed my cheek and hugged me and made Hashim laugh with whatever he'd said about me in French. It was dark, but I thought I detected a change in Hashim's coloring when the friendly Frenchman patted him heartily on the shoulder, laughing and carrying on. Hashim rolled his eyes and shook his head.

Before he pulled out onto the road, Hashim placed my hand under his on the gearshift. We drove, shifting the car together, feeling the revving of the engine and anticipating the changes of the gears together. Forget about the dangers of kissing, if he thought this was appropriate touch, he had no idea what it was doing to me. *Oh, my God*, it was the most erotic thing I'd ever experienced.

Once in the driveway, he walked around the car and opened the door for me. He held my hand as we walked the few steps to the house. He took my keys in his free hand and unlocked the door for me.

"Would you like to come in?" I asked.

"No, I have some work to do before midnight."

"Well, thank you again, Hashim; tonight was wonderful. I'll see you tomorrow."

He put one hand on my waist and his other on the back of my neck which made my head fall back involuntarily. I blinked dreamily up into his eyes as he leaned over and kissed me. I was smiling when he released me. "Goodnight, Caroline."

CHAPTER 8.5

Joyful is the person who finds wisdom, the one who gains understanding.
For wisdom is more profitable than silver,
and her wages are better than gold.
Wisdom is more precious than rubies;
nothing you desire can compare with her.

— Proverbs 3:13-15

Caroline's declaration was not a surprise, but the fact she spoke it aloud to me, was. It explained a couple of things, like why she did not have a serious boyfriend and why she was not on the prowl like most young women. I appreciated the attention she had paid to herself tonight. Sure, she looked pretty, but I dared not speak it. *Pretty* was not the right word. *Lovely, engaging, prepossessing.* The valet, the maître d, and nearly every man as we entered the restaurant took notice of her. She paid them no attention, but she knew I was proud to be with her. What man wouldn't be?

She liked good wine; we had that in common. Our waiter, Leo, was most complimentary, but thankfully she could not understand him, especially at his ribbing. I was not accustomed to being made the butt of jokes, and he had read our situation well. Even in jest, his comment struck a nerve. "The lady is not accustomed to such finery, but she could easily become so," he had said. "I warn you, my friend, her finery may be beyond even you. A lifetime might not be enough to appreciate it." He was laughing, but his words were true.

The drive home was interesting. I had not anticipated her pleasure; the electricity between us was intense. That had not been my intention. I should have known her affinity for driving would please her in other ways, as well. In heels, she was a couple of inches taller, and I only had to lean over slightly to kiss her goodnight. I kept my hands securely on her waist and neck. I would keep firm control of myself for both of our sakes. She trusted me. Besides, what significance could come from a few months of friendship and kissing?

***

My mind was surprisingly focused, and I worked intently until midnight. I slept, woke at five, and ran. The morning was muggy and heavy again, but I managed the eight miles; my goal was to reach ten before the end of the week.

Billy was getting out of his truck when I arrived, but he looked at me cautiously as he walked toward the carport. "Good morning," I said as I approached the house. I was still winded from running. Billy nodded once, acknowledging me, but did not look friendly. "Hashim Emir, your new tenant." I said extending my hand out in greeting.

Billy remembered his manners and shook my hand. "Billy Sweet. Caroline didn't tell me she'd rented the place. Are you a student?"

"Yes. By coincidence, your sister and I have classes together." He raised his eyebrow like he did not believe in coincidences. Truth be told, neither did I.

Billy was taller than his sister by several inches, with her same light eyes, brown hair, and fair skin. He had the build of a firefighter, and I suspected the agility of a former athlete. He stood like a soldier as he assessed me more closely. I did not blame him; I was a foreigner, a stranger, living in his home. He had been trained to be cautious, if not paranoid, of men who bore my likeness. I was no threat, but he would need convincing more than Caroline.

CHAPTER 9

I felt giddy after our first *friends who kiss* dinner. I couldn't remember the last time I'd felt this way. I kicked my shoes off and flopped onto the sofa and stayed up until three watching more episodes of that show on Netflix. I cleaned the kitchen, washed my face, and went to bed. I fell asleep immediately and slept past noon on Thursday.

When I finally got up, it took two large cups of coffee to get me going. My car would be ready before four, so I would ask Hashim if he could take me on our way to class. Billy was home when I got up. He was mowing the grass. I watched him for a little while and wondered if I should tell him about going to dinner with Hashim last night. How could I explain the closeness I felt for a man I'd met only six days ago? I could hardly reason it in my own mind, much less speak it out loud. I would wait and introduce them and then gradually allow our friendship to be seen. Yes, that would be a good plan. Hashim would understand; he would be cool about it, especially with our professors and in front of Krissa.

I jumped when Billy burst into the kitchen, hot and sweaty. I was so distracted by my thoughts that I hadn't heard the mower shut off. He slammed the door and poured himself some cold tea from the fridge. He swallowed it in two gulps.

"I met your tenant this morning. What's his story?"

"He's here for the geropsychology program."

"Yeah, he said you have class with him." It was obvious Billy didn't like that fact. He poured himself another glass of tea and wiped his face with the bottom of his t-shirt. "Anything else I need to know about him?"

"He moved here from D.C. He's lived all over the world and speaks several languages. He works from home with computers and tech stuff."

Billy nodded, considering. "Hey, where's your car?" he asked like he just remembered not seeing it.

"In the shop, getting some work done. It died Saturday night. It'll be ready this afternoon."

"How did you get to work? Did Krissa drive you?"

"No, she was working Saturday night. Hashim brought me."

"Has he been driving you all week? Why didn't you call me at the station?"

I shrugged. "It wasn't a big deal. He replaced the starter on Sunday and it's been running fine. He said the belts needed to be replaced so we took it in yesterday morning. I told them to fix whatever they could for five hundred bucks. It's all good."

"What did he charge you?"

"Just for the part. He knew I was in a bind; he was being generous."

Billy scoffed. "That's it?" Billy asked skeptically. "So, he moves in one day and is fixing your starter the next? He barely knows you and he's already fixing your car and giving you rides?" I didn't like Billy's tone. It was angry and condescending. He was being protective, but his tone made me feel stupid.

"It's not like that, Billy." I crossed my arms and frowned.

"With our luck, he's a damn Arab, probably here on a terrorist mission," he said loudly.

"Keep your voice down!" I whispered harshly through clenched teeth. "I need the money, and he paid three full months in advance. Be cool, okay? Can you please try and be civil? He's not an Arab and he's not even Muslim." My own voice rose to match his. "Thanks to him, I can cover my tuition, my car is running, and I put extra in savings and some away for Momma." I was angry and defensive. It wasn't a tone I used very often, especially with my big brother.

Billy stood back and considered me. "Sounds like you've spent some time with him, gotten to know him." My cheeks were flushed with anger, but I couldn't hide the blush that spread from my neck to my ears. I needed to tell him something so that he wasn't presuming the worst.

"I have," I said defensively. "We've eaten together a few times." *Exactly six*, I thought to myself.

"You invited a complete stranger into our home and gave him food?"

"He was just getting settled. I was being hospitable. I'd made soup and there was plenty."

"You are such an idiot!" He threw his hands in the air in exasperation. "You could have been raped or murdered! You don't know what men are capable of!"

I waited for Billy's temper to settle before I said, "He's really nice, Billy. You don't even know him."

"I don't have to know him. I know his kind."

I hated to fight with Billy. It made my stomach ache. He was being protective in his paranoid way. His Marine Reserve unit had been deployed twice, with a third deployment pending. He'd seen stuff. It affected him. His best friend was taken out by a sniper during his first deployment, and his other best friend suffered from PTSD. It altered Billy, hardened him.

I swallowed my anger and decided to change the subject. "So, when is Zin coming over?" I asked.

"She'll be here after school tomorrow."

"Good, I'll get to spend some time with her before I go to work."

Billy took a deep breath, releasing his earlier frustration with me. "I need to tell you a couple of things." I looked into his eyes; they were serious. He aged before me, looking more like my father than my brother. "They've moved up our unit's timeline."

"How long?" I asked.

"Six weeks. Early October." I nodded solemnly and had to bat back the tears that stung my eyes. I knew it was coming, but I was looking forward to having until Thanksgiving, at least.

"What else?"

He took another breath. Whatever he was about to say was worse than his deployment news. I braced myself. "I'm going out with Krissa tonight when she gets out of class."

I shook my head disapprovingly. I didn't have the right to tell my older brother what to do, or who to spend his time with, but he could read my expression clearly. He didn't bother to say anything else to plead his case. "And you called me an *idiot* for sharing soup with Hashim." I laughed out once, darkly.

Just then, there was a knock on the door. It could have only been Hashim. I glared at Billy. "Be nice," I whispered. I stepped forward, but I was still in my bathrobe, so he moved past me to answer the door.

"Good afternoon," Hashim said politely to Billy before he turned his eyes to mine. "Do you need a ride to get your car before class?"

"Yes. It should be ready by four. I think they close at five-thirty."

"I can be ready before five," he said.

"Would you like a cup of coffee or a glass of tea?" I asked, cutting my eyes toward Billy, daring him to challenge me.

Hashim sensed the tension between us and I felt certain he had heard our argument. "Thank you, that's gracious of you." He stepped forward and Billy had no choice but to back up and allow Hashim to come in. Well, he could have protested and looked like an ass, but I think he was considering how I might retaliate against Krissa.

I poured Hashim a cup and placed the sugar and cinnamon next to his mug. Billy looked hard at the two of us. I reached for the half-and-half from the fridge and couldn't help but smile when I turned back to them. Hashim was amused.

He took a sip of his coffee. "Thank you, once again delicious." He winked before he took another sip, but Billy didn't see. Hashim placed his mug on the counter in front of him and stood to his full height, looking directly at Billy. "I would like to clear up a common misunderstanding. I'm not Arab. I was born among my father's family in Pakistan and my mother is of Turkish descent. I am not Muslim and I pose no threat to you, your country, or your sister. I am here to study and work, and with your knowledge, spend time occasionally with Caroline, outside of class."

Hashim put out his hand like he was meeting Billy for the first time or he was making a gentlemen's agreement. Billy assessed him with caution, but after a few moments, put out his hand and shook it. They were both tall men, muscular and lean. Billy had definitely inherited the Sweet's handsome features. We had the same coloring, but my beauty paled in comparison to his. My daddy was a real looker, even as he approached his sixties. Billy relaxed and stepped back, satisfied, somehow. I felt small with them both standing a head taller than me, and I felt like a freak of nature in contrast to their insane attractiveness. One room couldn't contain it.

Hashim finished his coffee and left us. I dressed and readied myself for class and work. "Have fun tonight," I said to Billy before I left with Hashim, and genuinely meant it. We both deserved some fun.

CHAPTER 10

"This doesn't make any sense," I said. The ticket read $1100.47 total, but the amount due was just under $500. It even included a new muffler. The advertised discount coupon took off $100 and then there were several other discounts listed, like a *Customer Loyalty Discount*. I had been using this mechanic for years, but I'd never seen a receipt like this before. "It can't be right." I felt foolish asking to speak with the manager, but the perky receptionist couldn't give me any answers.

She just smiled and batted her eyes at Hashim. "He's out until next week," she said apologetically.

"Come on, do not worry about it, now. We need to go; we do not want to be late for class." Hashim was right. There was a line forming behind us.

"Thank you," I said to the receptionist and stepped away from the counter.

"Bye," the receptionist almost sang and waved and smiled again at Hashim. He turned me suddenly toward the door.

"Did you have anything to do with this?" I asked before we made it to my car.

"To do with what?" he asked innocently.

"For why my car cost so little to fix," I demanded, forcing the receipt in his face.

He didn't say anything. He didn't have to. He knew I knew. He was wavering between telling me the truth and remaining silent. "It needed to be done. The noises were unbearable. It was the right thing to do for all our sakes. Please accept it as a gift. I did not intend to offend you."

I was conflicted. A part of me wanted to fight about it, but he was generous and considerate. I took a deep breath and released my agitation. "Thank you, again. I appreciate it. Please deduct it from the remainder of your lease." I took his hand then and forced him to look me in the eye. I smiled slightly so he didn't feel like a disciplined child. "Hashim, in the future, just be honest and tell me. I don't like surprises and being caught off guard. I truly don't like things being done behind my back."

He kissed my hand. "Agreed."

Our Thursday class, Healthcare Economics, was going to eat me alive. It was boring and the professor droned on and on in his monotone economist way. Krissa sat attentively in class. She actually loved business and economics and anything to do with making money. She raised her hand at appropriate times and asked informed questions that only made the professor talk more. It was painful.

Krissa gave me a brief hug and bolted out of class as soon as we were dismissed. She was eager for her date with Billy. I was relieved to have a few moments alone with Hashim. He walked me to my car and I complained loudly about the semester's reading requirement. "This is going to be so hard! I barely got out of undergrad econ. My brain already hurts." Hashim laughed at my drama.

"Economics is important. I can help you. My parents both studied economics. I understood the basics before I could read."

"Of course, you did," I said sarcastically, unlocking my car and opening it. "You've never really mentioned your parents before." I was surprised and curious.

He smiled, distracting me, and helped me remove my backpack. He put it in the back seat and took me in his arms. He hugged me and kissed the top of my head. "Have a good night, Caroline." He then took my face in his hands and kissed me.

***

My shift went smoothly and Momma slept well. Hashim was stretching when I got home. "Breakfast?" I offered.

He shook his head. "No, I have a call. Business. Would lunch be possible?"

I shook my head and yawned. "We have Zinnia tonight. She'll be here after school. Maybe tomorrow, then."

He gave a quick nod and an even quicker kiss. "Sleep well, Caroline Sweet."

Zinnia's arrival was a breath of fresh air. Children bring a different level of energy into a household. Zinnia had asked for rollerblades for her birthday after digging my old pair from the hall closet. Mine were too big for her, so we got her a pair of her own. We went outside and rollerbladed for an hour before dinner. Billy walked and ran alongside her. She had improved a lot in the past month, but he was still cautious with her.

We made mac and cheese for supper, the homemade kind with a variety of cheeses. It was one of Momma's best recipes, so I would bring her some tonight. We also made sliders with Hawaiian rolls. What kid could resist tiny burgers that fit so easily in her hand. We played cards until I had to leave for work. Slapjack was dangerous at any age and Billy and I were fiercely competitive. Zinnia Sweet was no exception to that trait; she was getting good.

"Are you staying one night or two?" I asked.

She looked at her daddy and smiled proudly. "Two."

"We plan to go see Momma tomorrow after our movie. We'll be home when you get up," Billy said. "Zin wants to grill tomorrow, so I'm thinking hotdogs and chicken sausage."

"Sounds good," I said and kissed them both goodbye.

I hesitated outside Hashim's door before I left. I wanted to knock and give him a kiss, but I heard him speaking. He must be working; I didn't want to interrupt him. He was speaking a language I'd never heard before. It was clipped with short syllables, and he was speaking like he was impatient and frustrated, but that could have been the language.

It was so interesting to hear him speak. Then he laughed. I smiled, still listening through the door. I wondered now if he were talking on the phone with someone on the other side of the world. He must have friends all over. Then doubt darkened my thoughts; he must have *girl*friends all over, too. Were they his lovers? Did he miss them? Their touch? Their long legs?

I shook the images of model-like goddesses from my mind and, thanks to Hashim, got into my not-such-a-piece-of-crap car. *We are just friends who kiss and touch appropriately and eat food without tots*, I repeated like a mantra all the way to work. I was terribly unconvincing.

Saturday morning, I arrived home later than usual. My replacement had called to say she had sick kids and was waiting on her mother-in-law to arrive. It was nearly eight-thirty. Hashim wasn't stretching when I arrived home. I felt a little foolish, but I really wanted to see him.

Zinnia and Billy were eating breakfast when I walked into the kitchen. She was all smiles. "Look, Aunt Caroline, I lost another tooth." She proudly produced the small, white nub. "Does the tooth fairy come to your house, too?"

I caught Billy's playful, daddy smile. "Absolutely! It's been a while, but I'm sure she can find her way back here," I said. For some reason, their familial exchange caught me right in the feels. There really wasn't anything better than the love between a father and daughter.

Zinnia got up suddenly and asked if she could call and tell her mommy. Billy went to unlock his screen, but Zin took the phone from his hand. "I know how; it's my birthday."

"You might want to call Jen later and ask her what the going rate of teeth are these days."

Billy laughed. "Already did."

***

When I awoke several hours later, I found a note from Billy. They went to the park and then they'd go by the grocery store. He said we'd eat by seven. It wasn't even four. I went out to find my laundry folded neatly in the laundry basket. "*Hashim*," I sighed to myself.

"Yes," I heard his voice behind me. I jumped and screamed, and a stream of curses flew from my mouth. Hashim froze and his eyes widened in shock. He put his hands up in surrender. "My apologies."

My hand flew to my chest and my heart beat hard from the startle. "You need to give a body some warning," I said a bit too forcefully for the small space of the laundry room.

"I will remember that." His lip twitched slightly like he was amused with me; then he laughed.

"Stop it! It's not funny!" but I knew it was.

He lifted the basket from the dryer and waited while I opened the kitchen door. He went in first and placed the basket on the table. The coffee was from Billy's breakfast. I poured it into a mug and was about to put it in the microwave when Hashim stopped me.

"That will not be good. May I?" he gestured to the cup in my hand.

"Sure," I said unsure of what he planned to do with my coffee.

"I will need a pot and the milk."

I watched as he poured what remained of the coffee into the pot. He opened the spice cabinet and added a few spices to the coffee. He added sugar and then gradually added the milk as he increased the heat. When he was satisfied, he took the spoon and sampled the steaming contents. His eyes did that same thing when he had tasted the soup. Both were satisfying and familiar.

He poured each of us a mug and pushed mine towards me. I held the warm mug in my hands and savored the aroma. Hashim waited patiently for my response. I closed my eyes and took a sip. It was delicious, creamy, sweet, and rich. It was both stimulating and relaxing. "Mmmm," was all I could say.

"Much better than microwaved coffee, yes?"

"Yes! Delicious!" I gestured for him to join me at the table. When I sat down, my robe gapped slightly exposing my inner thigh. Hashim's eyes fell and he saw everything and quickly looked away. I remembered then that I was not dressed and my short gown was the entire reason I needed to wear a bathrobe. *For Christ's sake, C, you aren't even wearing underwear.* I blushed and pulled my robe closed.

I took in a quick breath and decided to strike up a conversation, totally unrelated to my thigh and panty-less self. Awkwardness wasn't hard to overcome when I could fill the silence, right? "I think I heard you working last night when I was leaving." He nodded and seemed to appreciate my course of action. "Are you an interpreter?"

He thought for a moment. "You might describe it like that, but that would just be scratching the surface. What I do is significantly more complicated." He stopped to consider, not like he had to put it in simplified terms like I was too stupid to understand, but like he was deciding whether or not he could trust me. His eyes tightened slightly at the corners. He was bothered at the conflict behind his eyes.

"It's okay, you don't have to tell me. I was just curious; it sounds interesting." I looked down at my coffee and tucked my hair behind my ear before I took another sip of his brew.

"It is interesting, but I am unaccustomed to being asked to explain my work. It is highly specialized and I enjoy the challenges." He smiled proudly before he continued. He almost looked relieved that he was going to tell me more. "I help organizations interpret and translate. I've been working for the past ten years. It is one of the reasons I went to university early." He then became more animated, almost excited. "It was never enough, though. I always thought that I was missing something, another dimension, so most recently, I have developed voice-recognition, interpretive software."

"Wow!" I said impressed.

"Thank you. I think so, too."

"Too bad you can't just read people's lips. You know, just hold up your phone and press an app and have it interpret the person's face for you. That would make some great spy software, huh?" I said dismissively and laughed.

Hashim blinked and pursed his lips and looked at me seriously. He nodded to himself and hastily finished the last of his coffee. His thoughts were far off. He stood and rinsed his mug in the sink. "I need to work. Thank you for the coffee." He excused himself and left the kitchen in a hurry. Not two seconds passed, and he knocked.

I stood and walked to the door, wondering why he left so abruptly. "Yes? Did you forget something?" I asked as I opened the door.

"I forgot to ask. Would you have dinner with me tomorrow?" He spoke normally, but his mind was still distracted and working behind his eyes.

I wondered at his intensity. Why did it frighten me a little? I pushed that feeling aside and nodded. "What time?"

"Six and would you please wear your hair down?" I nodded again. I guessed he was tired of always seeing me in scrubs and pony tails.

CHAPTER 10.5

But the path of the righteous is like the light of dawn,
which shines brighter and brighter until full day.

— Proverbs 4:18

I could not believe the rush of thoughts that flooded me. I had learned even more of Caroline in a matter of days. Walls were thin. Humans assumed that a wall protected them and their words. We were all foolish and took them for granted, walls and words.

She had defended me against her brother's suspicions that I was a spy or a terrorist. She argued and pleaded on my behalf. She had used words like *kind* and *generous* and *nice*, but perhaps she was merely projecting her own personality onto me. I had done nothing, really. Everything I had done had been for purely selfish reasons. She was the kind and generous one.

It was so easy to tell her things that I told no one. I had mentioned my parents and divulged something so personal about myself and my upbringing. I was usually more guarded. She would not be able to assume anything from what I had said, but it was strangely pleasing to tell her things, to make her coffee, and to allow her new experiences.

She startled easily and knew how to curse. That thought made me laugh. My thoughts were racing in a million different directions, now. It always happened like this with pivotal ideas. She had no idea what her casual statement had stirred in me. I had to get away from her to think. She would have thought me a madman if I had allowed this process to begin in her presence.

I had to free the jumble and chaos in order for it to run its course. Once I caught the stream, the random thoughts settled to the bottom, and then I could

86

begin the real work. I trusted the way my mind sifted through the insignificant. Maybe another run would help.

Two thoughts, two directions, two possibilities were warring. Just as one thought would take precedence, the image of Caroline smiling in her bathrobe pushed it aside. The next thought took the lead, but then Caroline's exposed thigh derailed it completely. It was barely a second before I had looked away, but it was enough to burn into my memory. I had been with her for over an hour without kissing her. Missed opportunities were intolerable.

I closed my eyes and tried to clear my mind, but that just made it worse. Her shape, the curve of her hips and backside, how her breasts rose and fell when she gasped or laughed. I wondered at the taste of her skin, when suddenly, the two warring thoughts merged into one. *Ingenious*, I thought.

CHAPTER 11

Momma ate her mac and cheese and chicken sausage like a little kid. She was awake at two when I took my break. She sat with me in the lobby and we talked and ate together. She didn't know me tonight, but she thought I made good company. She liked the food and asked for the recipe.

She told me about how hard it was to work there, the long hours, and having to spend nights away from her family. She told me about her children and how proud of them she was. It was odd to hear her say my name and have no connection to the person sitting next to her.

She asked me if I had any children. I told her no, that I wasn't married. She nodded and patted my hand. "Do you have a fella?" she asked and then answered her own question. "Why of course you do, a pretty girl like you. Is he handsome? Does he treat you like you deserve?"

I smiled and nodded. "Yes, ma'am, he is; he does," I assured her.

She took my hand in hers and looked down at them for several moments. They were so similar. I wondered if she noticed. "Caroline," she said so familiarly that I was taken by surprise. "Did you know you and my daughter have the same name?"

"Yes, ma'am." I smiled, but this conversation was such a hard mixture of love and pain.

"I hope you and your fella have a happy life. I can tell you love him. My sweet Caroline, you are going to have beautiful babies with that beautiful man," she said. "Can't you see it?" For a second, I could, even if it were just playing pretend with my momma. "Oh, my, look at the time. Do you mind seeing me to the door?" she asked like she had just stopped in for a visit.

By the time I got Momma back to her room, she was exhausted and despondent and frustrated that I was fussing over her. She slapped my hand away twice and non-verbally huffed her impatience towards me.

I drove home Sunday morning, feeling drained from the emotional rollercoaster that was my mother's condition. I never knew when the last conversation would be or the last words she'd actually speak to me. I stayed up and ate breakfast with Billy and Zinnia. I helped Zin get ready for church and braided her hair. Her toothless grin was so adorable. She was delighted to wake and find that the tooth fairy had found her tooth. Billy would be at the fire station for the next three nights. I waited to go to bed until after Billy and Zinnia went to church to meet Jen.

***

I slept hard, harder than usual, and when I awoke, I was a little disoriented. My phone was buzzing; it was Krissa.

"Hey," I answered groggily.

"Whatcha doing tonight? I want to go out." she said. I hesitated. There was something important I was going to do. "Are you awake?" she pressed impatiently.

"Yeah, give me a minute." I sat up and rubbed my eyes and saw my dress hanging on the bathroom door. "I can't go out tonight. I have plans."

"*You* have plans?"

"Don't act so surprised. I make plans, sometimes."

"Sometimes, like never. Really, go out with me. Reschedule. I'm going to be bored while Billy's at the station."

"Nope, can't." I was smiling, then, thinking of my evening ahead. I was getting that giddy feeling in the pit of my stomach. It felt fluttery and excited just thinking about it.

"Are you going out with Hashim?" she asked teasingly. I was so thankful she couldn't see my face at that moment, but she was observant enough to know I had a huge smile on my face.

"Yes," I giggled.

"Oh, girl," she giggled and then her voice was serious like an older, wiser sister, "I've already warned you. Please be careful. I don't want to see you hurt."

"We are just going out to dinner. That's pretty harmless."

"No offense, C, but he's a few steps above your paygrade." I really hated that phrase, *No offense*. I was offended. I was offended every time I heard it.

"What's that supposed to mean?"

"Where are you going? What are you wearing?"

"To dinner. A dress."

"Where?"

"I didn't ask."

"You're so naive." Her voice was condescending and impatient, like she was speaking to a child. "Caroline, do you even have condoms?"

"No! Why on earth would you ask me that? We aren't having sex; we're just going to dinner!"

"C, please, I'm sorry. I'm just concerned for your wellbeing. He's beautiful, sure, but there's something edgy about him. You know? Dangerous, like his intensity is hiding something dark."

"Yeah, he's pretty intense, but I think it's because he's so freaking intelligent." I needed to reassure her or maybe myself. "I'm okay, Krissa. I appreciate your concern. Hashim isn't going to take advantage of me. Please, don't worry."

"So, what are you wearing?"

"The green, knit dress you gave me." Silence. "You don't approve?"

"There's no shape to that dress. It's so plain. You can't even see your figure."

I gave a little chuckle. "I don't understand. One minute you're warning me to be careful and the next you're telling me my dress isn't alluring enough. It's really confusing."

"Yeah, I can see that. Sorry. I'm coming over; I'll help you get ready."

Krissa left just before six. She did my makeup and agreed that my hair was prettier down, flowing just past my shoulders and holding the curls, even in the late-summer humidity. Krissa convinced me to wear heels. I would have to be mindful of every step, but I agreed. I wore the same jewelry as I had before.

Hashim didn't compliment me with his words, but his approval was in his smile, the intensity of his eyes, and the way he put his arm on my back possessively and protectively whenever he stood beside me. He wasn't wearing a blazer tonight but tan slacks and a dress-shirt that felt like butter against his chest. I was distracted by its texture when I momentarily braced myself to regain my balance when I got out of his car. There was no valet.

We had driven over an hour to the closest big city. Tonight, we were eating Italian. It was a small, family-owned restaurant. I was surprised to see several families with their children. They were obviously related somehow. They were speaking mostly Italian, but the younger children were all speaking English.

"Are we crashing a family party?" I asked.

"No, they eat here on Sunday evenings. That is the grandmother and her sister. I am pretty sure they are from southern Italy, but the older gentleman, I cannot quite place his accent. I am almost positive that he is not a first-generation immigrant like the grandmother."

Even amid the chaos of strangers and kids, I felt oddly welcomed. The food was amazing and the wine, if possible, even better than the bottle the week before. I felt warm and happy. I loved pasta in most any form. The bread was hot and the sauce, spicy and savory.

Hashim had spent two summers in Italy when he was twelve and thirteen. He studied art and opera in Rome, but he was more entertained by the food and confessed that the second summer was his first encounter with the opposite sex.

Between courses, he took my necklace in his hands. "Do you always wear this?"

I looked down and shrugged. "Most of the time, why?"

"Is it common to wear the wedding bands of your deceased relatives on a chain around your neck?"

I shrugged again. "Aunt June wore Pawpaw's, Momma added hers and my daddy's when they passed, and I guess I'll add Momma's when that time comes," I said looking down at the collection of rings.

"What is the inscription?" he asked, examining my daddy's wide gold band in the light.

"Proverbs 18:22. It's from the Old Testament. *The man who finds a wife finds a treasure, and he receives favor from the Lord*," I recited from memory. Daddy had told me a thousand times.

He looked at the band in between his fingers and muttered something under his breath. I didn't ask him to repeat it, but it sounded like, "You will make a good wife, someday, Caroline." His tone was a little sad with hints of regret so I ignored it. I didn't want his mood to shift away from the liveliness of the restaurant.

Absentmindedly, I lost count after my third glass of wine. Our waiter opened a second bottle, but I didn't remember how much of that was left at the end of the meal. I was too distracted by the children and the food and Hashim's hands. He touched my hand all through dinner. He scooted closer to me in the corner booth. Our thighs touched and it felt nice, not dangerous at all. But when he casually put his hand on my thigh during dessert, my eyes widened, and I instantly felt small and vulnerable.

He understood my expression and moved his hand. He placed his arm around my shoulder, a safe distance from my thighs. He pulled me in and kissed my temple. My trust in him returned. I couldn't remember much beyond dessert. There was laughter, and his shirt was so soft. I dreamed about his beauty and his eyes and his kiss and the dark-eyed, dark-haired children at the restaurant.

***

It took me a long time to wake up Monday. My head throbbed and the sunlight from the bathroom was painfully bright. I inhaled and could smell Hashim's clean scent close to me. I opened my eyes suddenly. He wasn't there, but his shirt was. Panic washed over me; my mind raced through last night's dinner. How had I gotten there? I checked myself, and thankfully, I was still wearing my dress. Where were my shoes? I pulled the covers away and was more relieved than anything to find my underwear exactly where they should be.

<u>CHAPTER 11.5</u>

The man who finds a wife finds a treasure,
and he receives favor from the Lord.

– Proverbs 18:22

Favor, I scoffed. My mother would have absolutely loved to know a young, common, Gentile woman was quoting scripture to her free-thinking, heretical son over Italian. It was almost comical. I had refused to make my bar mitzvah. I saw no reason, even then, to follow a faith and a god whom I saw no proof of in my world. Nevertheless, I could not argue with Caroline's faith or her resolve to pray. It was real to her, and I had met enough spiritual leaders and devout believers to know when their belief was authentic. Whether or not I found any value in it was of no consequence. It was in them and undeniably what defined their character.

I thought nothing of the way I had touched her all evening. She was approachable and at ease. She smiled and it was obvious she loved the food and the wine and the friendly, extended family surrounding us. Even in her American-style clothes, her dress tonight was feminine without revealing anything of her shape or her curves. She was shrouded like she was wearing an abaya. I simply wanted to know those same thighs from the morning were still there. I knew I had erred, as soon as I saw the look in her guileless eyes, the mixture of fear and innocence. I took my hand away and placed it around her shoulder instead.

When she stepped from the booth, I knew instantly that she was unable to walk on her own. I encouraged her to sit back down, and I took her heels off one at a time. Her feet were adorably bare, the way I expected to see them every day.

She put her arm around my waist, and I gently guided her towards the door and out to the car. She was giggly and silly from the bottle of wine she had consumed without my being aware. I had not been paying attention to the wine; I had been paying attention to her. She stroked the fabric of my shirt periodically, pleased with its texture. She turned toward me and watched me drive her home in the dark. The wine had clouded her vision, but it was as though she could see right through me.

"You are so beautiful. I really like your eyes. No, I really like your smile more. Do you like my smile?" she asked dreamily.

"Yes, Caroline, I like your smile.

"I like to see your teeth when you smile," she giggled. "Do you like my teeth when I smile?"

"I like your face, but I like your toes better," I confessed.

She giggled again and sang, "This little piggy went to market and this little piggy ran wee, wee, wee, all the way home."

She finally fell asleep as we entered her neighborhood. I lifted her from the car and guided her feet toward the door. She was unable to do more than hand me her keys. I knew that I could not leave her in her current condition to even find her bed, so I scooped her up into my arms and carried her down the hall toward the bedrooms. I stood, unsure for a moment, realizing that I had no idea which room was hers. Billy's truck was not outside, so I knew he was not home.

I could instantly tell that the room at the end of the hall was hers. Her robe was lying across the foot of her unmade bed. But even if I had not seen the robe, I would have known it was her room. Her presence was everywhere, her scent especially. As soon as I lifted her into my arms, she placed her head on my shoulder and nuzzled her face into my neck. It would be so easy to turn and kiss her, but I refrained. She was intoxicated and vulnerable, and I had promised her that I would not use the attraction she held for me against her.

I laid her gently in her bed, but she continued to hold onto my shirt. "Hashim?" she whispered.

"Yes, Caroline," my voice broke a little in the whisper.

"Thank you," she said and kissed me gently on the mouth.

I had to brace myself though when she wrapped her arms around me and pulled me down on top of her. I gently eased myself away from her, but she still clung to my shirt and to my mouth.

"Are you going to stay with me?" she whispered.

I swallowed, torn between that question and the temptation of her words and her lying there, knowing I could convince her so easily to give herself to me. Power is a heady thing. I loosened the buttons of my shirt and gently slipped out of her grasp. I wondered briefly if this was what Joseph experienced at the hands of Potiphar's wife.

I stood over her, half-dressed. She rolled over slightly taking in my shirt affectionately into her chest like a child clinging to a beloved stuffed animal and sighed. The hem of her dress went up, exposing the creamy, pale skin of her thighs. I reached for her comforter and covered her all the way to her chin. I stood back looking at the lumpy form in the middle of her bed and knew that no amount of coverings could shield me from her attraction. I suddenly had an over whelming desire to run.

I took her keys and locked her inside of her house and hurriedly found my running shorts and shoes. It was not even midnight, but the neighborhood was quiet and the warm, humid evening felt like I was running through water. I pushed myself a full ten miles before I allowed myself to go anywhere near her home. Walls and deadbolts and comforters were no protection for what I was feeling toward Caroline. Even as I ran and sweated and exhausted myself, her scent remained; the taste of her kisses was still fresh on my tongue. I took a hot shower and brushed my teeth twice before I was able to fall into bed and escape in sleep. When my alarm sounded at five, I did not need to run; I needed to work. I could see everything coming together.

<u>CHAPTER 12</u>

I busied myself with chores and errands for a few hours on Monday. I made myself a sandwich and got ready for class. I didn't see or hear Hashim all day. Before I left for the grocery store, I found my keys and heels on the counter with a brief note from Hashim.

Thank you for a lovely evening. You were sleeping.

I wasn't really embarrassed that I had gotten inebriated, but I was concerned that maybe I had done or said something to offend him. He seemed distant and preoccupied during class. Krissa monopolized most of my attention, begging me for details of our date. She didn't like my outline of the evening and told me that I was a horrible storyteller.

"Can you cover for me Wednesday night?" Krissa asked me. "Billy'll be off and I want to see him." My glance instinctively moved to Hashim. I wasn't sure if he would ask me to go out again on my night off.

"I will be working long hours this week to prepare for a meeting. I leave Friday morning and will return late Sunday night," Hashim said. I was surprised at how hard it was to hide my disappointment. Krissa looked hopeful that I would say yes now that it was clear I would have no other options.

"Yeah, I'll work for you," I said begrudgingly.

The rest of the week was monotonous without anything to look forward to. Hashim said he couldn't even spare time to have breakfast with me. He did walk me to my car after class and he did kiss me as had become our habit when Krissa wasn't nearby. As though he could sense my worry, he told me that he was starting a new project and needed to work to finish the initial contract. He assured me that this trip was unavoidable and that he couldn't spare the time or distraction while he prepared. I tried to be understanding, but I felt like he was holding me at a distance. How odd that I had come to expect his attention in a week's time. I felt a little foolish.

CHAPTER 12.5

Do you see a man skillful in his work?
He will stand before kings; he will not stand before obscure men.

– Proverbs 22:29

I had kissed Caroline briefly after class on Thursday night. I would be at the airport before she was home from work Friday morning. I drove two hours to the designated airport where a chartered plane waited. I was flown to a small, private airstrip in Virginia and was then helicoptered by military to the Pentagon. Kennedy was a better agent and handler than Marshall. I preferred most militaries over the private sector. Like the spiritually devoted, those trained and disciplined had sworn fealty. They understood loyalty and honor differently than those who had never fought or faced death for something beyond themselves. Although private sector paid better, I did not trust all of my work in the hands of the greedy bastards Marshall represented. I was satisfied to throw him the scraps every-so-often to keep him appeased.

"Emir," Kennedy said as he shook my hand in greeting. "What you've managed to produce has been incredible. Whatever you've got going on, keep it up. It's working."

"Thank you," I said.

Kennedy led me through the security protocols and waited while I was all but body-cavity searched. "Everyone's gathered. We're eager for your updates and the interphase. When do you think you'll have the finished product?"

"That is part of the reason I asked for this meeting." Kennedy nodded, not forcing me to repeat myself. He could wait to hear it with everyone else.

The committee, made up of both military and appointed, was pleased with my progress and my assurance that the first phase of this contract would be completed months ahead of schedule. They also agreed to renegotiate my terms for the additional phase that I would begin working on immediately. I left them eager and almost salivating at the prospect of their being given first access to such technology.

Hands were shaken, smiles returned, goodwill given, and assurances of their loyalty. I had played this game often enough and witnessed first-hand the rise and fall of good graces. For now, I was seen as a hero, but as soon as my job was done, or in the unlikely chance that either party reneged on their end of the deal, I would become an enemy of any given country in a matter of seconds. It was a tenuous line I walked.

I met with the tech team, assigned to my project. They were the ones who opened the highly-secured portal regularly for me to dump my files into the Pentagon's mainframe. We had only met once before, but we held a mutual respect.

The three of us worked straight through the next thirty-six hours, napping occasionally when the transferring took longer than twenty minutes to complete. I could sleep in peace on the return flight. Kennedy kept us fed and provided a steady flow of caffeinated beverages.

The weather was not cooperating and delayed my flight by a couple of hours. My thoughts returned to Caroline and her welcoming smile, and I was saddened that I would not see it again for another twenty-four hours. I was delirious and exhausted. Why was she the only thought to mind. I slept until I felt the pressure change as we prepared for landing. I secretly hoped Caroline would hear me and welcome me home. I was obviously sleep deprived.

CHAPTER 13

Hashim left Friday morning. He said he had an important meeting to attend and wouldn't return until late Sunday night. I worked Friday and Saturday, wrote a paper and studied for my first exam.

Sunday evening was so weird. I made dinner and Krissa came over. I was hoping they would go out again, but they decided to stay in and watch a movie. I could tell Krissa had every intention to stay the night. She'd brought in a twelve-pack and microwave popcorn. It was gross to watch their interaction and obvious foreplay. I was used to Krissa's flirty behavior, but it was borderline nauseating to watch my brother return her attention.

I tried to watch the movie with them, but, even in the dark, I was too distracted by their groping to concentrate on the plot. I finally went to my bedroom and tried to read a chapter from my *Economics of Aging* textbook. Surely, that text could remove any sexual thoughts from the reader's mind. No use. I put in headphones, too, but then I heard a loud bang and drunk whispers and giggles. They'd bumped into the wall or missed the door or maybe were doing it already in the hallway.

I pressed the spot on my forehead between my eyebrows, but it didn't relieve the growing tension. Increasing the volume didn't help, either. I couldn't handle the giggles and sex sounds coming from Billy's room. I decided to go outside to have some peace. I sat down on the concrete and leaned my head against the door. Hashim must have heard the door open. He opened his door, cautiously, and stepped out under the carport.

"Caroline, is that you?"

"Yes. When did you get in?" I hadn't heard his car.

"A little while ago. What's wrong?"

"Can't sleep." He came and sat next to me and nudged me with his elbow, playfully. I wasn't in the mood. Then we both heard the sounds from inside the house. They were embarrassingly loud.

Hashim chuckled knowingly. "I understand why you are unable to sleep. Would you like to come in?"

I shook my head. "No, that's not guaranteed to be any better."

"Why not?" He almost sounded offended.

"Alone in your apartment? The probability of kissing? The sounds of sex fresh in my memory? Being freakishly repulsed and turned on at the same time? Pick one," I said sarcastically.

"I see." He paused. "It is good to see you; I thought I would have to wait until tomorrow evening."

I smiled at that. "It's good to see you, too. How was your trip?"

"Exceedingly promising. It feels good to know my work is useful and productive. It is not often a man's work is appreciated."

"I appreciate you," I said quietly and it stirred the air between us.

"I know," he said and put his arm around me and drew me into his side. He kissed the side of my head.

We heard a squeal and more inappropriate laughter. "Can we get out of here, please. I can't handle this. I know it's normal behavior, but I don't feel right knowing what happens between my friend and my brother."

"Would you like to drive?" he asked.

Those were magical words. My spirits were instantly lifted. "Yes! Please!" I turned to him smiling for the first time all weekend and kissed him briefly on the lips. "Thank you." I could see him smiling back at me in the dark.

***

I was speeding, flying around corners, drifting, squealing happily on the straight-a-ways. They were genuine and more heart-felt than even Krissa's. I was burning up Hashim's gas. We would need to go back into town soon. It was then that I caught the flashing lights from the corner of my eye.

"I'm sorry," I muttered. "Shit! I don't even have my purse," I confessed.

"Don't worry. Let me handle this," he said reaching for his wallet.

As the officer approached, I rolled down the window and saw the young officer clearly. "Hey Eddie," I said not believing my luck.

"Hey Caroline, where you headed?"

"Just driving."

"How have you been? It's been a while."

"Good, and you?"

"Can't complain. Nice ride."

"Thanks," I said smiling. "I'm enjoying it."

"I can tell. Are you avoiding another date rape scenario?" he asked, looking directly at the dark-skinned man in the passenger seat.

"No, not tonight," I said and cut my eyes toward Hashim. "He's just letting me drive his car for fun."

"Have you been drinking?" Eddie asked.

I rolled my eyes. "No. Are you going to give me a ticket?" I asked.

He almost grinned, considering. He laughed a little and shook his head. "I think my supervisor would frown at that. He would make me pay it, regardless. You left quite an impression on him."

"Thanks. I'll be law-abiding and bring it on home."

"Thank you. You're making my shift easier. Have a good night, Caroline. Be safe; I'll see you around."

"You, too, Eddie." I gave a little wave before I rolled up the window. "Oh, my gosh! I can't believe that just happened!" I covered my embarrassed face with both of my hands and laughed uncontrollably.

"Who was that?" Hashim asked.

"Remember the story about my ex-boyfriend? Well, that's him. Ironic that he's in law enforcement." I giggled. "We should probably go home, huh?"

"Yes." Hashim nodded. "Unless you have more ex-boyfriends who can refuse to give you a ticket for speeding or reckless driving."

Once we were home, my heart sank a little. Krissa's car was still parked in the driveway. "Do you think they could still be at it?" I asked.

"I doubt it."

"Thank you," I said. "I really needed this." We unbuckled ourselves but neither moved to get out of the car.

"Me, too," Hashim said, taking my hand from the gear shift and kissing my palm. "It felt strange not seeing you for a few days."

"I know, right? Strange what you can get used to in a short period of time." I leaned against the back of the seat looking into his eyes. He cupped my cheek in his hand and I anticipated his kiss. I liked the way his beard felt on my face. I liked the way he held my neck securely, grounding me, keeping me near him. I thought about something while we kissed. I leaned back and looked at him. "What time do you usually go to bed?" I asked.

"After midnight. Why do you ask?"

"Geeze, it's nearly three. I've kept you out half the night. I'm sorry. I wasn't thinking, and you probably have work tomorrow. I can't believe I've been so selfish."

"Have I complained?" he whispered as he kissed down my neck.

"No," I said in a breathy whisper. *This is new*, I thought, but he wouldn't receive any protest. I liked too much the way his beard and lips felt against my neck.

"Then do not worry," he whispered near my ear. He returned his lips to mine and we kissed for a few minutes more. He kissed me again at the door and I stood on my tiptoes and pressed myself against him, wrapping my arms around him. He moved his hand to the small of my back and the intensity of our kissing changed. I suddenly didn't want to be separated from him. He moved his lips from mine, but instead of moving away like I usually did, I began kissing his cheek toward his ear. I took his earlobe between my teeth and exhaled. I continued to kiss down his neck, all the while pulling him closer. I felt strong enough to climb his lean torso and broad shoulders.

His scent captivated me. I had selfishly slept with his shirt all week. I knew how creepy that sounded, but in his absence, like an addict, I justified my need for him. His shirt was nice and all, but I lost myself at the source. My senses were reeling. My hands were everywhere as my lips and tongue tasted his skin for the first time. If I had been a vampire, I would have sucked him dry. Warmth flooded me and awakened a desire deep within me; I had yet to experience anything like this in my twenty years.

"Caroline." I heard my name being said, but I ignored it. "Caroline." This time it was more insistent and I felt Hashim pulling away from me. "Goodnight, Caroline," he said firmly, and before I could protest, I was standing in the kitchen, dazed and confused.

CHAPTER 13.5

Above all else, guard your heart, for everything you do flows from it.

— Proverbs 4:23

Damn it! What the hell was that? I shut the door and tossed my keys onto the counter. I opened the fridge and guzzled orange juice straight from the container. My heart was racing like I had just sprinted a couple of miles. I suddenly needed to take a long, hot shower and manually relieve myself of the feelings Caroline had suddenly stirred within me. We had been kissing often for the past couple of weeks, but she never took the offensive.

If I were a weaker man, less self-disciplined, I would have lifted her up and carried her into my apartment. She wanted me to; I could sense her need and desire. For the first time, I imagined her lying in my arms, naked beside me, panting, with a light sheen of perspiration from the physical exertion of our lovemaking. How had one kiss altered me so entirely.

I knew better. It had not been one kiss. It was weeks of kissing, romantic dinners, and driving. It was being apart for three days, intense meetings, and the anticipation of being with her again. It was also the sounds coming from her house. She was annoyed by her brother and friend, but no one could deny the power those sounds had to make one more attuned to his or her own sexual desires. My assurance to protect her virtue just became that much harder. *Caroline.* My phone vibrated on the counter, drawing me back to the present. *Marshall,* I said his name like a curse in my mind. I answered it, not thinking.

"What?"

"Good morning," he said.

"It's still night where I am," I said flatly.

"How were your meetings in D.C.?"

I said nothing. How did he know? Nothing had been in my name. Kennedy set the meeting; he had chartered the flight. He did not know where I was, either, but I would not be hard to find. The boiling passion Caroline had stirred in my blood only moments ago turned to raging anger. Curses in every language flew through my mind. I had yet to formulate my exit strategy. Again, I had become lax.

"Emir?" Marshall's voice was biting. "You know it won't be long. I think this might be my opportunity to set a personal record. I'm feeling lenient, so I decided to give you a head's start. I'm close, man, really close. I can feel it."

"Perhaps I should thank you."

"Perhaps you should."

I ended the call and threw the phone against the wall, shattering the screen into a million pieces. I knew better. Ironically, my first thought was not of leaving but for the girl asleep under the comforter, barefoot, behind thin walls. *Caroline.*

CHAPTER 14

I didn't see Hashim again until class. He was still distracted, but even edgier than before. He looked tired, but I knew that was my fault; I'd kept him up half the night. We spoke very little and he didn't mention anything about Sunday night. He walked me to the car and kissed me, but it was cautious like he was afraid of being seen or being attacked again.

I was ashamed of my behavior. I had made it clear that I wasn't going to have sex, but that was easy to say and be sure of when I wasn't attracted to anyone, when I wasn't kissing anyone. I felt like such a tease. I was filled with lustful passion for a beautiful man. I wondered if this burning was sent directly from the depths of hell. Hashim didn't ask me out again. Neither of us could spare the time. The third class was proving to be too much. We studied some together before midterms, but he was just doing it as a favor to me. There wasn't much he needed to review.

Krissa and Billy spent every spare moment they had together, and Krissa slept over nearly every night when he wasn't at the fire station. Thankfully, they had tempered their passions and kept things respectfully quiet when I was home. It wasn't hard to admit they were actually good for one another.

Momma's condition was deteriorating rapidly. Her doctor changed her medication, but we both knew medication wasn't the issue. Most likely her brain was misfiring like tiny, little, struggling fireworks in the gray abyss of her decaying brain. She didn't sing anymore. She didn't even hum my song anymore when I kissed her goodnight. She barely spoke at all. The lovely, friendly crinkles around her eyes when she smiled were replaced with scowls and frowns. She even spit at me. It was awful to watch. Billy couldn't stand it either. He tried, but finally said he wouldn't go back; he couldn't go back. I understood and didn't judge him. That wasn't our mother, the woman who raised us; that woman was gone. I needed to let her go and grieve her passing. It was just so god-awful slow and painful.

By mid-October, the heat was finally gone for a few months. Billy was leaving soon and spending every moment he could with Zinnia and every night with Krissa. Although I hated surprises, I preferred quick, spur-of-the-moment. I hated long goodbyes, agonizing deaths, and waiting for the inevitable. I hated the teetering unknown of friends who kissed.

One evening, Krissa came by to get something from Billy's room. It was pretty late, but I heard Hashim's voice through his door when I walked Krissa out. The carport light needed to be replaced, so I was standing in shadow.

I didn't hear Hashim behind me, but I knew they were his hands around my waist. I smiled when I turned in his arms. His eyes were wide in the dark. He pulled me further into the shadow of the carport near the laundry room. He placed his hand gently over my mouth and whispered into my ear.

"Caroline, I am sorry." His words were breathy like he'd been running. His heart was beating through his chest. I sensed his fear, his desire. I shook my head, not understanding what he was doing to me. He pulled me closer into his embrace and I could feel the fear and panic in me rising.

"What are you doing?" I tried to ask, but he couldn't hear me with his hand over my mouth. I shook my head and tried to get away from him. I didn't like the way he was holding me forcefully in the dark. He jerked me abruptly and shook me to get my attention. I knew instinctively not to fight him; he was much bigger and stronger than me. I was afraid, but when I looked into his eyes searchingly, I knew I wasn't afraid of him.

"Do exactly as I say. Go into the laundry room and hide. Do not come out, no matter what you hear, until I get you myself. Do you understand?" he whispered through clenched teeth. My eyes were wide now, searching his for answers. He was holding me so tightly and I couldn't breathe with his hands around my mouth. His intensity frightened me but I nodded, unable to deny the truth in his eyes. He was possibly more frightened than me. He lowered his hand from my mouth, trusting that I wouldn't scream. I didn't have breath to breathe, much less scream. He unlocked the laundry room and stroked my cheek briefly as he eased me through the crack in the door. "Hide."

I heard him lock the door behind me. I was standing in the dark of the laundry room that also served as a small storage space for tools and the lawnmower. I had to think; fear had clouded my judgement. He told me to hide. He was afraid; he was afraid for me. I crawled low under the shelves, in a space too cramped for even my compact size. My heart was beating in my ears. The laundry room door had a metal grate near the base to let the heat escape. I could hear a man's voice that I didn't recognize.

"Emir. Who's the girl?"

"None of your concern."

"She's not your usual type. I only caught a glimpse, but hell, even I'd do her. When do you expect her to return?"

"She will not tonight," Hashim said flatly.

"Convenient."

"She is nothing." I heard him say dismissively. That hurt a little. "So, you found me; why are you here?" Hashim's tone was unsettlingly cold.

The other man made a comment that I couldn't discern through the door in my state of terror. I took a couple of deep breaths to settle the incessant beating between my ears. I wanted to hear what this stranger was saying to Hashim.

"She is my landlord, nothing more." His words were strong and direct. He sounded so convincing. The fear that gripped me was laced with doubt, and insecurity was even greater than fear. His words were believable and I knew them to be true.

"We warned you, Emir, not to repeat your last mistakes; you seriously have an issue with women." *Women.* I hid silently and hoped he would forget about me. How could I face him again? My rapid heartbeats fought hard against the strangling doubt in my chest. Tears ran down my cheeks.

"You could have called." Hashim said.

"No, sir. You are much too important to call, and besides, you avoid my calls. You warrant a personal visit and constant supervision. I'll be watching everything from now on. You could make this so much easier if you'd just come in for good and tell us what we want to know."

Their murmurs and tones sounded tense, but indiscernible. I waited for a long time until nothing else was said. I was hovering under the shelf, cramped and sweaty in the small space. It felt like forever before Hashim opened the laundry room door. I was afraid and hurt, not physically, but ashamed at the relief that gripped me when I heard him unlock the door. I squinted when my eyes were thrust into light by headlights passing down our street. When I opened my eyes, I could make out the shape of him in complete shadow.

"Are you alright?" he whispered.

I nodded. "Who was that?" I asked at nearly the same volume.

He shook his head and placed one finger over his lips, giving me warning not to say anything aloud. He helped me come out from the small space under the shelves. He pulled me into the kitchen and locked the deadbolt. He hit the play button on an old cd player we kept on the kitchen counter and music played loudly before he led me outside onto the back patio.

I was shaking, but I managed to keep it together enough not to scream or speak at all. He took my hands and turned to me. He brought them up to his chest and exhaled slowly. His heart was beating strong. He leaned his head down and breathed against my cheek and neck. Involuntary shivers ran down my spine. His intensity had frightened me before, but I needed answers only he could give.

"Who was that?" I breathed into his ear. My voice came in breathy gasps.

He leaned in closer and wrapped his arms around me. "Take a deep breath, Caroline. You are safe. I will not let him get to you."

I trusted his words, but they didn't give me answers. I settled myself in his embrace, finding courage. "Please, tell me."

He took a deep breath and drew me closer before he whispered low into my ear, "Private sector. Your entire house may be bugged. We need privacy."

I looked up into his eyes pleadingly. *Privacy*, I could do that. "Wait here," I mouthed in the shadow and touched his chest gently with my finger. I'm not sure why, but I walked back into the house. It was pretty dark so I didn't think anyone would see us leaving the backyard. My mind was racing. I grabbed some water bottles and a blanket, the turkey Lunchables™, a bag of fresh veggies and a flashlight. I opened my backpack that was hanging on the barstool and dumped everything inside. I powered off my phone and slipped it into my back pocket. Once I was outside, again, with Hashim, I motioned with my head the direction I intended to go. He silently followed me through the yard and into the small cluster of trees.

It had been years since I'd been to the fort but I knew the way well, even in the dark. I could still feel the air on my face as I ran through the trees to beat Billy there. The faint scar on my cheek was from the time the branch slapped me when Billy outran me. Daddy had allowed us to carry off the extra lumber from the addition.

Hashim didn't ask where we were going, but when we came to the small clearing, he laughed low under his breath. I opened the makeshift door and went inside. I turned on the flashlight which illuminated the entire space. Something scurried and jumped from the window to escape. I jumped as I turned to see Hashim had followed me into the fort. His form was hulking and intimidating in the shadows of the small interior. He looked around and took the blanket from my arm. He understood.

"Privacy," he said flatly.

"Yes," I said in a shaky whisper.

He opened the blanket and deftly shook it out in one motion, making it fall gracefully onto the earthen floor. I knelt down and placed the food from my backpack onto the blanket. Hashim knelt down beside me. I diverted my gaze and focused unnecessarily on the food; I offered him a water bottle. He took my hand instead and willed me to look at him.

"Hashim," I whispered; my stomach hurt so bad.

"Caroline, please let me explain."

I didn't want an explanation. I wanted him to take me in his arms and reassure me. I wanted him to tell me he wasn't a spy, and he wasn't here to hijack a plane or bomb a building or murder innocent people. I wanted him to tell me I wasn't crazy like my momma and Aunt June, and that he cared for me. I knew deep down he was good and had a conscience, but I wasn't sure he knew that.

"I am sorry I made you hide; I regret you had to be frightened of me. Marshall is not a good man; he is dangerous." He said the words like he needed them to sink in.

"Who is he?" I asked again.

"He is a handler. He has been assigned to bring me on full-time into his organization."

"You work for him?"

"No."

"You worked for him before?"

"Not directly."

"Was it illegal?"

"Yes, by most countries' standards." He shook his head not really wanting to give any details. "What I do is very specialized. There are probably only about a dozen of us in the world. We freelance; we work for ourselves, aligning with an agency or country as is needed. My services and abilities are highly coveted which means my position is quite lucrative. The only downfall is that I am rarely afforded protection, except from the country or agency with whom I am currently contracted. Once the contract is completed, I become fair game."

"Lucrative, like money?"

"Yes, among other things."

"Like what?"

"Cars, houses, women, drugs, protection, whatever you want."

"You've had all of those things?" He closed his eyes and took a deep breath. His words, *she is nothing*, made me pause. "I'm sorry that's none of my business, and that's not why I brought you here. I thought you could use the fort to clear your head." I shook off the darkness and lightened my tone. "Billy and I built it as kids," I said completely changing the subject. "This was once the best place in the world."

When the flashlight flickered and dimmed, I scrounged on a low shelf for a box of matches and a candle. I was surprised when the matches ignited. I found another candle and secured them together on an old metal lid and placed them in the center of the blanket. We might need the flashlight for the walk home.

"Nice." he said and took another deep breath. He leaned his head back against one wall. He opened the bottle of water and took a sip. I watched him as he retreated far away with his thoughts.

I opened the bag of vegetables and crunched loudly on a carrot breaking the deafening silence. I saw his lip curl up slightly. "Sorry," I muttered around the carrot in my mouth. He was amused when he opened his eyes and looked at me. All of his fear was gone.

"You cannot help it. You make noise, and I hear everything. Even when you are still and reading, you make noise."

<u>CHAPTER 14.5</u>

Pride goes before destruction, a haughty spirit before a fall.

— Proverbs 16:18

I refused to consider he would find me so soon. I had done everything I knew to cover my tracks: low profile, simple, cheap. It was too easy for him. Marshall had to have people working on the inside.

Crunch, chew, swallow. I could not help but be amused, but I did not understand her reasoning. I had held her roughly and frightened her. I made her hide and locked her in a laundry closet. I brought danger into her home, and how did she repay me? She made me a picnic. She thought to bring me provision and take me to the one place she knew no one would find me.

She refused to look me in the eye and focused unnecessarily on the crackers and meat and cheese in the tiny, compartmentalized tray she balanced on her lap. She had not run to me or clung to me or screamed or cursed at me. She was avoiding me, though, and she had every right to do so.

"Caroline," I finally said and she gradually lifted her eyes to mine. She swallowed nervously and took a small sip from her water bottle. "I am sorry."

"What are you sorry for?" she asked.

"Bringing danger to your doorstep. Forcing you to hide and be silent." She shrugged, dismissively like it was nothing. "Caroline, what are you thinking?" She shook her head, refusing to tell me. "I want to know," I pressed. She shook her head more adamantly and her eyes widened again in fear. "Please, I want to reassure you."

She looked hard into my eyes. Her light eyes were shadowed in the dim candlelight; they looked both vulnerable and determined. She blinked like she was holding back tears. "Are you *sorry* for spending time with me?"

What a ridiculous question. What was she asking? Had I given her any indication to think that? "No," I said.

"Are you *sorry* for being my friend?"

"No."

"Are you *sorry* for kissing me?"

"Why would you ask me that?" My voice rose slightly with this line of questioning. "What would make you doubt any of that?"

She gave a slight shrug and lowered her gaze onto the cracker she held in her hand. "You haven't asked me out again and you don't kiss me or agree to eat with me very often. I don't know... what you said tonight to Marshall. I understand. Really, I do."

I ran my hands through my hair and squeezed the back of my neck. *What the hell was she talking about?* This had nothing to do with kissing her or the time we spent together. This had everything to do with Marshall finding me and him using her to get to me. I said nothing for several, long seconds.

She suddenly grabbed her backpack and made to leave me alone. She tossed me the flashlight and said, "Follow the break in the trees. You'll see the house. I'll leave the patio light on for you."

"Caroline." My voice sounded pleading. She shook off my voice, so I grabbed her leg when she tried to stand. She came down hard against me and pushed herself away. I kept hold of her calf so she could not scurry away. "Listen to me," I demanded. "I do not know what you heard tonight, but I was careful to give nothing away. Marshall cannot know about you. He will use everything he knows against me. He already knows too much."

"But you said, you said I was *nothing*."

"Oh, Caroline," I said in a hard, humorless chuckle. "Nothing? You think I meant that?" I pulled myself closer to her, clutching her thigh and then her waist. I forced her to look at me. "I have not asked you out or eaten with you because I have had no time. Your presence has filled my mind with new ideas and more clarity than I have had in years." I was scaring her again, but I needed to make her understand. "I want to kiss you more than I care to admit, but even I have my limitations. When you kiss me, I want more, more of something, something I have already promised to protect. Do you have any idea what that does to me?" The question was purely rhetorical, but she nodded with complete understanding.

I loosened my grip on her and gently brought her into my side. I wrapped my arms around her and breathed in her scent. She was still not close enough to suit me. Moving her legs over mine, I scooped her into my lap and cradled her against my chest. She lifted her eyes to mine, and for the first time all evening, I knew she trusted me again. I lowered my lips to hers and she welcomed my affection. Her arms held me securely around my neck. I wondered who was comforting whom. We tempered our passions, satisfied to cling to one another, and at some point, we fell asleep lying together in each other's arms.

CHAPTER 15

"Caroline," I heard Hashim's voice. He was shaking me gently. I rolled over and opened my eyes. I was not naturally a morning person; truth be told, I was a person who slept hard and hated to be awakened. I never knew where I was when I first opened my eyes and it took my brain a few seconds to adjust.

"It is nearly five. I need to get back to the house. I cannot break from my routine." I shook my head not understanding. "I run at five; they will be watching." The memory of last night flooded my mind and I understood.

I nodded and pushed myself up from the hard ground. I would definitely regret that later. My body was already sore and achy from the stress of hiding under the shelf, but our impromptu campout only made it worse. Hashim brushed the loose hair from my face and kissed my forehead. "Good morning." He smiled. I think he was trying to reassure me.

"Morning," I said and was thankful he hadn't kissed me on the mouth. "What's next? What do I need to know?"

"Nothing for now. Stick to your routine and be mindful of your surroundings." He slid my phone from my pocket and turned it on before he handed it to me. "Unlock it."

I opened the screen and handed it back to him. He typed in a number and handed it back to me. I looked at the contact he had just entered. "Aunt June?" I asked and then laughed. "Perfect, no one would ever guess." I said sarcastically.

***

The next three days were bizarre. I went through my routine like a robot with only intermittent texts from Hashim. I saw him in class, and when he walked me to my car. It was hard not to touch him. I helped Billy get everything ready for his deployment. I cooked dinner for everyone on Sunday night. Even Zinnia was allowed over on a school night.

Our farewell was subdued, yet heartfelt. Zin cried when Jen came to pick her up. After I loaded the dishwasher, I hugged Billy hard, but I didn't cry. I wished him well before I retreated to my room, giving him and Krissa the rest of the night together. He would be gone long before the sun. I wanted to see Hashim and wished we didn't have to worry about what Marshall might see. I wished I could dig a secret passageway to the apartment. I texted him that Billy would be leaving early in the morning. I also asked if I could see him. He gave no reply.

Monday night, after class, I went to work as usual. I think Momma knew Billy was sent away again. She had a familiar, wistful look in her eye. Maybe she was just mirroring mine. I made the usual rounds and decided to take my break in her room; it was about two in the morning. She wasn't awake, but it made me feel less alone to sit near her. I played music low for her from my phone. I had a playlist of all of her favorites. I zipped my cooler bag and stood to give Momma a kiss when I heard loud whispers in the hallway. I looked up to see Hashim burst through the door into her room. The head nurse was right behind him. She looked angry and threatening even on her best days, so I shrunk back around Momma's bed when they forced themselves through the door.

"Caroline," they said at the same time. The nurse's tone was in warning, threatening me that this crazy man would cost me my job; Hashim's tone was pleading.

"I've got it," I assured the brooding nurse. She eyed me cautiously and gave Hashim a threatening glance.

"You have five minutes," she warned him.

He gave a quick nod and then turned toward me. He took two steps and then looked down at the sleeping woman between us and frowned. "Is this your mother?" he asked.

"Hashim, meet Momma. Momma, Hashim," I said flippantly. "Why are you here?"

"We need to go," he whispered.

"What? Where are we going?"

"I need to get you away for a while. It is not safe."

"My shifts? School? I can't just leave," I protested.

"Please." His eyes were begging. "We have to go; I cannot leave you." His words were insistent. Frighteningly demanding.

"Okay, give me a minute. I need to get my things and let them know I'm leaving. I'll be back in ten minutes."

"Five would be better."

I ran down the hall and found my station manager. This was insane! She gave me one look and knew something was terribly wrong. "There's an emergency. I have to go. My friend…," my voice wavered. "I'm sorry; can you cover for me?"

"Sure thing, honey, is there anything I can do?"

"I don't know. I'll let you know when I find out."

I ran to my locker and grabbed my backpack and the few personal items that seemed to have accumulated over the years. There was a photo of my family and another one of me and Momma and Aunt June. I crammed them down into my bag and slammed the locker.

When I returned to Momma's room, Hashim was holding her hand and whispering something into her ear. It was so unusually out of character and yet endearing. He looked up at me and said, "I was telling her what a lovely daughter she raised."

I walked around to the other side of Momma's bed and kissed her forehead. "I love you, Momma. Goodnight." She didn't smile or acknowledge our presence. Her roommate stirred, then, and we took our exit.

Hashim had parked across from me in the parking lot. He ushered me to my car and followed closely as we drove separately to the house. He was out of his car before me and pushed me towards the house. I unlocked the door and he hurried me inside.

"Stop!" I demanded. "Please, talk to me."

Instead, he pulled out his phone and texted me.

Passport?

I shook my head.

"Of course, not," he muttered and typed again. *Birth certificate clothes toiletries.* He took the keys from the counter before he stepped close to me. "It will be okay," he whispered and kissed me briefly on the mouth.

At that very moment, I wasn't sure I trusted him. He had that distracted look behind his eyes again. He stood back from me abruptly and texted again. *Hurry. Be ready.* I went straight to the filing cabinet and pulled out my folder for school; it contained my birth certificate. He had asked if I had a passport. How far away were we going to have to go to get away from Marshall. How long was *a while*?

I pulled down a duffel bag from my closet and began packing. I heard the door unlock and I called down the hall. "Hashim?"

"No, C. Sorry to disappoint you. It's just me. Why aren't you at work?" Krissa asked.

"Didn't feel well."

"Billy's not gone a day and you're already calling your neighbor over?" she asked teasingly. Then her eyes fell upon the duffel bag on my bed and the stack of clothes I was cramming into it. "Where are you going?"

I stammered. "I'm going away for a couple of days. Hashim has asked me to go with him on business," I lied, and then I realized something. "How did you get in?" I asked.

"Billy's key. I just got off work; I came to get my things."

"Did you lock the door?"

She shrugged. "I don't know, why?"

"Because you don't want to make it too easy for me to get in." I recognized Marshall's voice immediately. My stomach lurched. He was standing just outside my bedroom door with his hands behind his back like he might be holding a weapon.

Krissa stepped to the side and eyed him. "Who, the hell, are you?" Krissa asked, seemingly unphased that a perfect stranger was in my house in the middle of the night.

"Which one of you is Caroline?" he asked leeringly at Krissa.

"Wouldn't you like to know?" she asked and bowed up to him like she was the bouncer at Pete's.

"No, don't," I said to Krissa, but she ignored me.

"You need to get the fuck out of here, asshole, before I call the cops." Krissa already had her phone in her hand.

In the next second, Marshall lunged toward her and whipped the side of a gun across her face. She staggered back and fell onto the floor. I stepped away from the bed toward the bathroom. I thought maybe I could get us both safely in there. I knelt down beside her. "Krissa?" Her nose was bleeding and her cheek was raw from the rough grip of the pistol. She was breathing but not responding.

"Thank you for answering my question," Marshall said as he grabbed my ponytail and pulled me to my feet. He wasn't that much taller than me, but he was strong and I couldn't get my footing right away. He shook me slightly and I regained my balance. *Hashim was coming back. Hashim was coming back. Hashim was coming back*, played through my mind, frantically hopeful. Then the realization came that maybe Marshall had gotten to him first, but if that were true, why would he be wasting his time with me? Instead of pulling away, I pressed myself against Marshall, taking the pressure from my neck and hair. It also gave me better balance for self-defense. Marshall took it completely wrong. "That feels nice," he said, moving his forearm around my neck. The gun was near my left ear. He released my ponytail, then, and groped my breasts and stomach and all the way down between my legs.

"Enough!" I grunted. I pressed my back side and hips further into his pelvis and hunched down into a squat, securing my balance and taking him onto my back. I tossed him over my shoulder and onto the floor. He looked up at me surprised and then offered me a demonic grin. I turned to run for the door, but he caught me and pulled me down. I kicked and scratched and screamed! He was on top of me, pinning me down with his knees. I thrust my hips upward and kicked and wriggled. He just smiled and stroked the side of my face with the gun.

"You're not as pretty as the other one. I'm honestly a little disappointed, but you're a fighter. I can see why that would attract Emir; he likes the feisty ones."

I was more angry than afraid. I wriggled and moved some more, trying to get free. Marshall just laughed, taunting me, and then leaned over and kissed me. I bit his lip, but he wasn't dissuaded. He pressed his chin to mine, forcing my mouth open. I gagged as his tongue entered my mouth. I cried out, but my voice caught in his throat. There was nothing I could do. I closed my eyes and prayed fervently to be delivered or for the wherewithal to get myself and Krissa out safely.

Instantly, the pressure lifted from my face, and I saw Hashim pulling Marshall away. He was gripping him around the neck and dragging him toward the door. Marshall was still holding the gun. Hashim forced the gun from his hand and it fell and skidded across the floor and under my bed. Marshall turned and the men exchanged blows. Marshall wasn't as tall as Hashim but managed a few good punches to his ribs and stomach. Hashim was able to use his height and longer arms to his advantage. He punched Marshall in the nose and blood gushed out.

Krissa lay unconscious. When she wouldn't respond, I hurriedly zipped my bag and dragged Krissa toward the door. She stirred. I pulled her some more, and then I caught the glint of steel from the corner of my eye. Marshall had pulled a knife and Hashim's shirt was bloody on one side. I had to do something.

I looked frantically around my room and found Aunt June's carved cane propped up against the side of my dresser. I lifted it and swung it hard at Marshall's head. I missed and caught him in the shoulder. He turned to see what hit him, but I was ready again. I swung and hit the side of his head. He blinked and staggered back a step or two before he and the knife fell onto Krissa. I screamed, and Hashim grabbed me around the waist when I lunged toward my friend.

"No!" he bellowed into my ear and pulled me away. Blood had already begun seeping onto the floor around them. Krissa's eyes widened in horror and she gasped, spewing blood from her mouth. Her eyes dulled instantly.

"Krissa!" I screamed and put my hand over my mouth in shock while I tried in vain to wriggle from his embrace. In frustration, Hashim lifted me up in one arm and grabbed my duffel bag with the other. He carried me from the room, screaming hysterically. I don't know how I had the sense to grab my backpack from the counter as he carried me out of the house. Habit, maybe? Reflexes? He all but threw me into his car and slammed the door.

CHAPTER 15.5

Hatred stirs up conflict, but love covers over all wrongs.

– Proverbs 10:12

Thankfully she stopped screaming before I got into the car. She was definitely showing signs of shock. Her breaths were shallow and her lips were nearly as pale as her skin. She was shaking. I concentrated on getting her as far away from the house as fast as I could. I told her the first time she had ridden with me that I never wanted to repeat the scenario of driving at this speed, but there I was, again, running for a life I wanted to protect more than my own.

I was certain at least one of Marshall's associates was dead. I was not certain about the other. He was down and I heard Caroline screaming, so I was satisfied with unconscious. I felt horrible that Krissa was lost to Caroline and especially that she had to witness it. It was an unfortunate accident. I knew Marshall was most likely still alive, but we would have a couple of hours' head start.

Just as I was pulling onto the interstate, I heard Caroline's weak, shaking voice. "Hashim?" I turned to her voice. "Are you still bleeding?"

I looked down onto my shirt. "Only a little," I said. "Did he hurt you, Caroline?"

She shook her head. "Krissa," she muttered and rocked slightly. "Krissa. Krissa. Krissa!" I took her hand and it felt cold and clammy. Her light eyes resembled dark orbs; her pupils were dilated. "Pull over!" she screamed. "I'm going to be sick!"

I pulled over onto the shoulder, skidding on the gravel. She threw the door open wide and heaved the contents of her stomach onto the grassy edge. She

125

turned completely and placed her feet on the ground, heaving and heaving between her knees; vomit thrust violently out of her. I put my hand on her back to comfort her, but when I reached to move the matted mess that was once a ponytail from her shoulder, she went rigid. She heaved once more and then grabbed the elastic from her hair and flung it out the opened door. With shaking hands, she wiped her mouth and stroked her hair. She repeated this gesture over and over again, panting and rocking.

I got out and walked to the other side of the car. I pulled a jacket from the backseat and forced it around her. I was careful not to slip in the vomit as I placed her legs back into the car and buckled her in. I shut the door and returned to the driver's seat.

"Caroline, look at me. We are going to find a safe place to clean up and rest. I need you to hold on a little longer. Do you understand?" She nodded but her eyes were hollow.

She took my words literally and grabbed onto my forearm and finally rested her hand in mine. The pain from the cut in my side was searing, but it was a shallow wound. I needed basic first aid; Caroline would need more than that. We both needed a shower, and I needed to reformulate my plan. How was I going to break this news to her? I thought that we would only need a few days, a week at the most, to circumvent Marshall, but now I knew this was a permanent relocation. Instinctively I had run east; I always ran east.

CHAPTER 16

I tried to close my eyes, but the scene replayed over and over behind my eyelids. Ruthless... Meaningless... Cold blooded... I wasn't even embarrassed that I had thrown up so violently. It was gross that I actually preferred the taste of my own vomit over Marshall's breath and tongue. I had reached for the cane to help Hashim. It felt good to make contact with Marshall's head, a solid hit, but at what cost? It was my fault Krissa was dead. We'd been driving at least a hundred miles an hour. The faster and further we drove, the better I was able to breathe. The warmth of the jacket helped. Hashim's scent grounded me. When he said he needed me to hang on, I knew I could do that. I willed myself to calm my breathing and forced my heart to steady its paces. Once I had a handle on my physical state, my mind soon followed a logical progression of thoughts.

"Hashim, where are we going?"

"A hotel. I promise to stop in the next fifty miles."

"After that?"

"I will tell you as soon as I know."

"Are you a soldier?"

"No."

"A secret agent?"

"No."

"A criminal?"

His hand tightened around mine. "No, Caroline, I am none of those things. I am a fool who trusted in the honor of thieves. I swam beyond my depths and nearly drowned, but I will make this right." He answered my questions but didn't take his eyes from the road.

"How did you learn to fight like that?"

"Different places."

"You looked like you knew what to do, like you'd done it before." I watched his face carefully.

His hand tightened again. "I have, but I am not proud of that." He swallowed.

"Have you killed people?"

He took a deep breath and exhaled slowly. "Yes, but I am not proud of that either. It was necessary."

I was out of questions while I reflected on what he told me. He slowed the car and exited off the highway into the parking lot of a small hotel. It was nearly daylight. I waited in the car. Hashim needed the jacket to hide the blood on his shirt. He pushed his hands through his hair and looked presentable, like a guy who had been driving all night.

I was disgusting. There was dried vomit on my pants and my shoes. My hair was a mess of knots. I had been groped and violated; I felt dirty. I quickly assessed my physical needs. I suddenly needed to pee, and I was extremely thirsty. Hunger would soon follow.

I could see Hashim talking with a young man working the counter. I saw him point back toward the convenience store and the gas station at the other end of the parking lot. Hashim's expression waned as he approached the car. It was like he saw me for the first time all night; I must look hideous.

"Are you hungry?" I nodded. "What would you like?" he asked as he pulled into the gas station.

"Water. I'm really thirsty. Maybe some granola bars or some Pop-Tarts?" I asked tentatively like a child.

He caught the change in my voice. He turned to me and placed his hand on the side of my face. He rubbed my cheek with his thumb. "Caroline, you may have whatever you want." His piercing eyes and his hand on my cheek warmed me more than his jacket, but I knew he was lying to me without realizing it. He could never give me what I wanted because, at that very moment, I wanted to be at home.

128

"A new toothbrush, too. I think I forgot mine." He gave a quick nod and locked me inside the vehicle.

***

I carried in the bags he handed me from his purchases at the convenience store and placed them on the desk. Hashim carried our duffel bags and put them on the floor near the closet. The room was clean and welcoming as far as hotels went. The sun was just coming up.

"Do you want to eat or shower first?" Hashim asked.

"Shower, please." He handed me a bag from the convenience store. Inside, it contained a toothbrush and toothpaste, mouthwash, a bright pink razor, ladies shaving cream, tampons, deodorant, and feminine hygiene wipes. He must have cleared the entire shelf. I looked at him, questioningly.

He shrugged. "I wanted you to have whatever you might need." I took my duffel bag to the bathroom and ran the shower as hot as I could stand it. It felt good to rid my body of the scrubs and sneakers. I threw them into a pile under the sink. I looked down at the chain and rings that fell between my breasts and felt decidedly grateful. I stood in the hot water and washed my hair and scrubbed down my entire body twice. The hotel shampoo and conditioner weren't half bad. I wrapped a towel around my head and dried off.

In the bathroom mirror, I noticed a few bruises forming along my shoulder and arm and ribs. They were faint and not too tender. I brushed my teeth and gargled. I parted my hair and brushed it straight down. The easy waves would naturally come as it dried. I reached into my bag and found pajama bottoms and a t-shirt. I also found a pair of socks. I almost felt human.

I was so thirsty, now, and my stomach was growling. My physical needs distracted me from the reality I needed to face. I took a deep breath and opened the door into the room. Hashim stood formally when I entered the room, like I was royalty or something. He didn't smile, but his eyes weren't filled with disgust like before. He pulled out the chair next to the small table where he had placed an assortment of items in front of me: Pop-Tarts, granola bars, a bag of miniature candy bars, creamy peanut butter, Doritos, water bottles, and bananas.

I laughed a little as I sat down and examined my feast. He had most all of my favorites. "How did you know?" I asked, pointing to the bag of chocolates.

"Chocolate has proven medicinal properties that counteract stress or at least help one deal with it. It also tastes remarkable with the peanut butter." He smiled tentatively, reading me. "Will you be alright to eat alone if I take a shower, now?"

I nodded. "I can manage." My voice sounded more confident than I felt.

He leaned over and kissed my forehead. He was satisfied with my reply. He turned on the lamp between the beds before he shut the curtains and checked the locks on the door. He carried his duffel into the small bathroom and shut the door.

I sat facing the food before me; the shower was loud through the thin walls. Although it was my habit to pray before meals, I was too numb and too hungry and thirsty. I closed my eyes and breathed; God would hear my heart because he already knew everything. I reached for the water first. I guzzled down half the bottle before I peeled a banana. There were no spoons or forks, so I unwrapped one of the chocolate bars and used it as a make-shift spreader. The combination of peanut butter and banana and chocolate was familiar and relaxing.

My thoughts went to Krissa as I sat there, alone. I had seen plenty of death working in a nursing home, but seeing murder was a completely different experience. Seeing my friend's murder, knowing it could have been my own, only added to the terror. Tears ran down my face, but I wasn't hysterical like I had been a few hours ago. Should I be bothered at how I was accepting all of this?

Krissa was dead. Billy was on a plane to the other side of the world. Momma was in another world, and I was in a hotel with a relative stranger who had killed people but had saved me. I wondered if I should call the cops or grab my stuff and his keys and leave. His keys weren't anywhere to be seen and my stuff was still in the bathroom.

I wiped away my tears quickly when I heard the bathroom doorknob jiggle. Hashim came out of the steamy bathroom, shirtless, wearing only loose-fitting linen pajama pants. He looked like a cologne ad from GQ. His chest was covered in dark hair that also covered his abdomen and continued along below his navel. He was breathtaking, and I was sitting there, gawking at him with wide eyes and sucking peanut butter from the make-shift chocolate spoon. He walked toward another bag on the desk and dug around until he found what he was looking for.

"Would you help me, please?"

"Sure," I said and stuck the candy bar down into the jar of peanut butter.

"I need you to glue the cut, and I bought some butterfly bandages. Can you do that?"

I nodded swallowing the peanut butter from the roof of my mouth. The gash on his side wasn't that deep, but it was a couple of inches long and would be irritated if he didn't get it sealed.

He flinched once. "Does that hurt?" I asked.

"No, your fingers are freezing!" he exclaimed.

"Sorry, I'm almost done."

He walked to the mirror and examined my work. He seemed satisfied and put on a white t-shirt and turned back toward my feast. "Have you had enough to eat?" he asked. I nodded. "Are you tired?" I nodded again, but I wasn't sure if I could sleep. "I have been awake for over twenty-four hours, but I want to make sure you are okay enough for me to sleep. We will need to be on the road again in a few hours."

"Where are we going?" I asked.

"I should have word before we leave."

I looked around the cheaply decorated hotel room and resigned myself to be here for the next few hours. I looked at the double beds and wondered if I would actually be able to sleep in the same room with him. I went to the bathroom again and brushed my teeth to get the peanut butter and chocolate taste from my mouth, but it just left a weird blending of the flavors with the toothpaste. I felt physically and emotionally exhausted, but I froze when I stepped back into the room and faced the beds. My hands felt cold and my feet wouldn't move forward. Hashim looked up at me from his phone.

"Are you alright, Caroline?"

"No," I whispered.

"What do you need?"

"I want to go home," I said.

"That is not possible."

"I know."

He walked toward me and put his arms around my shoulders and held me close to his chest. I let him comfort me. I let him hold me. I let him put me in a bed, and I didn't protest when he lay down beside me. I didn't protest when he held me like he'd done in the fort a few nights ago. I needed him.

CHAPTER 16.5

Do not forsake wisdom, and she will protect you;
love her, and she will watch over you.
The beginning of wisdom is this: Get wisdom.
Though it cost all you have, get understanding.

– Proverbs 4:6-7

It was a long time before I fell asleep. Caroline was accustomed to sleeping in the day; I was not. Her presence helped me reason and know my thoughts, but it did nothing to help me sleep. I wondered if her stillness was normal and if she was truly resting peacefully. She needed a passport. With that, we could be on a flight to Dubai before midnight. Father would be there, but he would understand. *Caroline would like Dubai,* I told myself. I was a terrible liar.

Dubai was an immediate fix, but it was not permanent. I needed to make this permanently secure. Kennedy could arrange it, but not as things stood. It would not matter that she was an American citizen and that she had rights. She had nothing with which to bargain; she was expendable. My contract protected me. My parents had established their own protection which also extended to me, but now I needed to extend all that I had to Caroline. My heart quickened at that thought, but it was the only option I had.

Once that choice was made, I managed to sleep until two in the afternoon. Caroline stirred easily, so I suspected she had not slept soundly. She did not move until I did. I rolled away from her and went to the bathroom. When I opened the door, Caroline looked up at me. I could not read her expression. She was standing, barefooted, making coffee in the tiny, hotel coffee pot, and eating a Pop-Tart.

"Good afternoon," I said. She gave a quick nod. I was unsure if she was being generally unfriendly, or if it was due to the lack of sleep and stress. I diverted my gaze.

"I just need coffee," she grumbled. She peeled a banana and poured the coffee into the paper cup. She dumped in a packet of sugar and powdered creamer and stirred it with the little wooden stick. She took a sip and made a face like she was forcing down medicine.

"Not so good?" I asked. She shook her head. "How did you sleep?" She shrugged. I hated seeing her like this. "Is there anything I can do?" I asked. She shook her head and turned away, fighting back the urge to cry. She took another gulp of the horrible coffee and placed the paper cup down with such finality, resolving herself into the acceptance of another day. I wanted to go to her and hold her and comfort her, but she had added an extra layer this morning. She was shrouded in resignation. I hoped resignation would not soon become defeat. I wondered if I would ever see her smile, again.

CHAPTER 17

Hashim snored, not like an old man snore, but like a light, low buzzing in my ear. I hadn't noticed it the other night in the fort. I could tell he didn't go to sleep for a long time. He just lay there next to me, holding me. I dozed on and off but didn't sleep soundly until I knew he had fallen asleep. I woke up about one, but I didn't move; I couldn't move. What the hell was I doing there? Where the hell was I letting him take me? This was ridiculous, but I knew no other options. I trusted him to see after me because he had already proven himself capable. I had trusted him from the beginning, but I wanted, no, I needed to know him better.

The room was still darkened from the thick curtains when Hashim rolled out of the bed. I got up two seconds later and attempted to make coffee. The hotel room coffee pretty much sucked, only adding insult to my waking. I would make the best of it and prayed that the rest of the day and night would be better. When he opened the bathroom door, he was dressed. He offered a few brief comments about coffee and sleep, and then stated flatly, "We need to go."

I walked past him and into the bathroom. I dressed quickly and brushed my teeth. I looked to my pile of vomit-laden clothes and sneakers and wrapped them in an extra bag from the bottom of the garbage can. I washed my face and realized then that I had no makeup or toiletries, except for what Hashim had purchased for me. Thankfully, the circles under my eyes weren't too dreadful. I brushed my hair, but when I went to pull it back into a ponytail, I froze, flooded by the memory of Marshall grabbing my hair and everything that passed after that. Waves of nausea came over me and I lost my breakfast and the hideous coffee into the toilet. I patted my face with a damp washcloth and brushed my teeth again. Tears burned in my eyes but didn't fall.

Hashim wasn't in the room when I came out of the bathroom. The food and his bags were gone. My heart sank for the briefest of seconds like I had been abandoned. Surely, he wouldn't just leave like that. I jumped when I heard the door. His response when he saw me was overwhelming. He slammed the door and ran to me. He held my face in his hands and looked into my eyes.

"I apologize," he said, "I should have told you I was going to the car."

"I threw up, again," I confessed. He nodded, understanding. He stood to his full height, then, and held me. The burning tears that refused to fall earlier, came easily, relieved to be released. Hashim sat me next to him on the edge of the bed and just held me. He rubbed down my hair and my back soothingly. I didn't allow myself to wallow and soon rallied and thanked him. "What should I do with my shoes and uniform?"

"We can put them in the trunk. We cannot leave any trace of ourselves, here."

Once in the car, I made a great effort to consider my current situation as a new adventure. Not like a vacation, because I rarely had ever taken one. Momma and Daddy had taken us to the beach a couple of times when we were kids. We had camped some when Billy was in Boy Scouts, but mostly we spent summers and holidays with grandparents.

Hashim drove through a Starbucks and got us each a venti. My attitude was instantly improved. He then drove more reasonably than he had last night. He didn't get it past ninety on the interstate.

"Where are we going?" I asked.

"Montgomery."

"Alabama? Why Alabama?"

"Two reasons. One, it is the closest passport office. Two, we will not have to wait."

"Wait for what?" I asked.

Just then he answered his phone.

CHAPTER 17.5

The prudent keep their knowledge to themselves,
but a fool's heart blurts out folly.

– Proverbs 12:23

"Yes, this is Emir. Tell Kennedy I am coming in. No. No, I'm not alone. There will be two of us." I hesitated slightly, knowing my next words would alter everything, but it was the next logical question from the voice on the other end. "My wife." I could feel her stare boring into the side of my head. When I ended the call, I turned and looked at her. She looked horrified.

"You're married?" The indignant tone in her voice stung. I had not wanted to say those words aloud before I had a chance to talk with her.

"No, Caroline, I am not married, but we will be when we get there." She looked at me incredulously. I turned my gaze back to the road.

"We? Like you and me?"

"Yes," I said and reached to take her hand. She pulled it away and moved as far away from me as possible.

"Bullshit! This is not happening! We hardly know each other!" She shook her head. "I'm not getting married!"

"We are getting married. Please accept that," I said flatly. "It is the only way I can see. They will protect you if you are my wife but for no other reason." My voice was firm but pleading.

"I don't know if I'm in love with you," she said dispassionately, almost surprised with the thought.

A humorless chuckle escaped my chest. "I do not know that, either, but we are neither repulsed, so you can choose to love me later, if you desire or not.

Right now, my only concern is your safety. I do not want you to end up like Krissa."

She put her hand over her mouth and fought back the urge to gag. "Krissa," she whispered into her hand. She leaned her head against the window and watched the landscape pass in a blur. She was silent for a very long time; the sky outside was growing dark. I was surprised when I felt her gaze return to me.

"When?"

"In the morning. We will check in at the hotel before midnight and sleep. Once everything is finalized, we will go to the passport office and do whatever we need to do there. We will most likely be in Montgomery a couple of nights."

"Who will marry us?"

I shrugged. "I am confident there is someone there who can make it official." I could tell she did not like that answer.

"This isn't anything like I dreamed my wedding day would be." She turned her gaze away from me again and looked longingly out the window.

The silence between us was painful. I felt horrible for what I was demanding of her, and I berated myself for having to ask, but I wanted to know. "What did it look like, your wedding day?"

She delayed her reply for what felt like she may never speak again. "You really want to know?" she finally asked.

"Yes."

"It's probably what all little girls dream of. My wedding day would be magical, filled with anticipation and love. I never wanted anything too fancy, but I'm wearing a beautiful dress and my hair is piled high on my head with ringlets all around my face. I would stand before God, beside the man I loved, and promise to love him forever, and I would have no doubt he loved me more than anything. We would be there with our family and friends. We would dance and eat cake. There would be flowers, lots of flowers." Her voice wavered slightly and she grew reticent again.

"I am truly sorry that I cannot give you exactly what you want."

"You wouldn't be able to give me that, regardless," she said sullenly.

"If circumstances were different, perhaps I could."

She shook her head. "I have no family to speak of: Billy is on the other side of the world, my only friend is dead, and my groom isn't sure he loves me. So, no, you have no power in that regard."

Her words struck me like a whip. They were true and the resignation shrouding her earlier returned. I took a deep breath. I would do everything in my power to make tomorrow memorable, and with any luck, it would make her smile.

CHAPTER 18

"Hashim?" I finally spoke again. "May I make a request?" He looked over at me and gave a brief nod. He seemed relieved that I had spoken, again. "I won't marry you without a pastor. I don't want a civil servant to marry us. It won't seem right, somehow."

"That sounds more like a demand."

"I guess it is, but if I have to go through with this, I would like it to be real and binding. Not just a piece of paper that we sign to make official. I want God's blessing over us because I sure as hell need his protection and his grace." My voice sounded desperate, edgy. "Can we stop? I'm hungry and I need to go to the bathroom. I'd like to drive for a while, too." I said. He pulled off at the next exit that had about a dozen places to eat. "Sonic," I said. He didn't question me.

I was stressed and needed comfort food. I needed tots! I needed a lot of tots! I jumped out of the car and ran to the bathroom. When I returned, I ordered a large chili-cheese tots and a Dr. Pepper. I scarfed them down and felt reasonably satisfied. Hashim had a burger. He didn't *scarf* anything. He also agreed to let me drive. It was nice to release my pent-up energy behind the wheel. I got it to 100 mph a few times, but there was too much traffic to maintain that speed for any length of time. Hashim texted and worked on his phone the entire time. He didn't seem phased at riding at that speed. Maybe he trusted me.

We stopped once more before we made it to Montgomery. Hashim took the wheel again and drove us straight to the hotel. The valet greeted us and the bellman took our bags. I had never entered a hotel this nice in my entire life. My eyes were wide and my mouth gaped a bit. It was spectacular. Light, instrumental music played in the background.

"Mr. Emir, welcome. We're pleased to have you stay with us," said a petite blond behind the counter. She smiled and blinked her eyes toward Hashim. She looked at me for the briefest of seconds, and I was suddenly very aware of my faded jeans and oversized hoodie. I looked down and saw my chipped toenail polish and worn flipflops. I tucked my hair behind my ear self-consciously. This stranger and I both knew I didn't belong. "I will have the bellman show you to your suite," she said, never altering from her friendly tone.

She handed the bellman an electronic keycard and we followed the young man toward the elevators. He didn't press the buttons but scanned the keycard. We entered and rode to the only floor that was accessible from this elevator. When the doors opened, I realized we were being taken to the Presidential Suite. I eyed Hashim, but he wasn't looking at me. There were men in dark suits standing in the hallway. The man standing closest to the door gave a brief nod to Hashim. They didn't say anything else. The bellman brought our bags into the suite and gave us a tour of the rooms. I couldn't take in all of the beauty at once. The fabrics, the textures, and the colors were amazing. The bedrooms were spacious and covered in beautiful wallpaper and crown molding. The light fixtures were all crystal. There were fresh flowers in vases and the bathrooms were nearly as big as my entire bedroom. I could have fit my queen-size bed in there.

Hashim looked to me to choose the room I wished to sleep in. I picked the first one I saw. The bed was covered with a thick down comforter and too many pillows to count. The bellman turned down the covers and arranged the decorative pillows at the foot of the bed. He said that breakfast would be delivered at seven as had been requested. It was nearly midnight.

The bellman offered an appreciative nod after accepting Hashim's tip. "Please let me know if there is anything else; we want your stay to be a pleasant one," he said as he backed out of the suite with a flourish.

"Who are those men outside?" I asked.

"Guards."

"Why are there armed guards outside of our room? Outside of our suite?" I clarified.

"How could you tell they were armed?"

"I just guessed. Guards are armed, right?"

"For your protection. I need to sleep and I need to know that you are safe while I do so. Do you have everything you need?" he asked.

I nodded. "This place is amazing," I said.

"Do you like it?" he asked, looking around and then back at me.

"Yes, but I don't belong here."

"Why do you say that?"

"Look at me, my hair, my clothes. They wouldn't even let me in the back door of this place if I weren't with you. This is more luxury that I've ever seen in once place, even in a magazine."

"*Luxury*. Luxury is easily afforded for me. This is how I was raised. I hope you can accept that." He took my hand and kissed my palm. "Goodnight, Caroline. We will need to leave tomorrow at nine." He then walked me to the door of my room. I looked up at him, expectant. I wanted him to kiss me. I wanted him to hold me. Being honest with myself, I wanted him to sleep next to me, again, but I knew he wouldn't. He kissed my forehead and then tilted his head to the side considering. His eyes softened and he kissed my mouth.

"That's better," I whispered and my lips tilted slightly into a grin.

"Yes, it is," Hashim whispered back to me before he kissed me, really kissed me, for the first time in several days. "Goodnight," he said again and shut the door between us.

I took a quick shower and wrapped myself in the bathrobe that was hanging in the bathroom closet. It gave me a whole new definition of the word, *soft*. I didn't even bother to put on my pajamas. I liked the way the bathrobe felt against my bare skin. I walked toward the bed and eased into it. It was the softest, most cloud-like sleeping surface. I think I was asleep before my head hit the pillows. I know I dreamed, but I couldn't remember anything. I know I slept hard because it took a while for Hashim to wake me up the next morning.

He finally whispered, "There is coffee and fresh strawberries and real cream." I nodded but didn't want to leave the bed. I think my hips had permanently molded into the mattress. When I didn't move, he kissed my forehead and my cheek. He tickled my ear with his breath, but I only sunk further into the pillows to get away from him. He laughed a little and kissed my neck. He was determined to get a reaction from me. When his lips made it to my collarbone, he stopped suddenly and sat back. "Caroline, what are you wearing?"

That caught my attention and I quickly assessed my current state. I was awake in seconds. The bathrobe was no longer on my body. It must have come loose in the night. I opened my eyes and pulled the covers up to my chin. "Get out! I'm not dressed!" I screamed and kicked to get him off of the bed.

Hashim stood suddenly and then bent down. He tossed the bathrobe onto the foot of the bed and walked out into the living room. I wrapped myself quickly and sat on the edge of the bed. The weight of the day's agenda crashed over me like a lead balloon. I rose and stiffly walked into the living room. I sat down at the table, and he poured me a cup of coffee. I stirred in the cream and sugar with a lovely, silver spoon. I took one sip and sighed. It was the best hotel coffee I had ever tasted.

"Good morning. Thank you for joining me," he said sounding amused, but I couldn't look him in the eye because the blush covered me entirely. I felt nervous and awkward and small. I focused on the coffee and the food in front of me. Everything was delicious.

"Are you nervous, Caroline?" The amusement wasn't in his voice anymore. I nodded, but I still didn't look at him. "Caroline," he began, but I kept my eyes on the bright red strawberry between my fingers. "Caroline, please look at me. I wish to know your mind."

I knew I was being petulant, but I couldn't help the way I felt. I took a bite of the strawberry to delay my response. I placed the green leaves that remained on the china plate. "I'm freaking out! This is all freaking me out!" I raised my hands to illustrate everything around me in case he wasn't able to see what I saw. "I just slept in the most amazing bed, ever! This bathrobe is more comfortable than anything I own." I stood and stepped away from the table. "I don't have anything to wear, today, so I'm considering getting married exactly as I am right now!" I let my hands fall in a gesture to be sure he knew that I was wearing a bathrobe. When I looked at him, his eyes flickered with amusement. I groaned in exasperation and placed my hands on the sides of my face and paced the floor back and forth. *Breath, C. Just breathe.* ·

Once I'd gathered my wits, I faced him and found my voice. "Hashim, I need to know exactly what sort of marriage this will be. What am I agreeing to?" He cocked his head to one side and considered. I could see the distraction of thought behind his eyes. He didn't know what to say. "You don't know, either, do you?" My stomach tightened. "Have you even thought this through?"

He didn't like the way I had challenged him. He thought I was underestimating him, doubting him. "Yes, Caroline, I have thought it through. You will be my wife and responsibility. I will be your husband. Once this union is consummated, everything I have will be yours as well."

"Consummated? Like sex? We can't consummate anything! What about birth control? I don't even know if you've been with anyone else. I suspect you have, but I haven't, and I don't know what the hell to do with that." His eyes tightened at the edges. "I hardly know anything about you. What about your family? What will your parents say? Do you want children? Where will we live? Where will we go? Do you even celebrate Christmas?" I could feel myself beginning to hyperventilate. His eyes couldn't contain it anymore and the flicker of amusement spread across his face and he laughed at my irrational statements. "Stop it!" I demanded. "This is not funny!" I screamed, but it was funny and stupid and his smile made me smile. I rolled my eyes; I was a complete goofball!

"Caroline," Hashim began, again, and he walked toward me and placed his hands on my shoulders. "I promise to take care of you. I promise to make this day as memorable as possible. I would never expect you to get married in a bathrobe. Trust me; I've taken care of everything." He smiled down at me and I smiled back at him. "I cannot tell you where we will go or where we will live, but I will as soon as I know. As far as my family, you will meet them in time. Having a passport gives us more options." He took my hands in his and squeezed them gently. He then led me to sit next to him on the posh sofa. He grew solemn and looked me in the eye. "I have been with others. You are right to assume that, but I have not been with anyone since I met you. I have never felt this way about anyone. I will be faithful to you, Caroline." I didn't know what to say. When he spoke like that, I couldn't help but believe him. "Furthermore, if you want children, and decide that you love me, I will give you children. I have never celebrated Christmas, but we can celebrate any holidays you deem worthy." He continued to hold my hand as he slid down onto one knee in front of me. I was frozen. I couldn't breathe. He was actually proposing to me. "Caroline Sweet, will you marry me?" His eyes were burning with sincerity. He was asking me like I had a real choice.

My heartbeat quickened and emotion caught in my throat. "Yes." It was the only word I could say.

He smiled up at me; his playful eyes returned. He reached his hand around my neck and pulled me gently toward him. After days of not being kissed, I felt his joy at being accepted and our mutual joy of kissing again. A few moments later, he pushed me back. "Take a shower; they will be here soon."

CHAPTER 18.5

Who can find a virtuous and capable wife?
She is more precious than rubies.
Her husband can trust her, and she will greatly enrich his life.
She brings him good, not harm, all the days of her life.

— Proverbs 31:10-12

A tall brunette entered the suite with a rolling luggage carrier filled with dresses and boxes. A rather flamboyant man followed her with a roller case in tow. I introduced Caroline to Manuel and Jessica. I trusted the three of them could sort through the details. I left the suite with one of the guards to take care of myself. I needed a new suit. I hated it, but I would have to buy off the rack today.

When I returned to the suite, I was ready. The men's store manager was more than eager to help me before regular hours. The promise of a sale and generous tip for his inconvenience was enough to motivate most everyone. My shoes were polished and my tie was perfect. I knocked on Caroline's door. "Are you almost ready? We need to leave in fifteen minutes."

"Perfection cannot be rushed," Jessica said, shooing me away from the door.

I stood, waiting, reflecting on our earlier conversation. Even in her innocence, she was bold to speak her mind and share her concerns; I simply had to ask. Of course, she was innocent, but she was not naive. I did not take this commitment lightly. How could I convince her? I would have to convince her over time.

Everything she questioned made me smile. I could provide and afford any worldly thing her heart desired, but she was not asking for material things, she was asking for assurances of commitment and responsibility of a vow, of the eternal. This would not be a marriage of convenience; it would have to be a marriage in every sense of the word. The truth seeped through my thoughts like rain over parched ground. She would one day be the mother of my children. She would be the kindest, most loving mother to our children. I could see her singing and playing and teaching them. As soon as she asked, I knew I had to foster respect and affection between us so that she would honor this commitment.

Finally, Jessica opened the door to Caroline's bedroom. Manuel escorted her out, formally. Her hair was done up, elegantly, with long ringlet curls encircling her face. Her makeup was subtle, but her eyes were even more captivating than usual.

She was wearing a long-sleeved wrap dress. The background was cream-colored, but the fabric had splashes of blue flowers all over it. It was simply lined and feminine and suited Caroline's shape and personality perfectly. She was wearing open-toed, wedge sandals, and her toes were painted a slightly darker pink than she had done herself.

She waited for my response. I nodded approvingly and smiled. We both thanked Jessica and Manuel and I saw them to the door. I then turned to Caroline. "Are you ready?"

She nodded. "Thank you," she said and her tone was heartfelt and sincere. I smiled at that. She had no idea what else I had in store for her.

When we arrived at the federal building, our guards ushered us upstairs to a meeting room. An older, African-American gentleman entered the room and eyed us both carefully. He was tall, dark-skinned, and had hands large enough to hold both mine and Caroline's at the same time. He took one look at the two of us and shook his head like he knew something was not quite right.

"They tell me the two of you want to be married, and you won't do it unless you're married by a preacher." His voice was deep and gravelly. Caroline nodded and gave a little smile.

"I am Caroline and this is Hashim."

"Have the both of you come here on your own free will?" He looked at me briefly, but his eyes were all on Caroline.

"Yes, sir," she said.

"My name is Reverend Bartholomew Jones. I am a research clerk. I have a passion for history, but a calling to preach. I am the pastor of an ecumenical outreach in downtown Montgomery. We mainly tend to the needs of the homeless and less-fortunate. It's been a while since I've had the honor of conducting a marriage ceremony. Do I meet with your qualifications, ma'am?" He stuck out his hand in greeting and Caroline took it.

"Yes, thank you," she said.

Reverend Jones called our guards to stand as witnesses. He eyed us all speculatively and began in his rich voice, "Dearly beloved, we have come together in the presence of God to witness and bless the joining together of this man and this woman in Holy Matrimony. The bond and covenant of marriage was established by God in creation, and our Lord Jesus Christ adorned this manner of life by His presence and first miracle at the wedding in Cana of Galilee. It signifies to us the mystery of the union between Christ and His Church, and Holy Scripture commends it to be honored among all people.

"The union of husband and wife is intended by God for their mutual joy, for the help and comfort given each other in prosperity and adversity, and, when it is God's will, for the procreation of children and their nurture in the knowledge and love of the Lord. Therefore, marriage is not to be entered into unadvisedly or lightly, but reverently, deliberately, and in accordance with the purposes for which it was instituted by God.

"Into this union Caroline and Hashim now come to be joined. If any of you can show just cause why they may not be lawfully wed, speak now, or else forever hold your peace." Reverend Jones looked around the room like he might be hoping someone would come in at that very moment.

"I charge you both, here in the presence of God and the witness of this company, that if either of you know any reason why you may not be married lawfully and in accordance with God's word, do now confess it." Again, he waited, but when neither of us said anything, he continued.

"Caroline, will you have this man to be your husband; to live together with him in the covenant of marriage? Will you love him, comfort him, honor and keep him, in sickness and in health; and, forsaking all others, be faithful unto him as long as you both shall live?"

"I will."

"Hashim, will you have this woman to be your wife; to live together with her in the covenant of marriage? Will you love her, comfort her, honor and keep her, in sickness and in health; and, forsaking all others, be faithful unto her as long as you both shall live?"

I had the distinct impression that the reverend was threatening me with his words, but I would not be dissuaded, and said, "I will."

"Will you witnessing these promises do all in your power to uphold these two persons in their marriage?" He looked to our two guards. "Never mind, you two will be on your own."

He took our hands and joined them. "Repeat after me: In the name of God, I, Hashim, take you, Caroline, to be my wife, to have and to hold from this day forward, for better, for worse, for richer, for poorer, in sickness and in health, to love and to cherish, until we are parted by death. This is my solemn vow." I was surprised that my voice spoke clearly over the God and love parts.

"In the name of God, I, Caroline, take you, Hashim, to be my husband, to have and to hold from this day forward, for better, for worse, for richer, for poorer, in sickness and in health, to love and to cherish, until we are parted by death. This is my solemn vow." Caroline's voice was strong. She meant every word.

"Are there rings?" Reverend Jones asked.

Caroline had already answered, "No, sir," when I produced a small band of gold from my pocket. Inscribed were the words *Proverbs 31:10-12.*

"Yes," I said and placed the gold band in the pastor's large hand.

While Caroline was distracted, gathering her belongings from her locker, I had stolen the woman's ring right off of her finger. It was a completely random thought in a moment of crisis, that led to extreme action. I had no idea why, but instinctively, I knew there was a chance that Caroline would not return or ever see her mother again. I was determined to take her as far away as possible, and I wanted her collection of rings to be complete. Forgiveness was easier to receive than permission.

"That's Momma's," Caroline said accusingly. "How did you get that?"

"I took it before we left."

Tears welled in her eyes, and she took a deep breath to settle herself. "You had no right."

"Will you forgive me?"

She rolled her eyes, indignantly, and took her hand from mine. I was afraid she was about to bolt and refuse to go through with the ceremony. Instead, she took the clasp of the chain she wore around her neck and removed her father's band from it. She laid the thicker gold band next to the one I had produced.

Reverend Jones held the rings together in his firm grasp like he could fuse them together, like he had the power to forge us together. "Bless, O Lord, these rings as a symbol of the vows by which this man and this woman have bound themselves to each other; through Jesus Christ our Lord. Amen."

He handed me the smaller band. "Place it on her finger and repeat after me: I give you this ring as a symbol of my love, and with all that I am, and all that I have, I honor you, in the Name of the Father, and of the Son, and of the Holy Spirit.

"Miss Caroline, please do the same. I give you this ring as a symbol of my love, and with all that I am, and all that I have, I honor you, in the Name of the Father, and of the Son, and of the Holy Spirit." Caroline's eyes never left mine.

He took our hands again and held them together between both of his. "Now that Caroline and Hashim have given themselves to each other by solemn vows, with the joining of hands, and the giving and receiving of rings, I pronounce that they are husband and wife, in the name of the Father, and the Son, and the Holy

Spirit. Those whom God has joined together, let no one put asunder." His voice rang out loud and clear.

"Dear Lord, it is with the utmost faith and earnest that I pray your blessing over these two. Watch over them. Keep them bound to one another. God the Father, God the Son, God the Holy Spirit, bless, preserve and keep you, Hashim and Caroline; the Lord mercifully with his favor look upon you, and fill you with all spiritual benediction and grace; that you may faithfully live together in this life, and in the age to come have life everlasting. Amen."

With her head bowed, Caroline repeated the word, "Amen." She had accepted every word this man spoke. She was bound to me by her god, the God of Abraham, and his son, her savior, Jesus. My heart beat strongly, watching the transformation take place before me. It would be naïve of me to think that I understood the depth and breadth of what those words would come to mean if we had any future together.

"Caroline and Hashim, having witnessed your vows of love to one another, it is my joy to proclaim you to be husband and wife. Hashim, you may kiss your bride."

I suddenly felt the weight of every word we had just declared and every word this stranger spoke over us. My mouth felt dry and apprehension gripped me. Caroline was looking into my eyes expectant. She smiled, encouragingly, and I kissed her, sealing the vows we made.

CHAPTER 19

Morning traffic was backed up all over the downtown area. Our guards offered to drive us to the passport office, but Hashim said that we only had a few blocks to walk from the federal building where we had been married. Reverend Jones made it real for me. He brought God's presence there on our behalf. At the conclusion of our brief ceremony, he wished us well and kissed my cheek before he left us to resume his usual duties at the FBI. Odd, but Hashim had spared no expense or inconvenience to make this a memorable day, indeed. Jessica and Manual had helped me get ready this morning. They made me laugh and smile and pampered me. Jessica had picked dresses and shoes from her boutique for me to choose. She said that Hashim had sent her pictures of me the evening before. It must have been while I was driving.

Hashim held my hand as we walked to the passport office. The day was sunny and pleasant. I didn't pay any attention to the guards walking in front and behind us. My eyes and attention were all on Hashim, my husband, and soon, I decided, my lover. The breeze caught me as we rounded the corner of a building. It made me catch my breath, but it wasn't just the breeze. It was the thought of making love with him at some point in the very near future. He looked down at me when I pulled into him to escape the wind. He wrapped his arm around me, then, and drew me closer into his side. It was both a protective and an affectionate gesture. I smiled. What a story this would tell in my old age. I could just see the eager faces of my grandchildren, awaiting another tale.

"So, Grandma, where were you married?"

"Your grandpa and I were married at the FBI building in Montgomery, Alabama. We were on the run from a dangerous man who wanted to force your grandpa to do illegal things."

I chuckled to myself, at the thought. Hashim looked down at me questioningly. I didn't say anything. He wouldn't understand. I had spent more than half my life with the elderly. I loved their stories. I loved imagining them young and full of life, living out their adventures, and there I was beginning my own.

The passport office was bustling; there were people everywhere. A man approached us, wearing a dark suit. He was older than us, but not by too many years. I suspected he was in his early thirties. He had the bearing of a soldier like Billy, but the refinement of an executive in his tailored suit and shiny shoes.

"Emir," he said smiling and thrust out his hand toward Hashim.

"Kennedy," he replied, smiling. "Thank you for making this happen."

Kennedy looked at me and smiled. "Some things are worth it." He put out his hand to me. "Mrs. Emir, it is a pleasure." It was the first time I heard my new name spoken. I swallowed nervously and smiled. "My name is Steven Kennedy. As you can see, it is my job to make sure your husband is taken care of. That courtesy now extends to you." He gave a little wink before he released my hand. He was charming; I liked him instantly.

"Thank you, but please, call me Caroline."

"Very well, Caroline, they are waiting for you in the office. I've also begun the process for your Social Security Card. It will take a couple of days for the paperwork to be finalized. I will need for you to stay local. Can you sit still that long?"

Hashim nodded. "I think I can manage."

Once we were in a private room waiting to be seen, Kennedy and Hashim spoke in hushed tones. Their faces were stern and I couldn't tell if they were disagreeing or if the topic was just so serious that it displeased them both. I wondered if Hashim was giving Kennedy the details of Marshall's attack. Kennedy excused the two guards who had spent the entire morning with us. I wasn't sure if he was sending them out for a break or if he didn't want to be overheard. I strongly suspected it was the latter.

A middle-aged woman came in at the same time and took me away to have my passport photo taken. She was a no-nonsense sort of woman and almost looked bothered that she had been asked to treat me differently than the lines of people waiting in the lobby. I followed her directions and spoke very little. She was like a stern librarian, daring me to return my books late. I found I stood and sat up straighter in her presence.

"Mrs. Emir," she finally said, "I have been asked to collect your fingerprints and a DNA sample."

"Is that routine for a passport?" I asked.

"No, but Mr. Kennedy has requested it. Were you not made aware?" she asked with pursed lips.

"No, ma'am, I wasn't, but do what you need to do." I smiled nervously. I decided I would draw the line at being tagged with a chip or a tracker like they did in movies.

After she fingerprinted me, she swabbed my mouth and asked me to spit into a small vial. She then offered me a wipe to remove the ink from my fingertips. "Come this way," she directed. I stood and followed her down a long corridor toward a ladies' room. "Disrobe. The agent will be with you shortly."

I shook my head. "Disrobe? Like take off my clothes?" I asked. This felt odd and really, really uncomfortable. "I'm here to get a passport."

She nodded. "Yes, among other things."

I shook my head, again. "No," I said. "I won't. Take me back to Hashim and Mr. Kennedy." My voice rose a little.

"Mrs. Emir, please," she said less formidably than before, trying to pacify me.

Two men passed us and looked at me and this woman as they walked by. Another group of people were approaching. "Take me back to my husband, or I will make a scene," I said through clenched teeth. It was the first time I had referred to him as *my husband*, but it was the truth and the words felt strong; I felt strong saying them. He was most definitely my husband and I wanted desperately to be near him.

The woman looked at me and down the hallway toward the group approaching. She obviously didn't want to call my bluff. "Very well, come with me." She went a different way than we had come and finally opened the door to the room where Hashim and Kennedy were now speaking more animatedly. They stopped immediately and turned to me when the woman opened the door.

I ran to Hashim. He had to see the fear on my face. "What's wrong?" he asked. He put his arms around me, shielding me from the woman I ran from.

The woman eyed Kennedy, her disapproval for my unwillingness to comply evident. My library books were definitely past due. "She refused to disrobe and wait for the agent," she said. "She threatened to make a scene." Her eyes were telling.

Kennedy didn't seem phased in the least. He smiled. "That's understandable. Don't worry. We'll take care of it," he said dismissing the woman. "Please tell Agent Reeves to meet us in here." The woman nodded and left us.

"What is this about, Kennedy?" Hashim asked.

"We need to conduct a standard intake. You know the drill. The FBI building has better facilities, but those guys don't always play nice, so I figured it could be handled here. I'm sorry, Caroline, I should have explained things better."

Just then, a woman opened the door. She, too, was wearing a dark suit. She wore pumps and carried a small case. Her dark hair was twisted into a bun at the back of her head. Her dark eyes and lashes were intriguing; even with minimal makeup, she was beautiful. She smiled as she entered.

"Kennedy," she said in a friendly tone. "It's good to see you, again." She put out her hand in professional courtesy, but there was more to her greeting. She eyed Kennedy. I wondered if they had a history.

"Agent Reeves," Kennedy replied and took her hand and they shared an air of familiarity. It was hard for him to conceal his attraction for this woman. "Let me introduce you to Hashim Emir and his wife, Caroline." She turned to us and smiled warmly.

"It's a pleasure," she said and shook our hands.

"Agent Reeves is a physician. She will be conducting the intake. She will need to examine you, Caroline, for any identifiable markings, scars, birthmarks, that sort of thing. She will also take your vitals and general health history."

"We will take blood and tissues samples and collect DNA," Agent Reeves clarified.

I looked to Hashim. He didn't look happy, either, but gave a quick nod in acknowledgement. "The other lady already took my DNA and fingerprints," I said. My mouth was dry and I wasn't sure I could offer them any more saliva.

"Where would you be most comfortable, Mrs. Emir?" Agent Reeves asked. *At home,* I thought. "I'm sure these two will step out and give us some privacy, or would you prefer your husband stay?"

Blush covered me entirely at the thought of Hashim seeing me naked for the first time. I knew I probably wouldn't be completely naked in this room, but I also didn't want anyone else present, either. I looked up at him. "I'm fine. Will you be right outside?" He nodded.

Kennedy moved closer to me and said kindly in a low voice, "Caroline, this is for your protection. We don't want you to end up like your little, blond friend." My eyes went wide and I nodded. Hashim must have told him about the attack.

Hashim kissed my cheek and squeezed my hand gently before he and Kennedy stepped out into the hallway. At that, Agent Reeves took an electronic tablet from her case and began typing information into the various screens that popped up.

"Please, have a seat. This will take a few moments. I will begin with asking you some questions." That was a complete understatement. She asked me over a hundred questions about my medical history, my parents and grandparents, and my sibling. She asked me about my menstrual cycle, sexual partners, and then skipped a few parts that didn't apply to me because I'd never had sex. She pulled a pair of gloves out of her bag and put them on. She opened her case completely, exposing the usual physician's tools. She slung her stethoscope around her neck and instantly looked like a doctor. She asked me to sit on the edge of the table so that I was at a better height to be examined. She checked my ears and eyes and throat. She felt the glands in my neck and around my collarbone. She checked my reflexes and finally took my blood pressure, drew three vials of my blood, and cut a clipping of my hair. "Mrs. Emir," she began.

"Caroline, please."

She smiled and looked into my eyes. "Caroline," she corrected. "If you would please remove your dress, I would like to document your body. It would be helpful if you begin with any known markings, like tattoos, childhood scars, broken bones, or birthmarks."

Everything up to this point was clinical and normal. This felt decidedly odd. She examined me carefully, looking over every part of me. She looked under my arms and traced her findings. She asked about a couple of scars and how they had been made: stitches over my eyebrow when I was ten, the branch across my cheek while running to the fort, a broken wrist roller blading, skinned knees and a few moles and freckles.

"May I ask what all of this is for?"

"It's for identification purposes, only. Once you're in the system, your information is cataloged, and we have references in the event your body needs to be identified. It's standard."

"Identified, like if I'm dead?"

"Of course, but also if you're seriously injured and unable to speak, or if you misplace your passport and need assistance from Kennedy or any other agent in the network. It's ultimately for your protection. You may get dressed now."

Agent Reeves put everything neatly into her case while I retied my dress around myself. I couldn't help feeling apprehensive at the fact that she'd just taken bits of me and they were all in her little case. *For your protection* had taken on a whole new meaning from the moment Hashim told me to hide in the laundry room. That wasn't even a week ago.

CHAPTER 19.5

Let love and faithfulness never leave you;
bind them around your neck, write them on the tablet of your heart.

– Proverbs 3:3

My time alone with Kennedy was not pleasant. He wanted the details of our leaving Caroline's house. He excused the guards, immediately, when I eluded to a leak in his department. I wanted to give him that information face-to-face. I could see the anger in his eyes when I told him that Marshall knew of the flight to Virginia and my meeting with the committee at the Pentagon. He listened while I told him my plans for Dubai and why I thought it was the safest place to go.

"The committee doesn't want you to leave the country. They want this badly; you don't want them getting nervous. I ask that you reconsider your plans to go to Dubai. I like you, Emir, please don't ask me to force my hand on this one. Miami's not an option?"

I nodded once, acknowledging what all he had already done for me, not because he had to as my handler, but because he wanted to. I would not disappoint him. "I can work in Miami, but as soon as it is finished, I will take her away and work on the particulars of the next phase elsewhere."

Kennedy nodded his ascent. "Thank you. You've just made my job considerably easier."

"Who will be at the hotel?" I asked.

"Dawes."

"Can he see after the car?"

"I already have someone else on that. Why don't you fly? We can have a plane ready for you as soon as you have Caroline's passport."

I considered that. "I'll let you know." The drive would give us more time together and more time before I would have the *pleasure* of introducing her to my mother. I groaned internally at the thought.

"I need to be getting back. You have everything you need here?" Kennedy asked, returning my thoughts to the present.

"I think so. Thank you. I mean that."

"I know. I confess, it's been a first for me, Emir. Passports, documents, chartered flights, fancy hotels, sure, I've done that a million times. Finding a preacher amid thousands of federal employees was like finding a needle in a haystack." He laughed. "Spending your wedding night behind guarded doors will definitely be a first for you." He smirked and then looked at me more seriously. "What gives, Emir? Why her? Why all of this?"

Kennedy looked down at the ring on my finger. I had been touching it and moving it back and forth around my finger the entire time we talked. I put my hand down, realizing that Kennedy had noticed too.

"I have been asking myself those same questions since the day I met her," I replied honestly.

"I hope you figure it out. Good luck. You know where to find me." Kennedy shook my hand and patted me on the shoulder. "Your men are downstairs waiting."

Agent Reeves came out then, too. "She's ready," she said to me. "Agent Kennedy, will you see me out?"

"Yes, I was just leaving, myself," he said, and I watched as the two of them walked down the hall together.

I opened the door to see Caroline standing with her arms crossed over her body. It did not look like an angry or defensive stance but like she was holding herself together. She looked up at me and smiled, relieved to see me.

"Can we go, now? I don't want to be here anymore," she said.

"Are you hungry?" It was nearly noon and she had had little more than coffee and strawberries for breakfast.

"I could definitely eat. I think some fresh air would do me some good, too."

"Are you alright, all things considered?"

She shrugged. "*All* things considered? Yeah, I'm okay. Were you able to make a plan with Kennedy?"

"Yes. I will tell you more about it after we have eaten."

Our guards were waiting for us near the main entrance. They walked with us to lunch and waited while we ate at an outdoor café. They made themselves blend in as best they could, and I was relieved that they did not hover over us. The weather was pleasant for October and the sun was bright in the clear sky.

Our food was delivered. We had ordered salads and wine. Caroline took my hand and bowed her head. She whispered a prayer over the food and thanks for the day. She was thankful, and we ate in companionable silence. While we waited for our waiter to bring our check, I thought I would give her some insight as to what she could expect in the near future. I took her hand and stroked her fingers. I looked at the narrow band around her finger and traced it with my thumb.

"You and I will remain at the hotel until we receive your documents. We will then go to Miami. We will stay there until I finish my work. That will take a few weeks. We have the option to fly or drive to Miami. Which would you prefer?"

"I've never been on a plane before." I could not tell if the prospect pleased her.

"Would you like to fly, then?"

"I think I would." She smiled.

We took our time walking back to the federal building. "Is it far to walk to the hotel?" she asked.

"No, just a few more blocks. Would you like to walk?"

"Yes, I would." I could not tell if she was enjoying the time out of doors since we had not seen sunlight in a few days or if she was avoiding getting back to the hotel too soon. "It's such a pretty day," she commented.

She paused in a few store windows and marveled at the buildings around us. She was unaccustomed to a large city and I could see where it might be enjoyable for her to take in the sites. She let me take her hand and lead her as we walked along downtown. She let me put my arms around her. At a particularly long crosswalk, surrounded by strangers and our guards, she caught my eye and smiled. I wondered what she was thinking. There was something in her look that made me want to scoop her up, throw her over my shoulder, and run back to the hotel with her. Instead, I gave her a quick peck on the cheek. She blushed like I had read her mind.

We walked into the hotel and directly to our elevator. The guard had the keycard. "We are relieved of our duties, here," the guard said. "Your team is waiting upstairs." He handed me the keycard to the elevator.

"Thank you," I said and ushered Caroline into the elevator ahead of me. I scanned the card and the doors closed.

Standing in the elevator, alone for the first time except for the few moments in the room where she had been *documented*, I suddenly felt a tightening in my abdomen and a fluttery feeling in my chest. "Hashim," she began. Her voice sounded nervous and small. She had to be feeling the same. I said nothing when I turned to her; she could feel the change in the air between us as we stood in the small space, moving upward toward our suite. Her eyes were wide and intentional, looking into mine. She leaned back against the railing of the elevator wall. I knew better than to touch her. The air was combustible and the slightest spark could prove incendiary. Instead, I placed my hands on either side of the brass bar behind her and bent my head slightly to kiss her. She closed her eyes and sighed; only our lips were touching. It was an incredible feeling. The slight altitude change made my ears pop and I felt light-headed, riding with my eyes closed. She reached out her hands and held onto me for balance until the elevator came to a gentle stop and dinged. I opened my eyes and looked at her as I begrudgingly released her lips. Could she read the intensity in my eyes?

"Oh shit," she panted.

I was satisfied with that answer. I turned to focus on the doors that were opening. Dawes and his team would be waiting for us. I moved in front of Caroline to give her a moment to check herself. She was flush and her ears were pink, but other than that, she was perfectly presentable. I heard her take a deep breath before she allowed me to take her hand and lead her from the elevator.

"Emir," the taller, guard said as we approached him from the elevator.

"Dawes," I said, giving him respectful acknowledgment as we approached the Presidential Suite. He shook my hand and patted my shoulder. He had been assigned to me from the beginning. He and I had spent many days together. He was easy and confident.

"I want you to know I had to leave a hot date behind; seems you were more of a priority. Kennedy sent me as soon as we heard from you." He glanced at Caroline. "Well, now I get to guard the honeymoon suite," he said wryly. "Tell me what you want, whatever you need; I'll be with you until you're safe in Miami." He looked down at Caroline, again, and raised his eyebrow approvingly. "Good afternoon Mrs. Emir. It's a pleasure. I'm Dawes. My men and I are here to protect you. You have nothing to worry about."

Caroline gave a slight smile and blinked. Her eyes were wide. "Thank you. Please call me Caroline," she said. She released my hand and put out her hand to greet Dawes. His words did nothing to comfort her current apprehension. Her concerns lay behind the doors of the suite; she had little concern for the men waiting and guarding us on the outside. I wondered if she thought me to be her only threat at that point.

I stepped forward when one of the other guards opened the door for us. I stepped to the side to allow Caroline to go ahead of me. She hesitated and took a deep breath. The look of shock on her face was apparent. The shroud of resignation returned. She ignored the eyes of the four men in her presence and focused solely on the opened doors. She was paralyzed in fear or was she waiting.

Dawes tapped my shoulder and gave me a knowing glance as though I was missing something. What was he telling me to do? He gestured his arms in a sweeping motion reminding me that it was customary to carry the bride over the threshold. Of course, how could I have forgotten? I knew that tradition had long-standing roots in this country and many countries around the world. I smiled thinking of the many reasons and superstitions attached to the custom for why a bride must be carried over the threshold, but in this instance, it was because the bride was unable or unwilling to carry herself. Caroline did not look surprised when I scooped her up into my arms. She looked relieved.

CHAPTER 20

I leaned my head into Hashim's chest as soon as he picked me up. I was so nervous and flustered and barely able to speak after the kiss in the elevator. It was a relief not to have to hold myself together and walk into the suite. His arms were capable of holding us both until I could get my shit together.

He kissed the side of my head gently and I lifted my face to his. He kissed me and I heard the door shut behind us. The finality of that sound echoed in the huge suite. Hashim put me down and steadied me before he released me. I was still holding onto him, our gaze locked, when I was suddenly assailed by the scent of flowers. I blinked and looked around. There were flowers everywhere! He must have bought out an entire flower shop. Every surface had a vase or bowl or bouquet. Roses and daisies and carnations. Tulips and violets and irises. There were flowers I didn't recognize, but they were all beautiful and fragrant. It was amazing!

I put my hands over my mouth taking it all in. I shook my head disbelieving. He put his hand around my waist and led me toward the center of the room. On a table, sat a small, layered wedding cake. It was elegant and too beautiful to touch, much less eat.

"Wow!" I laughed into my hands. The sweet aroma of cake and icing drew me toward the table. I reached out my finger tentatively to sample the edge of the icing. I licked my finger. It tasted even better than it looked. Rose petals had been scattered over the delicate, white icing and onto the table encircling the cake. The petals continued over the table and onto the floor in a trail leading toward Hashim's room. Hashim watched me as I took it all in. The suggestion of what lay along that path made my heartbeat quicken and it was still racing from the kiss in the elevator. It would surely explode if it kept this pace.

"That can wait," he said, understanding.

"Can I have a few minutes?" I asked.

"Of course. I will be here."

I went through my room into the bathroom where I had showered earlier. No petals led to that bed. I looked at myself in the mirror. My cheeks were flush, of course, and my hair was windblown from walking around downtown. The ringlets had eased into waves around me face. I removed the pins and brushed through my hair.

I kicked off the wedges toward my duffel bag. Being barefoot on the cool, tile flooring settled me. Barefoot was better, always better. I went to the bathroom and brushed my teeth and applied some gloss from my backpack.

I felt more like myself, again, well, my new self, my newly married self. A stream of explicatives passed through my mind at that thought. *I'm married. Hashim is my husband.* The thoughts made me catch my breath and I held tightly to the edge of the sink while I regained my composure. I looked down at the gold band on my hand and clasped my hands together attempting to draw strength from it.

I finally sat on the floor next to the tub. I couldn't stand on my own. Momma and Daddy had been married for thirty years. They wore these bands and found strength from the words inscribed within them, but they loved one another when they got married. Did I love Hashim? Did he love me? I vowed today to love him. I found peace in the fact that vows didn't say I already loved him, but that I promised *to love* him, like God already knew my heart and my insecurities.

I bowed my head over my knees and prayed. I didn't exactly know what to say, but I knew I needed something that I didn't currently have, that only God could provide. I didn't want to make Hashim worry, but I knew I had been in the bathroom a long time. Sure enough, there was a knock at my door. He was probably dealing with his own doubts about what all had transpired today and didn't need the added stress of me hiding out in the bathroom. I opened the door and he smiled when he saw my hair down and my bare feet.

"Better?" he asked.

"Yeah, sorry. I just needed a few minutes."

"Me, too." I noticed then that he had removed his coat and tie and had rolled up the sleeves of his shirt.

"Can I have some water?" I asked.

"Sure. There is a fridge near the bar."

"We have a bar?" I asked. "With wine?"

"Yes," he chuckled.

"Can we cut the cake, now?" I asked. Hashim frowned at me. "What?" I asked.

"Caroline, would you stop asking my permission for everything? You are not a child; you are my *wife*." His words caught at the end. He swallowed and took a deep breath. "I know you feel as though you have few choices at this time, but you do. You may use the bathroom and eat and drink and sleep and even shower on your own timeline."

"Yeah, I guess I needed reminding of that." My tone fell flat. I closed my eyes because his list was shorter than I realized. My eyes stung a little when I thought about all that I no longer had a choice in: school, work, home, Billy, Zinnia, and Momma.

Hashim shook his head. "That sounded better in my mind."

I shook off the funk that threatened me. "It's okay. I understand." I was in an amazing place, surrounded by flowers; there was cake, and a beautiful man was waiting patiently to consummate our marriage. I blinked hard and turned toward the cake. "I'm going to cut our wedding cake, now. Would you like some?" I asked assertively.

His eye approved of my efforts. "That is better, and yes."

The hotel had champagne chilling in a stand near the bar. Hashim poured us each a glass while I cut the cake. The cake was delicious; the champagne was, too. I had only tasted champagne once at a friend's wedding. It tasted nothing like what I currently sipped.

We sat together on the luxuriant sofa, sipping champagne. The cake melted on my tongue. The sweetness of the icing blended with the bubbly sips of the champagne. After my second slice of cake and my third glass of bubbly, I knew why it was sipped and not done in shots like tequila or whiskey.

I curled my legs under and settled into the sofa against Hashim. It was relaxing. He ran his fingers through my hair, distractedly, like he was a million miles away. We had never had the luxury to sit together like this. We shared meals and we rode in the car and we sat together in class. I leaned over and poured myself another glass of champagne.

"You might regret that later," he warned.

"What? The champagne? But it makes the icing taste so good."

He shook his head. "Consider yourself warned. The bubbles are nice, but they wreak havoc on your brain later."

"Okay, so I've been warned." I took another sip, challenging him playfully. He smiled. "What now?" I asked. He didn't know quite how to reply to that. "I mean, are we stuck here in the hotel room until we leave or are we allowed to go out?"

"We can go out but not alone. If either of us go anywhere Dawes will be with us. He's like an annoying shadow, but you will get used to him. Do you wish to leave? Would you like to go out for dinner?"

"Not particularly. I was just wondering what the next couple of days would look like. Have you known him very long?"

"A few years. He is good. There is no one else I trust more."

"Not even me?" I asked coyly.

"I have trusted him longer." He leaned in and kissed me, holding the back of my neck. I really, really liked it when he did that. The combination of the champagne and the kissing was very pleasant, even sweeter than the icing and champagne.

"You really trust me?" I asked. He nodded as he kissed the tender skin beneath my ear. It was hard to concentrate with his lips moving down my neck. I was decidedly married to this man and even more decidedly willing to have sex with him, which probably happened before he married me, but still, I needed to know. "Enough to tell me why Marshall is really after us?"

He hesitated slightly but continued to kiss me. "Yes, I promise to tell you everything."

I moved my hands around his neck and breathed into his hair as his lips moved across my collarbone toward the dip between my breasts where the dress crossed over me. "Like you promised to love me, today?"

He stopped dead in his tracks and drew back from me. "What is that supposed to mean?" he asked cautiously.

"I want to know that the word *promise* means the same thing in both contexts. Do you mean it the same way?"

"I rarely say things I do not mean, Caroline," he said sternly.

"Well, do they mean the same thing?" His dark eyes bore through me, but I held his gaze. I would not be intimidated and I would not go further until I had his assurance.

CHAPTER 20.5

May your fountain be blessed and may you rejoice in the wife of
your youth. A loving doe, a graceful deer – may her breasts satisfy
you always, may you ever be intoxicated with her love.

– Proverbs 5:18-19

Her lips tasted like the sweet combination of icing and champagne. She was relaxed and content for the first time all day. She felt like herself to me for the first time in days. I took new liberties as I kissed her. I was determined to coax her with kisses. My focus was to have complete access to her thighs.

She asked if we could leave. I did not wish to go anywhere. I liked where we were; I liked where she was, close and barefooted with her hair down. She asked if I trusted her. *Of course.* That was a ridiculous question. I had no reason to doubt her. I had already resolved to tell her everything. It was conditional, though. Like everything else, it would be hers once she was mine. I was making progress in my seduction when she caught my attention, when she pressed with the word *promise.* I had promised today to love her and I had just promised to tell her the truth. How could she question that? Had I not been a man of my word?

"Caroline, do you doubt me?"

"No, but I also know that you have done everything today for me: the flowers, the cake, the minister, the dress, and my hair. You've gone overboard to make today memorable for me. You even made vows and promises in the presence of God, whom you claim no affiliation. I know you meant every word; it's just a lot for me to accept. Of course, I trust you; I have since the day I met you. I appreciate you, and I am very grateful to be alive and here with you. I miss my old life, but I'm not unhappy to be here with you. I just want to know that they mean the same thing. I don't expect them to happen immediately; I need reassurance, that's all."

I kissed her instead of answering her. She accepted my kiss and my words. "Yes, Caroline, they mean the same, and over time, you will come to know everything. Are you satisfied with that?"

"Yes." I kissed her more. Her lips parted and she allowed me to kiss her deeply. She sighed as my hands roamed her back and down her ribs to her waist. Her hands were around me, untucking my shirt and moving along my bare back. My hand moved over the tie of her dress tempting me. I slipped off my shoes and eased her onto her back as I tugged at the tie. She stiffened.

"No. Please. Stop," she panted. I looked at her to gauge her reaction. Was she refusing me outright? "Not here. Please. Dawes. What if they come in?" she asked between kisses.

"They will not come in," I assured her and kissed her neck again and her collarbone and down her sternum. Her dress gaped more with her on her back and I could see the lace of her bra. I refused to be distracted again.

"I don't want my first time to be on a sofa, even a sofa as comfortable as this."

"I would never presume to, ever, on a sofa." I hope she did not hear the indignancy in my voice, but what could she expect? Her only near-sexual experience was in the bed of a truck.

The insistence of her hands cooled. "I don't have any condoms, either," she whispered.

"Caroline," I said exasperated. "What else are you worried about?"

"I don't know. I'm so confused; I'm not sure what I want." She covered her face with her hands and tried to roll away from me. "I'm spending my wedding night on the run, in a strange place, surrounded by armed men. Bodyguards? What the hell am I doing, Hashim?"

I eased her up into a sitting position, but I refused to let her move away from me. The loosened dress was tempting and taunting me. If I could just untie it, the rest would be easy. I moved my hand through my hair and took a deep breath.

"Caroline, will you allow me to make love with you?"

"Yes," she whispered.

I sighed in relief. "Then would you please stop worrying and allow me, *your husband*, to make love to you, *my wife*. Relax." I stroked her hair and the side of her face. I rubbed my thumb over her lips before I kissed her again. She did not interrupt me, again, for several minutes. She unbuttoned my shirt and rubbed her hands all over my chest and back. She kissed my neck and pulled her hands through my hair to the base of my neck. She allowed me to move my hands over her thigh and her hip to her waist. She moaned low when I moved my hand to the small of her back and pulled her closer, slightly arching her hips.

When my hand moved to the tie, she stopped me again. "No," she said and placed her hand over mine. "Not here."

I had had enough! I stood and looked down at her, lying on the sofa. She shifted her dress over her legs modestly. I had not planned to move her to the bedroom until she was truly ready, but she gave me no choice. In frustration, I lifted her into my arms and followed the path of rose petals to my bedroom.

"Thank you," she said. I considered laying her on the bed, but I would not be so presumptuous. "Would you please lock the door?" I put her down on her own two feet and turned to lock the door behind us.

CHAPTER 21

Finally! Privacy. A locked door. No one listening right outside. Hashim exhaled as he locked the door, but he took in a breath just as suddenly when he turned to find me slowly loosening the tie of my dress. He'd been trying to do it for the better part of an hour with no success. I grinned, slyly. "Would you care to do the honors?"

He took the two steps towards me and loosed the tie at my waist. At the same time, he loosened my dress and placed his hands on my bare skin, I stroked the black hair on his chest. I never knew what a hairy-chested man would feel like, but it was soft like the hair on his arms and his legs. I especially liked the way it parted down his chest to his abdomen and came to a point below his navel just above his belt buckle.

He was distracted by the lace on my bra and deciding between which direction he planned to pursue first. I bit my lip considering. Would he allow me to undress him? I had unbuckled plenty of belts, not for sexual reasons, but to help old men dress and undress. This was very different, but the buckle was exactly the same. It was easier than I thought to kiss and be kissed while our hands moved over one another.

I unbuckled his belt, unbuttoned his slacks, and loosened them around his hips before he knew what was happening. He moved my arms and forced the dress from my back. He lifted me up and I wrapped my arms around his neck and my legs around his waist. He kissed me hard while he stroked over my backside. He clung tightly to my thighs and hips. He walked me to the bed and gently eased me down.

I laughed when I realized that I was lying on a bed of rose petals. "Stop," I said. "I can't do this."

"What?" Hashim demanded, frustrated that I had told him to stop, again.

"No! Not that. The roses petals. They're everywhere!"

I sat up and pushed an armful off of the bed. I reached for the covers and pulled them away, exposing the sheets. Hashim's bed was a king with even more pillows than mine. The mattress hugged my hips like mine had done last night. The pillows sucked me in and under like a cloud. I lost myself under his weight as he slipped out of his slacks and onto me. All the while, the kissing continued; the touching continued. Our underwear was lost somewhere in the sheets. My body was doing things it had never done before. I was breathing and panting and moving with his body in ways that were unexpectantly pleasing. He kissed me and gently caressed my breasts. He kissed down my entire body until he found my thighs. His beard tickled and I giggled, until he gently bit the inside of my thigh. I screamed, but it was mostly in pleasure. He laughed and did it again.

I expected what would happen next, but I didn't expect the pressure and pleasure that came with it. He distracted me with his hands in places that I had hardly ever touched myself. I heard the drawer in the nightstand open and a faint tearing sound. *Condom*, I thought. I wasn't sure how I would respond. Would I be noisy and boisterous? Would I be quiet and timid? Would I actively participate or would I just lie there and allow him to do everything?

I realized instantly that whatever happened, at that moment and throughout, I had very little control over myself or my voice or my heart or my response. It was a little bit uncomfortable at first, but when I relaxed, it got easier. I followed his rhythm, gradually finding my own. His breathing was steady like he was running until the very end. The intensity between us increased until I thought I was going to explode. He held me close like he was hanging on for dear life. I felt the spasms of his body carry over and continue into mine.

"Oh my God!" I exclaimed just before he collapsed on top of me. "What the hell was that?" I panted.

Hashim's deep chuckle pressed me deeper into the bed. It took him a couple of seconds to speak. His breaths were measured and strong like when he was stretching after his run in the mornings. "The. Ultimate. Goal." Before I could ask him anything else, he put his fingers over my mouth. "Shhh." He closed his eyes. A few seconds passed before he eased himself from me and rolled me onto my side beside him. He kissed me gently on my forehead. We held one another close and waited patiently for our hearts to settle. Mine felt full and a little bit overwhelmed. I buried my face in his chest while tears leaked from my eyes and down my cheek and onto the bed. He looked into my eyes, then, and smiled at me. "Are you alright?" he asked.

I nodded because I was alright. I was better than alright. I smiled and kissed him. "Thank you. That was worth waiting for." He smiled and his eyes looked heavy like he was drugged. "Does sex make you sleepy?" He nodded and closed his eyes again. "Are you hungry?" He nodded again. "Can I," I began and he opened one eye at me. "I mean, I am going to call room service. I'm starving." He smiled sleepily and let me find my way to the bathroom.

There were robes in his bathroom, too. *Convenient*. I settled into the robe and walked out into the living room. I looked everywhere for a room service menu. In my searching, I discovered the champagne was all gone; the cake nearly devoured. Luckily, I found some mixed nuts, a bag of chips, and some fancy peanut butter crackers in the bar. I also found a couple of bottles of water and a bottle of wine and a corkscrew. Things were definitely looking up. I would wait and figure out room service when Hashim awakened.

I sat on the comfy sofa and found the remote to the tv. Cable. *Yes!* I found an old, black and white movie and cuddled into the cushions and the bathrobe. I was definitely asking for one of these robes for my birthday. I gradually ate through the snacks and alternated sips of wine and water. An hour later, I cried, again, but this time it was because of the movie. That ending always made me cry. I was wiping away tears when Hashim entered the room. I looked up and smiled. He was wearing a matching bathrobe.

"Did you sleep well?" I asked.

"Why did you leave?" he asked.

"I was hungry," I confessed.

"Did you call room service?"

I shook my head. "I couldn't find a menu."

He nodded, understanding. "There is no menu. You simply pick up the phone and tell them what you want."

"Anything?"

"I have yet to be denied, but then again, I have never asked for anything out of the ordinary."

"So, I can pick up the phone and ask for a PB&J on white bread and they make that for me?"

"Yes."

"A BLT on toast?"

"Yes."

"Chili cheese tots?" I challenged.

"No, not that. They draw the line there. I am confident they have no tots." He laughed. "Really, what would you like?"

I looked at my devoured snacks and the half empty bottle of wine. The water bottles had been emptied first. "I'd like a turkey sandwich with swiss cheese, lettuce and tomato, mayo and mustard, on whole wheat toast with a dill pickle on the side."

"Sounds good." He walked to the phone and called downstairs. He ordered two of the same. He sat next to me on the sofa and wrapped his arms possessively around me. He looked at my wine and snack wrappers on the table. "That looks like quite the feast."

"I was hungry."

"Is this wine a good pairing with crackers and chips?"

"Excellent," I said and giggled. The wine was definitely having an effect on me.

The food was delivered and we ate and watched another old movie. I went to the bathroom and brushed my teeth and then cuddled next to Hashim. I was feeling sleepy now; the day was catching up with me. I watched until the end, but this one didn't make me cry. The next movie was starting, but I fell asleep before the opening credits.

When I awoke, I was in Hashim's bed, wrapped in the bathrobe with his arm over me. His light snore was at the back of my head. I smiled and cuddled my back into his chest. I slept peacefully until the morning sun peaked around the curtains. I stretched and yawned and found my bearings. I only had to think for a moment to remember where I was. Hashim's scent was all around me, and parts of my body were sore that had never been sore before. I heard the shower running. All of these things made me smile. I could still smell flowers from the other room and coffee. Mmmm. There was most definitely coffee.

I sat up and adjusted my robe. The coffee wasn't two steps away from me on a cart. I lifted the covers from the plates and there lay an omelet and toast and fruit. I covered the food and focused on the coffee. I poured myself a cup and stirred in the cream and sugar. It was just as good as it had been the morning before. I saw my hand as I reached for the toast. Seeing my wedding band made me smile. I was a married woman in the Presidential Suite of a fancy hotel in Montgomery, Alabama. I was no longer Caroline Sweet; I was Caroline Emir. That part made me smile, too.

Hashim stepped out of the bathroom, then, wrapped in a towel, his dark hair glistening from the dampness. I was staring. I was admiring. I was lusting after the man that was now my husband. That lava feeling flooded me again. I just stood there, holding my coffee, unable to do anything else. A sly grin spread across his face. "I was going to serve you breakfast in bed, but you beat me to it."

"The coffee," I said.

"Good morning," he said, casually. He found the linen lounge pants he'd worn our first night together. He didn't bother to put on his t-shirt, though. His chest was distracting and I wanted very much to touch him. I wondered if he would mind eating breakfast with my hands stroking over him.

I refilled my coffee and nibbled on the fruit on the tray. He ate most of the omelet but offered me a few bites, and I ate the toast. I went to the bathroom and realized that my razor and deodorant and my duffel bag were all in his bathroom. He must have moved them while I was sleeping. I slipped out of the bathrobe and took a long, hot bath in the huge tub.

There were scented oils and bath salts and a variety of lotions and shampoos to choose from. I smelled amazing and felt all smooth and fresh. I wondered if I should get dressed or just stay in the bathrobe. Nothing I had packed was as comfortable as this robe; I opted for the robe.

Hashim was texting on his phone when I came out. He also had his laptop opened; it was obvious that he was working. I was going to walk past him through the bedroom door to give him privacy and not disturb his work, but he caught me with his free arm as I passed and pulled me onto his lap.

"You are not getting away that easily."

"I thought you were working."

"I needed to make some notes. I had an idea and I wanted to save it before it eluded me."

"Was it a good one?"

"Yes, you have that effect on me." He closed his laptop and set his phone down. He leaned me back and kissed me. "Good morning, Caroline."

"Good morning," I said and kissed him in return, my hands stroking over his chest and down his arms. I rubbed my cheek on his chest and nuzzled my face into his neck. He loosened my robe and took his time becoming reacquainted with my body. I was happy to have the robe because chills ran over every inch of my skin. I couldn't stand it anymore; he was driving me crazy. "Hashim, please," I begged.

"Please, what?" he said between kisses, taunting me.

"Please," was all I could say.

"What do you want, Caroline?" I couldn't say it out loud, but I wanted it. I couldn't demand it in words, but my body was screaming for him to be inside of me. Why was he making me beg? "Tell me exactly what you want."

"I want *you*," I finally said. "Please, I want you."

"Good. I want you, too."

I pulled him over into me and we slid from the chair onto the floor. I was on top of him, now, kissing him and reaching for the tie of his lounge pants. I was crazed with passion, singularly focused, straddled over him. I didn't care that we were on the floor. I didn't care that we going at it like rabbits. Hashim, apparently, didn't either. This time was hard and fast and more intense than the night before. At the end, I cried out and collapsed on top of him. It was the most incredible feeling in the entire world. Hashim held my hips and urged me off of him abruptly, quickly pulling up his pants and sitting up from the floor. "Caroline, we cannot make a habit of that."

I looked at him bewildered. I knelt down next to him and wrapped myself protectively in the robe. "Why?" I asked, not understanding. I felt self-conscious and ashamed. "I thought that was what you wanted when you opened my robe," I said defensively.

"Yes, that was what I wanted, but unless you want to get pregnant, *that* is not allowed!" His tone was firm, almost harsh.

"Why didn't you stop me?" I asked.

He laughed, dryly. "I tried." He sounded frustrated.

"Are you angry with me?" I asked.

"No. I was unprepared and taken completely by surprise. It will not happen again."

"Which part?" I asked sarcastically. My pride was wounded, but I really did understand. I was so stupid. Sex without a condom was a very different experience than sex with a condom. Sex that I initiated, too. *Wow!* Both situations had their pros and cons. I should have known better. Maybe I should consider birth control pills or something more reliable than condoms that would ensure spontaneity.

He stood and looked down at me. "Get dressed. I need some fresh air. I need to run."

The only clothes I had packed were jeans and t-shirts, a hoodie, and some underwear. I had no makeup and nothing to fix my hair. I needed to wash my clothes if I planned to wear my bra another day. Hashim took one look at me and shook his head disapprovingly. He was wearing running shorts and a t-shirt.

"Is that all you have?" he asked as he tied his sneakers.

I nodded. He'd married a complete idiot. "I guess I should go shopping. Do you think there's a Target or Walmart around here?"

He rolled his eyes. "No, I doubt it. I can take you shopping with Dawes as soon as I run."

I shrugged. "I can go by myself with Dawes. There's probably a drug store around here; I need some makeup, too. You can run with one of those other guys, right?"

CHAPTER 21.5

The words of the reckless pierce like swords,
but the tongue of the wise brings healing.

– Proverbs 12:18

I ran with Preston and left Caroline with Dawes. He rolled his eyes when I told him what she needed. "Do not take her to any thrifty department stores. She is allowed to go into any boutique she likes. She needs everything, all the lady stuff."

"What am I supposed to do while she tries things on?"

"Be charming and flirt as much as you want with any woman other than my wife."

"What's her budget?"

I looked at him blankly. "Dawes, she needs to buy nice things to wear. Make sure she has some dresses, too. You know what I like. Please, I need to run; my head is about to explode. I will meet you; this will not be all on you." He gave a nod and an amused smirk. He was such an ass sometimes. He knew he would love every minute of it.

The rhythm of running was exactly what I needed. Caroline's presence gave me clarity and my brain worked overtime, but I needed the time away from her to actually put those ideas into the proper applications. My fingers were eager to be on the keyboard working, but they liked the feel of Caroline better. My tongue and lips could form hundreds of thousands of words in numerous languages and dialects, yet, all they had done for the past twenty-four hours was taste the sweetness of my bride.

My head expanded from the ideas that had begun in the night: random thoughts of a suitcase to hold her new clothes, fabric falling over her hips and swishing back and forth as she walked, and the way wine tasted on her lips. Algorithms. Her words begging for me. Programs. Input. Data falling into place. Me falling onto the floor. Laborious hours of translations. Run. Breathe. Run. Pace. Breathe. The steady rhythm of her breaths under me. The sporadic beating of her heart this morning. Contrast. Run. Breathe. She caught me completely off guard. Fearless. Passionate. Strong. I had never had unprotected sex. I was too cautious, too careful, too calculating. Press on. Another mile. Utterly helpless. Contrast, again. The most amazing feeling in the world!

I ran for nearly an hour. I made it eight miles. Preston could have gone longer. That was good to know. I would run with him again in the morning. We should have Caroline's passport before noon and be at the airport immediately after that. By the end of the seventh mile, my head was clearer. Running was an amazing anesthetic. I showered and texted Dawes. They were still at the first boutique.

Bring me a sandwich. Starving. He was much more demanding in text than in person.

Get your own, I replied.

Preston showered while our third guard escorted me to meet Dawes and Caroline. They were less than a block from the hotel. Caroline was in the dressing room when I arrived.

"She's impossible," Dawes said. "She refuses to buy anything. She says everything is too expensive and won't buy anything from that pile until she talks to you. She has no idea, does she?"

I shook my head. "It is both a blessing and a curse."

Dawes laughed and excused himself. "I'll be back in thirty."

Caroline came out of the dressing room wearing a skirt and blouse. She was looking at herself in the full-length mirror, considering the fit, when she caught my reflection. She smiled. "What do you think?" she asked.

"I like it. Dawes says you are having trouble deciding."

She walked toward me and coaxed me so she could whisper into my ear. "The prices here are ridiculous. This blouse costs eighty bucks! There aren't any shoes for less than a hundred and fifty. I have never paid more than fifty and those were on sale." I sighed inwardly. She was being thrifty, how adorable. "The underwear, alone, costs more than my shoes. Can't you just take me to Target? I already know what size bras and brands of underwear and socks I wear."

"That is not convenient. You can go to Target in Miami. Get what you need for now."

"What exactly do I need for now?" she asked.

"That looks nice," I gestured to the outfit she had on. "Do you like it?" She nodded. "Pick a week's worth of outfits, one dress, and shoes to match. Remember, it will be considerably warmer in Miami."

The saleslady was relieved to be sorting through the pile in hopes of an actual sale. Caroline was decisive about what she liked and refused to get underwear there. She said they looked uncomfortable. She only found two pair of shoes. She wanted a pair of sneakers. We asked that they deliver everything to the hotel. We walked to a cosmetics store and she purchased a few items. She also found an athletic store for her sneakers. I happily paid over eighty for the ones she liked. She was happy they were on sale. The intimate apparel store was entirely distracting. Dawes tried to sit in the plush pink chair and look casual, but he finally said he would wait outside. The two salesladies were extremely helpful and asked Dawes if he'd like them to try on anything for him to get a better idea of what he might like to purchase.

"I thought that only happened in movies," he said before he walked through the glass door and waited on the sidewalk.

Caroline liked this store. She wanted some pajamas and a nightgown. She also liked some of the perfume. I had a hard time not imagining Caroline wearing every lacy item that hung on racks and rods. The tables were laden with stacks of lace panties and thongs and every delicate thing that I could imagine touching and removing from her.

On her third trip to the dressing room, I almost followed her in to help her. I caught myself just before the sales lady stopped me. "Sir, men aren't allowed back there."

"Caroline," I stammered, "I will be outside with Dawes. I need to discuss something with him."

"Too much?" Dawes asked as I stepped outside.

I exhaled. "I have never done that before."

"Yeah, it gets pretty intense after a while. Doesn't seem to have the same effect on women. I wonder if they really like any of it, or if it's just to drive us crazy."

"Any word about the passport?"

"Tomorrow morning at the earliest."

***

Finally, we were making our way back to the hotel when Caroline remembered she needed some items for her hair. We backtracked to the drugstore. I tossed another package of condoms and some deodorant into the small shopping cart that Caroline insisted on using. She examined the items in the cart and then looked at me sheepishly.

"I'm sorry again for this morning." I had no reply. "Are you still upset with me?"

"No."

"Are you sure?"

What kind of question was that? "No, I am not upset with you. What would make you think that?"

"You haven't touched me since."

Her mouth went down in a pout and she diverted her eyes. She was right; I had not touched her. I pushed her off of me and told her to dress and I went to run. I had not kissed her before I left. I had not kissed her when I saw her at the store. I purposefully removed myself from the store that made me have too many thoughts of what I wished to do with her and smelled like everything feminine and intoxicatingly sensual. I had not even taken her hand while we walked back toward the hotel.

"I apologize. It was not my intention. I have a great deal on my mind today," I confessed.

"Do you need time alone to work?" she asked.

"Yes, but that can wait until we get to Miami." That seemed to please her. I paid for our purchases and the three of us walked back to the hotel. I made a point to hold her hand. She seemed pleased by that, too. She spoke with Dawes with casual familiarity. She laughed with him and thanked him for his helping her. She took nothing for granted and expressed her appreciation.

We ordered room service and watched another black and white movie. I held her bare feet in my lap and rubbed her toes. She muttered some of the lines with the actors. I watched her more than I watched the movie. She laughed at the right times and cried at the end. Her new clothes arrived at some point along with a courier with her new Social Security Card. I reached for the remote and turned off the television. She looked at me.

"Are you tired of watching old movies?"

"No, I want to tell you about Marshall."

She half smiled. "Thank you. I would like to know."

I took a deep breath because I knew I would have to start at the very beginning. "It began three years ago. I was working on a small project for the U.S. Government. It was the same time I met Kennedy and Dawes.

"About a month after I completed that project, I was contacted by another handler in the private sector. Until this point, I had only worked with government agencies. Even while I was at the university, I worked on teams. I made a name for myself, and before I graduated at eighteen, I was working independently. I prefer to work independently, so I freelance. I completed two jobs with this handler and the men in charge were very pleased. I was compensated accordingly."

"Like money?" she asked, like she had in the fort, lightening the mood. I had become very serious.

"Yes, like money, a lot of money." She nodded. "That handler was soon replaced by Marshall. He had a job that he was insistent that I do. They had two others working on it, but they were unable to break the code being used. It was not a code, exactly, it was the stringing of a specific sub-dialect of an isolated, indigenous tribe woven into random gibberish. I had no knowledge of the language when I first began, but it only took about a month to make enough associations from other related languages. In the course of the relays, I realized that it was not generated from isolated tribesmen; it was electronically generated.

"Someone was using this to transmit and conceal other information. The information they were transmitting was connected to two political coups. The current leaders of both of those countries had been assassinated. I could hear the story unfolding as to whom was behind the incidents. I told you that my parents were economists. That is only partly true. They met at university while they were both studying economics. Beyond that, their knowledge and areas of expertise are vast and highly coveted. They are political economists and have diplomatic immunity in many countries. They advise world leaders and have had opportunities to lead governments out of financial and political unrest. They are both adored and hated by the same countries they have saved from utter ruin. I know more than how to interpret. Thanks to my parents, I know how to read the political and economic climates of most any given state. My involvement in this particular job with Marshall soon made me realize that I had swum beyond my depths. I gave them a portion of what I had interpreted, but they strongly suspected that I was holding out on them. They knew there was more and they were right.

"Less than a year later, I began my current project with Kennedy. I had worked with him in a general sense, but not as closely as I do now. I was arrogant; I thought I could do this job with Kennedy and straddle between your government and the private sector. My job with Marshall was writing updates for something I had set up for his agency years before. It was completely unrelated to the other job. When word was received that I was back in circulation, they demanded that I return and give them everything I had left unfinished. They began threatening me, determined to have me finish. Everyone I came in contact with was now under constant observation. I had already made plans to begin classes this semester, so I was foolish to think I would have more time.

"Marshall has become increasingly bold, but I suspect he acts more in desperation. He infiltrated my home in D.C. and killed someone with whom I had been spending time. Her death was accidental, much like Krissa's, but he was using her as leverage. The night she died, I left D.C. Thanks to Dawes, I got out, but I did not go far enough. I should have left the country, but I was still working with Kennedy. Maybe things would have been different if I had kept Dawes nearby."

At the mention of another woman and Krissa's death, Caroline moved her feet underneath her and sat up straighter. She withdrew from me and into herself. "I thought if I kept a low profile and focused on my studies and my contract, everything would pass. I was ignorant, and now we end up here."

CHAPTER 22

I sat silently for several, long minutes. I didn't know what to say. His story sounded reasonable. I just couldn't imagine how he thought he'd be safe living in our little college town. I could have guessed that from movie plots. For the first time, I questioned his intelligence. The other thought that drilled into my brain was of course the mention of another woman *with whom he had been spending time*. That was unpleasant and made me increasingly jealous. I didn't like that feeling, either, but now she was dead, just like Krissa, just like I could be, too.

"I am sure you have questions."

"Did you love her?" I asked. It was the only question I could formulate.

He shook his head. He wondered at that being my first question when I could have asked a hundred others. "No. I have never loved any woman." *Except you, Caroline*, was what I wanted him to say, but he didn't.

"Would you have married her to save her? I asked.

"No, that is just you, Caroline." I felt somewhat satisfied with that statement, but then he cocked his head to one side and remembered something unpleasant. "I later found out that she was working with Marshall. He had gotten to her long before she was able to get to me."

"Did you tell anyone else what you discovered?" I asked.

"What do you mean?"

"Does anyone else know why Marshall is after you? Have you given that information to anyone else? Does anyone else know that you can understand the transmissions?" I pressed. He shook his head.

"I have only told Kennedy bits and pieces. He knows that Marshall upped his game, but I have divulged nothing of what I know. You are the only person who knows those details. Kennedy suspects that it may be more than I have told him, but he has yet to press me for details. He was not particularly concerned. His government would protect me, regardless. They want what they want and tend to overlook transgressions when they do not directly affect their cause. Marshall only knows the bare minimum of what I uncovered. He is greedy for more, but I refuse to give him that power."

"Are his employers worried you might sell that information to someone else? Are they afraid you'll tell on them?"

"I have not thought of it that way. I want them to leave me alone to work and complete the tasks at hand. I hate the distraction."

"This is really serious, Hashim, two women are dead and it's obviously not going away. Is this all just an inconvenience for you?"

"Marshall will become bored or be removed from the picture, entirely. Leadership changes like the wind. It will pass soon and you will be safe."

"What happens once I'm safe? Am I free to resume my life?" I asked with an edge to my voice.

He looked offended. "You want to go back?"

"Of course, that's my life and *if* I'm safe, why can't I go back? I have my studies and my job. Momma and Billy. I'll only have a semester or two left before graduation after I repeat this one."

"You would leave me?" The look in his eyes was devastating. He had just told me everything. He was completely transparent, and I asked if I could leave him.

"Damn it, Hashim, this isn't fair! You took me away from everything I've ever known and thrust me into a completely different world *for my protection*. I want to be home and safe, and when you said that it'll all pass over, I just thought maybe that meant I could return." I caught his eye, then, holding his gaze. His look of bewilderment made me feel guilty. I moved in closer to him, and the intensity of his eyes softened when I took his hand. "Whether or not this passes as soon as you hope, you're making me doubt my entire path. You're making me want things that I've never desired before." The truth of those words hung between us.

"What do you desire, Caroline?" His voice was low and husky.

Blush spread over my face and neck. "Stop it, Hashim! Don't make me say it!"

"I like knowing specifically what you want. I choose not to exclude you in anything. You now know more about me than any other person, including my parents, including Dawes, and he has watched after me for quite some time."

"You aren't afraid this entire place is bugged; you think we have complete privacy?"

"You tend to be paranoid. They swept for bugs before we arrived."

"You don't think they'd placed their own?"

His thoughts were running behind his eyes, again. "A conspiracy theorist, also?" I shrugged. "Are you ready for bed?" he asked.

"Yes, I could sleep," I said unwilling to be the first to suggest we make love again.

Once we were in the bedroom, Hashim made up for the lack of affection he'd shown me throughout the day. Maybe he was more comfortable with private affection rather than public displays. I could temper my desire for him in public if it meant that we stored it all up for when we were alone. Alone, behind locked doors, was amazing. Alone, behind locked doors, left me panting and making noises that I'd never made before.

Condom was burned into the front of my brain, and I waited patiently, well, somewhat patiently, until it was in place before I came completely unhinged. The release of physical pleasure was a beautiful way to end the day, and I collapsed into heavy sleep a few hours before midnight.

***

An unfamiliar hand was over my mouth, and suddenly my eyes flew open. I struggled, but that same unfamiliar hand had arms that were holding me down. "Caroline," the voice whispered into my ear. The room was dark. It sounded like Dawes, but I wasn't sure. I reached over, but Hashim wasn't lying next to me.

"We have to go," the voice said. I shook my head because it was the only part of me I could move. "It's Dawes. We need to go. Do you promise not to scream if I let you go?"

I nodded and he released me. "Hashim?" I mouthed close into his ear. He was still pressed over me, holding me down.

"Packing." I nodded in the dark and he eased off of me, pulling me up. I clung to the covers when I realized that I was naked. Dawes came back for me. "Get up!" he demanded just above a whisper.

"Robe?" I asked.

He muttered a curse and threw a robe at me. "Come on!"

I didn't waste any time. I wrapped the robe around myself and had no choice but to let Dawes lead me out of the bedroom by my elbow. I heard steps behind me and knew it was Hashim by his scent and the sound of his breaths. Dawes led us across the hall to the elevator. Everything was dark and silent. I was confused; was there a power outage? If so, why were we taking the elevator. Hashim shoved in behind Dawes; he was carrying everything in his arms. I suspected it was our duffels and my new clothes. I could barely make out either of the men's figures in the dark. I stood so small and frightened between them. Dawes was holding onto me with one hand and I was pretty sure a gun with the other. We went all the way to the basement, past the lobby floor, and into a parking garage.

"Can you carry her?" Hashim asked.

"Yeah, no problem," Dawes said sarcastically, and as soon as the elevator doors opened, I was thrust over his shoulder. I was too afraid to scream, but I wasn't expecting to be carried like a sack of potatoes. Blood rushed to my head, but I held onto consciousness. He took a few steps toward a black SUV. He opened the door and threw me inside and slammed the door behind me. I gathered up the robe around me and made an attempt at modesty. I looked up and Preston was in the driver's seat. I heard the back hatch close and Hashim joined me in the back seat at nearly the same time Dawes closed the door to the front passenger's side. Preston drove out of the parking garage and onto the deserted street. It was still the middle of the night. I clung to Hashim or was he clinging to me? I was so frightened, but relieved to be with him.

"What happened?" I asked when I'd found my voice. Every other part of me was shaking.

"Marshall," he said flatly and pressed my hair down along the side of my head.

Preston drove smoothly at top speed. "Where are we going?" I asked.

"The airport," Dawes answered for Hashim.

"Miami," Hashim said matter-of-factly.

Preston drove straight onto the tarmac. Dawes dragged me out of the SUV and pushed me toward a small airplane. I turned to see Preston with Hashim and the bags. My bare feet stumbled on the cold pavement and Dawes scooped me up again and carried me into the plane. He plopped me down onto a leather seat. "Stay!" he demanded. I did as he instructed and sat shaking until I saw Hashim come in with Preston and Dawes. They threw the bags on the floor behind the seats. Dawes closed the doors to the small aircraft while Preston eased through the tiny cabin and into the cockpit. It felt like I was inside a flying minivan. Preston put on a headset and I felt the plane's engine come to life under me. "Buckle up!" Dawes demanded before he joined Preston as co-pilot. He put on a headset as well.

I fumbled for the buckle. My hands were shaking, but I managed. My entire body was shivering. My bare feet were nearly numb from the brief moments they had touched the pavement. The air was cold blowing from the vents in the small cabin. Hashim placed his hands over mine and looked at me for the first time.

"You are freezing."

"And scared."

CHAPTER 22.5

Faithful are the wounds of a friend,
but deceitful are the kisses of an enemy.

– Proverbs 27:6

Scared was an understatement. Her eyes were wide and she looked completely disoriented. She would not stir when I tried to wake her. I received Marshall's text after two a.m.; passport or not, it was time to move. I dressed and asked Dawes to see after her while I packed. All my efforts to make her comfortable, to make her safe, and to have nice things were thwarted. Here she sat, shivering, shaking, barefooted, wearing nothing but a damned bathrobe. I held her hands to keep them warm. Preston spoke low into the headset; he drove the plane toward the runway. Dawes looked back to make sure we were buckled. I nodded once. I put my arm around Caroline and tried to make her comfortable against me. The plane turned and taxied down the runway. She leaned her head back and closed her eyes. She took a deep breath as she felt the force of takeoff. We were airborne in seconds. There was little to do to get a small plane off the ground.

I sighed, relieved to be in the air. The likelihood of Marshall getting to either of us, now, was minimal. She yawned to relieve the pressure in her ears and opened her eyes. She looked past me out of the window. She was curious, but the night sky revealed very little. We would be landing just after sunrise. She would enjoy that. She adjusted herself in the seat and pulled her feet under her. I removed my jacket and laid it over her legs, giving her both privacy and warmth. She pulled the collar of the robe up to her neck and crossed it over herself.

"Where are my clothes?" she asked.

"In the back; in the bags."

She looked at me and sighed. "Any hope of getting to them?" she asked.

I looked up to Dawes and Preston. It was not a good idea to be moving around and adjusting weight midflight. I shook my head. "The flight will last less than three hours. You can take care of everything when we land."

She crossed her arms over her chest like she had at the passport office. The shroud covered her once again. She eased from under my arm and leaned over toward the window. Like in the car when I told her we were getting married, she wanted to be as far from me as possible. I knew she needed time to process everything. I convinced myself she would be fine once she prayed to her god and reasoned through her fear. I made no efforts to touch her or coax her from her mood. There would be time enough for her to accept our circumstances.

Dawes turned and caught my eye. He made a gesture with his chin towards Caroline, an unspoken question. I lifted my shoulder in a slight shrug and shook my head. I could not begin to understand all the complexities she must be reasoning through, and I did not wish to provoke her in such a small space. Dawes pulled something from his pocket and tossed it onto my lap. It was a small currier's envelope.

"Came by messenger just after you two went to bed. I was going to give it to you first thing in the morning. I guess, it's the second thing, now," he said over the hum of the engine.

I opened the envelope and held Caroline's passport. Finally! Possibilities unfolded in front of me. I felt elation to hold the Holy Grail. I checked the information inside and smiled when I looked at her photo. Not many people could claim such a beautiful likeness on their passport, including hair and make-up done by professionals. I opened the passport to her photo and held it up next to her head and pointed. Dawes laughed at the contrast of her current state and the photo, and I smiled, too. The contrast was quite comical. His expression changed, and I was suddenly and forcefully elbowed in the ribs.

"Give me that and stop laughing!" she exclaimed and grabbed the passport from my hands. She glared at both of us. Dawes turned to face the front of the plane, but I could still see him laughing. "What the hell, Hashim! This isn't funny! This is all your damned fault! I can't believe you're making fun of me!" She opened the passport and looked at her photo. She leaned back over toward the window and moved her fingers over her likeness, wistfully. Her eyes looked sad and I could feel strong emotions radiating from her. She blinked hard and swallowed holding back the tears that I knew were about to fall. Sure, I had hurt her feelings, but she was already deeply wounded.

"You know what?" she asked. I leaned in toward her to hear her better. "It's the only wedding day photo I have and you aren't even in it." She closed her eyes and pressed the photo to her chest. She turned her body toward the window, leaving her back to me. She covered her face with her arm. Grief and regret attacked my chest like she had volleyed her emotions directly into my heart. I ran my fingers though my hair in frustration and leaned back against the leather seat, exasperated.

I did not make a habit of having my picture taken. My parents had only a few photos of me as a child. Photos were not important to them and photos of their children could be used against them. I had not thought that would be important to her, but I should have known better. "I am sorry, Caroline. I should have been more considerate," I said, putting my hand on her shoulder.

"Humph," she muttered. I thought she was dismissing me, but it was the beginning of a sob.

Dawes snuck a peak behind his shoulder. His expression was just as guilty and sad as mine. He mouthed a curse and rolled his eyes. Preston must have heard his curse and turned to look over his shoulder to see Caroline in a crumpled heap sobbing. He shook his head and closed his eyes, feeling her grief; the entire interior of the aircraft was brought down by her misery.

I let her cry. I put my hand on her shoulder but she refused to move any closer to me. After an hour, though, I could stand it no longer. "Please, Caroline, talk to me. I hate seeing you like this." She sniffed and wiped her face with the sleeve of her robe. I had nothing to offer her.

"I'm sure you do," she said sarcastically. "I'm nothing like the beauty in that passport, your precious passport." Her words were biting.

"We were just kidding," I said. "You have to admit the contrast."

"Yeah, I admit the contrast," she said mockingly, her light eyes burning. Her voice rose over the droning of the plane's engine, but Preston and Dawes kept their eyes fixed forward. "That girl actually looks happy. She wasn't thrust from her bed in the middle of the night, frightened half to death, and thrown into a car and a plane and whisked off to only God knows where! She's had coffee and strawberries; her teeth are brushed, and she's wearing underwear! Yeah, I admit the contrast!" She looked away and brushed through her hair with her fingers trying to remove the tangles. It only formed static electricity and made the waves of her hair stand out more. I had yet to decide if I were more intimidated by Crying Caroline or Angry Caroline. Neither one was pleasant, but Crying Caroline at least was generally more consolable than her angrier counterpart.

By the time we touched down at the private airstrip, Caroline was in slightly better spirits. I nudged her to catch the sunrise as it gradually made its debut; the streams of color danced over the clouds on the horizon. The colors were magnificent and her light eyes shown bright taking it all in for the first time. She watched out the window as we made our descent. She had that same far-away look like when she drove. I suspected she would like flying the plane herself.

A car had yet to arrive when we landed, so I found her bag immediately. I could not bring her into my mother's home in her current state. Preston and Dawes waited outside the plane while she dressed. "Here," I said handing her the bag. She reached in and found an outfit. She put on a skirt and a knit top. She slipped on the pair of wedges she had worn on our wedding day. She found her makeup and a hairbrush. There was nothing she could do for her hair. She had not worn it in a ponytail since the night we left, but I knew she was battling with what to do about it. She brushed through it again and finally just tucked the

195

sides behind her ears. She shoved the bathrobe down into her bag and hefted it to zip it.

"Is there a bathroom around here?" she asked.

"Yeah, I think there may be one over there," I said motioning toward a small hanger. She grabbed her toothbrush and made her way out of the plane, determined to feel as normal as possible. Preston and I followed her while Dawes waited for the car. She came out of the small bathroom and greeted me civilly. She almost smiled. Preston and I took turns after her. A couple of mechanics meandered around the hanger. Dawes whistled when he saw the car approaching. I shook Preston's hand and thanked him. He would be returning the plane to Montgomery and be relieved of his current duties. Dawes would remain with us indefinitely. Caroline smiled, admiringly, when she saw the BMW approach.

"Is this yours, too?" she guessed. I gave a quick nod. I was thankful she was talking and not screaming at me. Mizhir pulled up beside us. He was an older man with gray at his temples and wisdom in his eyes. He had been with my family for a long time. He managed the gardens and the cars and was exceedingly patient and good-natured.

"Welcome home," he said as he greeted me with a friendly smile.

"Mizhir, it's good to see you. You remember Dawes, and this is my wife, Caroline. Caroline, this is Mizhir. He is a good man; you can trust him."

Mizhir could not conceal his surprise and gave a clap of his hands in celebration. "A wife? Congratulations!" He took Caroline's hands in his and lifted them to his forehead, offering his service to her.

"It's nice to meet you, Mizhir."

"The pleasure is mine," he said.

Dawes and I saw to the bags. Dawes rode shotgun and I rode in the backseat with Caroline. I could tell she liked this car. It was not a sporty model, but it was a luxury model. She felt the trim along the seats and inspected every inch of the interior with her eyes. She took my hand in the space between us and gave it a little squeeze. Perhaps that was a sign that she would forgive me. She liked flowers and cars, good wine and Doritos. I had also been able to please her sexually. I felt confident I could keep her content with coffee every morning and that short list for a while at least.

"Is she in residence?" I asked.

Mizhir nodded once. "Your father has been delayed. He was expected at the end of the week, but I think it might be another few weeks before he returns."

"Does she have plans to meet him?" I asked. He shook his head.

We pulled into the back entrance of the property. It was no less guarded, but considerably less obvious an entrance. Mizhir drove up to the back entrance of the house near the pool. He let us out and I gathered our bags. Dawes went with Mizhir and would stay in the guest house again. I walked past one of the outside guards and put our bags on the marble, tiled floor. Caroline followed me into the house. Her eyes were wide with wonder and apprehension at everything she was taking in.

I took her hand and kissed her fingers. "This is our Miami home. It is also my mother's primary residence. I have the pleasure of introducing you." I smiled but she doubted my confidence. "We will stay here until my work is finished. In the meantime, think about places you want to go; consider it an extended honeymoon." She smiled a little at that. I walked her to the kitchen to find coffee. She would definitely need coffee before we greeted my mother. It would make everything easier. "This is Nita," I said as we entered the kitchen.

The squat Cuban woman wiped off her hands and squealed her delight in Spanish. "Hashim! You don't call! You just show up for breakfast!" She grabbed my face and kissed both of my cheeks in greeting.

"Coffee, please," I replied in her native tongue.

"And who is this?" she asked with a glance toward Caroline as she pulled two mugs from the cabinet. She hesitated because I had never brought a woman to her table before. She set everything in the center of the kitchen table and poured the coffee.

"Caroline, my wife."

Nita's eyes opened wide and she set the pot onto the table suddenly and made the sign of the cross over herself. "*Su* esposa?" she asked like she had misheard me. I nodded. I was not sure how much Spanish Caroline could understand, but she jumped at Nita's exclamation. She jumped again when Nita screamed in delight and grabbed her forcefully and hugged her. She then kissed Caroline's cheeks. She made us sit down while she resumed the serving of coffee. She rambled on in Spanish and produced breakfast items: eggs, toast, and fruit. She spoke English well enough to communicate with Caroline but spoke more Spanish to me. Caroline drank her coffee and smiled and laughed with Nita. Satisfied that she had fed us adequately, she sat next to Caroline. Nita took Caroline's face in her hands and looked deeply into her eyes, like she could see into her soul. Caroline did not pull away from the woman's intense gaze. Nita released her at the end of her examination and nodded her approval to me. "You choose, well," she said in English. She patted Caroline's cheek and then patted mine before she left the kitchen with a tray for my mother.

"I like her," Caroline said as she drained her second mug of coffee.

"Me, too."

"Will I meet your mother, now?" she asked.

"Soon, but first, I will take you to our room. You can freshen-up there. I want you to be at your best before you meet her."

"Thank you."

CHAPTER 23

What a night! I had completely lost it on the plane, but even with all of that, flying was an amazing experience. I realized a few things, though. Hashim and Dawes had a good relationship; they bantered and joked like old friends. Another thing, Hashim had not mentioned that we would be meeting his mother. I guessed by the layers of security, that he and Kennedy felt this was the safest place to work, but I felt exceedingly uneasy about his hesitation to mention his mom. Lastly, the Miami house was bigger than the hotel we had just stayed in. The grounds were immaculate and there were armed guards all over the place. I counted six on the way in from the back gate. I did not have a good feeling about this, but I was more accepting of the security guards than meeting his mother. I heard dogs barking in the distance. I wondered if they had kennels for pets or if those were guard dogs. There was a pool and a guest house and servants' quarters, I imagined, too. I had willingly entered a compound, a heavily guarded, luxurious compound.

Then there was the car, *oh, the car*, I sighed inwardly. I was a complete idiot. I thought I was smart and capable of reasoning, but he knew he had me at the damn car, okay, and Nita's coffee, too. I was such a sucker. I had lusted after him and his car from the first time I laid eyes on them.

We walked up the back stairs onto the second floor. He showed me into his room. It was spacious with a king-sized bed, a seating area, and an office nook. The bathroom had a garden tub and a shower with multiple nozzles and showerheads. Hashim showed me to the closet and moved a few of his clothes over to make room for mine. He cleaned out a couple of drawers and said I could unpack later or he'd ask one of Nita's girls to help me get sorted.

"Do I have time to take a shower?" I asked.

"Yes, I plan to take one as well."

"Would you like to join me?" I asked, wondering if he would actually accept my invitation. "It looks large enough for the two of us."

My feelings toward him were so conflicted. Exhaustion, stress, and isolation made my need for connection overpowering. Being with him would help remove the rush of emotions that I couldn't imagine wading through. Sex cleared my mind and right now I needed that desperately. He smiled at me, and before I finished my statement, he was kissing me. Pressed up against his clothes in the closet, he was kissing me. The emotions and fear and adrenaline from the middle of the night returned, and I was consumed once again, but this time, I channeled all of my feelings toward Hashim in the form of need and desire.

We entered the bathroom and he locked the door behind us. I turned on the shower and began undressing. The steam rose and covered the glass of the shower and the mirrors. I found my razor and stepped into the shower to begin shaving my legs and underarms. Hashim entered and washed his hair and his body. It was so distracting to watch him bathe that I was afraid I might cut myself. Hashim moved from under the showerhead and placed me under the hot water. He lathered his hands with shampoo and washed my hair. His hands moving over my scalp forced goosebumps to run along my entire body. He let the lather run down my shoulders and over my breasts. His long fingers and palms traced every surface of my body, bathing me, washing me, forcing my eyes to close when he returned his lips to mine.

He knew exactly what I needed to be brought back from the past six or so hours. I think he needed the reconnection as well. He was prepared. I was not. He lifted me against the tile wall and I wrapped my legs around his waist and my arms around his shoulders. He took me there, in the shower, steamy and wet and gasping in the echoing room. The sound of the water ran in the background. The hot water streamed over Hashim's back and onto me. Our bodies pressed together, fused in the steam. When he finished, he stood for a long time, holding me against the wall. He pressed his forehead against mine. I could feel a struggle forming in his mind. I tilted his head so that I could see into his eyes. I looked at him searchingly. Surely, I could find the answers there. The water sounded so loud, now, in the silence between us, the intensity of our passion temporarily abated. He wrapped his arms around me and held me close into him.

"I have never had this feeling before," he whispered. "It is you, Caroline, and I have no words," he panted.

I closed my eyes and held his head more tightly. I didn't want to release him; he was vulnerable and transparent and I wanted to cover him entirely, to protect this fragile state of things between us. I kissed his head and breathed in his scent. I hoped it was enough, but I knew it wasn't. "I love you, Hashim," came out in a sigh. My hand flew over mouth. *Oh my, God, no*! I thought. *No! No! No!* But it was too late; the words were already out.

He leaned back and looked at me. I couldn't read his expression. He eased me down from the shower wall and set me firmly on my own two feet. The thoughts behind his eyes were racing. He didn't smile, but at least he didn't look angry or disappointed. He stepped back like I had just shattered him in his fragile state. He turned back into the spray of the showerhead and rinsed again like he was washing off me and my words. My stomach ached from the rejection, or should I say, the lack of response. My eyes burned but I refused to cry. I didn't expect him to say he loved me in return; hell, I didn't even expect to say those words aloud myself. They just slipped out. I wanted him to know that he was safe and that I would protect his heart; I understood his struggle.

I slipped out of the shower and dried off. I could just pretend it didn't happen. I could swallow my pride and resume this facade of a marriage. I went back into the closet and dressed. I sat on the floor and put on my makeup and brushed my hair. I scrounged in the bag for my new shoes, strapped them on, and adjusted the buckle. I stood and looked at myself in the full-length mirror at the end of the closet. *Well, C, you clean up pretty well for a kept woman.* I leaned over and dried my hair more with the towel. When I lifted my head from underneath it, Hashim was standing, watching me in the mirror. I looked up into his eyes in the reflection. They were softened and apologetic.

"Is that really how you feel?" he asked.

I thought about it for a few seconds. "Yes, at that moment and if I'm honest, probably for more moments that that." And there it was, the truth, laid out between us. *I loved him.*

"I cannot return your words," he said, regretfully.

"I don't expect you to. That wasn't the agreement between us. I didn't intend to say them, but now that I have, will you forgive me and perhaps in time accept them?" My stomach ached waiting for his reply. He said nothing but he nodded. "Are you angry with me?" I asked.

"No."

"Good. I guess that's a start." I could hear the strain in my voice.

I returned to the bathroom while Hashim dressed and hung my towel on the hook. I brushed my teeth and found a hairdryer and dried my hair. "Ready?" I asked when Hashim emerged from the closet, fully dressed. "Do I need to know anything before I meet your mom? You know, you could have mentioned her before we were on her doorstep. What have you told her about me?"

"Nothing."

"You've put us both at a disadvantage," I accused.

"You are probably right, but I would rather you each make your own first impression. Our marriage will surely come as a surprise to her. Whatever you do, be yourself; do not let her intimidate you." He took my hand and kissed me, not like in the shower, but like friends who kissed and I found that I liked that just fine.

CHAPTER 23.5

The wise woman builds her house,
but with her own hands, the foolish one tears hers down.

– Proverbs 14:1

I love you, Hashim. Her words. No one had ever spoken those words to me much less over me. Their weight was so heavy. *Love* was not a word spoken in my home. I acknowledged that my parents must love one another and they must love me, but I had no memory of ever being told so. Caroline had undoubtedly been told that she was loved from the time she was born. She was loved and in turn was loving. She did love me; there was no denying that. Her kindness towards me from the beginning proved that. Romantically, she was captivated by me. Physically, she could not resist. The truth of the words in the shower, though, pierced me. My care and concern for her had deepened, but *love* eluded me. She could feel my struggle and my desire. I needed her, her strength, her touch, but her *love*; that, I was not prepared to receive.

Mother was downstairs, reading her papers in my father's study. She lowered her reading glasses when I entered the room and smiled. My presence was a pleasant surprise. She moved gracefully from around the desk to greet me. She kissed both my cheeks and held my face in her hands, looking into my eyes.

"Hashim, you are home," she said in Turkish.

I smiled and replied to her in kind. "Yes."

"When did you arrive?"

"This morning."

"For how long?"

"A month, maybe more. I need to work; I have deadlines."

"Your sister arrives next week; this will please her. Once your father arrives, we will all be together." I smiled at the idea of seeing Sefa. I had not seen her since the last time Dawes and I were at the house together. This would indeed be good timing. Sefa would be a good distraction for Caroline while I worked.

"Mother, I brought someone I want you to meet."

She raised her eyebrow as I stepped out of the study and led Caroline in by the hand. "Mother, this is Caroline. Caroline, this is my mother, Ecrin Emir," I said in English. My mother's face was pleasant and almost friendly as she expectantly eyed the light-eyed, Caucasian woman at my side. She acknowledged youth and beauty, I was sure. "Caroline Emir," I clarified, putting the emphasis on her last name, "my wife." My mother rarely showed emotion; she was factual and concrete and stoic. She could carry herself in most any circle in the world and never be shaken, but as my words settled, her pleasant exterior hardened as she critically examined the petite woman at my side. Her eyes turned on me, full of disappointment and arrogance.

Regardless of how she received the news, I knew her response would be the same. Ecrin Emir was possessively proud of me, her son. She would be disappointed in my choice; she always was. She may not have shown her emotion, but she could show her disappointment with every fiber of her being. She would be disappointed that I had married without her involvement. If she had a choice, she would prefer that my father arrange my marriage, but I had disqualified that idea long ago. My father disagreed with her and thankfully, she had no power to force me to do anything; she never had. This would have been so much easier if my father were home. He was more reasonable; he would understand.

"What do you mean by this?" she asked in Turkish, purposefully excluding Caroline from the conversation.

"I would like you to welcome my wife," I replied in kind, again. I did not wish for Caroline to hear everything my mother would say, now that she had set the precedent.

"You could not see to give me warning? You come home for the first time in months with *this*, and you expect me to welcome her?" She gestured a hand toward Caroline. "What do you mean by bringing this infidel into your father's home?"

"We are not Muslim, Mother," I scoffed.

"She's obviously not a Jew." She glanced dismissively toward Caroline.

"Under most pretenses, neither are you," I argued.

Caroline put her hand on my arm to get my attention. "English, please," she whispered to me. "I can't understand anything you're saying." She did not need to hear all of this, I was sure. She may not understand the language, but she definitely understood my mother's gestures and her tone and the obvious disapproval. My mother hesitated when she saw me respond to Caroline's touch with familiarity. Her beautiful green eyes glared at the exchange between us.

"Mrs. Emir," Caroline, began. "It's a pleasure to meet you." She stepped forward bravely and put out her hand in greeting.

My mother regained her composure and took Caroline's hand. "I wish I could say the same."

Caroline removed her hand from my mother's like she had been burned by her touch. Caroline stood to her full height and took a deep breath. "Truth be told, ma'am, I don't want to be here anymore than you want me to be. This wasn't my choice, but I think this house is big enough that I can stay clear of you for the time we have to be here. Don't worry, you won't see me again." Caroline turned on her heels and stormed out of the study. She steadied her gait until she reached the staircase and then I heard the light tapping of her heels as she ran up the stairs. I glared at my mother and turned to follow Caroline. That had not gone well for any of us.

CHAPTER 24

Ecrin Emir was the most beautifully formidable woman I had ever met. I could see their likeness as soon as I entered the room. I could see so much they shared. Her eyes were green and not Hashim's milk-chocolate brown, but other than that, I saw all of their shared magnificence. Watching them argue about me, their intensity, her fury. Seeing her disapproval as soon as he introduced me as his wife and feeling her utter disgust that her son had married me. I couldn't tell her, but at that very moment, I felt the same.

I ran straight back into the room, through the bathroom, and into the closet. I kicked my shoes toward the wall and slid down on top of my duffel bag. I pulled out the hotel bathrobe that was shoved down among my belongings. I receded into a corner of the closet into a small ball on the floor and covered myself entirely with the robe. I was exhausted, ashamed, and humiliated. I had never felt so much self-loathing. I heard Hashim looking for me. I knew it was childish, but I wanted to hide. I wanted to be alone. He could take his time finding me; I wasn't making it easy for him. He'd just brought me to the mouth of the lion and held me over the pit. She had no warning; how would any mother respond? I heard Hashim open several doors down the hall. I heard him call my name, but I ignored him. Soon, it was all quiet and I was able to fall asleep. I slept there, peacefully, for a long time.

***

When I woke up, it was late afternoon. I went to the bathroom and flushed the toilet and washed my hands. I brushed my hair and teeth and walked into the bedroom. Hashim was sitting at his desk working. He looked up from his work.

"Do you feel better now?" he asked.

"A little. How long did it take you to find me?"

"Not long, but you were sleeping. I did not want to disturb you."

"I'm still pretty disturbed, so thanks for letting me sleep. I needed it."

"Are you hungry?"

"Do I have to eat with your mother?"

"It is customary."

"Then, no, I'm not hungry," I said. "I'll be fine. You do what you need to do."

"Be patient; she will come around and accept you in time." He was making an effort to be encouraging. He sucked at that. He also sucked for thinking his mother would ever accept me.

"Are you going to be at that for a while?" I asked.

"Yes. Do you need, otherwise?" he asked.

"I'm going to unpack. Where's the laundry room? I need to do a load."

"Just leave them on the bathroom floor. Nita's girls will get them in the morning."

"I can still do my own laundry," I muttered and returned to the closet.

It didn't take me long to unpack and get my few toiletries organized. At the bottom of my duffel I found my phone, but I couldn't find my charger. "Hey, Hashim, do you have an extra phone charger? My phone is dead."

"No, mine is different," I heard him reply from the other room.

I placed my phone on the shelf of the closet. I'd get one when I went to Target. I also wanted to look for some shorts and a sweater. "I'm going to go to Target tomorrow. I need a swimsuit and a phone charger. Do you need anything?" I asked.

"Tell Dawes. You may not leave without him," he said flatly.

I knew I was distracting him, but I really didn't care. "Does Marshall know we're here?"

"I have no idea, but I am not taking any chances."

"I'm going to go and walk around, get some fresh air."

"Stay on the property." He turned and returned to his work.

I scoffed a little at his final comment. Like I could get past the armed guards. I walked down the hallway from our bedroom and looked into all of the empty rooms. They were lovely, spacious, and incredibly well-decorated. I walked down the back stairs to the kitchen. Nita was there, again. She looked up and welcomed me.

"Miss Caroline, are you hungry? Dinner isn't until seven. Would you like something now?"

"Yes, please. May I make myself a sandwich?"

"Of course, but I can make it for you."

"I'm good," I said. "Where's the bread?" I asked.

She showed me the pantry and the fridges and where I could find whatever I might need. She showed me the freezer and where she kept the ice cream. I made the sandwich and poured myself a huge glass of milk. I sat at the table where I had eaten breakfast and felt instantly better. Nita cooked dinner and busied herself around the kitchen. When she passed again, I asked her where the laundry room was. She almost looked offended that I wanted to do my own laundry, but she showed me just the same. I went outside and walked around; I found the pool and the guesthouse, or what I thought would be the guesthouse. Dawes answered the door. He looked so different than he did in his dark suit. He was wearing a t-shirt and jeans. He looked casual like a regular guy.

"Would you be able to take me to Target tomorrow? I need some things."

"Sure, what time?"

"Whatever is good for you. I have no plans."

"Alright. I run with him at five and we can be there when it opens. Meet me here by seven-thirty."

"Thanks," I said.

Hashim may have sucked at several things, but he did not suck at working; he worked a lot. I had to remind myself that he worked while I slept and I had worked nearly every night while he slept. He only ate occasionally with me and took me out a few times. I decided to be patient; the more he worked the sooner he would complete this job and the sooner we would be away from there. His attentiveness in Montgomery would definitely not be the norm. Without anything better to do, I turned on the television and clicked through a million channels. Hashim had headphones on and didn't seem to mind. He pulled off his headphones at six-thirty and dressed for dinner. He kissed me briefly and then went down to dinner for seven. He worked again when he returned. He didn't say anything about his mother or her demeanor. I was glad he didn't say anything because I was determined to just avoid her.

At eleven, he joined me in the bed. I wasn't sure how our nights together would be. We'd made love in the shower that morning, but he wanted more. I corrected myself, mentally. We had not made love because he did not *love* me. Perhaps we were married friends who kissed and had sex. I suspected that his affection was his way of making up for the way his mother had treated me, but I found our physical contact compelling. He merely had to touch me and kiss me and I was his. It was like the first time he took my hand and led me from the restaurant. He claimed me and I was ill-equipped to resist, or maybe I wasn't trying.

I felt Hashim leave the bed the next morning. Five a.m. was not a real time. Running at five a.m. was absurd. I slept until Hashim came back. He kissed my cheek and went to shower. I got up and dressed and brushed my teeth. We went downstairs to eat together. Nita greeted us with coffee and a cheese omelet. She could speak English, but she and Hashim were accustomed to speaking Spanish. She made him laugh. Breakfast was easy. I met Dawes outside at seven-thirty. He was wearing khakis and a blazer over his shirt.

"Is that to conceal a weapon?" I asked referring to his jacket.

"Yes," he said.

"How do you run with a gun?" I asked.

"Carefully," he said dryly.

"No, really, how?"

"It's a significantly smaller weapon." He laughed.

I walked with him to the garage, well it was actually a warehouse of cars, like a showroom. I gasped. "Are these all Hashim's?" I asked.

"Pretty much."

I sighed. They were amazing, beautiful cars. There was the BMW that we had ridden in from the airport. Next to an Audi like the one Tony Stark drives in *Iron Man*, was a yellow Porsche. I was drawn to it like a magnet. "It's beautiful," I said affectionately stroking the hood of the car. I looked up and saw a Rolls and a Maserati. "These, too?"

"No, those are his father's, except the Jag."

"The Jag?" I asked looking around for it. My hand was on the Porsche, but I could feel the pull of the Jaguar, a deep silver, gray convertible. I think I drooled. I left the Porsche behind momentarily and began walking toward the Jaguar. It was calling me like a siren. I just wanted to touch it.

"That's his mother's," Dawes warned and I stopped dead in my tracks.

"Of course, it is," I said despondently. She would have the one car in the entire garage that I would give my left arm for.

"You two hit it off, I take it."

I sighed dramatically. "What car are we allowed to take?" I asked changing the subject.

"Whichever one you want."

"The Porsche; I choose the Porsche!" Dawes smiled. He liked that idea, too.

Dawes didn't say anything as we made our way out of the compound, but I figured if we were forced together, it was polite to make conversation. "So, what do you do around here all day?" I asked as he drove.

"I run with him and I take you shopping."

I rolled my eyes at his flippant reply. "No, really."

"I swim and workout; I watch sports and movies and I shoot at the range. Sometimes, I read. Sometimes I find a sparring partner; the guards are all pretty good fighters. They rotate frequently, so I have a constant selection of fresh meat. Honestly, watching after Emir is a pretty cushy gig. I have no complaints."

I didn't spend too much time shopping. I bought a bag of Doritos, two swimsuits, a sweater, and a phone charger. I also bought a pair of headphones so

I could listen to music. I didn't think Ecrin would approve of me belting out show tunes from my bedroom; I also knew it would distract Hashim. I passed through a clearance rack of shorts and picked out a few of those, too. On my way to the register, I passed a display of books and inspirational materials. I backed the buggy up and glanced over the selection. I thumbed through a couple of Bibles and tossed in a classic, leather-bound NIV. Dawes raised an eyebrow at my selection. "I need all the help I can get," I said. He remained neutral; his face revealed nothing, but I thought I felt him smile behind me, like maybe he understood. As we approached the car, I asked Dawes, "Can I drive home?"

"You know how to drive stick?" he asked.

"Yes, I'm a competent driver," I assured him. "Do you know any back roads home?" He shook his head. He was so boring; he made me drive the speed limit and go the most direct route home.

Once we were home, I patted the Porsche affectionately. She was beautiful and I liked her best. I would need to tell Hashim. I didn't disturb him, though. He was wearing headphones and his fingers were flying over the keyboard. I found my phone in the closet and plugged it in. I sat down and waited in there alone. It was quiet and I was sure not to bump into Hashim's mother. I folded my new clothes and swimsuits and sat on the floor of the closet. It was surprisingly peaceful there like my own little retreat. I opened the bag of Doritos and ate them while I thumbed through the pages and read a few passages while my phone charged. It took a little while for my phone to charge enough to even reboot. There were several messages and texts from the center. They were probably all wondering where I was. I listened to the messages from the nurses, checking on me.

"Where are you, Caroline? You missed your shift again. Are you sick, honey? Do you need anything?" Then a day later, "Caroline, it's your momma. She's not responding. Hospice is taking care of everything. Please call us." The next message, "Caroline, it's your momma. Honey, I don't want to say this over the phone, but she passed away last night in her sleep. Please call us. We're worried. Where are you? There are plans to be made. How do we get ahold of your brother?"

I continued to sit on the floor of the closet, numbed. That was three days ago. Tears flowed down my cheeks and onto the open Bible on my lap. I snatched the Bible like a teddy bear and clung to it, hoping and praying for strength. I knew her passing was close, but I didn't know it would be days. I had been grieving her loss for the past couple of years, so it wasn't like a shock to know she was physically gone; it just felt like a continuation of the void that had been there for a long time. I dug out the photo from the bottom of my backpack and looked at it for a long time. I held Momma's wedding band, now my wedding band, around my finger and said a prayer and thanked God for her. I prayed for Billy and the shock that would follow when he found out I wasn't even there. When we knew he was going to be deployed again, we made provision to have Momma cremated. Billy paid for everything so that I wouldn't have to make any decisions or worry about any details when the time came. Momma's remains would be taken care of.

Hashim found me in the closet, crying, over a bag of chips and the Bible on my lap. I guessed he realized I hadn't come out for a while or maybe he heard me crying. He knelt down and asked me what was wrong. I explained, but I didn't cry again. He held me for a long time which I appreciated. "Do you have to do anything?" he asked.

I shook my head. "No, Billy took care of it, months ago, before he left. It's just so final, you know?"

"Yes, I do," he said and kissed my head. I was quiet for the rest of the day. He didn't make any demands of me, but I knew he was watching me on and off, keeping tabs on me. I put in headphones and listened to Momma's playlist. I think it was like my own little homage to her memory and the things we shared.

CHAPTER 24.5

Whoever brings ruin on their family will inherit the wind,
and the fool will be servant to the wise.

– Proverbs 11:28

The woman was dead. The only other person Caroline had in the world, now, besides me, was her brother. Her mother had been unable to do anything for her daughter for a long time, so why did her passing make me feel the weight of an even added responsibility? She had been crying when I found her, but she did not cry any more for her mother in my presence. Caroline had done everything possible to see to her mother's comfort before she passed. Surprisingly, she seemed at peace.

I ate dinner again with my mother which was anything but peaceful. Last night's dinner was a continuation of her disapproval and disdain for the situation; I had little appetite. Tonight, our conversation was more civil, yet not any less frustrating for either one of us. She would not see my side of it. I could not tell her the details of what precipitated our marriage, only that it was necessary.

"No, she has not trapped me; on the contrary, it is I who has required it of her."

My mother's assumption that Caroline had tricked or ensnared her son was probably more palatable to her than the thought that I might find Caroline attractive and desirable on her own merit. My mother's arrogance and derision for Caroline only served to make me desire her more. I was like a rebellious teen, doing everything in my power to want the very thing my mother would not accept. She said that in time I would grow bored with her and come to my senses. I laughed. I could not see that happening for a very long time.

"Did you at least have the sense to sign a pre-nuptial agreement?"

"There was no time for that, Mother, and I would never ask that of Caroline."

She scoffed at that. "You are so naïve, son, to think she will not grasp at the air if she thinks it will secure her." She sat for a few minutes, focusing on her meal. "Hashim," she began in a milder tone. "Does that Dawes go with you everywhere, now, or is it necessary."

"It is necessary," I said, confirming her concern.

"I see, now, why you come to Miami." She did not approve of my need for additional security, but she understood. "I will not require the details of you, but does that have anything to do with your hasty marriage?"

I nodded once.

"Very well," she said, and I considered her tone a first step in acceptance. She could possibly accept chivalry over stupidity.

By the third night at dinner, we neither made any mention of Caroline. Mother only spoke of Sefa's arrival and the expectation of Father's return in the span of our combined visits. She cordially invited Caroline to join us for dinner on Sefa's first night. "Please. We will make a party of it. Your Dawes may dine with us, also. I remembered he was here when Sefa last visited." She spoke of politics and government economies. She spoke of the stock markets worldwide and other topics of interest, but her disapproval seeped through every word and onto me.

CHAPTER 25

The next few days eased into a predictable rhythm: Hashim ran, we ate breakfast, he worked and worked and worked some more; I watched television and swam; I read and spent time in the closet alone with my thoughts. In the evenings, he ate dinner with his mother. He usually returned in a huff and took out his exasperation with her on me; to be more precise, he was determined to have sex with me every night in spite of her.

Psychological projection is a powerful way for a person to avoid processing his or her undesired emotions by *projecting* them onto someone or something else. It was probably terribly dysfunctional on my part, but his emotions were strong and his projection even stronger. I absorbed every bit of him and felt more connected to him than before. I came to expect his desire for me in the evening, anticipating and craving him more and more. I was definitely forming an addiction.

Without much stimulation during the daylight hours, I became exceedingly bored. I was used to working long shifts and sleeping and studying. That had been my life for as long as I had memory. I didn't even have the luxury of cooking for myself or for anyone else. I hung out in the kitchen with Nita and the housemaids. Her *girls*, as they were referred to were not her daughters, but fresh, young girls from either Mexico or Cuba. They didn't speak much English, but they didn't yell at me to get out. Even if they had, I probably would have ignored them. That went on for a couple of days until Ecrin told Nita that I wasn't allowed in the servants' areas any more. I thought Nita was going to wrestle me over my laundry one morning after Ecrin was insistent that I not be allowed to do that, either. Maybe Nita should be Dawes' next sparring partner.

I swam at the pool as much as I could, but I was too fair to sunbathe. I used a gallon of sunscreen every time I went out in the middle of the day. The weight room was nice but I had never really worked out before. I noticed that Dawes spent a great deal of time there. Climbing stairs and taking care of my patients was my only real exercise. Now that I was in a huge house on a heavily guarded property, I accepted that I was going to have to figure out what I could do to occupy myself. What did women of leisure do? They did charity work and visited social clubs, lunched with friends, got their hair and nails done, and shopped. I didn't do any of those things; I honestly didn't know how.

"I have nothing to do," I complained.

"Take a walk through the gardens," Hashim suggested. "Find Mizhir. He'll either be in the gardens or the garage. I'm sure he can talk your ear off about the flowers."

Mizhir was in the gardens where everything was lush and green and blooming. Miami had a very different climate than we had back home where everything was dry and dying this time of year. Mizhir welcomed me into his little flowering world. He laughed and delighted in everything I asked and observed. He invited me to return after lunch. He had an area that he was particularly fond of that he wanted to show me. When I returned to the garden, Ecrin was speaking to him. He was nodding humbly as she spoke. Mizhir looked up at me and smiled as I approached. Ecrin turned to see what had distracted him.

"Caroline," she said as though my name tasted like the little bit of baby vomit that comes up after a huge burp.

"Mrs. Emir," I said with as much cordiality as I could muster.

"This is unacceptable. Please find something to occupy yourself. I cannot have you distracting my staff from their duties. Their work is important to the running of this household."

"Yes, ma'am," I said and looked apologetically at Mizhir.

I turned and left the two of them. I refused to go back into the house. The only place I had found true solace was in the closet, under the bathrobe, and I would have to pass Hashim to get there. So, I found myself in the garage. I went straight to the Porsche and sat in the driver's seat. I closed my eyes and imagined driving around curves at high speeds with the windows down and feeling the air blow my hair around. The keys were in the ignition, taunting me. I wanted to start the car and drive a hundred miles an hour out of there. I could bust out through the back gates. I wondered if the guards would actually shoot at me. I really didn't care at that very moment.

I stroked the steering wheel and the gearshift lovingly. "You want to go, too, don't you? You feel absolutely trapped in this garage. It's miserable, isn't it?" I asked the beautiful car like she would answer me. "I think we should just go; to hell with the rest of them. I'll bet you feel completely out of place among these cars. You don't belong here, either." I closed my eyes and resumed my daydream. I heard a light tapping on the glass and opened my eyes and was instantly relieved to see Mizhir and not Ecrin. I made to open the door to get out of the car.

"Meetha?" Mizhir's kind voice spoke a little over a whisper. I didn't know what that word meant, but it didn't sound like *get out*.

"I'm sorry," I apologized and moved away from the car and shut the door. "I don't want to get you into any more trouble."

He shook his head. "There is no trouble, here. This is not her domain. The gardens and the house are hers, and I respect that, but the cars are not." He smiled encouragingly. "Were you praying or speaking directly to the car?"

I laughed, embarrassed that he caught me. "I was talking to the car, but I should have been praying."

"Did she speak to you?"

I laughed again, but he was serious. "Not directly, but I get the sense she really wants to go and run as fast as she can." I could feel tears prickle the back of my eyes.

"Do you like to drive?" he asked.

"Yes, but I don't get the opportunity very often."

"That can be arranged, you know?"

"Really?"

"Yes, meet me here in the morning. I will make it so. I cannot go with you, alone, but that man, Dawes, is allowed to take you most anywhere you choose to go. Please ask him to meet us here at eight in the morning."

"Thank you, Mizhir. You just made my day."

"It is my pleasure, meetha Caroline." He took my hands and did that thing with his forehead again.

I went straight to the guesthouse to find Dawes. He came to the door wearing a t-shirt and his swim trunks. "Going for a swim?" I asked.

"Yes, when I'm finished. What do you need?"

"What are you doing?" I asked smelling the light scent of something familiar. I stuck my head into the doorway to get a better look.

"I'm cleaning my weapons, why?" he asked slightly impatient with me.

"I recognized the smell. I couldn't quite place it. It's been a while since I've cleaned a gun, but that smell doesn't leave you."

"You know how to clean a weapon?" he asked skeptically.

"Well, rifles, anyway. My brother and daddy hunted quite a bit. They let me help."

"Do you shoot?" he asked.

"Yeah, I mean I haven't done it in a long time, but I know how. Why?"

Dawes shrugged. "Do you want to come in?" he asked, like maybe my interest in guns raised his estimation of me.

"Sure," I said and went into the guesthouse. It wasn't exactly what I expected, but then again, I had never been in a guesthouse before. It was open with lots of widows looking over the pool and a section of the gardens. The dining and kitchen areas were larger than my house and the living area seemed more spacious, too, given the open floorplan. "How many bedrooms do you have here?" I asked.

"Two." Dawes made his way back to the dining table. Lying on a towel, were six handguns. They were all unloaded.

"Is that your running gun," I asked, pointing to the smallest one.

He looked at me like he was considering whether or not he should answer me. "No, that one is." He pointed to the one just slightly larger.

"Where do you hide that one?" I asked, pointing again at the little gun.

"If I told you, then it wouldn't be hidden, would it?"

"I guess not."

"What do you want, Caroline?" Dawes didn't seem the type for small talk.

"Mizhir said I could drive the Porsche tomorrow. He said I could take it out at eight, but only if you go with me."

"Why would he let you do that?" he asked, resuming his gun cleaning.

"He caught me talking to the car. He agreed that she needed to be driven." Dawes picked up a larger weapon and examined the barrel and wiped down the grip with a rag. He checked the sites. He then picked up a revolver and did the same thing. "Did you shoot today?"

"Yes."

"May I watch you next time you go?"

"What would Emir have to say about that?"

"I really don't know. I don't have to ask his permission for everything. I figure anything is fair game as long as I'm not disturbing his work, or the household staff, or seen by his mother.

"You must really be bored." he said.

"Exceedingly," I sighed.

***

The next morning was better. I didn't tell Hashim where I was going because honestly, I didn't know. I did say that I was going with Dawes after breakfast. He didn't seem phased by that information at all. He probably thought I was going back to Target. That could not have been further from the truth.

Dawes and I stood in the garage, waiting on Mizhir. He was looking inside the engine of the Audi. He stood to his full height and closed the rear hatch. "Are you ready?" he asked.

I looked to Dawes and he shrugged. "Sure," he said, "where are we going?"

"The track," Mizhir said. "Meetha would like to drive." He gave Dawes a look. I didn't know who Meetha was, but I suspected that he was referring to me not the car. Dawes looked a little put out that he was telling him to let me behind the wheel again.

I squealed and clapped and skipped happily to the Porsche. "Thank you, Mizhir. May I name her Sunshine?" Mizhir laughed his happy laugh and Dawes rolled his eyes as he got into the passenger's seat. I followed Mizhir to a local track. Apparently, precision vehicles needed to be maintained differently. He took them out periodically to *run*, he explained. He handed me a helmet and let me ride with him through the paces for the Audi. Mizhir was concentrating on maintaining the vehicle at a top speed, but his smile was nearly as big as mine as we rounded the track. When he brought the Audi to a stop near where Dawes waited by the Porsche, he looked over at me.

"That was amazing!" I exclaimed and reached over and hugged him.

"I'm glad to please you, Meetha. Now, for you to drive."

"Me? I can drive the Porsche?"

"Most certainly. *Sunshine* would appreciate your delicate touch."

I jumped out of the Audi and straight into the Porsche. Dawes shook his head disapprovingly. "No," he said firmly. I was too full of adrenaline to care for his caution. I completely disregarded his eyes boring into the side of my head. Mizhir joined me in the passenger's seat and talked me through the process and what he wanted me to do. He was such a patient teacher; no wonder the flowers did exactly what he wanted them to do. Once we made it to the second lap, he let me increase and maintain the speeds at intervals. At 110 mph, he let me maintain that speed for nearly an entire lap, surging to 120 mph on the straightaway. My heart was racing, but my breaths were steady. My hands held securely to the steering wheel and I focused on the road ahead of me. My smile was permanently fixed to my face and spread all the way down to my toes.

On the fourth lap, Mizhir instructed me to gradually reduce the speed, again holding it at intervals. I came to a stop next to the Audi. Dawes didn't look angry with me; I think he looked a little bit impressed. He couldn't help but smile back at me when he saw me get out of the car. I radiated everything wonderful in the universe. Mizhir took the helmet from me. "You both feel better, now?" he asked referring to me and the car.

"Yes, sir. Thank you from the bottom of our hearts. That was exactly what we needed." I hugged him, again. I loved this humble, flower-growing, car-driving man who had given me a pet name.

"Oh, meetha Caroline, it is my pleasure," he said with that same reverent nod.

Dawes insisted on driving us home. He said I was too keyed-up to be trusted behind the wheel. I didn't argue. It would probably look better with him driving back into the compound. I thanked Dawes for taking me. He just shook his head and retreated to his guesthouse. I felt exhilarated, satisfied, and exceedingly thrilled as I entered the house. I skipped through the kitchen and made myself a sandwich. I put my finger over my lips to signal to Nita not to fuss at me for breaking the kitchen rules. I grabbed a bottle of water and snuck the sandwich up the back stairs. Hashim was, of course, working, but in my joy, I was suddenly consumed with a desire for him. I placed the sandwich on a table near his desk and wrapped my arms around him. I breathed in his scent and kissed the back of his neck. Perhaps Hashim was not the only one guilty of projection.

CHAPTER 25.5

A wife of noble character is her husband's crown,
but a disgraceful wife is a decay in his bones.

– Proverbs 12:14

"Ah," I sighed as I felt her arms around me. She stirred the air each and every time she entered the room, but I took little notice of her most of the time. This time, though, the air felt very different, easier maybe, lighthearted, happy. I removed my headphones and slid my chair back to ease her onto my lap. I looked into her eyes; she was smiling. She kissed me, releasing some of the joy from her morning. I could tell she was happy, and for the first time in days, she wanted me to share in that happiness.

"I made a sandwich; would you like some?" she asked.

That was the *Caroline* that I found so entirely attractive, the willing, bright-eyed, unafraid version of herself that shared her food with me. "That would be nice. I could take a break; it's been a while since you have served me food." She acknowledged my words with a peck and offered me half of the sandwich from her plate. I examined it and took a bite. "Where did you go with Dawes this morning?" I asked when I had finished eating. She offered me the bottle of water to take a sip after her.

"Mizhir let me drive the Porsche!" she said excitedly. "I love her; she's beautiful, and she runs like a dream." She sighed happily. "Why didn't you tell me about your cars?" I could not help but smile with her. I knew from the first time she rode with me that, given the chance, she would choose the Porsche. I was unable to answer her because, in her excitement, she was kissing me. I straddled her legs over me and let her distract me for a long time. She ran her

222

hands over my shoulders and through my hair. Her touch was so familiar to me, now.

"I named her Sunshine. I hope you don't mind," she said between kisses.

"Who did you name Sunshine?" I asked.

"The car. I love her and I think she loves me, too."

"Is that the same kind of *love*?" I asked not thinking before the words came out.

She sat back and looked at me considering. She had asked if *promise* had meant the same and now I had blurted out the question of *love*. "No, Hashim, it doesn't mean the same at all," she said seriously and then her light eyes flickered with seduction. She kissed me more intentionally and with much more passion for me than she had for the Porsche. I was close to giving into her entreaties when I heard the signal from my computer. The processing I had been waiting for was now complete. I hated to put her off, but I had a deadline.

"Caroline," I said, "I need to get back to work." She did not release me. "Caroline," I said more insistently and pushed her away. She sat back and looked at me dejectedly; she did not like to be dismissed. She pouted and refused to look me in the eye as she silently made her way to the closet. I hated watching all of her excitement melt again into resignation. She reemerged a few minutes later wearing a two-piece swimsuit. Her light eyes only glanced over me slightly as she passed. Her displeasure was all my fault; I could not blame my mother this time.

***

A few hours later she returned, wrapped in a pool towel. "Caroline," I called.

"Yes? Give me a second, I'm changing."

I followed her into the closet. "I need to speak to you about something."

She looked up, wrapping her hair in the towel. She gestured for me to untie the back of her swimsuit. I was a little surprised at how easily she dressed and undressed in my presence, now. She wrapped herself in the same bathrobe from the hotel while she fished through her drawer for underwear. Thankfully, Nita took care to wash it every few days.

"Mother requests that you and Dawes join us for dinner tonight." She looked up at me hesitantly. "My sister will be here for dinner. I would like you to meet her."

"Your sister?" she asked, clarifying. "You have a sister? You've never mentioned her; I thought you were an only child." Her tone was sharp.

I shook my head and frowned. She knew so much about me, yet still knew so little. "I have a sister. Her name is Sefa; she is a few years older than me."

"When did you plan to tell me?" she asked, still edgy. "Where does she live?"

"It has not been a priority to speak of her. I believe she arrives from South Africa, but I am not completely sure. That is where she was going the last time we spoke."

"What was she doing in South Africa?"

"She is a physician, a pediatrician, with the World Health Organization, among other things."

"Just a minor detail of your life that you forgot to mention? *Hey, Babe, I have a sister.* She's probably six-feet tall, gorgeous, and performs brain transplants in her free time." I grinned a little at her response. "What?" she demanded.

"You guessed two out of three; I know nothing of brain transplants."

She rolled her eyes in exasperation. "Great! Do I really have to go to dinner? Can't I meet her later? I'm sure she's not just coming in town for dinner from so far away."

"She will be here for a couple of weeks, but I think it would be an opportunity to honor my mother's request."

She rolled her eyes, dramatically. "I don't want to," she said flatly.

"Caroline, I am asking that you please join me for dinner. It is important to me, and Mother has assured me that she will welcome you to the table."

She huffed loudly and sat down cross-legged on the floor. "Why would I think she would welcome me to her table? I'm not allowed in the kitchen or the gardens. Your mother is hostile to say the least, and while you're working every waking hour, I'm resigned to spending my entire day in here," she gestured to the closet, "or at the pool, and so far, I've only managed to freckle."

I disagreed, her skin had a pretty glow from the sun. I walked toward her and knelt down in front of her. I touched my fingers to her cheeks. "The sun has kissed you," I said and kissed each side of her face.

"Stop distracting me. You aren't going to get your way that easily. What do I get if I go to dinner with you?" She crossed her arms over herself determined to guard herself against my persuasion.

"Like a trade?"

"Yes."

"What do you have in mind?"

"I want to go to Disney World." My expression was stumped. "You told me to be thinking about where I would like to go, and I want to go to Disney World."

"Yes, I said that, but I meant like London, Dubai, Stockholm, or Paris? *Disney World* is the one place you want to go?"

"Yes, I've never been and it's really close." she said matter-of-factly.

I thought for the briefest of moments. This could work. We could be in Orlando in an hour, easily, by plane. "Agreed. Disney World is a fair trade for dinner with my mother tonight. Your best dress and your best behavior."

She smiled. "Thank you. That gives me incentive. I won't disappoint you." Little did she know, but she had yet to disappoint me. I did not think her capable.

***

She looked stunning. She wore her best dress and matching shoes. Her hair was pulled up on one side and the natural waves flowed down and past her shoulders. We took the main stairs down to the dining room. She was nervous but seemed to be fine as long as I held her hand.

Dawes met us outside the dining room. He gave a nod of approval in Caroline's direction. "I liked that one, especially," he said, referring to the dress she had tried on while they were shopping.

"There you are, Little Brother," Sefa said as she came down the stairs smiling. "Ammi warned me that you had a surprise." She cut her eyes at Dawes briefly and approached me to kiss my cheek. She then drew back and looked for a few moments at Caroline. Sefa patted my cheek, affectionately, looking deeply into my eyes. Her eyes and features mirrored mine. She spoke to me then in Urdu, my father's language, rather than Mother's Turkish. Sefa had begun that habit when she was seven just to provoke her. My mother had no allies, except for our father. "Little Brother, you have been very, very naughty. Ammi is most displeased." She smiled a cunning smile, like she approved of anything rebellious.

"Sefa, may I introduce my wife, Caroline," I said, turning the attention away from myself.

"Caroline," she said warmly. She took her hand and kissed both of her cheeks in greeting. "Welcome, Sister, it is a great pleasure to meet you. I look forward to getting to know you. I often wondered what sort of woman would capture my brother's heart." She laughed and entwined her arm into the crook of Caroline's elbow and led her into the dining room. "I have to say that you are nothing like what I imagined; I am most intrigued."

Mother joined us, then, and we all took our places at the table. I pulled out the chair next to me for Caroline, furthest away from my mother. Dawes pulled out the chair for my mother and then did the same for Sefa. "Thank you, Dawes," Sefa said like she finally remembered his name. Mother demanded that Sefa give us a detailed report of all the things she had done while she was in Africa. Mother reported on Father's progress; she eluded that she may need to meet him if the negotiations continued as they had. She neither spoke to Dawes nor Caroline directly.

Sefa was not so easily appeased. She asked them both questions and listened with absolute rapture of every detail they spoke. Dawes said less than

Caroline, but Sefa's warmth and genuine interest relaxed Caroline enough to speak her mind. She must really want to go to Disney World. "We need to go out," Sefa demanded. "Not tonight, but maybe tomorrow or the next. I have missed the clubs and bands. Caroline, please say you'll go." Surprisingly, she nodded. Sefa could woo just about anyone to her way of thinking. That was probably a trait that made her so good with treating children. She simply convinced them that whatever she asked of them was the most amazing thing in the world. She surely had that power over me.

CHAPTER 26

"That wasn't so bad," I said once we were back in the bedroom. Hashim followed me to the closet and began hanging up his jacket. He unzipped the back of my dress for me and I slipped it off and hung it on a hanger. When I turned back toward him, he was smiling.

"Thank you. I know that was not easy for you."

"Your sister is gorgeous, smart, tall, and very confident. I really like her; is that all for real or was she just putting on a show to provoke your mother?"

He gave a brief laugh. "She has perfected her ability to get whatever she wants." It was obvious that he did not want to talk any more about Sefa. He seemed distracted as I stood before him, wearing only my bra and panties. He put his hand on my bare waist and kissed me.

"I am sorry that I was unable to leave my work in the middle of the day. You made it very hard to focus."

I smiled, my joy from earlier today soon rekindled. "I was really happy after driving this morning." I wasn't sure how he would react to knowing how far and how fast I had driven. I would share that information later.

"I could tell." He kissed down my neck while I helped him remove his clothes. Unfortunately, they didn't make it onto a hanger. I would be sure to clean up before Nita's girls cleaned the room in the morning. I had accused Hashim of projecting his issues with his mother onto me, but I was just as guilty of projecting all of my feelings onto him. I was used to making the best of difficult situations. This was definitely a difficult situation, and I was determined to make the best of it. Thankfully, the time I spent with Hashim alone and naked was good for both of us. After making love, well, that was what

I chose to call it, but it was not the same for him, I knew I only had a few minutes before he would fall into a deep sleep.

"Hashim, what does meetha mean?" I asked.

"Meetha?" he asked curiously. "Where did you hear that?"

"Mizhir."

He smiled, sleepily. "Of course. He's using it as a pet name. It means *sweet.*"

"Aw, I like that."

"You should," he said sleepily and kissed the tip of my nose before he faded into sleep.

***

The next couple of days were wonderful. Sefa added an air of complete command to the house, but not in a bossy way. She made everyone at ease and she made everything enjoyable. She liked to swim, so I swam with her. She liked to eat, so I ate with her. She demanded that Dawes join us, too; he didn't seem to mind. We followed him to the shooting range the second afternoon. He seemed undaunted at having two women following him. He handed us each some ear protection and set up targets. I confessed at not having very much experience with handguns. He said he didn't have access to any rifles, but if we were there for any length of time, he would see what he could do. I was encouraged that we might do this again. Sefa held the weapon like it was familiar. We talked guns. We shot guns. We cleaned guns. Our conversation was like listening to Billy and Cooper after a hunt.

"You aren't afraid of guns," he commented.

"Why should I be? I understand how they work. I'm not an idiot and I'm not a sociopath, so they aren't really a threat, are they?"

I wasn't a very good shot with the handgun, but that was okay because I didn't need to be. It was like bowling; I went because that's what everyone else was doing, not because I particularly enjoyed the game. It was terribly morbid, but a few times I imagined the target to have Ecrin's face. I smiled every time I shot her through the head. Dawes was insistent that I improve my aim with each shot. I guessed if I hung out there long enough, with his instruction, improvement would be inevitable. I hoped that we could hang out more with Mizhir. I liked it better when we talked cars. I always preferred the cars.

Two nights later, Sefa demanded that we all go out. Ecrin had plans for the evening and Sefa saw it as the perfect opportunity. "Come on, Hashim, Caroline needs to get out of this house. She's not left it since I arrived," she began in English, but soon took to whatever language they spoke between them. It didn't feel like she was being exclusive, but that she knew she could coax him better with those words. I wished I had some secret language to coax him, too.

That night was extraordinarily fun. Going out at home always seemed like a chore. I felt like I was in Krissa's shadow, or if I was noticed by a guy, it was for all the wrong reasons. The music was lively, the drinks, ice-cold and sweet and flavored with a variety of rums. I noticed that Dawes never drank a drop of alcohol, but he smiled plenty and even danced with Sefa when Hashim and I were on the dance floor. In heels, she was his exact height.

The next day, Sefa decided that we needed to go shopping. When we entered the garage, she kissed Mizhir on the cheek and asked for the keys to the Jag. Mizhir didn't even blink when he handed them to her. Sefa noticed when I looked at Dawes and then to Mizhir. I knew Ecrin would have a small aneurism if she knew I had ridden in her car.

"No worries, Little Sister. She will know nothing." I couldn't take Sefa seriously; I knew better. This might be my one and only opportunity, so I embraced the temptation. I had to give Dawes shotgun because his long legs would have never fit in the backseat. Still, from that vantage point, I could experience everything: the wind in my hair, the smooth engine, and the sun and wispy clouds overhead. Sefa played music loudly as we drove.

After looking around in a few of Sefa's favorite boutiques, she demanded that we get pedicures. Dawes was not pleased by this change in plans, but he patiently sat at the nail salon, thumbing through a magazine. Sefa offered to let him get a pedicure, too, but he respectfully declined. As we approached the Jag, parked on the curb, Sefa handed me the keys. "Mizhir says you like to drive." I looked down at the keys in my hand and could feel the sweat cover my body. I shook my head like she'd just handed me kryptonite.

"I can't," I confessed.

"You can't or you won't?" she teased.

"No. I can't give her another reason to hate me."

"That's probably not possible." She smiled at me like she knew her mother couldn't hate me any more than she already did. "Go ahead," she encouraged. "It may be your only chance."

She had that same tone in English as she did when she spoke to Hashim. *Lord, have mercy.* I looked to Dawes, hoping he would be the voice of reason. He only offered me a shrug. I wondered if this was what it felt like to have a devil and an angel on each shoulder like in the cartoons. I thumped the angel off of my shoulder and hopped into the driver's seat. I don't know how Sefa and her long legs fit into the backseat, but she didn't complain. She leaned forward between us, and I thought I detected some stress in Dawes face. Maybe he was rethinking this after all. Forbidden fruit tasted sweet and I enjoyed every moment of the adventure. We brought the Jag home unscathed. I hugged the steering wheel and thanked God for beautiful cars. I patted Sunshine on the way out. She wasn't jealous at all.

We joined Ecrin for dinner the next couple of nights without incident, but the third night, she had had enough pleasantries. She had apparently found out about our taking the Jaguar to town and lit into us like we had done something criminal. I couldn't eat anything. Sefa dismissed her mother's tirade, but I felt horrible. Dawes, too. I couldn't tell if his reaction was anger or something else. I knew I shouldn't have, but Sefa was so damned convincing. Ecrin banished me, once again, from her presence and told Hashim that he was a fool to marry such a young, immature girl. She predicted his utter demise for such a foolish decision. She held nothing back and spoke in clear, decisive English. She didn't want me to miss anything she said.

I stood and shook off her words. I refused to stay there any longer and take her abuse. I had done wrong, but I refused to accept her curses upon me and my marriage. Her children were unable to get a word in edgewise. Dawes and Hashim stood when I stood, but I wasn't sure if they did that because it was proper manners or if they were afraid they might have to restrain one of us from attacking the other physically. I had no intentions of touching the vile woman. Her feelings towards me were equally matched with how I felt about her.

I walked toward the staircase. Dawes followed me. I could hear Hashim and Sefa berating their mother in a mixture of languages. Ecrin didn't let up. No amount of coaxing would ever return me to that woman's presence. Hashim could even offer to take me to the moon; it would never happen again. I would have a fridge installed in the closet. I could live on Pop-Tarts, sandwiches, bananas, and Doritos, forever, if I had to.

"Caroline, are you alright?" Dawes asked when I'd reached the second step.

I only turned slightly towards him. I was afraid that if I didn't go immediately, I would burst into tears and not be able to make it upstairs. I shook my head harshly. He put his hand on my shoulder. "You won't be here forever. You and Emir are safest here. Do your best to let him finish." I couldn't respond, so, instead, I closed my eyes and took a deep breath before I bolted up the stairs.

I grabbed a big pillow from the bed and kicked my shoes across the room as I entered. I jerked myself out of my clothes and went straight into the corner of the closet again and cried myself to sleep. When I awoke, and entered the bedroom, Hashim wasn't there. I glanced at the clock; he must have gone to run. He hadn't slept in the bed, either. It was the first night that he hadn't touched me. I was sick at the thought.

CHAPTER 26.5

Diligent hands will rule, but laziness ends in forced labor.

– Proverbs 12:24

"No," I flatly refused the suggestion of the person on the other end of the call. "That will not work." I was frustrated by this conversation. Nothing was working on their end. After months of transmissions, and now this. Things on this end were running smoothly; I could not understand what was missing. I was banging my head against a proverbial wall. I had not slept in several nights. I had not touched Caroline in as many days. The conflicts were pulling me in different directions. This project was at the forefront, but the clash between Caroline and my mother needled at my brain constantly. I ran and I worked; that was all.

I needed to be there, onsite, but I did not want to go. I knew leaving her would be harder than telling her, but I did not want to do that either. I knew, whatever her reaction, I would suffer. Kennedy called from the Pentagon with the details of the charter; I would be leaving before midnight. I went outside to look for Sefa and Caroline. Instead, I found Dawes and Caroline at the pool. They were playing volleyball. *When did they add a volleyball net to the pool?* The two of them were laughing and passing insults back and forth. I watched their interaction from a distance.

When Caroline made a spike over the net, she squealed and he grabbed her and forced her under the water. Just then, Sefa jumped in to her rescue. He was fighting them both. It looked like fun, but I did not like the way they were playing. I did not like the familiarity with which Dawes grabbed my wife and pressed her against the side of the pool while he fended off my sister. He then swung Caroline over his shoulder and was about to take Sefa down, one handed. My sister, even at thirty, was as playful as Caroline, at twenty. Everything was all a game to her. I stood at the edge of the pool, waiting for a break in their game. Dawes saw me first and released Caroline, placing her gently on the side of the pool.

"Emir," he said, jumping deftly from the water. He grabbed a towel and tossed it to Caroline before he took one for himself. He instantly returned to a state of duty and purpose.

"Dawes," I said flatly. I did not mean to sound so serious, but I was preoccupied with everything I was dealing with upstairs and then to find my wife slung over the shoulder of my guard, again, like he had done when he carried her from the hotel elevator. She did not seem to mind it this time. I asked for Sefa to excuse us. She did as I asked without argument. She understood.

After I explained my plans, Caroline asked, "May I go, too?"

"No. That will not be possible."

"How long will you be away?" she asked.

"A few days, maybe more. It is critical that I be there. I would not leave you if I had any other choice," I said meaning it, but I could feel her heart sinking.

"But your mother!" she argued.

"I will speak with her before I go. She speaks of leaving soon. Besides, Sefa will be here, and Dawes," I amended. "They will be good company for you. I trust them both. Even Mizhir and Nita will do everything in their power to keep you two apart."

"Dawes won't be going with you?" she asked.

I shook my head. "Preston will be here before midnight."

"Tonight?" she asked incredulously. I was not sure the emotion behind her eyes. Was it sadness, fear, or anger? She followed me upstairs while I packed. She asked if there was anything she could do but there was not. She sat on the floor of the closet, idle and sad. I wished there was time to take her in my arms and have my way with her, but I had too much to do to be distracted for even a moment.

She had fallen asleep watching me work for the last few hours before I left. Before Preston arrived, I kissed her cheek and went downstairs. If that was what *promise to love* felt like, then it was the most painful thing I had ever experienced, leaving her, knowing I would not sleep with her for as many nights as it took to finish. Getting onto the chartered flight to Virginia was agony. "Will you call me?" she had asked just before she fell asleep.

"I will try, but please do not expect to hear from me for at least three days. I would also appreciate you not wrestling with Dawes. It is unbecoming of a married woman to spend so much time with a man who is not her husband and in such an undignified way." She rolled over away from me after that. I suspected that she had been crying because I tasted salt on her cheek when I kissed her goodbye.

CHAPTER 27

The morning after Hashim left, I slept in. I hadn't even made it to midnight to give him a proper goodbye. I don't know what I was hoping for, but the past several days and nights had left me longing. Sefa was content to leave me alone for a few hours, but in the afternoon, she climbed into the bed next to me and joined me to watch television.

"Where's Dawes?" I asked.

"He's running, I think. He didn't say."

Rain was forecasted for the next few days which only added to my state of misery. I was sleeping and watching too much television; I was surely getting fat. Nita brought me food and Sefa brought me snacks. The second day that Hashim was away, I decided to make sure my phone was charged in case he decided to call or text me. As soon as it was charged, I received a reminder from my period tracker that my period was due. I never really kept track but relied on the app to remind me. My breasts felt tender, but that could just mean that it would arrive soon. It was stress; it had to be the stress throwing everything out of order. The third morning he was away, I slept even later as rain pelted down the windows at a steady rhythm. The fourth, even later than that. I felt so tired and napped again in the afternoon. I was probably coming down with something. I should ask Sefa; she was a doctor, after all.

Maybe, I was just grieving. I missed Hashim. Nita's girls insisted that I let them change the sheets on the bed, so they no longer smelled like him. The rain was making me sad, too. I knew I had not properly grieved Momma's passing, so maybe, just maybe, it was all crashing together like a pile-up on the interstate. There was too much to sort through, so I just laid around and ate too much and slept too much and let the television screen pulse images into my brain so I didn't have to think. I was watching daytime television and after a commercial for tampons, I remembered. My last period was at least a couple of weeks before we left. We'd had a test and I was cramping all the way through it. I was relieved when I got to work and everyone on my wing was already asleep. I had borrowed a heating pad and microwaved it and sat at the nurses' station all night. I remembered taking enough drugs to really knock me out the next morning.

Maybe it was too early to know, but I definitely needed to rule it out before I became hysterically paranoid. Early the fifth morning, I went to find Dawes. He was usually exercising at this time, so I looked for him in the weight room. He wasn't there. I went to his guesthouse to find him, instead, I found Sefa coming out of Dawes' front door.

"Good morning, Little Sister," Sefa said and greeted me with a hug. She traced the circles under my eyes. "Are you not sleeping well with my brother away? Come swimming with me after lunch. The rain has passed and the water is quite pleasant."

"Is Dawes in there?" I asked.

"Yes," she said and there was something telling in her eyes. Had she spent the night with him?

I knocked on the door and Dawes answered. "May I come in?" He moved out of the way and let me in, but I noticed his eyes followed Sefa for the briefest moment as she walked back to the house. Her scent and her presence were all over him. I diverted my eyes and looked down at the table; he was cleaning his guns, again. "Have you heard anything?" I asked.

"No," he said flatly.

"Take me to the drug store," I demanded.

"Tell Nita what you need. She will get it for you," Dawes argued and loaded a round into the revolver. He seemed edgier than usual with Hashim away.

I shook my head; I didn't want anyone to know. "Please, Dawes, I really need to get out of here and I want to go shopping for myself, and can you give me twenty bucks? I swear I'll pay you back. You can take me to Target, too. I just need to feel something familiar and normal."

"Why don't we go with Sefa, later, she'll even let you drive."

I shook my head, again. "No, I want to go with you, now. Please," I insisted.

"You know he hates those jeans," he commented when he noticed what I was wearing.

"Well, he's not here, is he?" I snapped, which was most of the problem; then I thought better of my mood. "I'll be sure not to wear them around him, but I like them; they're comfortable."

He looked at me considering. "Give me five minutes. I'll take you," he finally agreed. He went into one of the bedrooms and changed into jeans. He began putting a couple of guns together and loading them. He strapped on his holster and snapped in a weapon at his side and another at his back just above his waistband. He lifted his pantleg and strapped on a knife on one leg and a smaller gun on his other leg.

"Wow! Do you have to do this every time we go out?"

"Yes."

"Impressive. Can I get one of those?" I asked pointing down to his leg holster.

"Not on my watch."

"Can we take the Porsche?" I asked.

"Yeah, we can take the Porsche." He almost smiled.

I begged him to let me go into the drug store alone. "No, I'm not letting you out of my sight. Until I hear from Emir or Kennedy, you will just have to endure me." He knew I didn't like it. "I know about lady products; you don't have to be embarrassed."

I blushed. He thought I was embarrassed to buy *lady* products. "Okay, but just stay at the front of the store, or keep your distance, okay? I'd like to feel normal for five minutes."

"Make it quick," he said as we entered the store. He handed me a credit card. "Emir left this for anything you might need. He's going to be pissed if he finds out that I let you out of my sight for even a second."

Thankfully the aisles were just a hair taller than me and the pregnancy tests were kept near the pharmacy counter. He could only see my head moving and shopping. I felt like everyone was watching me as I decided which test to purchase. I was a married woman, for Christ's sake. There was no shame in purchasing a pregnancy test; women did it all the time. I felt so uncomfortable, though, standing in front of the barely sixteen-year-old girl checking me out at the register at the back of the store. I paid for the test and crammed the box down into my purse before I met Dawes waiting impatiently at the front of the store.

"They didn't have what you needed?" Dawes asked conversationally.

"No," I lied. "I'll check at Target," I said as I handed him back the credit card.

Dawes found a parking spot close to the store. "I need to use the bathroom," I said and made my way to the unisex-family bathroom. He rolled his eyes. I knew I was pushing my luck, but I did not want to take a pregnancy test at the house and have any traces be found by the maids or Hashim's mother, or even Sefa. I felt nauseated just thinking about it. I read all the printed instructions on the box. They seemed pretty self-explanatory. I peed on the wand and sealed it with the cap. I placed it on the toilet paper holder and read the entire inside packaging while I waited for the digital countdown. I didn't understand a word I read in the packaging, but it was something to keep my mind occupied while I waited. I glanced twice over to the test to make sure it was working.

I pulled up my jeans and washed my hands. I was sweating bullets in the small space, but that quickly changed as I watched the digital readout go from the countdown to **Pregnant**. I was suddenly cold and clammy and felt faint. My hand was shaking as I held the inoffensive wand to let the word become believable. It wasn't working. This was all my fault. This was all because I had attacked him that morning. Dawes became impatient and I jumped when he knocked on the door.

"Caroline, are you okay? You've been in there a long time." That's all I needed was for Dawes to burst through the door to find me freaking out in the Target bathroom. I knew he'd break it down if I didn't answer it, but I couldn't walk.

"Yeah, give me a minute," I called through the door.

I threw away all of the packaging and hurriedly wiped the tears that I didn't know I had cried. I shoved the second test from the box to the bottom of my purse and stuck the used one into my jeans' pocket. Dawes knocked again, harder this time. He was so impatient.

"I'm here!" I demanded as I opened the door. I couldn't look him in the eye.

"Are you sick or something? You were in there forever," he complained.

"No, I'm not sick," my voice threatened to give me away.

"Caroline, what's up? Talk to me. You're acting weird."

I just shook my head, dismissing his concern, and grabbed a buggy like I was planning on doing a lot of shopping. I really just needed something to hold onto and the big red buggy looked friendly and familiar. I made my way around the store. I needed nothing. I grabbed a bottle of water and a bag of Doritos and began eating them absentmindedly. I walked through housewares like I even needed a lamp. I walked through office supplies and sporting goods. I walked down the game and puzzle aisle and ran right smack into the aisle between maternity and babies. I froze, paralyzed with a half-eaten Dorito in my mouth. To my right were full-bellied mannequins and to my left were strollers and car seats and tiny, little, neutral colored onesies. I couldn't look anymore. It was all moving in towards me. I laid my forehead down on the handle of the shopping cart. *Breathe, C.* In through my nose, out through my mouth. Repeat.

"Caroline? I don't think you're feeling well. Come on, I'll take you home."

I shook my head. "Can't," I breathed.

Dawes put his hand on my shoulder. "What's wrong?" he whispered near my ear.

I motioned with my hand in a swirling motion over my head, gesturing to all that was around me. "This, all of this. I can't take it."

He looked around but seemed oblivious to the suffocating racks of big-bellied pants and baby socks. "What are you talking about?" He was getting frustrated, again. He took me by the arm and gave me a shake, forcing me to face him. "Caroline, look at me. What is wrong with you?"

I reached into my pocket and pressed the wand into his chest. He took it in his hand and rolled it over to read the tiny, digital screen. He was just as dumfounded as me. "Fuck," he finally whispered.

"Yeah, exactly," I said. He handed me back the wand. He didn't want to hold it, either.

"He has no idea." His words came out as a statement. I shook my head and stuck the wand back into my pocket. "I don't know what to say," he said.

I looked up trying desperately to hold back the tears. My lip quivered and I knew I was a goner. I felt alone and angry and guilty and overwhelmed. Hashim had left frustrated and angry. He felt torn between appeasing his mother and satisfying me. Our animosity distracted him and he wasn't able to focus on his work like he needed to. My heart ached, but I couldn't do anything to woo his affections. He hadn't touched me in days and then to accuse me of being *unbecoming* with Dawes. I stood in Target crying and I had no power to stop the flow of tears. Dawes put his arms around me and patted my back. It was a little like Billy hugging me. I knew it was his job, but Dawes was like a protective big brother.

"He'll understand," Dawes said trying to convince both of us.

I pushed away from him. "No, he won't. He's so careful, every time. He doesn't want a kid. He doesn't even want me." More tears. More feelings of hopelessness. "I was really happy in Montgomery. I felt hopeful, you know, like maybe I hadn't made a huge mistake after all. Then Marshall. Then his mother. Now this."

"Come on," he insisted this time. I grabbed the bag of chips and half-empty bottle of water. He snagged a box of tissues, the really soft kind, and handed me a couple while we waited at the checkout. He kept his hand on me as he walked me out to the car but stood for a second before he opened the door for me.

"Sefa?" I asked, looking up at his face. His eyes softened. He knew what I assumed after seeing her this morning.

"Yeah," he said, opening the door for me.

"Does Hashim know?" I asked once he was in the driver's seat.

He shook his head. "Not that he's made mention. I don't think that's something he would keep to himself." He chuckled low to himself. "He'd probably punch me in the face and send me on my way. It's fine for him to have a woman, but God forbid his sister has anyone, or me, for that matter."

"He's been so busy, he probably hasn't noticed anything," I said.

"This isn't the first time. We've been together before," he said, but it sounded like *before* was more like *a while*. "I like her, Caroline. I like her a lot. She's good like him, but softer, less intense, most of the time," he added with a smirk. Every Emir I had met so far was intense. "I was excited when Emir settled on Miami. I knew she'd come and we'd be here together. She always comes to Miami." It was the most words I'd ever heard him speak at one time, even when we talked about guns or cars. I guessed that him knowing my secret, and me noticing his, opened an unspoken trust between us.

"When do you plan to tell him?" I asked.

He laughed. "When do *you* plan to tell him?" he countered.

"About what?" I asked innocently, tucking my hair behind my ear and making my eyes wide and innocent. "I don't know anything about you and Sefa."

"I mean, about the baby."

Baby. I had not considered that, but it was a baby or would be when it arrived. I put my head down into my knees. "I'd rather tell him about you and Sefa. Want to make a trade?"

"No."

"Can we find a Sonic?" I asked, completely changing the subject. "I need some comfort food." He found a Sonic on his GPS and headed that direction. "Is there any way you can call and check on him? It feels like he's been gone forever."

"Yeah, I'll call Kennedy."

CHAPTER 28

We hadn't been back from our drugstore run an hour when Nita knocked on my door. "Drink," she demanded and handed me a mug of tea. "Ginger," she said. "You'll feel better." I sniffed the pungent tea. "Go ahead. Drink it," she insisted. "Once the nausea passes, you can eat. You have to keep your strength." She smiled and said something about niños and comida and amor.

Was this woman psychic? She knew I was pregnant and I needed food and something about love that I couldn't catch completely. I did as she instructed and sure enough it eased the nausea almost instantly. "Thank you," I said. "How did you know?"

She crossed her arms over her full breasts and raised her eyebrow. "A woman knows. I've had five of them myself, so it's a familiar look. It's a sense, you know?" I nodded. "When will he be back?" I shrugged. I honestly didn't know. "You don't seem happy. You aren't happy because he's not happy?" she asked.

"He doesn't know," I confessed.

"Umm, and the Lady Emir?" she asked sternly.

I shook my head. "Hell, no!" I exclaimed. "She already hates me enough. She can't know before Hashim."

Nita laughed. "Good. That's how it should be, but you are afraid." She examined my face carefully.

"Is it that obvious?"

Nita made the sign of the cross over herself before she took me into a hearty embrace. She spoke Spanish over me like a prayer. She drew all the fears and feelings from me. The tears flowed uncontrollably then. I found solace in her embrace; all of her motherly instincts and protectiveness washed over me.

"Caroline," I stiffened at the sound of my name. I thought for half-a-second that it was Ecrin, but then the softer lilt of Sefa's voice came. "Choti Behan," she cooed and I could feel her hand on my back. "Dawes asked me to check on you."

I buried my face further into Nita's shoulder and she whispered something in Spanish to Sefa. They each offered me an understanding sigh, but no words were spoken for a few minutes. Nita gave me one more encouraging squeeze and set me up to look into my eyes. "Children are a blessing," she said smiling, "even the unexpected ones." Nita stood then and patted my cheek. "Finish the tea; I will bring you some food," she said before she left me and Sefa alone. Sefa's eyes were full of delight. I wondered if it was because she knew a secret or because she was especially fond of the thought of a child. She was a pediatrician; she had to like children, right?

"How far along?" she asked in a professional tone.

"A little more than a month since my last period. Not long, maybe six weeks."

"You took a pregnancy test?" I nodded. She looked at me considering. "Would you like me to examine you?"

"You're a pediatrician. That's not weird?"

"Yes, I am a pediatrician, but I am a physician who has served in many capacities around the world. When you are the only doctor in a community, you treat everyone from the unborn to the aged. Would it make you feel better if I examined you?" she asked. I nodded, again. "Put your robe on; I will get my bag."

I lay on my bed and let Sefa examine me. She told me everything that she was going to do. I stared up at the ceiling, trying to relax. Her touch was delicate and easy. I had never had a vaginal exam before, so I wasn't sure if it would hurt and be the nightmare that my girlfriends always complained about when they went for their yearly checkups to get birth control. She pulled the glove from her hand and covered me with the edge of the robe before she offered me a hand to sit up.

"Everything looks and feels good. I think you are right on the timing. She cocked her head to the side, considering. You are probably looking to deliver sometime in July. It might be too early to detect a heartbeat, but we can go in for an ultrasound. I'll set it up." She sounded so excited about the prospect. "You should probably have some routine bloodwork done then, too." Her demeanor completely changed as she moved into her physician's role. She and Hashim looked so much alike when she was serious. "You need to eat plenty of protein, eighty to a hundred grams a day. Stay hydrated, limit caffeine, and keep swimming. Exercise and proper diet ensure a healthy baby." She smiled again, her playful nature returning. Her eyes danced. "Let's go shopping! You will need clothes."

I shook my head. "No, it's too early for that. I'm not doing anything until I tell Hashim."

"Shopping will help; it always helps," she pleaded.

"No, his being here will help." I could hear the sadness in my voice.

She sat next to me on the edge of the bed. "You have a deep fondness for my brother; I can see that you love him, but you are unsure of him."

"I'm not unsure of *him*. He's the surest thing; he's the only thing. He doubts his feelings for me and can't admit that he loves me or ever will, so how can I ask him to love a child?" I asked and felt the tears flow again.

"Children are different. They come into this world, helpless and needy, yet unknowingly, the most powerful force in a man's path. It is a great mystery how a man loves a woman, but how a man will sacrifice everything for his child, is an even greater one."

"You're very wise, Sefa. Thank you."

"Choti Behan," she cooed again, "no worries. Happy mothers make happy babies and I will do everything in my power to keep you both content."

CHAPTER 28.5

A single rebuke does more for a person of understanding
than a hundred lashes on the back of a fool.

– Proverbs 17:10

Finally! It was finished! I was exhausted and ready to return to Miami, but when I was completely honest with myself, I was ready to return to Caroline. We could leave. I was free from my current obligation. I had spent more time at the Pentagon than I had expected, but it was easier to work there and finish everything with the team. I had the luxury of minimal distractions and the necessary determination and motivation. Caroline was not coming in and out of the room, stirring the air, although I missed that the longer I was away. I had not slept a tremendous amount while working with the team at the Pentagon, so I looked forward to getting in bed with her. I longed to touch her and kiss her and enjoy the sounds she made when I pleased her. I desired nothing more than to feel her arms and legs around me and to fall into a deep sleep while breathing in her scent.

On the flight home, I wondered what Caroline had been doing in my absence. I wondered if she had moved into the closet permanently or if Sefa managed to get her into more mischief. I was hoping for the latter. Sefa was a troublemaker, but she was more fun than being alone. I had not heard anything from Marshall and hoped the threat had passed, but regardless, we would be leaving the country as soon as I could get Caroline packed. Kennedy had looked into the incident at Caroline's for me but discovered nothing. He found no police report, involving the death of a young woman. He had no trace from the contact

Marshall had made in Montgomery, either. We had no idea whether or not he knew we were in Miami.

Kennedy knew the Miami house was virtually impenetrable with all of its security, but he allowed Dawes to remain as a favor to me. Caroline was already comfortable with him and I did not want a stranger making her even more uncomfortable than she already was. I probably would not have been so quick to leave or stayed away so long had it not been for Sefa's arrival and their instant affection for one another. Sefa would protect her from our mother and Dawes would protect her from any other threats.

Over the course of my time at the Pentagon, Kennedy pressed me for a few more details of the Marshall incidents. He was cautious about me leaving the country. "Where do you plan to go?" he asked.

"I have no idea; I'm leaving that up to Caroline. I may not know anything until we settle. I will keep you posted, but as of now, we have no itinerary."

He did not agree with that plan and thought it best to stay stateside. I disagreed. "You aren't thinking Dubai, are you?"

"We have a comfortable home there, but again, I will defer to Caroline." It was an easy choice for me, but I had a feeling that Caroline would not choose *easy* or unfamiliar. I smirked a little thinking that if she had her way, she might desire to live at Disney World. She had earned a trip there. Kennedy questioned me again about Marshall and Miami, and for the first time alluded to the work I had done for Marshall. He had never seemed interested before, but I grew impatient with him. It was none of his concern and I was eager to leave. I had fulfilled my end of the contract, so I saw no reason to be detained any longer with his idle interest.

"Tell Dawes he's relieved of his duties," Kennedy called out to me. There was something in his voice that was edgy and controlling. He was likely as exhausted as I was from seeing this project through to the end. The past ten days had been brutal.

"Of course," I replied curtly and turned to make my way through the doors and onto the helicopter that would take me to the private airstrip. Preston waited for me at the airport. I thanked him again for flying me back to Miami. Preston was not anything like Dawes, but he was consistent and seemed confident in everything he did. Maybe in time, I would come to trust Preston as well.

I expected Mizhir, but instead, there was an agent in a black sedan waiting for me at the airport. Preston introduced me and I was driven directly into the front gates like a guest. It felt off, but I pushed it to the side. I was exhausted and not thinking clearly so late at night. I entered the house, silently. It was the middle of the night, and everything was quiet. I went upstairs to my room and found the bed empty. *Where is my wife?* I went immediately to the closet; she was not there, either, but I exhaled in relief that she was not sleeping on the floor and had not packed up all of her belongings. Her few dresses hung neatly and her duffel bag and cellphone lay on the floor next to her Bible; it was opened like she had been reading.

I left the room and went to find Dawes. My heartrate increased as I flew down the stairs and out the back door. Something was not right. The shades of the guesthouse were all closed, but I could tell there were lights on within. It was then that I heard music playing and Caroline's laugh and a squeal. I heard Dawes laughing, too. The panic of finding Caroline passed, but jealousy surged. I was not prepared for the anger that rose within me as I opened the door. Dawes moved instinctively in front of Caroline and briefly glanced at the door to his bedroom. He took a defensive stance and reached for a weapon that I had not seen. He did not draw the weapon, but he was prepared. I posed no physical threat, but he had to first reason that through his well-trained mind.

Caroline was oblivious to the standoff between me and Dawes. She was standing behind him in the small kitchen, cooking. *She was cooking for him. She was laughing with him. She was happy with him.* Dawes relaxed slightly and Caroline turned and caught sight of me. A huge smile spread across her face. "Hashim!" she exclaimed and hurried toward me. She stopped suddenly, when she saw my reaction to what I had seen when I opened the door. "What is it, Hashim?" she asked and tried to get my attention. I was glaring at Dawes, the traitorous son-of-a-bitch.

"What are you doing here in the middle of the night?" I asked Caroline. My tone was accusing.

"We're cooking a very late supper. I'm starving." She moved to embrace me, but I did not remove my eyes from Dawes. "I'm so glad you're home." There was genuine pleasure in her voice.

Just then, Sefa, came from Dawes' bedroom wearing men's clothing, *Dawes' clothing*. I looked at her and stood bewildered. "What the hell is going on here?" I asked.

Dawes looked at Caroline and then at Sefa waiting for one of them to reply to me. "Ah, Little Brother, you're home." Sefa said in her most appeasing voice, she walked directly to me and gave me a peck on the cheek. "Caroline didn't have much appetite today, but she's hungry now. We didn't want to make a mess in Nita's kitchen and suffer her wrath in the morning, so we brought the food over here. Would you like to join us? You must be hungry from a day of travel," Sefa offered like it was the most casual thing to do.

"Have you made a habit of this?" I asked.

"For a few days," Sefa replied with a wink, looking knowingly at Caroline with a smile.

I felt like I was interrupting something familiar and intimate. "Where is Mother?" I asked.

"She flew to Dubai day-before-yesterday. We have the entire place to ourselves." Sefa sounded utterly pleased.

I just stood there. "Hashim, would you please join us? It's ready." Caroline's tone was pacifying. I looked into her eyes for the first time; they were bright and welcoming. She reached for me again and this time I put my arm around her shoulder and allowed her to wrap her arms around my midsection, but it was far from the reunion I had been thinking of all day. She urged me toward the small table. I removed my jacket and hung it over the back of the chair. She had complete command of Dawes' kitchen. She plated up the food and handed the plates to Sefa who then served me and Dawes. It was all surreally domestic. I had never seen my sister carry anything to a table before, much less serve me. They were smiling and laughing like old friends, like sisters.

I looked down and saw roasted chicken, green beans, and tots. I did not know whether to be amused or irritated by the small potato bits. Caroline was the last one to the table. She carried a huge bottle of ketchup and her plate was mounded with tots. She smiled at me. "They have tots in Miami," she said like she had struck gold. Dawes and Sefa hesitated before eating until Caroline bowed her head and gave thanks. "Thank you, Lord, for this food and for bringing Hashim home safely. May you continue to bless us and keep us safe. Amen." She reached over and gave my hand a squeeze. "Let's eat."

I watched as Caroline and Sefa began eating. Dawes was more cautious and eyed me periodically. I could eat, so I ate while I tried to figure out what was happening. "Are you finished?" Caroline asked excitedly after she had devoured more than half the mound of tots and plenty of ketchup. She was referring to my work.

"Yes, it is done. I will continue to work, but the deadlines are more forgiving." Those words pleased her. "We can leave soon. Have you decided where you would like to go?"

"We can talk about that later." She cut her eyes toward Dawes and Sefa. Sefa smiled encouragingly and reached and dipped her tot into Caroline's ketchup playfully. Once we had finished our meal, Caroline rose and cleared the table. "That was so good," she sighed, satisfied. Sefa stood, too, and began loading the dishwasher with Caroline.

I was not surprised at Caroline, but I was shocked watching my sister. I had never seen her like this. She and Caroline were both barefoot, cleaning the kitchen. I realized that I knew nothing of how my sister lived her daily life apart from our family. I looked at Dawes, then; he was also watching the women in the kitchen. His face was impassive; he would not willingly reveal anything. He could feel me staring at him, so he turned his face toward mine. I had questions; he had answers.

Sefa returned to the table and took mine and Dawes' plates, interrupting our silence. "Perhaps you two would like to step outside and have a private conversation. You're putting a terrible damper in the air." She looked down at Dawes with an arched brow. "We will only be a few more minutes and then we can all call it a night."

Dawes lifted his chin to suggest we step outside. Caroline looked up when she saw us rise from the table. She smiled warily with a plate in her hand, when I said, "I need to speak with Dawes alone." We stepped outside and shut the door behind us. I walked toward the pool. The moon was bright overhead and illuminated the water. I could see Dawes' face clearly. "Dawes," I began courteously, but the strain was evident.

"Emir," he replied.

"Were you not expecting me?" I asked. It was obvious they were not.

"No, we haven't heard anything since you left. Kennedy relayed no information. I called him once at Caroline's request, and he said you were working. That's all."

I was not sure I believed him. I did not like the feeling of distrust that surged within me. Had Kennedy deceived me or was it Dawes? "I sent a message nearly every other day."

Dawes' eyes were suspicious. "No." He shook his head. "That can't be." He did not like the incongruency any more than I did. "What do you make of it?" he asked.

"I have no idea, but I would like to get to the bottom of it. I have suspected a mole in Kennedy's security for some time. Right now, I suspect you."

Dawes scoffed, "It's not me." There would be time to figure that out, maybe in the morning. I looked back at the guesthouse when I heard Sefa and Caroline laughing.

"All of this tonight, has this been your routine?"

"Caroline likes to cook and she needs to eat. We didn't mean any harm. She's a good kid and Sefa is terribly indulgent of her."

"Your job is to protect her not let her cook for you."

"I am protecting her," he said defensively. I was surprised at his tone.

"What do you mean by that?" I asked, putting us at even further odds.

"It was pretty awful for her when you left. She's made the best of it, but she's had a rough time. You need to do something. She's been dying here without any word from you. She's got nothing but you, now, and you haven't been much of a prize. Damn it, Emir, she loves you. Can't you see that she needs you?"

"But does she want me?" I asked sardonically.

"Yeah, she wants you, man. She wanted you to man-up and defend her against your mother's misjudgment. She also wants to know you aren't bored with her. There's a change in her; pay attention, Emir. You are so freaking smart, and yet you can't see what's right in front of your face. You come in all jealous and angry tonight for finding her in the guesthouse with me. Apologize for being an ass and deal with her. She's too good to let slip out of your grasp. She may not have any choice but to stay with you, but you could make it so much better for her. You need to give her a chance to talk to you."

He was way out of line and he knew it, but he obviously cared more for Caroline than he did for his job. "What does she need?" I asked defensively.

"She needs a friend and a husband and you haven't been much of either since Montgomery." I was seething in my anger. He was challenging me. He was protecting Caroline, protecting her from *me*. He took a deep breath to settle himself. "Yesterday and today were better. Your mother leaving was a huge relief to her, and today," he began, but then let his words falter.

"What of today?" I asked accusingly.

"Today was just better, a lot better."

I was affected by his words. I did not like knowing that my leaving had such an adverse effect on Caroline, but I knew how I felt leaving her and could only imagine her feelings would be that much stronger. I was such a fool. "And what of my sister?" My tone was measured and careful. "Why is she wearing your clothes?" I took a deep breath before I asked the question lingering between us. "Are you fucking my sister?"

Dawe's jaw stiffened at that, but he did not look away. "When it's convenient." I looked at him incredulously, trying to understand the meaning of his words. My fists clinched and I wanted nothing more than to punch him in the face. Then he realized how that had sounded and corrected himself. "When it's convenient, we spend time together," he clarified.

"You and Sefa? Together? How long?"

"Since the first time we were here together," he admitted.

"When did you think you might tell me?" I asked, through clinched teeth.

He shrugged. "When I was no longer assigned to your detail, when you no longer needed me in this capacity, or when and if Sefa ever decided that she wanted to pursue our relationship long-term."

"Three years is pretty long-term," I said sarcastically. Dawes only raised his eyebrows noncommittally. All this time, every time we were in Miami Sefa turned up. That one time in D.C., too. When I moved into Caroline's apartment, Dawes jokingly mentioned taking an extended vacation, and how he had earned it. I was completely oblivious. I had spent more time with Dawes than any other person, yet I still knew nothing about him. "What was so different today?" I asked, going back to his previous comment. The way he had said it needled at the back of my mind.

"That's a question for Caroline," he said, his eyes determined and concealing. I did not like him keeping her confidences. It made me rethink the treachery I felt upon entering the guesthouse.

"Tell me," I demanded. Dawes stepped back, sensing my anger and frustration. He put his hands out, palms up, signaling surrender.

Just then, Caroline came out of the guesthouse. Her brow furled, seeing the two of us at odds. "The kitchen's clean. We can go, now," Caroline said trying to lighten the mood between us. "Come on, Hashim, it's late." She tugged on my sleeve. I noticed she had my jacket folded neatly over her arm.

"You are technically relieved of your duties," I said low to Dawes before I followed Caroline into the house.

"I'll take my leave as soon as you two are on a plane," he replied in an even lower tone.

CHAPTER 29

It didn't take a week from my missed period for me to be in the throes of morning sickness or depression or both. I had walked down to the kitchen each morning and ate scrambled eggs only to be overcome by nausea and lethargy. I tried toast, but that was no better, so I gave up getting out of bed in the morning all together.

Kennedy told Dawes that Hashim was working but had no idea when he would be home. No call, no word at all for all of that time. Ecrin flew to Dubai to meet her husband and the change in the household was palpable. I felt retched in the mornings, but by early afternoon, I was better. Nita brought me ginger tea and toast in the mornings, but I couldn't stomach anything else until the afternoon. Dawes and Sefa and I cooked together in the evenings.

I felt the change in Dawes' stance while I was cooking and turned from the stove to see Hashim. I couldn't help but smile, but he was definitely not in the mood to find us all together. I wasn't sure if he were more upset to find me cooking food for another man or if he were upset at seeing his sister in Dawes' clothes. I hoped it was the latter. In a way, I was glad he saw us all like we had been for a week. Sefa and Dawes acted more naturally around me now that I knew they were together. They were easy and didn't make me feel like a third wheel. Dawes' tension seemed to rest solely on the fact that we had had no word from Hashim.

I had skipped through the house and had eaten with Nita and her girls that afternoon. Other than having to tell Hashim that I was pregnant, everything looked brighter. I asked Nita if I might cook dinner for everyone. She happily welcomed me into her kitchen now that Ecrin was on the other side of the world. Sefa and Dawes would surely join me for dinner at the kitchen table. I had napped, though, and skipped dinner completely. That's when we decided to cook at Dawes'.

Sefa had made an appointment for that morning at the imaging center. She assisted the ultrasound tech. Dawes followed us into the small examining room. He looked uncomfortable at first, until Sefa assured him that he would see barely more than what my bikini revealed. I reclined on a narrow bed. The tech asked me a few questions and typed the information into her computer. She then asked me to lift up my shirt and rolled down the waistband of my shorts, placing a towel there to protect the fabric from the clear jelly she squeezed onto my abdomen.

My eyes were wide and expectant, but no more than Sefa's. She held my hand, encouragingly. The tech moved her instrument around on my belly and found a little, dark oval. She took some measurements on the screen and keyed in the information. She then took still shots of that area. After a few moments more, she smiled a little and asked if I would like to hear the heartbeat. I nodded. My eyes pricked with tears as she played the audio. It was a rapid little swishing sound like flapping wings. My hand flew to my gaping mouth. Sefa wiped a tear that escaped and ran down my cheek. Her rich, brown eyes shown out as she smiled at me. I hoped so much that Hashim would smile at me again like that. Dawes' reaction surprised me the most. He stood behind Sefa as far from us as possible in the small room. As we listened to the swoosh, swoosh, swoosh, he walked toward the monitor to get a better look. His eyes were fixed in awe. "Wow," he whispered, "that's inside of you. That little bitty blob has a heartbeat."

"Yeah," I sighed. "It sure does. Can you believe?" I asked surprised at my reaction, full of expectation and joy.

"Can we go shopping, now?" Sefa asked breaking mine and Dawes' fascination.

"No," Dawes and I said together.

"Not until Hashim knows," I added.

So, that very day, Hashim arrived, or should I say, that very night. I had tucked the ultrasound pictures in my Bible along with my other two photos. I sat in the quiet of the closet on the floor. Physically, I felt different but no different than if I had a virus or some other kind of ailment. I honestly felt bloated and pre-menstrual and just really tired. The proof of the ultrasound, though, had altered me instantly. It made it real, somehow. How could I return to the life I had before? I had bound myself to Hashim when I married him, but now I was bound to him forever. Together, we had created another life. I had no idea how he would react or how long it would take him to accept the truth. I didn't linger long on the unknown, and thankfully, I didn't have to wait too long before I had the opportunity to tell him.

CHAPTER 29.5

The fruit of the righteous is a tree of life
and the one who is wise saves lives.

– Proverbs 11:30

Caroline took my hand and led me upstairs. She seemed content, almost happy. My mother's departure had obviously been a relief to her. Her ever-apparent shroud was tucked neatly away somewhere out of sight. She smiled at me, and I was drawn into her, anticipating the reunion I had longed for all day. I was thankful she welcomed me after being away so long. I pushed the hair back from her shoulder and put my hand on the back of her neck. She closed her eyes and took in a settling breath. She liked it when I did that. I pulled her closer and bent to kiss her. She wrapped her hands around my waist and pulled herself into me. I felt like a fool for doubting her earlier and the jealousy and frustration melted away.

Within minutes, we were nearly naked, lying together between the sheets of my large bed. Her scent and the feel of her body against mine was more intoxicating than wine. Her hands moved and caressed me gently. She kissed me and drew my focus to her lips and her hands. She was trying to be patient, but she was anything but. I reached toward the nightstand drawer to retrieve a condom. When I moved back toward her, she had gone completely rigid and her eyes were wide in the darkened room.

"What is it," I asked.

She took a deep breath. "You won't be needing that," she said in a whisper. She bit her bottom lip self-consciously, like she was considering something and was embarrassed.

I didn't understand. "Why not? Did Sefa get you birth control?"

"Not exactly, but we won't need contraception for a while. It's a little late for that," she sighed and looked into my eyes like she was trying to get me to read her mind. I did not say anything for several seconds. "Hashim, I'm pregnant," she confessed.

I sat up away from her and shook my head, denying her words. "No, that is not possible."

She frowned slightly like she thought this might be my reaction. "I know. You're incredibly careful, but it's the truth. I have proof." She smiled then and her eyes glistened. She reached for my hand, but I slid it away from her gently. Her smile faltered then and she diverted her eyes. She sat up abruptly and wrapped the sheet around herself before she eased from the bed. I was sure she was going to run and hide. "I'll be right back," she said.

I sat in the bed waiting for her. When she returned, she turned on the lamp. She sat on the edge of the bed and handed me a small stack of ultrasound pictures. I looked through them. Each one contained indistinguishable gray images with a large, dark mass in the middle and an even smaller circle within the dark mass.

"When did you do this?"

"Today. Sefa took me." She tempered her smile, cautious to hold her emotions as she read my reaction. "Don't worry, Dawes went with us."

Don't worry? She just told me not to worry. She said she was pregnant and told *me* not to worry. They both knew, Sefa and Dawes. They were all conspiring against me at dinner. No wonder Dawes protected her so vehemently and had refused to break her confidence. He was right to do so; this was not something any man would want to hear from another. I was suddenly exhausted, weighed down by her words and the proof in the images; the long day was catching up with me. She looked at me, imploring me with her eyes for some kind of reaction. I rubbed my eyes with my hand and brought my palm down across my face, smoothing my beard and finally resting it on the back of my neck. I let out a long, slow breath.

"I feel like I owe you an apology, and I've felt guilty, so guilty, knowing this is all my fault for attacking you like I did that morning, but today, hearing the heartbeat." She smiled, then, and her eyes had a far-away look. "I'm not sorry." She blinked like she was holding back tears, but she was not sad. Conflicted, maybe, but definitely not sad. Those were tears of joy. "I really missed you and I don't want you to be angry or disappointed. I've had a few days to process all of this, and I'm good. I know it's going to take you some time to accept it, but you told me the morning you proposed to me that if I decided to love you and wanted them, you would give me children." She was right on that count; I had said those exact words. "Just to be clear, I do love you, and I want this baby; I want it badly," she whispered, and I marveled at her determination and strength.

I do love you. Her words went through me again as they had done in the shower, but this time I did not deny them or their power. She was a completely self-possessed creature. Her eyes were expectant again, but when I gave no reply, she reached over and gently took the pictures from my hand. She turned to leave the bed, thinking that I probably needed some time alone with this, but I caught her arm so she could not leave my side. I was not going to let her go; she would not be alone and this was not her fault. I looked into her eyes, those same light eyes I had missed for days, even days before I left for Virginia. Unsure of the words that needed to be spoken, I kissed her instead.

Her relief that I was not upset with her or her news was unmistakable. I was neither angry with her nor had I rejected her. Surprised? Absolutely. Confused? Slightly. Disappointed? Yes, in myself, but never in her. She enveloped me with open arms and an open heart. She entangled her legs around me, and I was received into her as her entirety wrapped me lovingly. There was no caution between us and I could not tell where she began and I ended. Unprepared for the intensity of pleasure between us, she left me completely satisfied, satiated, quenched. If this was what it felt like to be loved by a woman, I could understand why wars were started and a man gave his all in the battle for a

woman: to defend her honor, to protect her virtue, and to capture her heart. I wanted her entirely.

I had barely slept three hours when I awoke at my usual five a.m. Caroline was unmovable in my arms and I had to roll her off of me. I dressed and walked downstairs, directly to the guesthouse. I knocked lightly on the door and Dawes opened it immediately.

"Run with me?" I asked.

"Give me a second," he said and stepped back to let me in.

I felt uneasy, like I was invading his privacy, but it was my damn house and my damn sister was probably still in his damn bed. I hesitated for a second, doubting my decision, but I wanted to run and clear my mind. He returned from the bedroom in shorts and a t-shirt; he armed himself and laced his running shoes before we went outside. We stretched briefly and started off in a light jog. Neither of us said anything for the first mile. I owed him an apology but hated having to admit my own faults. My words were paced with our breathing and the steady rhythm of our footfalls.

"Dawes, I am sorry for the way I reacted last night. I had no right, and you were correct in keeping Caroline's secret. Thank you for seeing after her."

"No problem," was his reply. "I'm relieved you know."

"About Caroline or about Sefa?"

"Both." I thought I saw him crack a smile. "Do you have a plan?"

"No. Caroline and I have not spoken of that."

"You seem accepting, almost like you're okay with it. I honestly didn't know what your response would be. I think she's been terrified you'd be angry with her, and it was frustrating not being able to convince her otherwise."

"How could I be angry with her?" I asked rhetorically. "It is Caroline," I sighed. "She has done nothing wrong but make love with her husband." There was that word, *love,* again. She had made love to me from the beginning. It was not simply a physical act for her; she had given all of herself to me. We ran in silence for another couple of miles. "I have a really uneasy feeling, like something is not right. I doubted you last night when you told me you had not received my messages, but I think it is Kennedy that I need to doubt as well. Be honest, was the hotel in Montgomery bugged?" I asked.

"I have no idea. The place was swept before I arrived. I didn't do it myself, so I can't tell you for sure. I was told it was clean, but if you have doubts, then so do I."

We made a large turn along our route. "Caroline suggested the place was bugged; I dismissed her as being paranoid, but the very night I told her about D.C. and Marshall, he texted me. I no longer think that was a coincidence."

"Hmmm," Dawes muttered to himself.

"How did you know we had gone to bed that night?" Dawes looked at me questioningly. "In the plane, when you tossed me the passport, you said it had arrived just before we went to bed."

He nodded, remembering. "I knocked lightly on the door, but you didn't answer. I entered, thinking you had called it a night. I was going to place the package on the entryway table, but then I realized that you two were far from sleeping. I backed up and shut the door behind me. I kept the package with me. Good thing, otherwise we may have both forgotten it in our hasty retreat."

"Kennedy was adamant that we go to Miami to finish the project. He blamed it all on the committee, but now I doubt that as well. Do you think someone on the committee is linked to Marshall in the private sector?"

"That might be easy enough to trace, but there's no way to be sure."

"Kennedy knows we will be virtually untouchable in Dubai. Surely, he is not working with Marshall." It was too hard to imagine that level of treachery after working so closely with him the past three years. We ran a few more steps, before I stopped suddenly. "Let us get back; I really have an uneasy feeling, now."

We had been lured into a false sense of security. My wife and the child she carried were sleeping in my bed, alone and unprotected, my sister, too. Dawes had to be thinking the same thing; we each sped our pace and made it back to the house in record time. I could tell Dawes' mind was racing like mine. "You need to go, now," he said like a command as we made it back to the house. I gave a quick nod and ran up the back stairs. Waking Caroline was like waking the dead. I kissed her, but she did not budge. I made three trips back to the bed between packing items into her duffel, including the robe and her Bible. I shook her gently and finally had to move her more aggressively.

I threw some clean clothes into my own duffel; thankfully my computer and equipment were still packed. I picked up the ultrasound photos from the nightstand and placed them in my wallet. "Caroline," I raised my voice, "get up!" Her eyes flew open at the tone of my voice. I leaned in and kissed her cheek; the rest I whispered in her ear in case anyone was listening, "Get up and get dressed! We are getting on the first flight out of here!"

She looked confused and exhausted. Her eyes were open, but her brain was far from connecting to the current situation. She yawned and blinked, processing my command. I laid an outfit on the bed beside her, along with a pair of sandals. "I need to shower," I said. She gave a brief nod and reached for the clothes on the bed.

She was dressed, standing at the bathroom counter when I got out of the shower. I dried off and wrapped a towel around my waist. She was packing her toiletries into her backpack. Her eyes were huge and vulnerable, again. I kissed her forehead and she leaned into me. She placed her hand on my chest and I closed my eyes; I could feel her touch all the way to my heart. She looked as though she was going to say something, so I placed my finger to her lips in warning. She closed her eyes and nodded. A half-second later she turned away from me and vomited into the toilet.

Great, nerves or morning sickness? I wondered. I held her hair back, away from her face, and let her heave her stomach's contents, which was very little, mostly clear liquid and air. I offered her a glass of water. She shook her head like that might make it worse. "I'm okay; it'll pass," she assured me. I helped her stand and she brushed her teeth. She gagged again over the sink as she spat, but she forced the wave of nausea past and gave me a quick nod like she was ready to go. She would need food and water. She would need rest. She would need to be settled as soon as possible.

CHAPTER 30

Hashim walked from the closet and handed me my passport, birth certificate, driver's license, and marriage certificate. I didn't realize that he had held all the proof of my existence the entire time we had been in Miami. I thought my license was in my purse. Good thing I never got pulled over while driving.

He then handed me an envelope. I held it up and gestured to it like a question. He leaned over and whispered into my ear, "In the event we are separated, this will be enough cash to get you anywhere you need to go. There is also a credit card. Use it for whatever you may need."

What was he talking about? We were not going to be separated. I shook my head denying his words and leaned back and looked into his eyes. He gestured with a nod for me to inspect the contents. I opened the envelope and gasped. It was filled with hundred-dollar bills and bills that I didn't recognize. There had to be at least twenty thousand U.S. dollars in that one envelope not to mention the other currency. I shook my head, again. That was more money than I made in a year. I couldn't take it. I tried to hand it back to him, but he shook his head. His eyes warned me not to argue.

I didn't like this; I didn't like any of it. I felt incredibly uncomfortable and my stomach ached. I didn't feel nauseated like before, but I had a really, really bad feeling that something horrible was about to happen. I had never felt this afraid before. He was doing what he could to protect me. He was doing everything in his power: money and flights for sure. He leaned in again, but this time kissed my cheek before he whispered into my ear, "I've also listed the address of our home in Dubai. That's where I want you to go." I reared back and glared at him, pushing him away from me. I shook my head adamantly. There was no way in hell I was going anywhere near his mother, again. He took my face in his hands and forced me to look into his eyes. "Say you will go," he whispered low and commanding.

I shook my head again and tears stung my eyes. They started as fear but soon turned to pure rage. "No!" I said strongly. He put up a finger in warning, but I didn't care who may be listening. "I'm not going anywhere without you, and I'm sure as hell not going anywhere near that woman! You need a better plan! If that's the best you've got, then I'm going home and you can't stop me!" I pushed his hands away and glared at him. He stepped back and examined me.

He shook his head. "No," he said flatly. "Please be wise. We have more than ourselves to consider now." He raised an eyebrow and glanced toward my midsection.

I rolled my eyes, seething. I covered my face with my hands and tried to get a handle on my breathing. His arms were around me instantly, but I refused his comfort. I pushed him away from me, but he only held me tighter. "It's all your fault!" I screamed as I beat on his chest. "Marshall! Krissa! It's all your fucking fault! Why the hell did I give myself to you? You're awful! I hate you so much right now!" I fought him like a feral cat; I was so hurt and enraged. Curses and tears flew from me. I wasn't strong enough to fight him for very long physically, and I shuttered as the wave of emotion began to wane. He only held me tighter and took whatever I threw at him. I was sobbing then, on the verge of hysteria. All the while, he held me tighter, willing me to release it all. He could take it; he could carry it for me. He was breathing steadily, forcing my breaths with his. I could feel the steady beats of his heart and the easy rhythm of his breathing, just like when he was on top of me, just like when I made love with him. *Damn him!* It was working.

"Shhh, Caroline," he whispered and stroked down my hair. He kissed my head. "My sweet, sweet, Caroline. Please forgive me."

I shuddered again and my breath caught in hitches. I took a deep breath and pressed against his chest solidly with the palms of my hands. He didn't need to ask for forgiveness. My anger had a short fuse; once it was ignited, it flashed but then was easily doused. "I don't want to do this alone. I want to be with you," I said, holding him just as tightly. I looked down and he kissed my forehead before I took one step back, gauging my balance and state of being. I turned toward the bathroom. I needed to pee and blow my nose, and I decided that I might be able to drink some water, then. I was suddenly parched.

I sullenly stashed the money in my purse and then packed everything into my backpack. Hashim picked up only two duffels. He apparently had more clothes wherever we were going. We walked down the back stairs and into the kitchen. He opened the fridge and handed me two bottles of water; he opened the pantry and pulled out a handful of protein bars. I pushed them into the side pockets of my backpack. I sighed imagining how vile those would be when I threw them up. "No?" he asked, reading my expression. I shook my head. "What then?" he asked looking around the shelves of the pantry. I pointed to the small shelf of items that Nita had gotten for me. He instantly disapproved but took them anyway. "This is unhealthy; you cannot live on junk food."

"I know, but I haven't thrown any of that up." He couldn't argue with me, so he grudgingly grabbed some peppermints, a couple sleeves of cinnamon Pop-Tarts, and the half-eaten bag of Doritos.

We walked out the backdoor toward the guesthouse. Dawes and Sefa were waiting there. Dawes had a backpack slung across his left shoulder. He was back in his dark suit, looking all professional and protective. "What's the plan?" Dawes asked. He looked at me; my eyes were puffy from lack of sleep and crying. He could tell I hadn't taken the news well. "So, it's Dubai," he stated reluctantly.

"Your guess is correct. Sefa?" Hashim asked looking at his sister. She wore dark sunglasses, a cross-body satchel, and a fashionable scarf around her neck and shoulders. A rolling suitcase was parked at her side. "Where are you going?"

"I don't plan to leave her, Brother," she said smiling at me. "I've contacted the charter. They'll be ready within the hour. We have just enough time to get there and get loaded."

"You told her?" Hashim asked Dawes. His tone was cautious and slightly angry.

"Yes, she was rather insistent," he said not daring to look at her directly. "Besides, it will be better for Caroline. She needs at least one ally in enemy territory." Sefa smiled her winning smile at Dawes. I wondered what language worked best on him.

Mizhir pulled the BMW around, then, and the guys loaded the bags in the back. "We will take it from here," Hashim said confidently.

I smiled sheepishly at Mizhir when he opened the doors for me and Sefa. He looked questioningly at our odd little party but didn't ask for any explanation. "Safe travels, Meetha."

"Thank you, Mizhir," I said and he bowed his head and shut the door securely behind us.

Hashim drove this time. He drove the car hard and fast toward the airport. "Caroline, do you have your phone?" Dawes asked. I nodded. "Give it to me." I dug around in my purse and fished out my phone. "Unlock it and open Emir's contact," he demanded before I handed it to him. He looked at me questioningly. "Really? That's an interesting code name." he said.

I rolled my eyes remembering that he was under *Aunt June* in my phone. "It's a joke."

"Clever," he said, but it sounded anything but. "This is my contact, now. If you need anything."

"Wait, you aren't going with us?" I asked.

"No, I've been officially relieved of my duties. I'm due back in Virginia." I was horrified at the thought. I had come to feel so safe with Dawes' presence. He could read the panic on my face. "You'll be fine," he assured me.

I looked to Sefa. She was willing to leave him for me. The rush of thoughts through my mind finally awoke me fully. My brain was beginning to make sense of everything. "Hashim, did Marshall contact you again?" I asked. I wasn't sure where the question came from, but the words jumped out in a rush.

"No, why?"

"I just thought it might be why we were leaving so suddenly. Did something happen in Virginia?"

"Nothing that I can put my finger on, but with Dawes returning, it is time. I have an uneasy feeling; I should have sent you away sooner."

I didn't like those words like maybe he possibly regretted bringing me along in the first place. I knew that wasn't true, but I couldn't help but doubt. I thought about how we left Montgomery and how we had left my home and everything that happened in both places. "Hashim, did you tell Kennedy that Krissa was a blond?"

"What?" he asked completely taken off guard. It was such a random question.

"At the passport office, at any point did you tell Kennedy Krissa was a blond?" My voice was insistent, almost commanding.

"No." He shook his head. "What made you think of that?"

I shrugged. "I don't know. I just remembered. He said something there, and at the time, I was too nervous to make the connection." I sighed. "The job is done, so you should be relieved, but you came home last night almost edgier than when you left. It wasn't the fact that you found us all together, so I wonder if it was something that happened while you were away." He and Dawes locked eyes in the rearview mirror. "How did he know?" I asked. "You were the only one who knew, you and Marshall. You were the only ones who could have known." I turned my attention toward Dawes. "Did you know?"

He shook his head. "No."

Their minds were racing. Mine was too foggy to make too many connections, but I knew my instincts were right. "Did Kennedy say anything to you?" I asked Hashim.

"Not directly, but he did press me for more details while I was away. He was arrogant with me, not his usual self. I thought it might be the exhaustion from all the days we were there working. I questioned his loyalty this morning for the first time. I am unable to make any connection to Marshall, though."

I sat quietly for a few minutes. "Is this something you can figure out from so far away?" I asked. I knew that he would not be able to solve this from half-way around the world. He shook his head slightly, his mind still racing while he drove. He could do this with Dawes. The two of them could figure this all out and confront both Marshall and Kennedy, but he couldn't do this if he were the least bit distracted by me. I closed my eyes, praying for discernment. My gut was screaming and my mind was racing. Was this merely intuition or was this an answer to my prayer? Pain gripped my heart and tears pricked my eyes, but that didn't make me alter the course of my mind. I knew what needed to be done. When I opened my eyes, it was like Sefa could read my mind. She was looking directly into my eyes. She gave me a brief nod of encouragement.

I put my hand on Hashim's thigh. He looked at me, trying to read my expression. He put his right hand over mine and gave it a little squeeze. He was reassuring me, but I was the one who needed to touch him so that he wouldn't doubt my words. We were getting closer to the airport by the second. Sefa put her hand on my shoulder, comfortingly, but I kept my eyes on Hashim.

"Hashim," I began, but had to clear my throat and take a deep breath before I could continue. "Pull over."

"Are you going to be sick?" he asked. I must have looked paler than I did seconds before.

"No. I don't know; I need some fresh air." He brought the car to a stop in a parking lot at the edge of the private airstrip. I opened the door and stepped out of the car and took a deep breath. Everyone, but Sefa, followed me. I looked into both of their faces. "I don't think this is the best plan," I said, stepping away from the car.

"Yes, it is. You will be safest in Dubai." Hashim reached for me, but I moved away. "You will not be watched constantly, and there is no way that Marshall can get to you."

I wanted to be encouraged, but I wasn't. "I honestly doubt that. If Kennedy is involved then his influence, combined with Marshall's, may be farther-reaching than either of you suspect. I also know that my being with you is a constant distraction. You won't be at peace until you get this resolved. I'm in no condition to help you, and I don't know what I could even do, if I were."

"What are you saying?" he asked, allowing his glance to linger on me.

"I'm saying that you need to stay here, and Sefa and I need to go." I hated saying the words. My heart ached and my stomach tightened all over, but I knew that it was the right thing to do and that made me strong.

"She makes a good point, Emir," Dawes said, breaking the silence. The tension was thick and uncomfortable. "If you stay, we can work this from both ends. You can work Marshall and I can work Kennedy."

He shook his head adamantly and looked away. He gripped his hands together, making his knuckles blanch against the pressure. He took a deep breath. He slammed the door to the car in frustration and stormed toward me. He grabbed my shoulders, but I didn't move. His hands were shaking, but I wasn't afraid of him; I knew he wouldn't hurt me. He was upset and trying to think clearly. I could see how desperately he wanted to find another solution.

"Look at me," I demanded. I was surprised at the steadiness of my voice. I put my hand on his cheek. "Please," I softened my tone, "Hashim, look at me."

After a few seconds, he lowered his gaze to mine. His expression was a mixture of anger and disbelief. He knew it was the right thing to do, but he was fighting it. "You know I love you, and I don't want to be apart from you. This will be agony for me, but you gave me specific instructions of what to do if we were separated. I promise to do exactly what you asked. I'll wait for you there. If it's as safe as you believe, then Sefa and I will be fine, and you can focus on everything you need to do here."

He put his hands on my face, then, his eyes piercing me all the way to my soul. "You are sure of this? And what of my mother?"

I wished I could smile, but my attempt faltered. Tears welled in my eyes and I sniffed reflexively. "I won't let her get to me; I'll do my best and pray." He couldn't smile either, but he could kiss me, and kiss me he did. He held me close and enveloped me in his strong arms. I didn't want to go and I didn't want to leave him, but my resolve didn't waver in the slightest.

CHAPTER 30.5

Listen to advice and accept discipline,
and at the end you will be counted among the wise.

– Proverbs 19:20

How on earth had I ended up with this woman? This strong, determined, unwavering woman. She was willing to face my mother again and exchange her freedom so that I could focus and make her completely safe. I held her close to me for as long as I could. I wished I could force her inside of me, somehow. I hated the idea of being separated again, but this time it was her choice, not mine, and that made it even harder, knowing she could leave me.

"You need to make it look like you've had a fight," Dawes said suddenly in a suggestive whisper.

I looked up at him. "What?" I could feel Caroline's face turn toward him, too.

"Caroline, when you're ready, I want you to push off from him and step back angrily. Then, when we pull up near the plane, I want you to try and slap him and curse at him, and then I want you refuse to let him get on the plane. Do you think you can do that?"

She shook her head. "Why?"

"If it looks like you've had a fight and that Emir is willing to let you go, you won't be as big a target. It gives us time. He has a reputation for not attaching himself, so I think it will be a believable scenario."

I rolled my eyes. "Is that really necessary?" I asked. "She is leaving with my sister."

He raised an eyebrow. "No one knows that, and thankfully she stayed in the car. I know it's a small thing, but if they're watching, then they're seeing us now. They see the two of you and it looks like you're trying to make amends, but if Caroline is willing to play along, it could look like something very different."

Caroline hugged me tightly. "I'm willing," she said and suddenly stepped away from me. She glared at me like she had done in the bedroom this morning. "This is horrible and I hate every bit of it but know that nothing I say for the next few minutes is true," she finished in a whisper. "Don't believe a word of it. When I say, 'I hate you,' it really means that I love you, and 'Get away from me' means I want you so close I can't breathe." I hated the way her lip quivered. I knew the tears that were about to flow were the Sad Caroline tears, but she would make them angry for show. "Dawes, this means, thank you." She flipped him off and stormed back into the car and slammed the door.

I was driving, again. We were seconds away from the charter service's hanger. "Give her the ring," Dawes whispered low in my ear from the backseat. I sighed. He was right. There needed to be no trace of her on my person. Unattached was believable. I held the steering wheel steady with my leg and pulled my wedding band from my finger. Perhaps the old adage about that finger being connected to the heart was true because as I twisted the ring over my knuckle, it felt like I was surgically removing it from my heart. My finger felt exposed and hollow. I wondered if the phantom pain would linger. Caroline's eyes were incorrigible. She held my hand with both of hers as I pressed the ring into her hand. I could feel her hands shaking. She leaned in and kissed my hand before placing the ring on her right index finger.

Dawes pushed off and began rummaging through the bags behind his seat. He pulled Caroline's bag over into his lap. He then turned again and I heard the familiar zipper of my duffel. I turned to see what he was doing. He had opened my bag and removed my computer and was placing it in Caroline's.

"What are you doing?" I asked. I was so angry that I spat the words at him.

"Take it and keep it safe. I will return him to you," Dawes leaned in and said to Caroline. He placed his hand on her shoulder. His words were a promise to her. She shook her head disbelieving that any of this was happening. Sefa looked at Dawes and wanted desperately to believe that he was doing the right thing. He handed her a baseball cap and she wrapped her hair up and placed the cap on her head. "Take her," Dawes said as a command to Sefa. "Take her far away and keep her safe. I promise; I will make this right."

I pulled into the hanger, then. It was empty except for the small jet and a couple of men working around the plane. "Make it convincing, ladies," he said and then uncharacteristically placed his hand on Sefa's cheek and leaned in and kissed her. He must have been confident that no one could see through the heavily tinted windows. Caroline looked satisfied, but I was taken completely by surprise. Caroline squeezed my hand and drew my attention away from Dawes and Sefa and back to her. Her light eyes were clear, now, confident. "Remember, take nothing I'm going to say to heart." I lifted her palm to my lips and kissed it.

I turned slightly toward her and put my hand over her heart, pressing her slightly into the seat. She closed her eyes in a long blink. I guided my hand downward and placed it over her lower abdomen. She took in a quick breath and I felt her muscles under my hand contract reflexively. I imagined holding the grayscale kernel in the palm of my hand. "Keep it safe," I said. Caroline's entire countenance changed. Her smile radiated a glow of pleasure at my acknowledgment for the child she carried. She kissed me, then, and I doubted for an instant that she would be able to pull this off, but she suddenly and abruptly opened the door and slid from the passenger's side. She angrily threw her backpack over her shoulder and then opened the backseat and grabbed her duffel bag.

"You're a fucking idiot!" she screamed! Her words echoed all around us. I jumped out and followed her toward the plane. "Get the hell away from me!" I pulled her hand and turned her toward me. The men near the jet looked up, cautiously watching our altercation. All they saw was a small, light-skinned woman being grabbed by a larger, dark-skinned man. Their protective instincts kicked in, and they approached us. From the corner of my eye, I saw Sefa emerge from the car. I forcefully pulled Caroline toward me and I took the opportunity to kiss her. She let me for a brief moment and then leaned her face back and made to slap me. It was rather convincing. I grabbed her wrist and held it tightly. She drew away from me and fear crossed her face. I could only imagine what a disturbing sight we made.

Dawes was in front of me then. "Let her go," he demanded. "She's not worth it." He gestured toward the men in the hanger. I dropped her wrist in frustration; the frustration was real. Dawes pushed Caroline toward Sefa. Caroline pushed hard against Dawes as though she would fight him, too.

"You're a sorry son-of-bitch!" she screamed. Sefa took her arm, then, and pulled her toward the plane. Caroline resisted. "I hate you! I hate you more than anything in the world!" It looked like Caroline was trying to get back to me, but she was letting Sefa pull her back as if her size and strength were no match for my sister's. Caroline held the duffel bag like a shield as she backed up the stairs into the small jet. She threw the bag in and turned toward us before she put up both middle fingers in protest against me and Dawes. I could hear her cursing and screaming insults until the door closed.

My response to her tirade was genuine; I stood dumbfounded. I had heard her curse before, but I had no idea she could speak that way. I stepped forward, and Dawes pushed me back forcefully. There were more men, now. The pilot and copilot were approaching the plane. They looked at the two of us warily.

"Everything alright, here, gentlemen?" the pilot asked with polite sternness.

"Yes, sir," Dawes answered. "We don't want any trouble. We'll be on our way." He pushed me toward the car. I was rethinking this decision. "Get in," he commanded as he opened the passenger side door for me. He could read the expression on my face; I was in no condition to drive. I watched as the pilot and copilot boarded the plane. I tried to see Caroline through the windows, but I only saw Sefa briefly before she pulled the shade closed. I imagined Caroline in a crumpled heap of inconsolable exhaustion, lying across the backbench of the cabin. Dawes pulled out of the hanger and back onto the main road leading away from the airport. He stopped in the same area as we had stopped earlier and turned the BMW around and parked. We both got out and leaned against the hood of the car to watch them take off.

"They're going to be okay," Dawes said. He sounded confident. "Where do you think she learned to swear like that?" he asked rhetorically. He almost sounded impressed.

I shook my head. "I have no idea. I startled her once in the laundry room and she lit into me like I was the devil, but that incident only surprised me and was mild in comparison. Thank you, again; your instincts continue to be right. What time is your flight?"

"5:30."

It was then, I watched the small jet taxi down the runway and into the sky. We watched until they were out of sight. "Take me back to the house. I need to eat. Why the computer?" I asked.

"You may need a reason to retrieve it. I was giving you an out. Call Marshall in a day or two; tell him you've had a change in plans and would like to reconsider his offer."

CHAPTER 31

"Close the blinds," I commanded. I couldn't see him again. I couldn't see the pain again on his face. My rant had taken everything I had; my blood pressure was up and I could feel a headache pressing against the throbbing of my pulse. Pretending was hard for me. My eyes burned from the raging, but not because I needed to cry. The pilot and copilot barely glanced my direction. I hoped they would still fly us, given my tirade.

"Dr. Emir, may we have a word?" the copilot asked.

I turned away and rummaged through my backpack. I found my headphones for an escape. I needed to calm down and relax. I plugged my ears with familiar tunes and completely ignored everyone else. I felt the plane leaving the hanger and buckled myself in. I realized then that Sefa was sitting directly across from me. She leaned forward and put a hand on my knee. I couldn't look in her eyes, Hashim's eyes, so I lowered my gaze remorsefully. Realizing that I wasn't going to give her any reply, she gave my knee a little pat and sat back and readied herself for takeoff. I crossed my arms over my chest and noticed Hashim's wedding band on my right index finger. I closed my eyes and rubbed it with my thumb. I then felt the change in the engines and the gentle force of the plane as it lifted off the ground. The combination of the change in cabin pressure and the realization that I was leaving the ground where Hashim stood forced the tears from my eyes. I didn't sob or become hysterical as I had done earlier, but the tears would abate for nothing. They flowed and flowed and flowed, and I did nothing to stop them.

A little while into the flight, Sefa forced a bottle of water upon me. "Drink," she commanded. I nodded obediently and unscrewed the lid of the bottle. She offered me a blanket. "Are you hungry?" she asked.

"No," I said and she frowned. "How long is the flight?"

"Less than three hours. We should arrive in New York in time to catch the morning direct flight. That flight will take about thirteen hours. You'll be comfortable and can sleep if you want. How are you doing, otherwise?" she asked.

I shrugged. "I'm numb."

"Numb might be better than feeling your heart being ripped out. You were quite convincing."

I scoffed at her compliment. "How can you leave Dawes so easily?"

Sefa gave a quick laugh and threw her head back. Her eyes diverted and she shook her head. Her smile was radiant. "He and I have had that discussion on more than one occasion. He calls into question my affection for him. He doesn't understand how I can be with him so entirely and then leave him just as completely. I cannot adequately describe it, either, but we each have our jobs to do, our callings, as you may. He is charged with protecting my brother and his incredible talents while he's working for your government. Maybe I'm being a protective older sister, but I find that worthy employment. He is not willing to follow me around the world and I don't think he'd be content without someone to protect or some mission to follow. He's incredibly loyal to Hashim and now to you. It's one of the many things I adore about him."

"Do you love him?" I asked, trying to understand. Their relationship was complex.

"Of course, I do." She seemed surprised at my question. "But love comes in many forms, Caroline. When we met, I had never had any significant relationship, perhaps a lover or two, but..." She dismissed the thought. "For the better part of my life, I focused on school and my work, and I've never lived anywhere long enough to establish a lasting relationship with a man. Men have had interest in me from the time I was thirteen, but I had no interest in them. I attended mostly all-girl schools, and I was content in myself until I met Liam."

I couldn't hide my surprise. "Is that his first name? I only know him as *Dawes*."

She laughed. "Yes, his name is Liam Patrick Dawes. Do you know where he's from?"

I shook my head. "I don't know anything about him except his enjoyment for shooting and we share an appreciation for cars."

"He's from Albany, New York. He's the eldest of eight children. His family is Irish and devoutly Catholic, so you can imagine our differences are extreme."

"Does his family know about you?"

"No, just as no one in my family has known about him until now. I think he's relieved, but it compromises his position. Relationships make us vulnerable and strong. It's a complicated maze, but we've made do."

"Is it because he's Catholic?" I asked.

"No."

"Do you have any affiliation?" I asked.

She did that thing with her eyes again, looking amused. "Did you know our mother is Jewish?" I shook my head. "She isn't a devout Jew, but she keeps her faith in her own way. I made my bat mitzvah when I was twelve. So, by choice, I became a Jew. I have since served with many people of faith around the world. They do good in the name of God, but worship and find salvation in very different ways. I have not proclaimed your Christ, but I see the benefits of that relationship in my Christian friends. I am not opposed to pursuing it further, but it would not be for convenience or for a man. I don't trifle with God."

"Me either." I said. We sat for a long time in silence before I confessed, "It hurts me physically to be away from Hashim. It has from the moment he kissed me. Do you ache for Dawes?" I asked, truly curious.

"That is understandable; your emotional attachment is notable. The emotional has obviously manifested into a strong physical relationship, so of course you long for what you know. Our relationship is not the way you describe. I probably have a bit too much of Ecrin in me, and we were raised in very different families with very different priorities. My desire for him is not merely physical. Liam has not asked me to alter my course for him; he would never do that. He has eluded to his desire to make a life together, but we have no clear understanding of what that may look like. I'm willing to be patient. Our lives are not conventional ones; we don't have the luxury to compromise."

I thought about her words and sat quietly for several moments. "I guess I have that luxury, the luxury to compromise, I mean." I felt small and self-conscious. I had compromised everything, and now I was on a plane that brought me closer to an even bigger compromise.

"You have compromised for the sake of peace; you've compromised to ease your husband's burden. You have not compromised anything of your values or your strength. You may have given up your home and a particular lifestyle with school and work, but you've not given up anything of real value. You are still completely yourself, altered yes, stronger, too, but still *Caroline*."

"Thank you. I needed reminding of that. I don't feel very much like the person I was just a few months ago. Speaking of work, how long can you stay with me?"

"I have no plans to return to Africa. I'm a glorified volunteer, so they can't really dictate my agenda. I've notified them that I will be on an extended leave of absence. They understand."

I rummaged then, in my backpack, and began eating some of the food that Hashim and I had packed. Sefa scrounged around and pulled out the other bottle of water and one of the protein bars. We ate in silence and spoke very little until we arrived in New York where there was a car waiting to take us to our next flight. We had barely an hour to spare when we arrived at the ticket counter.

Sefa purchased two first-class tickets on the next flight to Dubai. She allowed me to pull her suitcase and she carried the duffel. I followed her lead. I had never been through airport security. We went through all of the checkpoints without any delay. I had only been in an airport a couple of times to get Billy and drop him off when he flew back for Daddy's funeral. I had never been on the inside of an airport where you waited.

We boarded the plane. "Wow!" I said aloud. It looked like something from a futuristic movie.

"We are pleased to have you flying with us, again, Dr. Emir," the flight attendant welcomed Sefa, directly. "This way," she said as she showed us to our seats and took our bags. She lifted them easily into the overhead compartment. "Do you need anything from your handbags, or would you like me to stow them for you?"

Remembering the contents of my backpack, I clung to it. "No, I'm fine. I'll keep it."

The flight attendant smiled warmly. "Please let me know if there is anything you might need."

"Thank you," I said and sat down in the high-tech cubical. Sefa lowered the divider between our seats. "You know what?" I asked in a whisper.

"What?" Sefa leaned in like I was about to tell her a juicy secret.

"I may never be able to return to the real world. I've only been in two chartered planes and they were nicer than anything I've ever traveled in, and now this." I gestured to first-class seats on this luxury airline.

Sefa smiled. "I know. Isn't it fun?" I nodded conspiratorially.

We settled ourselves and readied for takeoff. "You know, Sefa, I plan to make the best of this. I have no intentions of being miserable; it's not my way. I'm not saying it's going to be easy with your mother and all, but I want you to know I appreciate you choosing to stay with me."

"Choti Behan, you are welcome."

"What does that mean, anyway?"

"Little sister."

I smiled at that. "I like that."

"Me, too."

We taxied down the runway, then. The sensation of taking off in a small jet was very different from taking off in a large, commercial airplane. The force was greater and I felt myself sinking into the seat. It took much longer for the plane to level off and I was suddenly overcome by waves of nausea. I took in a couple of slow, deep breaths before I felt Sefa's hand. She had an airsick bag opened for me. Good thing, because I threw up the protein bar. I was right; it tasted horrible coming back up. She reached over and opened a can of ginger ale for me from the side bar in my cubicle. There were also wet wipes and a straw. The wet wipe smelled like lavender, and within a few sips, the ginger ale settled my stomach.

"I'm sorry," I apologized.

"You're fine. You'll feel better after you sleep. I'll wake you when it's time for dinner."

Our flight attendant came around then and asked if we needed anything. I asked her to help me make out the bed. I put on the sleep mask and put in the earplugs. The white noise of the plane and the compounded exhaustion of the past twelve hours since Hashim's return were enough. Had it only been half a day since he returned? My heart felt saddened, but thankfully sleep afforded me a peaceful reprieve.

I didn't need much rousing when the smell of food wafted through our area of the plane. I sat up and lifted the sleep mask onto my forehead. I stretched. "I need to pee." I said and Sefa pointed to the bathroom.

The meal that was set before me when I returned was amazing. Fresh fruit, olives, bread, meat and cheese. There were things I didn't recognize, but I didn't really care what they were because it all tasted amazing. I ate everything from each little plate and dish, savoring every bite. I sat back and sighed. "That was delicious, exactly what I needed." Sefa smiled and sipped her glass of wine. "Am I allowed one of those?" I asked.

Sefa shook her head. "No, you aren't of age. They won't serve you on this flight."

"Am I allowed to have alcohol pregnant?" I asked.

"In moderation, but I would err on the side of caution and tell you to abstain until the second trimester. Honestly, I'd like you to abstain the entire time. You have enough stress. Let's not provoke it."

"Speaking of stress, how can I win your mother over? What's your father like? Will he be as hostile as Ecrin?"

Sefa's smile was consoling. "Please don't worry about winning Ecrin over. She will see you in time." She reflected for a few seconds before she continued. "Ammi and Abba are living embodiments of the fact that opposites attract. Ammi would have refused the Queen of Sheba for Hashim if she had not chosen her for him herself. Abba, Rana to you, is more understanding and eager for peace at most any cost. He has a great sense of humor and laughs and enjoys life."

"Like you," I interjected.

"I think so, but he is amazing and I can only aspire to have the same impact on the world as he has."

"Do you think he'll like me? Do you think he'll approve?"

"Yes."

"How can you be sure?"

"He and Hashim came to an understanding many years ago regarding his choice to marry or not. Since Hashim became a man, our father has questioned very few of his choices. He will be relieved, I think, that Hashim has married, and when he finds out that you are carrying his grandchild, he will be delighted."

I blushed. "What do you think your mother's reaction will be?"

"No worries; Rana will temper Ecrin. They are a good balance; you'll see. Together, they are better. Ammi is harder to handle when she's not with her husband. He grounds her; he grounds all of us. He will welcome you, and you will see a marked difference in how my mother treats you in his presence. For the most part, it will be genuine." I didn't argue, but I wasn't sure I believed her, either.

I decided to watch a movie. Afterward, I slept and then we were served a very late meal. I wouldn't call it breakfast, but I knew that the morning would arrive soon. I was pampered with hot, wet cloths and delicious snacks. It was so odd to never have darkness when my body knew it was supposed to be close to midnight. I wondered how many days it would take to recover from jetlag.

CHAPTER 31.5

A gentle answer turns away wrath, but a harsh word stirs up anger.

— Proverbs 15:1

The drive back to the house was quiet. Mizhir was surprised to see us return without Sefa and Caroline. He did not question me openly, but I could see the disappointment in his eyes. He adored my sister and I knew he would miss Caroline's presence, too.

"Are you free to drive Dawes to the airport?" I asked.

"Yes, indeed. What time?" Mizhir asked.

"We'll need to leave by two-thirty," Dawe's interjected.

"Will you be staying, then, Hashim?" Mizhir asked.

"Yes, for now. I'll let you know my plans in a day or two." Mizhir gave me a brief nod.

I walked sluggishly into the house. Dawes followed me to the kitchen. Nita scowled up at me as soon as we entered. "Where is Caroline?" she began in Spanish.

"She is not here."

"I know she is not here; I went up to bring her tea this morning and there's no trace of her. No clothes! Nothing!" Nita's voice was commanding and protective. "Did you send her away?"

I stepped back feeling the force of her anger and disappointment. "Yes, I needed to send her away."

She made the sign of the cross over herself. She rounded on Dawes next. "You, you let her go, too? You knew. You knew she was in no condition and still you let her go?"

Dawes backed up and shook his head. "No, ma'am, it's not like that," he protested.

Nita refused to hear any of it. "She was afraid you would be upset!" She raised her voice in angry Spanish. "She's too young to be on her own and take care of a child! You must do right by her!"

"Nita, please understand, it wasn't like that. She chose to go. It was necessary and it was her choice," I replied. I couldn't conceal the pain. Nita shook her head, dissatisfied. She didn't believe it, and honestly, neither did I. "She's safe and she'll be fine, I promise." *I promise.* I had to swallow those words before I could speak again. "Is there anything to eat?"

Nita looked at me angrily. She may have been deciding whether or not to serve me or whether or not to punish me with food poisoning. "Do you know where your sister is?" I nodded. "Will she not be returning, either?" I shook my head.

"Dawes will be leaving today as well; I will be the only one in residence for the time being."

She seemed disappointed in that news. I was suddenly her least favorite person, but apparently my responses appeased her enough to feed the two of us. Maybe she could read the pain I was unable to mask completely. Within seconds, she had mugs of hot coffee on the table; a few moments later, she slammed down plates of food in front of us. She would not easily forgive. Why was I surprised by everyone's protectiveness of Caroline? I had felt those same feelings the first day I met her. Had I not fixed her car the second day of our acquaintance? How things had changed in the course of a few months. Caroline only appeared vulnerable; I knew differently. She was incredibly strong and secure, but still appreciated the security of others around her. Obviously, Nita was helping her through her morning sickness. I had not thought to ask how she felt after she threw up this morning. Mizhir, too, was concerned for her wellbeing, though he would never be so bold to ask me or reprimand me as Nita had done. Cuban women were very different from Pakistani men.

I saw Dawes out to the car. I shook his hand and thanked him for everything. "I'll be in touch," he said.

I went upstairs then and looked around my room. The house was quiet, too quiet. I took one look at the unmade bed and the room we had left so hastily this morning. I lay on the bed, exhausted. Caroline's scent and the memory of our intimacy lingered all over the sheets. I sat up immediately; there was no way I could stay there, much less sleep. I walked across the hall and found a guestroom and decided I would sleep there.

It was much later in the day when I awoke. The sun ebbed in the afternoon sky. I needed to run, clear my head, and exhaust my body enough so that I could focus on the next step in the plan. When I walked back into my room, our room, Nita's girls had already been there. It looked like every other time I had ever entered this room: neat, tidy, and completely void of Caroline. My duffel lay in the corner where her belongings once lay. I opened all of her drawers, but I knew I had packed everything thoroughly for her. I was not a man who had ever cried, but if I knew how, I would have cried; I would have cried hard and for a long time. Instead, I ran.

I ran mine and Dawes' usual route. At about mile eight, I noticed a car behind me. At mile ten, the same car appeared in my periphery. I thought about sprinting the next mile to the gates, but decided I needed to see what this was about so I slowed my pace instead. The car trailed closely behind me. Finally, it passed me by and another car approached from the opposite direction. This car stopped in the middle of the road and blocked my way. I stopped and put my hands on my knees to catch my breath. The driver's side window went down and Marshall grinned.

"Afternoon, Emir. Seems you're alone this afternoon. I've been waiting for a long time to speak with you. You keep moving around and now you're hiding behind those gates. Are you ready to talk?" I looked down at the ground, mustering up the courage and breath I needed to be bold in this. I tilted my head to one side and gave a brief nod. I was not even faking the fact that I had little breath to speak. "Are you holding that little brunette captive in one of those rooms? She's really not your type, Emir; I don't know why you bothered to go to so much trouble for her."

I took a deep breath before I stood to my full height. I looked Marshall in the eye as I said, "No need to worry yourself with her. She has gone with no intentions to return."

"But you went to so much effort to protect her. Surely, she means more to you than that."

"She learned that I was not worth the risk; two women have died and she chose not to become a third. Besides, she no longer desired my company. I am too easily distracted and cannot afford the attachment." My tone was dark, but I detected no hint of remorse or regret in it; I hoped Marshall did not, either.

"Those were both accidents, you understand."

"Regardless, it was unnecessary." My disapproval was obvious.

Marshall glared at me. "You ready to finish what you started?"

I shrugged noncommittally. "Depends."

Marshall's eyes were calculating. "On what?"

"You tell me who's feeding you the information you need to keep finding me."

He scoffed and shook his head. "Not going to happen, Emir. Just know that there are more eyes watching you than you know. They allow me the privilege to find and speak to you directly, but there are plenty of fingers in the pie. They all want you; they want you bad." He laughed sardonically, then, "Too bad women don't pay as well, heh? You'd be a gazillionaire by now." Dawes was right; unattached was believable.

CHAPTER 32

The airport was crowded. I heard nothing familiar. My ears were in overdrive trying to process all the languages being spoken. Intermittently, I heard heavily accented English. Sefa took my duffel bag and put it on top of her rolling suitcase. She took my hand and led me through the crowded terminal. I was trying to take it all in. This place was amazing. I marveled at all of the shops and the way everyone dressed. It was fascinating. Once we were through customs, Sefa requested a visa application be sent to the apartment. She said that Rana had connections to ensure that I would be able to stay with them indefinitely. I didn't understand most of what she said to the woman, but I knew my own name even in a different language.

We took a cab to the apartment. I was too visually stimulated to take in everything: skyscrapers, bustling sidewalks, and crowded streets. The buildings were all unique and shiny. I had never been to a city this large; everything was so clean.

Once we were at the apartment building, Sefa introduced me to the doorman, Alham. He looked more like a cross between a bouncer at Pete's and a CIA agent. He wore a dark suit like Dawes and an earpiece. She explained to him that I would be staying with them and to welcome me accordingly. We rode the elevator to the top floor and a young man named Adi carried my duffel into the apartment. It was the most magnificent space I had ever walked into. The furnishings were sleek and modern with a staircase that spiraled down into the living areas. The furniture was low and white with minimal accent colors. There was a huge mirror on one wall above the dining table, a large abstract painting on another, and floor-to-ceiling windows made up the rest of the walls. They extended all the way up to the second floor, giving full view of the city's skyline and the full sun in the bright blue sky.

I guessed that the way I felt was associated with jetlag. I wasn't even sure what day it was, but I marveled at everything around me. Sefa stood behind me, then. "This is our home for now; I won't leave you," she promised in a whisper. I took in a deep breath and exhaled slowly. I needed to get my bearings. "Are you hungry?" she asked. I shrugged. I honestly didn't know. "You need to eat something and sleep. She walked to the fridge and opened it. She began placing items on the counter behind her. I didn't recognize anything but a carton of eggs and some cheese. I shook my head. Nothing looked the least bit appetizing.

"Are there any crackers? I think I could eat some crackers." Sefa closed the fridge and opened the pantry. She pulled out a box of crackers and offered them to me. They were savory and salty with a hint of herbs. They would be okay for now. She then offered me a glass of water. "Thanks," I said and sat on a tall stool at the bar.

Just then, a man in a striped bathrobe and slippers walked into the room with a furled brow. He was tall and very distinguished even in his pajamas. There was a bit of gray at his temples and throughout his beard, but he had Hashim's bearing. I knew instantly that this was their father. He looked cautiously at me before he addressed his daughter. "Sefa?" he asked, but I didn't understand anything else that he uttered.

Sefa turned. "Abba," she replied with a smile. She walked quickly to him and embraced him. Yep, that was definitely her dad. He released her and kissed her cheeks and looked her over like he was the proudest parent in the world. They spoke briefly and then Sefa took his hand and led him toward me. "Abba, this is Caroline. Caroline, this is our father, Rana Emir," Sefa said proudly, smiling her winning smile. She was proud to call him father and proud to call me sister.

He blinked and nodded taking in the information. I'm sure Ecrin had already given him an earful. He put out his hand in greeting; I did the same, but instead of shaking it, he took my hand in both of his protectively. I looked into his dark brown eyes. They weren't the same color as either of his children's. They were intent and focused, though, just like theirs. The Emirs were all very intense. He lifted his chin slightly as he spoke to me. "Ecrin has told me of your marriage to Hashim. I look forward to knowing you. Our son has made his choice, and we accept it. You are most welcome here, Caroline." He gave a friendly smile, and the skin around his eyes crinkled. He was a man who was accustomed to smiling.

I'm sure my mouth was gaping. This was nothing like what I expected. I expected more hostility. I expected to be held captive in a room and forced to wait in solitude for Hashim. "Thank you, sir," I said, but I couldn't find my voice. He could sense my apprehension and exhaustion.

"I have many questions, but they can wait. You will need to rest after such a long journey. Fatma will be here any moment to prepare a meal. You may tell her whatever you might need."

"Thank you, sir," I said, again, and this time, my voice returned.

He smiled down at me and it was easy to smile back at him. "Please call me Rana, and in time perhaps you will come to call me Abba as well."

He looked toward the coffee pot on the counter. It had clicked on just before. The smell of coffee permeated the kitchen and I was instantly drawn to it and then just as suddenly repelled by it. I jerked my hand away from Rana and jumped from the barstool. I thrust myself past Sefa and leaned over the kitchen sink. I vomited and heaved and spat. *Way to make a first impression, C.* I was so embarrassed. I ran some water into my hands and drank directly from them. I splashed the cool water across my face. Sefa dampened a washcloth under the water and wrung it out before she handed it to me.

Tears had begun falling, too. I let out a little sob. I felt horrible physically, mentally, and emotionally. I was a complete wreck. "Let me get you settled," she said and walked me up the stairs. "Abba, please bring her bags from the foyer. I will put her in Hashim's room." Sefa brought me through the bedroom to the bathroom. She began running water in a large tub and set out shampoo and soap and towels. "Do you need anything else?"

"Please apologize to Rana. I'm so embarrassed."

"He will understand." Sefa's eyes were so sincere and concerned for me. I tried to smile, but it didn't work. "I'll be downstairs if you need anything."

I nodded. "I think I may try to sleep some, if that's okay with you."

"Sure thing," she said and closed the door behind her.

The hot bath was welcomed. I hadn't bathed in at least two days and I couldn't remember when I'd last washed my hair. I wrapped my head in a towel and opened my bag. There, on top, lay Hashim's computer. I placed it gently on the end of the counter. Under that was my robe and clothes from Montgomery. I found my pajamas and hoodie and dressed. The closet was not as large as the one in Miami, but it was spacious enough and Hashim's clothes hung neatly. His t-shirts were folded and stacked next to his shorts. His socks and underwear were in the drawers below that. His shoes were placed in a row along the floor of the closet. He was here, but he wasn't. I didn't want to linger in the closet. It was too hard to see all of Hashim's belongings and imagine him wearing them. I tossed my bags onto the floor and shut the door. I would deal with the job of unpacking later. I looked around the room and the décor reflected the modern downstairs. The large bed took up most of the room. It was on a platform that looked like it was suspended from the wall. The wall of windows extended from floor to ceiling with long curtains to keep out the sun. I closed them all and the room was dark as night. I collapsed into a heap in the center of the bed and prayed until I fell asleep.

When I woke up, I stretched and yawned. I hadn't slept so hard that I didn't remember where I was; that had to be a first. There were two other rooms upstairs. Sefa's things were in one, and the other was obviously a guestroom. I wasn't sure if I should be reintroduced in pajamas, so I dressed and went downstairs.

A woman stood in the kitchen. She was wearing a long skirt, a long-sleeved knit top, and a hijab. She looked up and smiled. Her dark eyes were bright and welcoming. I couldn't tell how old she was, but her face was smooth. I would suspect she was in her mid to late twenties.

"Good afternoon," she said.

"Hello," I said.

"I am Fatma," she said clearly in accented English.

"I'm Caroline. Where is everyone?"

"They are out. Ecrin and Rana have business and Sefa has gone to the mall. She will return soon. They have asked me to watch after you. What may I get you?"

I shrugged. I still didn't have much appetite, but I knew I needed to eat. "What do you have?" She opened the fridge and began telling me everything available. She then opened the pantry. "Would you happen to have any ginger?" I asked. "I think ginger tea should settle my stomach so I can eat."

"Are you ill?" Fatma asked concerned.

"No," I said dismissively. I didn't need to get into the particulars with this stranger. I was heartsick and was now in a strange country, surrounded by strangers, and would have to wait out my time here, alone, until Hashim returned or sent for me.

"One moment," she said as she turned and began preparing the tea. She put on a kettle to boil. "We have dried ginger, no fresh, but I can make a tea from that. Honey?" she asked.

"Sure," I said, looking out over the skyline and the bright, blue afternoon sky. My eyes pricked with tears and I was instantly weighted by the vast distance between us. *God, please, keep him safe. Be with us while we are apart from one another. I can't do this, Lord; I don't have the strength.*

"For you," Fatma said, handing me the mug of steaming ginger tea.

I thanked her and sipped the tea. It was delicious. She smiled knowing that it pleased me. "You are Hashim's wife?" she asked.

"Yes. You know him?"

She smiled broadly. "Yes, I know Hashim." There was something telling in her eyes, and I didn't like the familiarity with which she said his name. She read my expression and sensed my uneasiness. She worked for this family; surely, she knew him. Why was I so jealous? Fatma smiled and blinked her long lashes.

"No misunderstandings, he is my cousin," she laughed. "Rana is my mother's brother. I work here when they are in residence; I attend the university. I have an apartment on campus."

"What are you studying?"

"I will soon be a daya."

"What is that?" I asked.

"A midwife," she said proudly.

"Convenient," I said wryly. I didn't plan to be here that long to need one, and I sure as hell didn't plan on delivering my child anywhere near Ecrin. Sefa would agree to take me somewhere else. She would help me find a way to get back to the U.S. and back to Hashim.

Fatma looked at me, her dark eyes sparkled with knowing. She had a pretty smile, but when her face was all that was visible, it was hard to tell what other beauty may lie underneath her dark covering. "Ah, yes, of course," she said.

She made no other comment but went to work making me a plate of food. She spread hummus over a piece of flatbread. She dolloped some yogurt onto the plate and drizzled it lightly with honey, alongside a few nuts and pieces of dried fruit. It was just what I needed, the combination of savory and sweet, crunchy and soft. Sefa came in while I was eating. She was smiling and carrying a few bags. She'd been shopping. "Choti Behan, I'm glad you are awake. How did you sleep?" I shrugged. She kissed my cheek before she placed the bags on the sofa. "Good, Fatma, thank you for feeding her. When you're finished eating, we'll swim." She loosened a light scarf from around her neck.

"Have you heard from Dawes?" I asked.

She shook her head. "No. I do not expect to and you shouldn't either. They will come when they can come. Please do not make a habit of asking me."

"But how long?" I asked impatiently.

"I have no idea, but we will make the best of the time we have here waiting. Today, we start by swimming," she said placidly. She didn't like the situation any more than I did, but she was better at dealing with it.

"Does Ecrin know I'm here?" I asked.

Fatma glanced at Sefa. I should have noticed the resemblance. They had a similar tilt to their eyebrows and curve to their lips. "Yes."

"What was her response?" I asked. Rana's welcoming that morning felt sincere, but I didn't know what power he would have to control his wife or her reactions when she found out I was carrying their grandchild. A wave of fear washed over me.

"She will welcome you here, Caroline. Be assured; Abba will see to it," she said confidently.

"Does she know?" I asked.

Sefa diverted her eyes and smirked. "Yes, as a matter of fact she does."

"How pleasant was it for you to tell her?"

"Exceedingly," she sighed. "You have given me one of the greatest gifts. Thank you for getting *knocked up* by my brother," she said, using the common American slang and she and Fatma laughed together at my expense. I glared at her. I saw no humor in it at all. "Fatma, come swimming with us. They won't be home for hours. Caroline and I will help you cook later."

I looked at them, surprised. How could Fatma swim in a hijab? I changed clothes and rode the elevator to the roof with them. The pool was completely enclosed by high, tinted glass walls and overlooked the city. We were in our own private area, unseen by the rest of the world. Fatma went into a small changing room and came out wearing a bikini more revealing than mine. I was shocked. Her hair was also uncovered and in a long braid. She was just as beautiful as Sefa.

"I'm sorry, but how can you wear that at the pool and are completely covered in the house?" I sounded so ignorant to myself.

Sefa and Fatma laughed. "It is okay, Caroline. I wear modest clothes because I do not wish to be seen by men or in mixed company, but in the presence of women or with men with whom I am in close relation, I may wear whatever I wish to wear. This is a private pool, so there is no risk of me being seen."

"Oh, okay. I was just surprised."

We swam for an hour. It felt great. Sefa said that she wanted me to swim at least an hour a day for exercise, laps and treading water. I didn't disagree with her. I had a feeling that between my pediatrician sister-in-law and now my midwife-in-training cousin-by-marriage, I would be their Guinea pig project.

I dressed and fixed my hair and knew that my next encounter would most likely be with Ecrin. I took a deep breath and braced myself for the worst. Sefa, Fatma, and I cooked dinner. Well, they cooked and I watched because they knew what we were having and I didn't recognize all of the ingredients. Fatma excused herself and left before Ecrin and Rana returned home. She said that she needed to study and prepare for class tomorrow, but I suspected she knew the evening might not be as pleasant as Sefa hoped. Ecrin and Rana arrived just in time for supper. Rana smiled and asked if I had rested adequately. Ecrin just looked at me; her expression was politely passive. I closed my eyes and silently prayed. We sat and ate in awkward silence.

When everyone was finished eating, Sefa rose from the table. I picked up her plate and took both of our plates to the sink. I began rinsing them and loading the dishwasher. Ecrin eyed her husband. "Rana, I wish to speak with Caroline, alone." I looked up from the dishes; Ecrin was looking directly at her husband. I then looked at Sefa and then to Rana. My stomach tightened. It would go down like this. I took a deep breath and tried to relax. I would be as respectful as possible, but I was not going to let her mistreat me or say ugly things about Hashim.

Rana looked at me with kind eyes. "I will be in the study. Please let me know if there is anything you need, Caroline."

"Yes, sir," I said and focused unnecessarily on the plate I was rinsing.

"Caroline, would you please join me. Sefa can see to that." Ecrin stood from the table and walked the few steps into the living room.

I looked to Sefa and she patted my hand encouragingly. Ecrin sat tall and graceful in the low, white chair. Her dark skin and dark hair contrasted in the modern room. I sat across from her in an identical chair. Her eyes were intently focused on me. I had no idea how this conversation would go. I took a deep breath to settle myself. Ecrin began and did not waste her breath on pleasantries. She jumped right into the heart of the matter. "Sefa tells me that you are with child."

"Yes, ma'am, that's correct." I held her gaze but not in a challenging way. Her eyes were captivatingly beautiful.

"You claim it is my son's."

I couldn't help but smile at that. "It is."

"You expect me to believe you?"

"No, ma'am, but it's the truth. I've never been with anyone else, so barring immaculate conception, he's the only option." I knew I was being sarcastic, but I didn't feel like I owed her any explanation. She had rejected me from the beginning, why were we even having this conversation?

"He took your virginity, how quaint." From the look on her face, it was anything but *quaint*. I couldn't tell if she were disappointed in him or in me at that moment.

I wanted to defend Hashim's choice. Maybe I was defending my own. My eyes pricked. She could see how vulnerable I was without him. I was putting up a brave front, but there were so many gaps in my veneer. "It didn't happen like that. He married me first. He did it to protect me, the marrying part. Neither of us expected this, but then again, my Aunt June told me all the time that sex makes babies. It wasn't like I hadn't been warned," I laughed and caught myself. *Not cool, C. Keep it together.*

She blinked and kept herself perfectly composed. "How old are you, Caroline?" Her voice was almost softened.

"Twenty. I'll be twenty-one just after the baby comes."

She gave a nod, considering. "Rana has made his decision clear, therefore, I must honor it. You are welcomed here while you await Hashim."

My mouth gaped open. I didn't believe she'd just said *you* and *welcomed* in the same sentence regarding me. "I'm sorry, Ecrin, but I have a hard time believing that after Miami."

She looked down and pursed her lips. She took in a deep breath and let it out through her nose. Once she had regained her composure, she continued. "You did not find me at my best, there. The news of your marriage to my son came as a great surprise. As you can imagine, a mother has certain expectations of her children and a hasty marriage is not one of them. Now, comes the news of a child. This, too, comes as a surprise."

"To all of us," I said in a low voice. The confession was genuine.

"What do your parents say about your marriage to Hashim?"

"Nothing. My daddy died when I was seventeen and Momma passed away the day after we were married. She had dementia and didn't even know me, so neither of them had much to say on the subject." The sarcasm came so easily.

"Do you have any siblings?"

"Yes, ma'am. My older brother is in the Marines; he's currently deployed in Afghanistan."

Ecrin only nodded once. "How long do you plan to be here?"

I shrugged. "I don't know. Hashim and Dawes have work to do, and it wasn't safe for me to go home or be alone in Miami. He thought I would be safest here; Sefa and Dawes agreed."

"It must be terribly dangerous if he thought Miami was unsafe for you."

I shrugged, again; I had no idea. "I have nothing to compare it to," I said as I rubbed Hashim's wedding band on my index finger reflexively. Ecrin's eyes fell onto my hand; she noticed my fidgeting, so I tucked my hands under my thighs. I didn't like the way she was examining me. I blinked but I didn't divert my gaze from hers. I refused to lose it in front of her.

She stared at me for a few seconds more before she asked, "Will you be comfortable in Hashim's room?" I nodded. "Please be at home, here."

"Thank you, but what exactly does that mean?" I asked.

She furled her brow, then, and gazed out the large, glass window, like maybe the answers lay over the lights of the darkened city. "Caroline, Rana has welcomed you, has he not?" Her voice was so stern like that should be enough.

"Yes, ma'am." My eyes followed hers like maybe I could find the answers there, too.

"You are welcomed into this family, now. This is your home as long as you need. We will treat you as one of our own children." I realized then that she was looking at me, again. I swallowed as I considered her words. I wasn't sure how I should take them. I didn't much like the way she had treated her children in my presence, and I wasn't sure if that allowed me to argue with her as Sefa did. I would've never spoken to my mother with such disrespect. "Caroline, I can understand your hesitation; Miami was unpleasant for both of us. Perhaps we can find a position of neutrality here."

For the first time, I could see why she and Rana were such effective negotiators. I tentatively agreed. "I think I can give that a try."

She seemed satisfied with that and gave a pensive smile. Ecrin then folded her hands on her knees. "You will need a physician while you are here. You will also need clothes. With your consent, I will have Sefa arrange an appointment for you. As soon as you need new clothes, I will see to that personally."

"Thank you, Ecrin," I said sincerely. She looked as though she were about to get up and dismiss me from our conversation. "Ecrin," I began, "may I ask you a question?"

She composed herself in the chair to receive my question. "What is it?"

"What made you change your mind, Rana or the fact that I'm pregnant?"

She offered me a knowing smile. She knew I was onto her and that I didn't quite trust her sincerity. "Even before you arrived, Rana asked me to reconsider my initial reaction to you. He suggested that I make an effort to make amends when I next saw you or Hashim. He also feared that in the event your union produced children, we might never have the opportunity to meet them. That would be most unfortunate for a child not to know his or her grandparents and for the grandparents to never know their grandchild. When Sefa told us this morning about the child, and since I learned more about your situation, I had to admit that my harshness was not completely warranted. So, to answer your question, it was a combination of things."

"Thank you for being honest with me. I plan to make the best of my time here. I don't want to be a burden."

Ecrin rose then, but the look she gave me was very different from the way she'd looked at me in Miami. Her demeanor was calm and for the first time, I felt slightly at ease in her presence.

CHAPTER 32.5

The discerning heart seeks knowledge,
but the mouth of a fool feeds on folly.

– Proverbs 15:14

I met Marshall the following day. He was eager to speak with me and impatient to come to some kind of agreement on behalf of the people for whom he represented. He seemed to be concealing his desperation as though he were under duress himself.

"Let's start with what we already know."

"And what would that be?" I asked.

"You know how to interpret those relays. You said you couldn't, but you can."

"I said that I could gather bits and pieces in a pattern," I clarified.

He chuckled without mirth. "You're a horrible liar, Emir. I wish you'd stop playing games and wasting time. You know what they want."

"I will not reveal what I know until I know with whom I am working. Full disclosure. In the wrong hands, this could be deadly. In the right hands, if there is such a thing, it could be too powerful. I do not wish to be caught in the middle of it."

"I was afraid you would say something like that. Even if I knew all the parties involved, I don't have permission to give you that kind of information. I do know that they want a way to trace it back to the source and extinguish it or use for their own benefit."

"Well, then, I think we come to an impasse. I will agree to stay here, in Miami, until your employers come to some sort of agreement or grow desperate enough to satisfy my condition. I have never made this request before, but then again, I have never dealt with anything this sensitive. Honestly, I do not wish to be involved. In the meantime, I will work on other projects."

"Is it true you're developing facial recognition technology for interpretation?"

I had only revealed that in one meeting to one committee at the Pentagon; Caroline did not even know. Someone was behind this; my thoughts instantly went to Kennedy. I would not give Marshall the satisfaction of knowing anything. I stood from the table in the small restaurant where we had agreed to meet. Marshall looked sullen. "You know they'll find a way to get to you. They'll find your weakness."

"How had they found yours, or did you go willingly into the pit of hell?"

I suspected that there were at least six men there watching me. I even suspected a woman at the bar; she was a plant to distract me. My gaze lingered as I slowly passed her; she was attractive in all the right ways. They definitely knew what I liked. I was doing it only for show, pretending to be interested. In another life, I might have stopped and introduced myself and offered to buy her a drink. Who was I kidding? I would have definitely stopped and done more than buy her a drink.

When I arrived back at the house, there was a package waiting for me. It was unmarked with no return address or postage.

"When did this arrive?" I asked Nita when she handed it to me.

"Soon after you left. It came by courier."

I opened the package. Inside was a cellphone that looked identical to mine. I turned it on and texted the only number listed in the contacts.

Received.

Aunt June, what a pleasant surprise.

I chuckled to myself. I may never live that down. **Any word on the delivery?**

Package arrived safely.

Met today. Will wait.

Be patient.

That was easy for him to say. I deleted the message and put the phone into my pocket. Without my laptop, I was unable to work right away. I inspected all of my equipment and decided, with some modifications, I could use the desktop in my parents' office. It was not ideal, but it was secure and would allow me to work for the time being. Converting systems was not my specialty, but without distraction, I would figure things out. I moved all of my equipment downstairs and began working.

In the days that followed, I was extremely productive. I ran and worked and ran and worked. A few nights I dreamed of Caroline and there was a nagging at the back of my mind every time I thought of her. Nagging had a negative connotation. Longing was a better description. Physically, I desired her more than I had ever desired any other woman. There was an aching, but I did not know if I should attribute that to regret or attraction. Mentally, I missed her candor and sense of humor. Emotionally, I refused to go there and avoided it. I could not afford to be vulnerable.

The truly nagging thought was about the leaks in Kennedy's security and Marshall's comment. I considered everyone on the committee and decided to begin my own investigation into possible connections to Marshall. Global Securities was the name of the company that Marshall represented. I suspected that it was just the front for many other companies, but it was the only place I had to start. I also began investigating the committee members who I had met personally at the Pentagon. Four of the seven members were military; three were retired, but by the way they dressed, they were not merely living off of their military retirement. Slowly, I began delving into the background of Global Securities and possible connections to the two. One retired general piqued my interest. He was the only member who had served on the same three committees with Kennedy. They were not openly chummy, but why would they be in that setting?

I made significant strides toward my program. It was easier than I thought to resume my natural work routine when there were no distractions. Thankfully,

Nita did not question me when I moved into the guestroom permanently. She cooked for me and kept my space tidy. She showed no pity, but I suspected she empathized with me; the vacancy had the shape of Caroline.

I could not afford the risk contacting my wife directly, so I received fragmented updates. Dawes sent one and two-word encryptions. He was more creative than I thought. He sent broken heart emojis and twice sent the following comments: **She still hates you** and **Don't waste your breath.**

My mother, though, was incredibly intuitive. She called, as usual, but for the first time since I was a teenager, I answered her call immediately. She made no mention of Caroline. She said that it was pleasant weather there and the forecast looked promising. She asked when I would visit next and how my work was proceeding. She said that Father was pleased with my most recent decision and looked forward to the increased responsibility. He wanted her to thank me on his behalf for the unexpected gift. "He is most delighted," she said. I knew from the tone of her voice that Rana had accepted everything about Caroline, and together, they were making her feel welcomed. The *increased responsibility* I took to mean they knew of her pregnancy, and that Father saw it as a gift. I was happy for Caroline that someone, besides Sefa, did.

CHAPTER 33

From the time we arrived, Sefa kept me busy. We swam daily and played tourist. She took me to museums and galleries. She took me to the beach and to the many gardens and fountains. A few times she took me to the theater and the opera house. I loved the music; the acoustics were amazing. Busy was better than overwhelmed and exceedingly better than depressed. Sefa was my activities director; Fatma was my dietician and pregnancy yoga instructor. Fatma also taught me to cook Hashim's favorite foods. Rana and Ecrin took to teaching me Urdu which was what they mostly spoke when they were together. Each evening at supper, Rana would teach me a new phrase. Gradually, I began to pick up their common words and phrases. I could tell, though, when Ecrin disagreed with Sefa because she would revert back to her native Turkish. I couldn't keep up when she made the shift.

I asked Sefa if I could go to the library to get some books about pregnancy and childbirth and refresh my knowledge of infants. It had been quite some time since I'd studied infancy and early childhood development. I felt like it was important for me to brush up on that since I'd focused so much of the past few years on the elderly and aging. Instead of the library, she took me to the bookstore, and we pretty much bought out the entire section.

My obstetrician was Dr. Mohamed. He was a middle-aged gentleman with a balding head and kind eyes. He was one of the leading physicians in his field. I thought it was overkill since this was not a high-risk pregnancy, but Sefa and Ecrin insisted that they only wanted the best for me. I didn't argue; after all, they were paying the bills. As much fun as Sefa provided, I grew weary of her constant attention. I just wanted to be alone sometimes, but I didn't want to seem rude or ungrateful. After a great deal of discussion, I finally convinced her to offer her services elsewhere. She happily began working a few mornings a week at a clinic near their apartment. It benefited us both to be separated for portions of the day.

Since leaving home, I had missed Halloween and Thanksgiving, and Christmas was rapidly approaching. I bought a tiny, little Christmas tree with ornaments the size of my thumbnail for the bedroom. I also constructed a nativity scene with figurines from the thrift store. I found a plastic camel for the wise men who were actually Halo action figures. Their gifts were odd pieces of jewelry. Baby Jesus had blond hair until I colored his head with a black Sharpie and dotted his blue eyes with the same marker. I wrapped him in gauze from the first aid kit and imagined my baby would have the same coloring. Hashim's dark hair and eyes would prevail.

The sun shone brightly outside every day and it rarely rained. I missed the seasons and cold fronts and frost on my windshield in the mornings. I missed the possibility of snow and road closures. I missed flannel shirts and fuzzy socks and the few times a year we were able to play outside in the snow. As much as I loved Christmas, I was somewhat of a purist. I hated when stores started putting up Christmas decorations before Halloween or the radio played Christmas music before Thanksgiving. I liked to celebrate each holiday individually.

One afternoon, I was looking through a magazine and came across a pattern for cutting out snowflakes. I hadn't done that in forever, and I admit that I got carried away and made about thirty snowflakes. I taped them to the windows in my bedroom so that when the sun was full, they cast snowflake-shaped shadows all over my bed and floor. I knew it was childish, but the simplicity made me smile.

I thought about how to get a card to Billy. I needed to tell him so much, and yet, I wasn't sure what I was allowed to say. I wondered if he was wondering about me. I wondered if he knew about Krissa. All of these thoughts sent my emotions toward dark places, so I quickly shook them off the best I could and decided not to think of them anymore. It made me hurt and have regret; my emotions were easier to deal with when I put them to the side and sifted them out one at a time.

CHAPTER 33.5

My child, pay attention to what I say. Listen carefully to my words. Don't lose sight of them. Let them penetrate deep into your heart, for they bring life to those who find them, and healing to their whole body.

– Proverbs 4:20-22

I had waited weeks to hear back from Marshall. He called a couple of times, but I stood firm on my desire for full disclosure. Kennedy called me once as well. It was his responsibility to check in with me periodically. We were under no deadlines, but he was a friendly handler who made friendly contact even during the down times. He asked about Dubai.

"That plan did not work out as I had hoped. Caroline left on her own accord," I confessed.

"Really? I'm surprised." I suspected he was not surprised at all. I was also sure that Dawes' report eluded to as much. "She seemed pretty attached. I'm sorry to hear it." His voice was the same and his words were the same, but my suspicion of him clouded his sincerity. I doubted he was sorry to hear it at all. "Look, I'm going to be out of town for the holidays, but if you need me, you know you can reach me anytime," he said.

The holidays, I thought. "Thank you, Kennedy. I hope to have something for the committee after the first of the year." That made a genuine smile return to his voice. "Happy Holidays, Emir. I hope it's not too lonely for you." His tone was suggestive like I would waste no time finding someone else, but my decision was already made.

I departed Christmas Eve and arrived Christmas morning. She had asked me on our wedding day if I even celebrated Christmas. This year, I would for the first time. Our anticipated reunion would be celebration enough for me, but I had no idea what an appropriate gift would be for Caroline. She would expect nothing and ask for very little. Would my arrival be enough? As I rode the elevator to our apartment, I was suddenly nervous and unsure of her response to me. How would she receive me? It had been weeks with very little correspondence. Father made her welcomed, but I hoped things were genuinely better with my mother. I had sent word through Dawes this time. I wondered if Sefa would relay the information or allow it to be a surprise.

My question was answered almost immediately. I opened the door to the apartment; it was mid-morning. I heard Caroline singing along to a Christmas carol on her headphones. I looked around the room; no one was there with her. I watched her for a few moments. She was, of course, barefoot, standing at the stove, cooking. She wore a long, knit top and leggings. Her hair was longer and braided loosely in a French braid. She was in her own little world. When she turned to reach for a bottle from the spice rack, I noticed the change in her profile. It had barely been more than a month since I had seen her and already she was altered: the swells of her breasts and the curves of her hips and the little paunch below her navel. She caught sight of me from the corner of her eye and turned fully to face me. Her mouth gaped slightly and she blinked disbelievingly. "Hashim!" She pulled her earphones from her ears and smiled and sighed, "Sefa said you'd come."

I walked toward her, but she suddenly turned from me. I stopped and was relieved that she had only turned to adjust the stove and remove the pan from the heat. I was close enough to her then that she could reach out and embrace me. I took her face in my hands and looked into her happy eyes. "Merry Christmas," I whispered just before I kissed her.

She smiled beneath my lips. "It is, now," she whispered in reply. I held her for a long time, taking in her scent and the feel of her hair beneath my lips. "I've missed you, Hashim," she said.

"I have missed you, too." She exhaled at that and moved in closer. "Where is everyone?" I asked.

"They're out. They usually come home early afternoon. Are you hungry?"

"What are you cooking?"

"Eggs; I can make more."

"I am not hungry." Other basic needs had taken over; hunger was the least of my desires. "Go ahead, eat."

She turned back to the stove, but I kept my arms around her. Now that I had her close to me, I wanted nothing more than to touch her. She plated the eggs and poured herself a glass of juice from the fridge. It was awkward walking so close to her, but she only giggled once when I had to move out of her way. We walked together to the bar where she sat on a stool and ate while I watched her.

"Stop it," she blushed. "You're making me feel self-conscious."

I dismissed her demand and smiled. "Hurry up and eat so I can do more than *look* at you." She blushed and flushed and could hardly swallow. She took a big gulp of juice.

I noticed my ring on her right index finger. "Have you worn this the entire time?" I asked.

She nodded. "Except when I swim."

"I thought for sure it would be hanging around your neck, again." She lowered he eyes and shook her head hesitantly. I did not like her diverting her eyes from me, so I gently lifted her chin to look at me. "What?"

"I thought about it, but you aren't dead, so I decided to wear it. It reminds me to think of you and pray for you, and especially, to hope for your return. I don't want to ever wear it around my neck again." She rubbed it distractedly with her thumb like it was something she did often.

"May I?" I asked and she allowed me to remove it, but then she took it from my fingers.

"May I?" she asked and took my left hand and replaced it on my ring finger. "I give you this ring as a symbol of my love." She smiled, playfully, repeating the words of our marriage vows. I scooped her up into my arms and held her closely, kissing every part of her that I could reach. I carried her to the sofa and she leaned into me, willingly. As I kissed her, I loosened her braid and ran my fingers through her hair. She straddled her legs over me and pressed me down onto the sofa. My hands were all over her, but I was frustrated by the long shirt and the leggings. I could only feel fabric, no skin.

She managed to untuck my shirt and rub her hands over my torso. "Let's go upstairs," she suggested. "I'll die if your parents come in and find us making out on the sofa." She didn't have to ask twice. I grabbed my bag and allowed her to pull me by the hand toward my room. I barely had time to shut the door before she had turned to kiss me. *Kiss* was an understatement. Her kisses came in a barrage and her hands were everywhere: removing my jacket, unbuckling my belt, and unbuttoning my shirt.

I was just as impatient for her as she was for me. I pulled her shirt over her head and took in a quick breath. Her breasts were full and round. I let my hand follow her curves all the way to her waist and then down to her thighs. She laughed and lowered her eyes to follow my hands.

"Crazy, right?" she asked.

"You are so different."

"Too different?" She waited to read my reaction. I could feel her pulling slightly away from me.

"No," I said, "I want to rediscover how you feel." She eased back into my touch then.

An hour later, she slid from the bed to go to the bathroom. She was tanned and toned and beautifully sculpted. While she was in the bathroom, I realized the changes she had made to my bedroom. There were snowflakes everywhere and a tiny Christmas tree in the corner, decorated with miniature ornaments. I had found her singing Christmas carols in the kitchen, but the display of toys I guessed was a nativity scene. I shook my head and smiled. She was determined to celebrate her savior's birth even amid a household of non-believers. There were no gifts under her tree. I wondered if she had given gifts to my family.

She returned, cuddled next to me, and put her hand on my chest. "They'll be home soon," she said. "I think it would be better if we were downstairs when they arrived."

"Why would that be better?" I asked. "It is not better for me."

She gave me a playful shove. "Everyone here holds modesty in high regard. I don't want to offend anyone. Displays of affection seem to be only for the home, well, in the case of this home, the bedroom. Maybe because your parents are the only couple, here, they rarely hold hands or kiss or hug in front of us."

I gave a low chuckle. "I have rarely seen my parents hold hands or kiss. They are respectful and kind with their words, but I would not describe them as affectionate."

"Besides, your mother has been better here with your father, and I would rather not provoke her by finding us in the bed together in the middle of the day."

"She's been better? What do you mean by that?"

"She's not hostile and she's not raised her voice once at me. She's been accepting of the baby. She's almost nice."

I laughed at that. "*Almost* nice?" I clarified. I could feel her smile. She combed through the hair of my chest with her fingertips.

"Hashim," she began, but then stopped herself.

I could tell that she had something on her mind. "What is it?"

She shook her head. "Nothing. Let's get dressed."

"You can ask or tell me anything. What is it?"

"We can talk about it later." She smiled sweetly and rolled over, out of the bed.

"Caroline, please tell me." I wrapped my arm around her, securing her to the side of the bed.

She turned back toward me and her words came out in a rush. "How much longer do I have to stay here? I miss you and I miss my home. I don't want to be impatient or ungrateful, but," her voice trailed off and tears welled in her eyes. She sniffed and blinked. "I don't want to have our baby in Dubai," she finally said.

I had no answer for her, and I knew my next words would wound her. I stroked her face and hair and drew her into me. "I am not here to take you home,

Caroline. I have no answers. I only came to wish you a Happy Christmas." *And retrieve my computer*, I thought. "A brief visit is the only thing I can give you for now."

She took a deep breath and sniffed again. She nodded. "I understand. How long can you stay?" she asked as she attempted to give me a smile.

"A week. I fly out on the second." She gave a quick nod and dressed like she had an important appointment.

***

I could tell she felt self-conscious about her changes, or maybe she was self-conscious about how much I touched her in my parents' presence. I cared not; I only saw power and felt her pull like she was her own planet aligning the rest of us around her. Even my mother bowed to her; it was magnificent to see. She was like an ancient fertility goddess with full breasts and I could understand why they were worshiped and revered. She was both voluptuous and alluring. I watched as she and Fatma cooked in the afternoon. They laughed and talked, and I watched the contrast of the two women, dark and light, covered and exposed, both smiling and commanding in the kitchen. My father smiled when he saw me with my wife. He spoke to Caroline in Urdu and she replied. It was a pleasant surprise, and I listened, proudly, as she and my father spoke.

After dinner the first evening, Father asked me to join him; he wished to speak with me alone. "Hashim, it is very good to see you. You look well."

"Yes, sir. Thank you for taking such good care of Caroline. I knew you would approve."

He humbly nodded his ascent. "She is a lovely girl, but so different. You know she does not belong here."

"Are you telling me that you wish for her to go?" I asked, unable to read his expression.

"No, she is welcome for as long as she likes, but I am concerned for her. She is not happy, not truly happy. She puts on a brave front for all of us, and I suspect has glimpses of happiness, but it is not easy for her to find joy here. She has bound herself to you and your absence is painful. I have never asked you before what dangers lie along your path, but I am concerned for you as well. You married her and sent her here for her own protection. Are you in danger as well?"

I thought for several moments about how to answer that. "Danger may not be the right word, Father. I am being heavily pursued, and I find myself wavering between their request and my hesitation to do what they ask."

"Is it immoral?" he asked.

"No."

"Is it unethical?"

"I think that would depend on the persons who have control of the information."

"Is it illegal?" His brow furled.

"Again, that would depend who made the law."

"Are you curious? Do you want to do the work they ask?"

I chuckled once. He knew me well. "You know that it is challenging for me to put something to the side once I have begun the work. My thoughts return to it often and I want to find a way to finish. The information is powerfully sensitive, and I have no idea who wields the power behind it. I am blind on both sides, so I refused to give them anything more until I know who is behind the request. In the meantime, they will use anyone and anything against me to bring me in. I am in no danger because they want the knowledge I have; unfortunately, they use those I care about to get to me."

"And you *care* for Caroline."

"Very much," I said firmly, but in a low tone.

My father's eyes were piercing, but not disapproving. He would leave me to my business, but I sensed his caution and his concern. He looked down at the wedding band on my hand. "As your father, I have examined myself often. I wonder if my life's path has allowed me to be the father you and Sefa needed. Have I done enough to guide you and influence your choices? Did I do enough to show you and teach you? There are times that I suffered the consequences of not making you the priority for much of your life. My work and the world's needs came before the needs of my children. You have been a man for some time now, and I have rarely if ever questioned you about the women in your life or the choices you have made regarding your work, but I need to know. Do you understand the responsibility of the vows you made?" he asked.

"Yes, sir."

His dark eyes were clear and focused on mine. "I could not bear to see that young woman injured in any way. You will be faithful to her? You will do right by her and the child?" My father had never spoken to me like this. He was not the serious one. He was never grave or commanding; that was Mother's role. Father had rarely ever challenged me, but I felt his remonstrance and his protection over Caroline. His careful eyes were examining me.

"Yes, sir," I replied again, but this time my voice was strong. "Had I known we would be in this situation, I would have avoided her, but from the beginning, there was something unusual and attractive about her. She was not easily ignored." I smiled at the memory.

Father smiled with me. "I understand. Your mother was much the same, still is for that matter."

"Which part? Attractive or not easily ignored?"

He laughed his hearty laugh and his dark eyes twinkled in their familiar way. "Both."

During my week with Caroline, we went to bed early and slept late. The only times we were apart were when she swam with Sefa or Fatma or when I ran. She said the morning sickness had mostly passed, but that smells occasionally sent her lurching over a sink or garbage can.

"Coffee, of all things. It's cruel. I love it, but now, the smell of it brewing is unbearable. I hope I can drink it after the baby comes. I miss it."

"Where is my computer?" I asked her a couple of days before I left.

"It's in the bottom drawer of your dresser."

"Do you have plenty of money?" I asked.

"Yes," she answered incredulously. "I haven't needed any of it. Your parents and Sefa have bought everything. They even let me get that tree," she said pointing to her little homage to Christmas.

"And the snowflakes?"

She shrugged and smiled shyly. "The weather never changes, here. I wanted it to feel like winter."

"It looks like you have been reading quite a bit," I said, gesturing to the stack of books next to the bed.

"Yeah, I want to know; I want to be prepared."

"What else do you want, Caroline?"

Her eyes flashed resentfully. "Why do you ask when you already know?" There was pain in her voice, masked in disdain, and she lowered her chin to divert her eyes. I pulled her closer towards me to comfort her, but she pushed herself away and sat up.

"I wish I could make you happy." My words were true.

"No, Hashim. You can't *make* me happy or miserable. That's on me and my attitude. Giving me what I want would please me, but it has no real bearing on my happiness or my joy. Not even you will have that power over me. I'm not miserable here, but I miss you. I'm not unhappy here, but I am homesick. I don't want to be alone when I have this baby. I want to be with you."

"Sefa," I began, but then caught her eyes.

"I didn't marry Sefa." Her words bit. "This isn't her child." Her eyes softened, then. "Please don't ask me again what I want or what I need. You take care of what you need to and don't return again until you plan to be with me and make a home together. Until then, please don't. It's too hard and I find myself missing you and you aren't even gone."

The threatening tears fell then in a torrent. I held her, but she refused to find complete comfort in my arms. She forced herself to be independent of me. I felt like I was the one grasping and clinging rather than her. My choices had altered her. My choices had hardened her. I pushed her hair from her face and wiped her tears with my thumbs. "Caroline, please. Please, do not hate me."

She pushed away from me. "Hate you? You think I hate you? To be so smart, you can be a real idiot. I don't *hate* you, Hashim, I love you. This pain is love not hate." She tapped the center of her chest like that was where she felt the worst. "It's what wakes me up in the morning and keeps me going. Love is the entire reason I left you; it's the entire reason I didn't get an abortion and a divorce in the same day. It's the whole reason I'm here." Her eyes changed, then. "Hashim, have you decided if you love me or am I just an easy fuck for the week?"

I released her. Her words stung like I had been stabbed. Frustration, anger, and the germinating seeds of bitterness rose in me like fire. I took her face in my hand, more forcefully than I had intended. Her eyes went wide in surprise and maybe a little fear. "Never, ever, speak of what is between us like that again. Do you understand me?" Fury laced every word. The way I was holding her, she was unable to reply. "You are the most important thing to me. *Love?* You want to know if I *love* you? What else could it be? I have never felt misery and pain and concern like this before." My words were laced with disdain and I felt a maniacal laugh rise to my throat. "I am driven half-mad with every thought of you. I am unable to sleep or eat or do anything without considering you. You have wormed your way into my heart and my mind, and I am completely possessed." I controlled the urge to squeeze understanding through my fingertips. I was venting my physical passions through tempered emotions and failing miserably. "You are a demon sent to torment me."

"I'm just a woman," she whispered and her eyes did something alluring.

"Are they not one in the same?" I muttered low through clenched teeth. She reached out and touched my forearm. My hand relaxed and her head lolled back as my hand moved slowly down her neck, finally resting over her heart. I could feel it beating in the palm of my hand. I put my other hand at the back of her neck and drew our foreheads together. "You are not a demon, Caroline. You are an angel sent to protect me, and I *love* you," I whispered before I kissed her.

CHAPTER 34

There is a contentment in knowing. There is security in hearing the words spoken aloud. Hashim loved me and I savored the kiss that followed. *He loved me.* I smiled all the way to my toes for the next two days and opened my body and my heart to him in new ways. I allowed him to claim me and heal the brokenness between us, even if it was just a temporary fix.

He held me tightly throughout the night; he would be leaving early for the airport. I hardly slept, wanting desperately to take in all that I could, storing it up until we were together, again. With great effort, he removed his ring and placed it back on my right index finger. He stroked my hair and kissed me gently on the cheek before he departed. I clutched my fist, holding fast to his ring. I had no power but to lie naked in the bed sobbing silently, listening intently for his footfalls on the stairs. The door shut solidly behind him, and I resigned myself to sleep.

***

At twenty-one weeks, another ultrasound was scheduled. Ecrin asked if she might come along. I was more comfortable with her; no, that was not the right word. I was cautiously relaxed in her presence, but I supposed I shouldn't deny her this experience. After all, she was this child's only grandmother. I lifted my shirt and exposed my belly. I had stopped wearing a two-piece bathing suit a while back because I didn't like the way the narrow waistband rolled under my protruding midsection. I knew quickly that I wasn't going to be a supermodel pregnant woman. I didn't just have a cute little baby bump; I was pregnant everywhere. I carried this baby in my breasts and in my hips, my thighs, and even in my feet. Now that my belly wasn't exposed to the sun, my light tan faded quickly, and it looked like a pale orb. I was surrounded by tall, beautifully dark-skinned people. I'm sure my belly was a stark contrast and surprise to Ecrin.

Everything looked normal on the ultrasound. The baby was healthy and all of its organs were exactly how they should be. "Would you like to know the gender of your child or would you prefer to be surprised?" the tech asked after she'd covered all of the important things.

I looked to Sefa and Ecrin. "I would like to know; would you?"

Sefa's smile was radiant. "Of course; that's why we're here."

I looked up at Ecrin. "And you?" She arched her eyebrow and gave a quick nod. She hadn't spoken a word since we entered the small examining room.

The technician resumed her work and found proof of the baby's gender. I didn't need her words. I could see proof as easily as everyone else. "A girl," she said sweetly.

I think my response would have been the same regardless. I was content with either a boy or a girl, but having it confirmed made the baby inside of me more real, more tangible. Having checked all of her vital organs, the tech could now show us the more fun aspects of my baby. She switched to 3D ultrasound, and I watched the monitor closely. The tech scrolled over the baby's hands and feet and stayed a long time on her face, showing us the details of her nose and mouth. My baby girl yawned and stretched and showed off for the camera. She then put her hand over her face and rolled over like she'd had enough. We were presented with about twenty prints and I was thankful to have them. I couldn't find the other ultrasound pictures anywhere. We must have left them in Miami.

"Are you thinking of names?" Sefa asked as she drove us home.

"Not really," I confessed. I was actually thinking about Hashim and how I missed him and wished that he was there with me. I was hoping to have some input from him on the matter. Days had turned into weeks and weeks had turned into months and still, Hashim had not returned. I stroked my belly absentmindedly and stared out the window. I was happy; really, I was. I was happy at the news and seeing my healthy baby girl, but there was always something missing and nagging at the back of my mind.

We stopped and ate at a small café. The café was conveniently located near a posh baby boutique, and Sefa was determined to buy her niece's first outfit. I had a feeling it would be the first of many firsts: first outfit, first shoes, first designer dress, first puppy, first pony, first car. Sefa was a mess with excitement and Ecrin wasn't too far behind her; although more reserved, she seemed pleased as well. I realized that it was the first time the two of them found no reason to disagree. They both enjoyed shopping and now had a unified purpose. This baby would want for nothing. I was relieved that their tastes were simple when it came to baby items. Nothing they liked was garish or Pepto-pink. They were practical and tasteful. They agreed on a pair of booties with yellow trim and a gown with pale yellow rose petals, made from the softest cotton I had ever felt. It was an elegant outfit.

"How big were your babies?" I asked Ecrin on the way home.

Ecrin blinked, surprised that I'd asked her a question directly. "Sefa was nine-and-a-half pounds and Hashim was ten pounds, two ounces."

"Wow! Those are big babies."

"What did you weigh at birth?" Sefa asked.

"Six pounds, three ounces, I think, but I was a couple of weeks early."

***

A few weeks later, Sefa drove me to the American consulate to begin the registration process for my unborn child. United Arab Emirates offered no dual citizenship for babies born in their country. I had been granted an extended visa at Rana's request, but my child would be an American citizen at birth. The day was sunny and bright as we rode in the convertible. It was steadily getting warmer and I understood that the summers would be hot and unpleasant. This Mercedes was not in my original top five, but I think I might need to reconsider my original list; the BRZ no longer ranked as highly as it once did.

The consulate was well-guarded by men in Marine uniforms; I instantly thought of Billy. I wondered what he might think about my marriage to Hashim. He'd probably be pissed, but there wasn't anything he could do about it. Maybe I could figure out how to get a message to him while I was there. The receptionist was friendly and directed me to the proper department. She asked that Sefa remain in the lobby. I filled out a bunch of paperwork and showed them my passport and driver's license and birth certificate about fifteen times. They even wanted to see my marriage certificate. I would have to come back with the baby after she was born to take a picture for her passport.

When that was all finished, I returned to the receptionist and asked if there was some way I could send a message to my brother who was serving in the Marines. The receptionist smiled and directed me toward a different department; she again asked that Sefa remain behind. I looked over my shoulder apologetically. I guessed Sefa couldn't go past the receptionist since she wasn't an American citizen. I was sent through several stations before I was introduced to a young woman in a Marine uniform. Her hair was up in a tight bun and she wore a serious expression. She keyed in several lines of text and then furled her brow.

"Mrs. Emir, if you would please follow me," she said as she rose from the desk. I followed her into another office. "Please wait here," she instructed and closed the door as she departed. The desk plaque read, *Lt. Col. Henderson.* I stood waiting. In a few minutes a woman in her forties entered the room.

"Mrs. Emir, I am Lt. Col. Henderson. Please, have a seat. My assistant tells me you have made an inquiry regarding your brother."

"Yes, ma'am. I've been away from home and I left no forwarding address. I wanted to get a message to him. I thought since I was here, and with there being so many Marines, I might as well check-in with him.

The lieutenant colonel opened her computer screen and I guessed she was searching for Billy's information. "When did you last have contact with your brother?"

"October. He was deployed in October."

She nodded and then I read her eyes. It was only a hint, but it was the same look her assistant had given just before she brought me in here. I could sense bad news was coming. When she took a deep breath, I knew it was bad. "Mrs. Emir, I hate to be the one to have to tell you, but your brother's unit was

320

attacked." She paused to read my expression. I blinked and swallowed. Her words didn't quite register.

"Attacked?" I asked.

"One of the vehicles in the caravan hit an IED. There were no survivors."

"No survivors," I repeated. She shook her head. "Billy's dead?"

"Killed in the line of duty."

I leaned forward and hugged myself. I couldn't breathe and I started shaking. When the lack of oxygen became uncomfortable, I breathed slowly, in and out, shakily. He was gone; Billy was gone. The baby moved and squirmed inside me. She didn't like this news, either.

"When?" I asked. My voice was faint and far away.

"January 30th. We tried to notify you. We were finally able to contact the mother of his child, Jennifer Martin. They made the arrangements for his remains."

My heart sank for Zinnia and Jen. I wondered if they were looking for me. I wondered if anyone was looking for me. I had been gone for nearly six months, and I hadn't seen Hashim since January. It didn't feel like there was enough air circulating in the small office. *Breathe, C. Don't lose it.* I leaned my head against the side of the lieutenant colonel's desk and tried to take deep breaths.

"Mrs. Emir, are you alright?" she asked.

I shook my head. I was definitely not alright. I heard her get up and open her office door. When she returned, she offered me some water. Why did everyone offer me water like it could fix anything? I took the cup from her hand but mine was shaking so badly that I couldn't hold it. I put my head back on the desk; my head didn't spin as much when it was down. A huge teardrop fell onto the floor. I watched it as though it fell in slow motion. It plopped and pooled onto the tile. Another fell and another. Pretty soon there was a small puddle next to my sandaled foot. I wasn't sobbing, but I was definitely crying harder than I had in a while.

Loneliness crept over me, that same feeling of isolation. I was alone. Except for Zinnia, I had no blood relatives left on the entire planet. My heart ached for connection; it ached for the feeling of belonging. I had yet to find that place of peace with Hashim. Then, as if on cue, my belly writhed and my baby kicked and moved. She didn't move suddenly or with any great force. It was like she was comforting me, reminding me that she was there and that I wasn't alone. I hugged myself again, returning the affection, and felt the deep grief shift slightly. I could breathe for the moment.

"Ma'am, is there anything I need to do?" I asked.

"No. Everything has been taken care of."

I nodded. "Would you please have someone walk me out. I'm not sure I can find my way back to the lobby." My voice was shaky.

"Are you sure you're ready?"

I nodded. I was sure. "I need to go. My sister-in-law is waiting for me. She'll be worried."

"I'll see you out."

I stood then and gathered myself the best I could. I still felt overwhelmed with the knowledge, but I didn't want to fall apart in front of this stranger. I also didn't want to have to be carried out. I wanted to go home and collapse in my own bed. A sarcastic sob escaped. Who was I kidding? I had no home and I had no bed of my own.

"Mrs. Emir, here, let me help you." Lt. Colonel Henderson took my elbow and helped guide me toward the exit.

Sefa looked up as soon as we entered the lobby. I must have looked horrible. "Caroline, what's the matter?"

"Sefa, please, take me home."

"Are you ill?" I shook my head.

Sefa turned on the lieutenant colonel, then. "What happened?"

"She received some unpleasant news. It came as a shock to her."

"What kind of unpleasant news?" Sefa demanded.

"Billy," I said, "my brother, Billy, is dead." My face contorted into a pained expression. "I need to go; please, Sefa, I want to go."

Sefa put her arm around me and held me close to her side. "What were you thinking?" Sefa exclaimed, rounding on Lt. Colonel Henderson. "You just drop this on an expectant woman?" Sefa's words were angry and protective.

"Sefa, let's go. Thank you," I said, and Lt. Col. Henderson gave a remorseful nod.

"You're thanking her? You're actually thanking her?" Sefa reprimanded me as she guided me through the front doors. We didn't have far to walk to the Mercedes. Sefa opened the door for me and I sat down. Once she was in the driver's seat, she turned toward me. "Are you okay, Caroline?" Sefa examined my face and then looked me over from head to toe.

I shook my head. "I need to lie down. I feel dizzy and I know it's going to hit me really hard, soon."

"I wish I had been with you."

"Me too, but there was no delicate way. Bad news is bad news," I said.

The sky was just as bright as when we arrived, but I couldn't take in the brightness. I closed my eyes and shielded myself from the sun. The beauty was a contradiction to the darkness of shock and grief. I often imagined that a candle stood on a pedestal in the center of my heart. I guess I took the song, *This Little Light of Mine,* literally when I was a child. The candle in my heart burned brightly most of the time. It kept me warm and made it easy to care for others and love them. I kept the fire burning through Daddy's death and Momma's illness; I even managed it apart from Hashim. Of course, I couldn't control the flickers that happened every time my heart was broken, like the fracture in my heart allowed a gust to threaten to blow it out completely. Gradually, I would seal the crack in my heart and the flame would return even stronger than before, but this time, I wasn't sure.

For the next week or more, I slept a lot. I swam and ate and slept. I said very little. Every time I tried to speak, tears threatened, so I remained silent. Sefa tried to get me to do more and go out, but I couldn't do it. Fatma tried to lure me to the kitchen with mouthwatering delicacies. The baby demanded I eat every few hours, so her needs won out over my need to grieve. I wanted comfort food. I wanted tots mounded with chili and cheese and milkshakes and a Sonic drive-in. I wanted to run into the woods, again, one last time, with Billy like when we were kids. I wanted to have a picnic in the fort and sing showtunes in the kitchen. I wanted to do normal things, familiar things. I wanted to study and go to school and work. I even missed my old, crappy, piece-of-crap car.

Grief, homesickness, exhaustion, a belly that constantly moved and expanded, they all contributed to my state of utter depression. I lay in the bed in the dark with my eyes wide, almost catatonic; sleep refused to linger. Sefa didn't understand. Hashim didn't know. Fatma didn't even try. I prayed, but it was no use, and music only annoyed me. *Come on, C.* My inner voice tried but was easily silenced. My heart was dark and cold. I'd lost my light. My joy was gone. Finally, I refused to go down and swim.

"Just send up some food later. I don't have the energy to do anything today," I told Sefa and Fatma when they each came to check on me.

That was the last straw. The very next morning, Ecrin came into the room and opened the blinds. "Caroline, get up," she demanded. Her voice grated like nails on a chalkboard. I didn't appreciate her tone. I closed my eyes against the bright sun and rolled over. Rolling over took a lot of effort, so the dramatic effect was lost. "Caroline, this is unhealthy behavior. Shower and dress. We are leaving in an hour." I covered my head with a pillow and tried to ignore her. That same persistent tone came through the pillow. "Caroline!" She said my name just like Hashim did when he was impatient with me. I let loose a stream of curses. I really wasn't particularly angry with Ecrin. Sure, I was annoyed by her, but my anger was generally targeted toward the universe and maybe a little bit toward God.

"If you refuse me, I will call the hospital and have you admitted for observation and psychiatric evaluation. It is in your best interest to get out of that bed." She couldn't be serious, but I knew there was a chance she was. I was honestly a little bit frightened by this intimidating woman. I removed the pillow and eyed her. I didn't trust her, so I did what she demanded. I rose from the bed tentatively and cautiously walked toward the bathroom. She actually had the nerve to follow me in there. I felt like an animal being prodded into a cage. She turned on the water in the shower for me and pulled a towel from the shelf.

"I can bathe myself," I said defensively.

"Good. I will get your clothes."

I undressed and stepped into the shower. The hot steam felt good to breathe. My hair was matted from not being brushed for several days, so it took extra conditioner to work through the rat's nest. Ecrin was waiting outside the shower for me with my robe. She opened it and allowed me to step into it. She kept her gaze diverted so she didn't embarrass me or draw attention to my belly. She handed me the towel and I wrapped up my hair. "Sit," she gestured to the vanity at the center of the bathroom counter. I eyed her warily, but I obeyed. She had a no-nonsense look on her face. She was in no mood to be refused. She unwrapped the towel from my head and began brushing my hair gently. She worked out the knots tenderly without pulling my scalp. I was surprised at her gentleness.

"Where are we going?" I asked.

"To buy some shoes."

"I don't need any shoes."

I sensed Ecrin's disapproval. "Caroline, I wish to tell you a story." I didn't look in the mirror at her, but she began anyway. "When I was a girl, my family's home was ravaged by war. My family fled from our burning home. I was suddenly a refugee." She allowed me a few moments to receive her words. "We were forced from our home in the night; my feet were covered only by thin slippers. Over the course of the next few days, I was forced to walk miles. My father carried me for a while, but then we were separated and I was sent with the women and children. He was taken with my two older brothers. We made camp where we could, but it was a day or two before we were able to find passage to a relative's home. I was cold and barefooted. I was hungry and exhausted. I had no possessions. You can imagine what that does to a child to have nothing familiar. My father was active politically and had some influence, but we lost everything and had to begin our lives anew. Nearly a year passed before we were all back together as a family."

I was drawn into Ecrin's story and gradually lifted my head to see her face in the reflection of the mirror. She didn't look at me as she spoke; she focused only on my hair. "I attended school and studied diligently. I worked and helped my family financially. Everyone contributed. As refugees, my parents had a hard time finding work. Without political connections, my father was forced to do menial tasks for meager pay. My mother fell ill and was unable to work. My brothers were both drafted into the military. Later, they died in the line of duty; it was while I was at the university." Her voice trailed off momentarily and I could tell that those memories were hard for her to share. "Do you know why I do the work I do?" I shook my head. "I have experienced the destruction firsthand; I know the pain that comes when there is discord. Agreement is a place of power because we can move forward together. There is strength in numbers. Peaceful accords save lives and there is a great influence when all parties are willing to cooperate. Children do not lose their homes in the middle of the night and families are able to stay together."

She was quiet then for several moments. "You feel isolated and alone in a foreign place. You have little trust and you feel abandoned. There is nothing familiar or known to you. Then, amid all of this newness, another rug is figuratively pulled from underneath your feet. You are left shaken and imbalanced. Lying in the dark will not help you any longer. Our days are numbered on this earth and we are wise not to waste them." She was looking at me, now, holding my gaze in the mirror. "Did you love your brother?" Could she be so cruel to ask such an inane question? I blinked back defiant tears as my reply. "I know you loved him; all sisters love their brothers. They are our first friends, first adversaries, and our first protectors. When we lose them, we lose a huge part of our identity; their lives are completely woven into ours."

"Why shoes?" I asked. I didn't want to talk about Billy or how homesick I was or even how much I missed Hashim.

She gave a humorless chuckle. "I had no shoes of my own for a long time. I borrowed shoes and was given hand-me-downs that did not fit properly. They were too small or too wide or even too old for any real use. I hated shoes because I never had appropriate ones. I saved every bit of money I could to buy my own shoes. I was fourteen and had been invited to attend a dance. It was the first time I purchased my own shoes and they were for a particular reason. Not only were they my first pair of heels, but I knew they gave me purpose and direction. We wear athletic shoes to exercise, formal heels for special occasions, boots for hard labor and for hiking mountains, and sandals for the beach. My heels empowered me for many years. I took care of them and wore them to my university interviews and again to my graduations."

Ecrin was now gathering bits of my hair and intricately braiding the damp strands. Her fingers worked nimbly. "I rarely see you wear any shoes, Caroline. Barefoot is fine, but it cannot be your entire way. I think it is time that you decide what sort of shoes you need and where you intend for them to take you. You swim for exercise and you wear sandals because they flatter your feet. You no longer need flattery; you need to be empowered. You are about to become a mother, and unfortunately, you may be doing much of that duty on your own since we have no idea when Hashim will be able to return to you."

What she said made sense even if it only added to my layers of sadness. What sort of shoes did I need? I had a pair of sneakers from Montgomery that I had only worn a couple of times, but I was growing a fetus not running a marathon. I dressed and put on the sandals that Ecrin picked to match my outfit, but she was right; they did not suit my current needs. They were pretty but not very practical.

Once we were downstairs, the valet pulled up in a black, Jaguar convertible with a pearl-white interior. Alham, the doorman-bouncer, opened the passenger's side door for me like he always did, and Ecrin drove me to the mall. It was the first time I had been alone with her and the first time that she had ever driven me anywhere. I had no idea what to expect.

"Ecrin, I really like your taste in cars. I confess that I'm a sucker for Jaguars and yours are amazing." She seemed pleased at the compliment. "I'm really sorry for driving without your permission in Miami. I just thought I wouldn't have an opportunity, again, or be able to get your permission."

She rolled her eyes a bit. "Experiences, such as they are, plant seeds of self-destruction. Bitterness is the most common to take root, but in my case, pride is my utter downfall. I am hoping that our outing today will help you avoid such pitfalls." She took a deep breath before she continued, "I was entirely disappointed in my son. I was angry with him and you received the brunt of my disappointment."

It felt strange to hear things like that from her. It almost sounded like an apology. It was so personal and contrary to what I experienced from her, directly. "Ecrin, were you specifically disappointed in his choice or in the fact he chose without your knowledge and consent?"

"Both," she said pointedly keeping her eyes on the road. I looked away, praying to all that was holy that this shoe-shopping trip wouldn't be completely fruitless.

On our way into the mall, we passed through the food court. I stopped suddenly when I saw an advertisement for a huge, bacon cheeseburger and a side of tots. My mouth watered and my heart leapt a little. Ecrin hesitated with me. "I want that," I said. She smiled approvingly, like maybe she'd won a bet or something. I was out of the bed, clean and dressed, in a public place, and now wanted food. If I actually bought shoes, she'd have hit the jackpot. We ordered food. Ecrin ordered a salad and I ordered the number seven meal. It was the most food I had eaten in a week. I could barely finish half of the burger. My stomach was probably shrunken, but also, the baby's position made it hard for me to eat a lot at one time. I did manage to finish the tots and burped loudly at the end of my meal. Ecrin raised her eyebrow and then gave a wry smile. She didn't approve but seemed satisfied at my satisfaction. I went to the bathroom and then we began our quest for appropriate shoes.

I was drawn to boots because I felt like I needed something rugged and strong and protective. A bad-ass pair of shit-kickers were comfortable and dependable, but they were hot and did not suite the climate at all. I could also imagine my feet swelling at the end of the pregnancy and not being able to bend over to pull them off; I already couldn't tie my sneakers. My second choice was a pair of rugged hiking sandals. They covered my toes for protection and were well-ventilated. The sole was thick and contoured and fit my arches comfortably. They also had the added bonus of being adjustable. I could make them suit my changing feet with straps and buckles. They came in an assortment of colors; I chose the ones that matched most of my clothing and were edged in black because they reflected my state of mourning.

Ecrin approved. "Until you find yourself, again, wear them from the time you rise until you go to bed. You can even swim in them."

"Thank you, Ecrin. I mean that; thank you." I wasn't able to smile.

"I know. You have never been disingenuous with your words." Her placating smile was sincere.

CHAPTER 34.5

A friend loves at all times,
and a brother is born for a time of adversity.

— Proverbs 17:17

I requested a meeting with Kennedy at the end of March. The committee was eager to see my progress. I imagined a pack of salivating dogs, eager for their next morsel. They were duly impressed. After the meeting, Kennedy and I ate lunch in the cafeteria. "How were your holidays?" Kennedy asked, cordially.

I was surprised by his question. "Fine, and yours?"

"Great, but Dubai has better weather than Vermont. It was wet and cold and overcast the entire time."

"You have family there?" I asked, diverting the conversation away from Dubai.

He nodded. "My kid-sister's in school there. She likes to ski; I like to give her what she wants." He shrugged dismissively. "Your family doing well?" he asked, politely. I nodded once. It would not have been difficult for him to know where I had gone. I wondered if he knew Caroline was there, too.

"What are you playing at, Kennedy?"

"What do you mean?" he asked innocently.

"I mean, why the sudden interest in my family? My travel? Dubai? This is not our usual course of interaction."

"We've been working together for years. I'd like to know you better. You seem more reclusive and less engaging than before. I can't afford to lose you as an asset and it's my job to make sure you're happy. It's obvious that you aren't happy. This guy, Marshall, threatens you, your wife leaves you, and from what we see, you're working and running, no women, no clubs, not even eating out. Don't get me wrong, the committee is beyond impressed with what you're producing, but *All work and no play makes Jack a dull boy.* We can't afford for you to become dull, Emir."

I understood his concern; by all accounts, I was not behaving normally. "I'm staying in D.C. for a couple of nights. I have some personal business to attend, and I will see Dawes as well. I can assure you that I will not be a hermit this weekend." That appeased him; he smiled and patted my shoulder as we parted company. He would be watching, and with Dawes' help, I was hoping to give him a good show.

I was driven into the heart of the city. The hotel was opulent and frequented by dignitaries from all over the world. Earlier, Dawes swept the suite for bugs. He dared not remove them, but we needed to confirm that they were there. I showered and changed clothes and walked the few blocks to the restaurant where we were meeting for dinner. Dawes walked up at nearly the same time with a gorgeous woman on each arm. One was a tall, curvaceous blond, and the other an equally tall brunet with dazzling blue eyes and a wickedly friendly smile.

"Emir," Dawes called to me and I joined them. "This is Alexandra and Kendrick, Alex and Ricki for short," he said introducing the blond and brunette in turn. Dawes never ceased to amaze me. I wondered where the hell he had found these two women. Reading the expression on my face, he leaned in and whispered, "Alex is my cousin and Ricki is her partner. They're with the LAPD." I assessed them differently, then. If they were cops, I wondered where they could possibly hide weapons in their designer dresses. The women were friendly, almost affectionate toward us and one another. The way he'd said *partner,* though eluded to the fact that they may also be lovers. This would make for an interesting evening.

Alex smiled and eased into me as she placed her hand in the crook of my elbow. "It's a pleasure to meet you, Hashim. I'm looking forward to a great evening."

"I am, too," I said honestly; my smile was genuine.

Alex and Ricki were excellent company. After dinner, the ladies excused themselves. "They are amazing. What are we paying them for tonight?" I asked.

Dawes laughed and shook his head. "Nothing, and we have them for three nights. Alex owes me a favor or a dozen. I've been her plus-one her entire life: every time she's needed a dance partner, an escort to a wedding or an honors banquet. I even took her to our senior prom. My family would never approve of her lifestyle, so I've buffered her from a great deal of ridicule. She moved to LA for a variety of reasons. They think she's focused on her career; she'll make lieutenant soon. Long story, short, she was happy to finally repay some of what she thinks she owes me."

We left the restaurant and went to a club. Sefa's favorite, I noted. The music was loud and the place was packed. I was happy for the distraction of noise and alcohol. Back at the hotel, the ladies soon retired. I gave Dawes the bed, and I contented myself on the sofa. I was up several more hours working. Dawes woke at five and asked if I wanted to run. I did.

The next evening was much the same. Alex kissed me on the cheek in public. Anyone watching would believe that we'd been intimate the evening before. Anyone watching would be envious of this woman's attention. It did not feel put on; she was good. I was almost convinced, myself. Ricki was not as affectionate with Dawes. They almost looked like adversaries at times. They had a past and I wondered if she were jealous of what he had asked of Alex. She was quickly appeased when I asked the ladies if they would like something new for our third evening together. We had reservations for dinner and I thought shopping would be a nice gesture.

"See, Liam, that's how a lady should be treated," Ricki said pointedly.

"I know how a lady should be treated, but until you act like one, I'll be damned if I offer to buy you anything." She blinked and flashed her wicked smile. Then she winked at Dawes and followed Alex into the boutique with me. He was smiling all the while.

Dawes and I had conversations each morning as we ran. He had limited contact with Sefa, which was their habit, which meant there was little contact for me as well. "Everything's fine, Emir. She's safe; you're safe. It's a win-win."

"I know, but I want it to be different. Have you learned any more of a connection? Have you been able to find out anything regarding Marshall?"

"Yeah, I found out Global Securities is a pretty tight outfit. I don't think we'll get anywhere with them. Kennedy hasn't done anything out of the ordinary, but with you having contact with Marshall, I figure at least one of them is satisfied. Kennedy's got a track on you 24/7, so be careful. You already know the hotel is bugged, and I would suspect he's got someone watching your every move." Dawes chuckled, then. "I wonder if Marshall's guys and Kennedy's guys ever sit and have coffee and compare notes. They've got to notice one another after a while."

"It seems like overkill."

"Hey, I want you to know, I'm up for a promotion. I won't be asked to pull Emir detail anymore."

It was about time, I supposed. Who would want this job for so long? "Congratulations. Where are you being assigned?"

"After some intensive training, I'll remain in Virginia. It's something I've wanted for a long time. I guess you could say I've been grooming myself for this position. My new post isn't as posh as the Miami house, but I'll make do." He laughed.

"Who will replace you?"

"I have no idea; there've been a lot of changes recently in our department, so I'm not sure." He cleared his throat like he had more to say. "I also want you to know that when this is all said and done, I plan to ask Sefa to join me."

I nodded. "She would like that. She will be due for a vacation from Caroline by then," I said amused.

"No, I mean, I plan to ask her to move in with me. I want her to make a life here. If possible, I'll convince her to marry me, but I'm not jumping the gun on that one."

I stopped suddenly and stared at him. "You want to marry my sister?" My tone was disbelieving.

"When she's ready."

I scoffed. "Are you sure you can handle that? She is unpredictable and slightly combustible, neither domesticated nor conventional."

He cocked his head to one side, trying to understand my meaning. "Are you trying to change my mind?" An air of defensiveness passed over him. Dawes was observant and rarely ever showed emotion or disapproval. He stayed in the background, unobtrusive, undemanding. He was serious and watched everything. He had been watching me for years, so he could easily read my expression and my tone. "Would you accept that? Would you support that decision?" Except for the night by the pool, Dawes never challenged me or showed any emotion. He handled every situation we had encountered, professionally, but the moment he kissed Sefa in front of me revealed a new dimension. He was asking for more than my acceptance; he wanted my approval.

"My initial reaction in Miami was to punch you in the face," I admitted, wiping the sweat from my brow with the back of my arm, "but had you taken me down, it would have been a huge blow to my ego." I chuckled.

He chuckled then, too. "Yeah, it would have been, for sure. Are you thinking about punching me, now?"

"No." I shook my head for emphasis. "I am happy for you. I hope it works out." It was hard to contain the smile that spread across my face.

"What?" he asked, knowing there was more.

"I relish the fact that Ecrin may one day be your mother-in-law. That is better than any lucky punch I could ever hope to deliver."

His jaw tightened at the threat. "Thanks, Emir, way to be a friend. You really know how to encourage a guy," he said sarcastically. "I'll race you back." He gestured with his chin and we set off. One thing was certain; he was a friend and I needed to do a better job appreciating that relationship. I also needed to consider that one day he might be family.

Our final night out with Alex and Ricki did not go as any of us had planned. Our dinner reservations had been unexpectantly cancelled. The restaurant was closed due to a kitchen fire. The restaurants nearby absorbed the overflow. We hailed a cab and decided to try another area of the city. Every place we tried was packed, so we ended up at one of my favorites. It was a family establishment and reminded me of the second restaurant I had taken Caroline when we were still friends who kissed. The wine and pasta were paired excellently with the company, but things felt off. If I had to be denied Caroline, I would be more content with my own company. Dawes excused himself a couple of times to take calls. He appeared distracted. He had worked all day and returned later than expected. The ladies had gone sight-seeing for the day, and I had worked. By the end of the evening, I had grown weary of the facade.

"I won't be able to drive you to the airport in the morning," Dawes announced after his second call. "I'm on a flight tonight. Can't be helped. Sorry, ladies. Do you and Ricki mind Ubering to the airport?"

"What time is your departure?" I asked.

"Our flight is at 7:45," Ricki interjected.

"I have a car coming at five, if you would like a ride."

"That'll work," Ricki smiled. "See, Liam, once again, you have so much to learn."

I shook Dawes' hand and thanked him. "When you can get a message out, please relay the usual." He gave a quick nod.

At three a.m., there was a knock at the door. Alex opened their bedroom door at the same time I opened mine. She looked solidly at me and for the first time, I noticed the family resemblance. Without makeup, the natural shape of her eyes and the slope of her cheeks were similar to Dawes, or it could have been her stance and the familiar way she held a gun at her side. "May I?" she asked and walked toward the door before I could get to it. There was a second knock and Alex looked through the peep hole. "It's not Liam."

I stepped forward and looked myself. "It's okay; I know him."

"Friend or foe?"

"Not sure."

"Let him in?"

"Yes, and pretend you like me again." Alex loosened her hair from the messy bun on the top of her head and shook out her blond tresses. She slowly blinked her eyes and was instantly transformed into coquettish beauty. I put my arm around her and moved her to the side protectively. She concealed her weapon behind me.

Kennedy stepped into the suite confidently and I could tell as soon as he entered that I should already be dressed and packed. He offered an approving nod toward Alex before he spoke. "Emir, get your things. We need to go."

"Where are we going?"

Kennedy's eyes fell over Alex, again, and I knew instantly that he would say nothing more in front of her. "Do you mind, excusing us?" I asked her politely. She removed herself from my embrace and gave an impish pout before she retreated into the bedroom with Ricki. The gun was nowhere to be found. Where had she concealed it?

"We have Marshall," he began in a low voice. "We'd like you to come in for the interrogation."

I was nearly packed, already, so it took very little time to dress and ready myself. I filled an envelope with cash and guessed that a couple thousand dollars each might ease Alex and Ricki's lack of sleep. I placed a neatly printed note on the table.

"You're leaving a note for prostitutes?" Kennedy asked.

"Not prostitutes. Merely leaving a token of my appreciation."

CHAPTER 35

With each passing day, I became more and more agitated. The direction my shoes were taking me was in direct contrast with where my body was taking me. I wanted to go home. I never thought myself terribly patriotic. I mean, my brother and father and grandfathers had all served in the military, I stood for the pledge and proudly sang the national anthem, but until I was so far away from home, I didn't know how fiercely proud and attached to my country I truly was. I was determined to birth my baby on American soil. Sefa thought that was a horrible idea and I was constantly reminded that it was a risk to travel later in pregnancy. The days were ticking away and I knew I needed to leave sooner rather than later.

I had the craziest dreams. Hashim was in danger, Marshall was lurking everywhere, and Aunt June was crocheting a baby blanket for an elephant. She rocked and sang and Momma kept giving her more yarn to crochet. They knew this baby was going to be huge. Waking after the crochet dream, I remembered a box in the back of the hall closet. Aunt June had made things for our future babies. I was determined to get that box and I became obsessed with how I was going to do that.

"You're just nesting, Choti Behan. Your hormones are in overdrive and you are thinking crazy thoughts. This is normal."

"I want to go home," I told Sefa.

"You promised to stay here. Have you forgotten that?" she challenged.

"We haven't heard anything for two months. Before that, it was some cryptic crap from Dawes. I'm tired of all of this. I want to go home." My voice was pleading, but I wasn't being whiney or impetuous. I had been formulating a plan in my mind for weeks, and whether or not Sefa went with me, I was determined.

Ecrin and Rana wrapped up their negotiations in Dubai and then flew to France with promises that they would return before the baby arrived. Fatma was busy with school and Sefa had steadily increased her hours at the clinic. Mornings were quiet and I slept and read and occupied myself the best I could. I had gone to the pool by myself more often for something to do. No one allowed me to leave the apartment alone. I knew my way around the city well enough and I missed driving, but I obeyed the house rules and occupied myself appropriately as I mentally made plans.

Adi was a young man who guarded our elevator. He was nothing like Alham, the bouncer-doorman, downstairs. Truth-be-told, I found Adi creepy and unnerving. Sefa said it was because he was prejudice against American women, but I couldn't help but feel like he was watching me all the time. Once Rana left, it got worse and I hated having to pass him each time I went to the pool.

After dinner one evening, I hatched my plan to Sefa. "Okay, so I've come to a decision. Since you won't let me go home to have the baby, how about we make a compromise." Her eyes peaked with curiosity. She had consumed a couple of glasses of wine and was relaxed reclining on the sofa.

"Go ahead, I'm listening."

"How about we fly to my house, get the things I want, and then return before anyone else knows we're even gone. The doctor said I had no limitations and I could do whatever I wanted. I want this, Sefa, please."

"How do you even know there's anything there for you? How do you know that the house is still standing? For all you know, they burned it to the ground to eliminate any evidence of your being attacked there." She didn't mention Krissa, directly, but I knew she was thinking it, too.

"I know, but I don't want to wait. If I'm forced to be here alone to have my baby then I want a bit of my family here, too. It's all that I have. If we go tomorrow, we can be back by the end of the week. We can be back before my next appointment."

She was easily swayed and I smiled at the possibility that she might say yes. Sefa blinked her long, dark lashes. God, she had Hashim's eyes. I prayed our child would have those eyes, well, at least those lashes. She would probably have everything of her father's, dominating genes and all. My fair complexion and light eyes would be lost completely. Regardless, she'd have my heart. She'd have all of my heart and love for music. Yep, she'd definitely have my love for music. Sefa hesitated, but I knew she was considering it. I knew she would like the adventure and feeling like she'd gotten away with something forbidden.

CHAPTER 35.5

The plans of the heart belong to man,
  but the answer of the tongue is from the Lord.
All ways of a man are pure in his own eyes,
  but the Lord weighs the spirit.

– Proverbs 16:1-2

"Where is Marshall?" I asked as soon as we were alone in Kennedy's small SUV.

"We'll get to him soon enough," Kennedy replied flatly.

"What does he know?"

"He knows you're with me. He's secure. You don't need to worry about him for the time being. We will go to him."

Kennedy headed west on the interstate. "He is not in the city?" I asked.

"No, he's being held nearby."

I examined him closely. Like before, there was something off about him. Caroline's words returned. "I never told you she was a blonde," I said. He eyed me considering my words and cocked his head to one side like he did not understand. "The woman at Caroline's who was killed," I clarified.

He nodded slowly knowing exactly what I was talking about. "You didn't have to; Marshall told me." His eyes were telling.

"How long have you two been working together?"

"For a long time, Emir, but when you refused to help Marshall, I had no choice but to step in. You have made this incredibly difficult for yourself. You're tampering with my retirement plan and I can't delay this any longer."

I considered how I might be able to take him down without killing myself in the process. Kennedy had increased his speed and we were rapidly leaving the city. "It took me a while, but through a series of connections, I found your sweet Caroline. She's been hiding all this time in plain sight with your family." He gave a low, caustic chuckle like he was surprised it took him so long to find her. "Now you have a wife, and I am suspecting that these are proof of a child," he said pulling the ultrasound photos from his inside, jacket pocket. I stroked down my beard with my hand. Those had been in my wallet since she left Miami. I was such an idiot.

His right hand was fixed on the steering wheel and his left hand then produced a gun. The gun was unnecessary. I had no choice but to help them now; I had no hope of saving Caroline or my child. *My child.*

"Where are you taking me?" I asked.

"Someplace safe where you can work without distractions. You'll find everything you need there. Put your phone on the dash and open the glove box. I'd appreciate you going ahead and seeing to that."

Inside the glove box was a blindfold bag, a pair of handcuffs, and an envelope. "Really? You expect me to put these on?" I was surprised at the humor in my voice.

"Yes, once you open that envelope, you'll be more inclined, I think."

I opened the envelope and there were pictures: Caroline with my mother, Caroline with Sefa, Caroline at the American Consulate with a woman in uniform, and finally, Caroline standing in the driveway of her house. I was completely thrown and shook my head disbelievingly. *No, that cannot be; she is in Dubai.* She held a box in her arms and looked like she was calling out to someone behind her. My heart raced and my hands tingled. *What the hell was she doing there?* I stared blankly at that last photo. Her face was the same, but nearly everything about her was different. Her hair was longer and wavier; her middle was big and round, expectant. Her lips were fuller and she smiled, radiant and beautiful.

"Dawes?" I asked, smothering the anger and disgust.

Kennedy laughed once. "Yeah, I couldn't have asked for a better plan if I'd devised it myself. You can't afford friendship in this line of work, so I'm very thankful his promotion went through. It was perfect timing; he's been sent to China of all places. Training. Convenient, wouldn't you say? No worries, though, keep your head up. You might be finished before he returns."

With frustrated resignation, I blindfolded and handcuffed myself but paid careful attention to the sound of the road as we drove. I could tell the interstate had not changed, and I suspected that we had not crossed over any state lines. Then, we suddenly exited from the interstate onto a small highway. I could hear no other vehicles, and the smell of the air changed, giving off the aromas of early spring, fresh grass, and budding trees. The road changed again into a bumpy trail. He was taking me further away from the city. Although I was unsure how time was passing, it felt like a couple of hours had passed since we exited the interstate, so I surmised that we were about three hours from D.C. He turned on the windshield wipers; it apparently had begun to rain.

Once the car was parked, Kennedy removed my blindfold, but I could see very little out of the rain-splattered windows. "Don't try anything stupid, Emir. If I don't return before nightfall, there are people in place who will not be so generous to your wife and child. They are directed to only observe for the time being. It took months, but I finally have people in Dubai. That fucking country is so hard to maneuver in. She's being watched constantly." I was relieved to know she had returned to Dubai, then. I sickened at the thought of her being exposed and vulnerable in her house or in Miami. Kennedy had no idea he had given me a small nugget of hope. Once out of the car, I realized that he had parked in front of a small cabin surrounded by thick woods. The overcast sky and drizzling rain reflected my mood completely. The cabin's roof was covered in solar panels and there was a pumphouse. This place was completely off the grid.

"You'll find everything you need inside." He walked around to the back of the vehicle and removed my bags and placed them on the porch. "It should be familiar to you once you're inside. I had everything brought in from Global

Securities. The relays are all recorded. I'll be back in a week with more provisions. Hopefully, it won't take much longer than that for you to figure out what we need and maybe do your magic with your software. Good thing you stayed in D.C. for a couple of days; it gave my men time to retrieve it all from Miami."

"Who are you really working for?" I asked. "Where do your loyalties lie?"

Kennedy cocked his head to one side, considering. "You're questioning my loyalty? How dare you? You, who prostitutes himself to the highest bidder with no affiliation to country or government, question my loyalty?" he scoffed.

I received the truth of his words. I had no loyalty myself, but I wasn't threatening anyone nor was I holding anyone hostage. "What is all this worth to you, anyway?"

"The more I know, the better positioned I am to present it to the most invested party."

"Are you working with Marshall at Global?" I asked, trying desperately to make the connection.

"Working with him? No, Emir, I'm not working *with* him. Global is entirely my operation; it has been now for quite some time. We run a variety of surveillance and happened upon those relays. Haven't been able to do anything with them until now."

"What do you plan to do with the information? Is it your goal to terminate the source?"

"That depends. I may find the source more useful than the information, itself, even more useful than you."

I looked down at my cuffed wrists and took in a deep breath. "When I am done; we are done, Kennedy." My voice was flat, and the threat was more than implied.

His expression slid into a menacing grin. "I know, but it's so worth it in the moment." I was growing annoyed at standing in the rain, so I took a couple of steps toward the cabin. "Hold on, one more thing." He produced a small box from the back seat. I turned to look at him and watched as he lifted a black and gray tracker from the box. He gestured for me to lift my hands toward him so that he could place it on my wrist. I was being placed under house arrest. *Damn it*, this device would tell him my every move.

I was seething as I heard the slight click of the bracelet around my wrist, I lifted my clasped hands forcefully, striking Kennedy in the jaw. He stepped back, surprised and a bit dazed. Before he could regain his bearings, I moved forward toward him again and was able to open my arms enough to loop them over his head and draw him in around his neck in a chokehold. He gasped and grunted and wriggled out of my grasp. I moved toward him again, but this time he was ready and blocked my attack. I was thrown off balance and together we tumbled to the ground. Without any real use of my hands, I had to rely on my arms and legs. I was larger than Kennedy and outweighed him by at least fifty pounds, but without my hands, I was no match for him. He could not afford to injure me, so he used only defensive moves. We wrangled and wrestled on the sloppy ground for several minutes before he could get away from me. I wanted him to know that I was not going down without a fight. Finally, he was able to get to the other side of the car, panting and frustrated, covered in grass and mud and the muck of the rain. His lip and nose were bleeding and he would have a nice bruise under his jaw.

I wiped my brow with my forearm and saw that he had also drawn blood. I smiled, taunting him. "I will not be handcuffed when you return," I said, feeling confident now that I could take him.

"Maybe, maybe not," he said and held up the key. I watched as he tossed it into the taller grass at the edge of the cabin. He gave me a quick, dismissive nod and entered the car and left me standing there in the rain. When I finally found the key in the knee-high grass, I was soaking wet and covered in mud. The cabin was nicer on the inside than the simple exterior boasted. There were two rooms. One had a bed and the other had a large workspace, a treadmill, and a weight machine. I showered and felt exhausted from the defeat of being so easily abducted and contained.

***

There were red birds nesting all over the property. I could see them outside the window working diligently to build nests with their mates. I had been at the cabin for six days and anticipated Kennedy's return with supplies. I had no plan to escape. The second phone that Dawes had given me had no reception. For the lack of anything better to do, I began the tasks at hand. It was tedious work and there were hours and hours of relays to decipher. Gradually, the tone and words to be interpreted changed and I would lose the content. It was frustrating, so I took breaks often to work out, but I dared not leave.

I expected Kennedy to arrive on the seventh day, but instead, food and supplies were delivered in the night. I was hidden, kept safely out of reach, and wanted desperately to contact Dawes. I would have even talked to Marshall at that point if it meant contact with another human being. The cabin was in the middle of nowhere, and without transportation, I was stuck for the time being. My only entertainment was watching the birds and the squirrels and occasionally a rabbit foraging for food and tending to their anticipated young.

I wondered constantly about Caroline and how she and the baby fared. I imagined her full breasts and rounded hips and a protruding bump larger than the one she had at Christmas, like I had seen in the photos. I remembered her sleek, tan body lying next to me and the nights we made love in Dubai. I knew that a woman's face and lips became fuller throughout their pregnancy and I could only fantasize about Caroline's lips, even fuller, as I kissed them. I wondered at feeling the baby kick for the first time. I envisioned our child and what he or she might look like. Genetically, my traits would dominate; the child would most likely have dark hair and a darker complexion, but I wondered if my mother's eyes and Caroline's eyes would somehow merge together. Maybe the child would have lighter hair, but I knew that would be nearly impossible. I was sure Sefa had already demanded an ultrasound; she would be impatient to know whether Caroline was carrying a boy or a girl. I honestly had no preference. The idea of a child had come as a complete shock, but like Caroline's love, the role of protector, provider, and parent gradually began to settle deep within the fiber of my being.

Day after day, I watched those damned red birds work diligently to build a nest for their young. Then, a pair of blue jays arrived and began doing the same. The blue jay was bold and would come and sit next to my window curiously watching me work. He was a nuisance and pecked at my window each morning like he was telling me to get up and make my own nest for my own mate, for my own hatchling. Like I did not already feel guilty enough. I watched as he boldly chased other animals away. He flew threateningly over squirrels and batted his wings violently when blackbirds encroached on his territory. He was an impressive defender of his mate. It was at those times I watched him most. I knew what I had to do.

Sleep eluded me for a couple of nights. The second week of isolation was brutal. Self-imposed isolation was what I had always created for myself, but forced isolation allowed the seeds of frustration to take root. The blue jay arrived at my window just as I had fallen into a deep sleep. I jerked up and cursed the bird. He was surely mocking me. How could this tiny, insignificant creature challenge me and hold me in account?

<u>CHAPTER 36</u>

Our whirlwind trip took its toll on me physically and emotionally. Physically, it took me weeks to recover from the flights and jetlag. I was exhausted as I entered the third trimester. I couldn't see my toes, my arms were too short to reach anything, and it took extra effort to do the simplest tasks.

Maybe the emotional toll was also affecting my physical well-being. I mistakenly thought that I could just go into my house, get the box from the closet, and be done with my life there. God, I was so wrong. I promised Sefa that we would not delay, but I had something important to do there. She had chartered flights and rented a car, a really nice car. My top five car list was evolving. She wouldn't let me drive, though, so the experience was wasted on me. Sefa drove straight from the small airport and we cautiously entered the house, but it was only musty and unused; there was no trace of a struggle or Krissa. Marshall had cleaned up well behind himself or maybe Kennedy had.

My piece-of-crap car was still parked in the driveway, dripping oil. Winter hadn't been kind to him; he was more faded and the tires were low and sagging. I took the rest of Momma's jewelry, a few photo albums, our family Bible, and my two favorite cookbooks. I wasn't saddened at leaving everything else behind, but it did tug at my heart a little more than I expected. I walked through Billy's room, but he wasn't attached to anything, and he'd never kept anything just for sentiment's sake. I wondered what became of his truck. I supposed the finance company repossessed it when he stopped making payments. I walked back to the fort and that's where I lost it. I had asked Sefa to give me a few minutes alone. She stayed at the house and watched me walk through the trees.

I stroked my belly absentmindedly and spoke out loud to my daughter. "This was my favorite place in the world growing up. We'll build you a fort one day, too, if you want. We'll have tea parties and play dress-up and we'll even sing, if you like that sort of stuff."

I looked around at the mismatched wood and the place we'd drawn and written our names. Most all of my childhood memories were wrapped up in these walls. Even though Billy was older than me, he never complained about keeping me entertained. How many times had we slept in the fort, telling scary stories and making hand shadows with our flashlights? If those memories weren't bitter-sweet enough, I remembered waking in Hashim's arms for the first time on that very floor. I shuddered feeling his protective arms around me and the security of waking with him. I couldn't take all the loss any longer. I leaned against the wall and slid down until I was sitting on the floor. Unable to even maintain that posture, I lay on my side and allowed all the feelings to press me down. It wasn't like the darkness and depression I felt after I received the news of Billy's death; it was more like I was releasing it all in the safest place I knew.

As though I were in an old-fashioned flower press, I let the weight of the grief press me down. I prayed to be delivered from the pull and energy that it took to carry. I had enough psych training to know I needed to release it all and leave it behind. What place could be better than to leave it here in the fort? I had struggled with my faith over the past few months and doubted if I would be able to regain my confidence, but lying there, I heard Psalms play in my mind. I knew without a doubt that I had returned for more than some hand-made baby clothes; I had returned to find my roots and some kindling to keep my inner light shining. When I finally rose from the floor, I felt like I'd lost all the weight from my shoulders, and I walked about a foot taller. It was there my inner voice returned. *You got this, C.*

***

We had been back in Dubai for well over a month when Sefa showed me the text from Dawes.

Is he there?

My heart sank. "What does he mean by that?" I asked.

"I think it means he doesn't know where he is." Her lips looked perturbed and she briefly resembled Ecrin.

I had known from my dreams that Hashim was in danger. Now, we had proof. I wondered if our escapade back to my house sent off alarms in different places. "Do you think this is our fault?" I asked.

"My little brother doesn't need our help to get himself into trouble. Liam had to go away, but when he returns he'll find him. No worries, Little Sister." I realized it was the first conversation we'd had completely in Urdu. She must be worried, because she'd slipped into her native tongue, and with my ease of understanding, I knew I'd been there entirely too long.

CHAPTER 36.5

There is a way that seems right to a man, but its end is the way to death.

– Proverbs 14:12

Food and provisions arrived once a week without my knowing who brought them or when they would arrive, like when I was in the shower or when I was sleeping. It was an eerie feeling, knowing I was being constantly watched and vulnerable in the middle of nowhere. I worked from daylight to well into the night, exercised three times a day, and slept. The relays were more complex than anything I had ever worked on before. Just when I figured out a pattern, they would shift, and within an hour, I would have to go back three hours to figure out the sequence and cadence. As much as I liked a challenge, it was ridiculous.

The content of the relays was random. It almost seemed like a news feed of sorts. I wondered if they were intended for a country where world events were banned or heavily censored. Depending on the country, that information was sensitive in its own right, but the highly sensitive information came in random tidbits and would have easily been misread or overlooked entirely had it not been for the algorithm that ran in conjunction to the interpretation software. Without that, I might never have figured out the shifts through the pattern. It made deciphering more reliable and timely.

Three weeks passed before Kennedy returned. I stepped out onto the porch wishing I had a weapon. He stood on the other side of his vehicle, a safe distance between us. "What happened to your returning in a week?" I asked wryly.

"After you attacked me, I decided you needed some time to settle down and focus on your work."

"What guarantee do I have that Caroline is safe?"

"She's fine," he said dismissively. "She's being watched constantly. I saw pictures of her this morning; she's getting huge. You should see her. Oh, but you can't." He chuckled to himself. "Was the scene at the airport your idea or hers?" I revealed nothing and stared coldly at him. "You even had Dawes convinced," he said under his breath. "So, how's the progress?"

"Nearly half-way. Do you know who is behind it?" I asked.

"We have a few possibilities. Have they revealed themselves?"

"No. Do you want what I have transcribed?" I asked through clenched teeth.

"Yes," he said greedily and stepped forward forgetting that I would like nothing more than to ring his neck. He hesitated and stepped back. "Copy it onto this," he said and tossed me a flash drive. "Make sure it's everything, Emir. No holding out on me this time."

A few minutes later, I returned and tossed it back to him. I purposefully tossed it where he would be forced to move away from the protection of the SUV. I stepped down from the porch and glared at him. He watched me cautiously as he tossed a backpack filled with supplies. I caught the bag easily and made no other efforts to intimidate him. I had no intention of attacking him right then, but he knew I had intentions, strong ones, and he would be even more cautious the next time he returned.

Another three weeks passed. I had no charger for my beard trimmer and my frequent workouts were building layered muscle. When I caught my reflection, I looked like a dark-skinned recluse. My hair was long and bushy and my beard was unkempt, but the most significant change was in my eyes. Impatience, contained fury, and an unwavering determination to get to Caroline were all singularly focused behind my dark eyes. I was unrecognizable even to myself.

Once my tweaked software detected the patterns in the relays, I was satisfied. The highly sensitive information had everything to do with vulnerable financial structures within Western governments. There were three strong possibilities as to the sources of these relays. From what I could induce, two were hostile enemies and one was domestic. This information could make or break First World markets. I translated the transfers as they were sent, concealing the highly sensitive information. I refused to make any of this easy for Kennedy. He was not smart enough to figure this out on his own, and I knew it would take a team to recognize the subtle changes. I would have to make a decision; I could not sit on this information in good conscience. I would get this information to the proper authorities one way or another, but not through Kennedy.

After completing the necessary interpretations before Kennedy returned, I had plenty of mental energy to devise a plan. Threatening my wife and child and isolating me would be his greatest regret. There were no weapons in the cabin, but I had found a screwdriver, a hammer, and an axe in the small pumphouse. I removed every scrap of metal I could find with the screwdriver and the claw of the hammer. I then constructed a weapon with a leg of one of the chairs. It was rudimentary but felt good in my hands. I also had the axe ready to wield if necessary. My plan was to maim and bind him, leave him, and drive the car back into town, but once I started swinging, would I have the self-control necessary to stop until he was dead?

That very morning, the blue jay pecked on my window as was his habit. He had been watching my every move. "Would you kill to protect your mate?" I asked him aloud. He bobbed his head and pecked along the window ledge. He paced back and forth and then stopped suddenly. His hidden eyelid wiped horizontally across his eye and he focused on me with a look like perhaps he already had. Even before Caroline was my mate, I had killed. I had killed to protect myself and to protect her, but now it was beyond personal protection. This time, if necessary, I would kill for love.

When Kennedy arrived, I was ready for him. My equipment was neatly packed in my duffle for a quick getaway, I removed the hinges from the door so that it would fall inward and hopefully throw Kennedy off balance. I refused to go out and meet him and ignored the horn.

"Emir," Kennedy called from behind the car door. "Emir!" His voice was more insistent the second time.

My non-reaction forced him to step onto the porch and instead of banging on the door as I guessed he might do, he reached for the knob. The trick with the door worked. With his gun drawn, he stumbled forward into the cabin. He lost his footing and one shot fired. I jumped but soon regained my focus and took a settling breath, relieved that I was hidden in shadow behind him. I swung my weapon and hit his arm, causing his gun to skid across the floor. Unprepared for my attack, he turned and threw his injured arm up to defend his face. I swung again and the nails and screws ripped into the flesh of his shoulder. He staggered back and gripped his arm reflexively.

"What the hell, Emir!" he bellowed, surprised at my attack. I swung again and again until he was lying huddled in a heap on the floor. Blood ran freely through his suit and he groaned and screamed in pain. My crude weapon was bloody and bits of fabric clung to the sharp metal protrusions.

He rolled over and pulled another weapon from his leg holster. He knew he had the upper hand. "If I don't make it back, you know she's done for. They'll have her in minutes and there's nothing you can do."

I stepped back but refused to lower my weapon. "It is finished, Kennedy. You have what you wanted. Release me."

"This is just the beginning, Emir. This was all to make a point; you're mine."

I refused to accept that. I refused to allow him to hold anything over me, and I would not work under duress. *Caroline would be safe,* I told myself; Dawes and Sefa would keep her safe. My absence would free her, but I needed to call his bluff. He could kill me if he wanted; that would be his loss. I walked toward Kennedy, determined, swinging my weapon loosely.

"Shoot me. Kill me, but I will not be forced to do anything against my will."

He could read the resolve in my expression and conflict flashed across his eyes. He would lose either way. Just then, I heard a familiar clatter. The bluebird tapped frantically against the window, flapping his wings and calling out. The cry was loud and piercing. It was just the distraction I needed. For the half-second Kennedy's attention was diverted, I swung my weapon again, sending him reeling in pain. Desperately, he shot at me, grazing my shoulder, and I swung again. I wanted nothing more than to finish him. He released another round, but I was over him; my foot firmly planted over his throat. Easily, I pried the gun from his hand.

Looking him straight in the eye, I forced the words through released rage, "No retirement plan is worth this."

"You wouldn't dare," he said, but he could read my intentions clearly.

"Remember when you asked me, 'What gives, Emir? Why her? Why all of this?' I know the answer, now. Love. I *love* her and you crossed a line when you threatened me with my own child."

His eyes widened in shock and disbelief as I raised the gun and shot him right between the eyes. I felt nothing, no remorse, no darkness. I grabbed my bag and ran toward the car, thankfully the keys were still in the ignition. I followed the path of the tires slowly through the woods. I had no idea where I was or how to make my way back to civilization, but I hoped I would soon intercept a signal. My second phone began vibrating all over the seat next to me. Text after text scrolled across the screen. Voicemails, missed calls, and more texts filled the screen. Rather than opening the GPS, I called Dawes, instead.

"Emir?" his voice called loudly. "Where the fuck are you?"

"I have no idea."

"Wait, where's Kennedy?"

"Dead." There was a brief moment of silence.

"Alright, I have you. You're only a couple of hours from me. I'm coming to meet you."

"How do I get out of here?" I asked. I had yet to find the gravel road. Both shock and relief hit me and my heartrate was sporadic; I felt cold and clammy as the adrenaline left my body.

"I'll talk you through it," he said confidently.

Two hours later, I was back on the interstate, driving ninety toward the exit where Dawes said we would meet. There was very little there but fields and an old, deserted gas station. I stepped out of the car to catch my breath when I heard the rhythm of helicopter blades above. Dawes jumped from the helicopter as soon as it touched down.

"That is quite an arrival," I said sarcastically, relieved to see him.

"You look like shit," he said. "Do you have any extra clothes?" I nodded and retrieved my bag from the car. "Change. You're covered in blood." I nodded again and stripped down right in the parking lot. Dawes eyed me for injury as I changed; I was virtually unscathed, except for the scratch where the bullet had grazed my shoulder. He examined it closely. "You'll need to tend to that." I nodded. He kicked my clothes into a pile and set them on fire. He then removed my phone and the gun from the front seat and wiped down the steering wheel and ignition. He popped the trunk and examined it closely. It contained food and water, ammunition, and several more weapons. There was also a first aid kit.

"I'll send someone for the car. We need to go."

"I am going to the airport," I said.

"*We* are going to the airport," he clarified.

"You fly helicopters, too?" I asked surprised to see Preston when I climbed into the back of the chopper.

He smirked. "I've flown planes since I was a kid. The military was kind enough to expand my training," he said. "It's good to see you, sir."

"You have no idea," I agreed as I buckled myself in. "Marshall?" I asked.

"No idea," Dawes said.

Within twenty minutes, my wound was cleaned and bandaged, I was dressed, and we were landing at the airport. It might be wiser to charter a flight rather than to wait for the next available direct flight. Dawes pressed to fly commercial. "Be patient. We'll be on a flight in a few hours. You need to get a shower and a haircut and trim off all that scruff. They'll think you're a terrorist for sure. You look awful."

I heard his words, but I was adamant. I had been cooped up in that cabin for weeks and I knew that Caroline was in danger. The cost was of no consequence. I was edgy and impatient; I needed to be in Dubai. I wanted to be with her. I needed to get to her. "Thanks, but no," I said caustically. "I am chartering a flight. I refuse to wait any longer." Dawes read the expression in my eyes and backed down.

CHAPTER 37

I liked the mornings when Sefa left early for the clinic and I was allowed to wake at my own speed. I rolled over to see if I might fall back to sleep when I heard someone downstairs. It must be earlier than I thought or maybe I had slept late and Fatma was already there. I dismissed it and closed my eyes in hopes of going back to sleep.

I wasn't resting as well as I had been. It was more difficult to get comfortable and stay comfortable during the night. At thirty-three weeks, I had nearly every pillow I could find propped around me, and then inevitably, as soon as I would get comfortable, I would need to pee. Once I took care of that and returned to the bed, settling all comfortable again, the baby would start kicking or have the hiccups for what felt like hours. It had been one of those nights. Most of the time, it was my only entertainment, so I would lie there, imagining my dark-skinned baby girl with long eyelashes blinking up at me. Hashim didn't know we were going to have a daughter, which saddened me. He should be relishing in this time with me, but then I doubted. I always doubted. Would he relish or would he retreat?

I stroked over my ever-expanding belly; she was sleeping peacefully, now. My short stature didn't leave much room for her to grow, so she grew out and around and under my ribcage. Sometimes it felt like she had squashed my stomach up into my lungs. I ate all day because I couldn't get enough calories in one sitting, and I panted all the time. The pool was the only place I had relief, but I looked more like a buoy bobbing about in the ocean than the Olympic swimmer I imagined myself to be as I swam lap after lap, every day.

I heard another sound then, unfamiliar and slightly unnerving. Maybe I was just being paranoid. We hadn't heard from Dawes again, so I was unusually edgy which was also influencing my sleep, or lack thereof. I quietly slipped from the bed and went into the bathroom. I wrapped myself in the robe that barely covered my belly, now. I walked to the door and opened it quietly. I could hear doors opening downstairs. I panicked thinking it might be a burglar, but then considered who would ever be able to get through Alham and Adi. I heard a grunt and a scuffle and something falling to the floor. Instinctively, I tried not to make a sound as I stepped back into the room. I went into the closet and hid. I crouched down behind Hashim's pants rack. Was I being foolish and paranoid?

"Caroline?" I heard my name muffled from downstairs. "Caroline, are you here?" The voice was insistent and edgy, but I knew that voice. I smiled through the fear and my heart fluttered. "Hashim?" I panted, relieved. Hashim was there! I called out again, "Hashim!" I found it hard to get up from the floor, so I crawled on my hands and knees until I reached the closet door to pull myself up. The door opened, then, and I looked up but not into the face I expected.

"Marshall?" I panted and shook my head. "No," I said confused and insistent. I was sure I'd heard Hashim's voice.

He reached down and pulled me from the floor. I screamed and kicked and fought him off the best I could. He jerked me and I stumbled into him. "Settle down! I don't want to hurt you!" he grunted.

"Hashim!" I screamed at the top of my lungs. Marshall put his hand over my mouth and moved me back into the closet. I wriggled my face away from his hand and bit him as hard as I could. He cursed under his breath and jerked my head back holding my hair as he'd done months ago. I reached back and scratched his neck. As before in my bedroom, Marshall was dragged away from me, and he released me. I fell onto the floor on my hands and knees. I felt my stomach tighten and the pain was unexpectedly abrupt. I couldn't focus on anything but the sudden pain. I gripped my midsection and tried to breathe. I couldn't even look up to see who had pulled Marshall away. They had moved into the bedroom and I knew they were fighting. From the sound of the last blow, the bed had collapsed onto the floor. Sounds of destruction echoed into the closet and I cringed not knowing who was winning.

I crawled to the closet door and looked out. I was still panting, but the pain had subsided. With the curtains drawn, the room was dark and I could barely make out the two men fighting. One toppled over the other and they were grappling and punching one another. From the shadows, it looked like Alham and he was dominating over Marshall. No wonder I thought I'd heard Hashim's voice. Alham could handle himself; I would be fine, but I was so disappointed that it wasn't Hashim.

Another wave of pain washed through me. Fake contractions had come in waves recently and I knew the familiar feeling, but this was different. I retreated into the closet, away from the chaos. In seconds, I was completely absorbed and focused on what was happening to my body. The pain even affected my hearing; everything was muffled and I felt dizzy and weak as my stomach tightened and my entire body went rigid. The pain passed again and I pulled on the lower hanging rod to stand. I needed to get out of there.

"Caroline! Caroline, what are you doing down there? Are you hurt?" Powerful arms reached down and pulled me to my feet. They took me forcefully and released me just as suddenly. "What the hell!" he exclaimed.

"I'm not hurt. I just had a hard time getting up." After regaining my balance and checking myself, I looked up into my rescuer's face, but it was not Ahlam. His hair and beard were long and untrimmed. His shoulders were broader and I searched his face. Though they were crazed, his familiar eyes widened with concern. I reached up and put my hand on his face. "Hashim," I smiled and tears flooded my eyes. "You're okay! You came!" He nodded solemnly and kissed my palm. His strong arms took me in his embrace and he held me securely. I cringed as another loud crash came from downstairs. "What's happening? Who's downstairs?"

"Dawes." That relieved me, too, and I eased further into his embrace. He kissed the top of my head and stroked my hair. I opened my eyes and saw the state of the bedroom. Marshall either lay unconscious or dead on the floor next to the collapsed bed.

"Is he dead?" I asked.

"No, but I am not concerned about him." He held me tightly and I breathed in all that I could of him. He moved my face towards his and he kissed me, moving his hand behind my neck and lifting me up onto my toes as I pressed in to deepen the kiss.

"Oh!" I exclaimed in pain and gripped at my belly. I leaned forward and gripped Hashim's arm. "Call Sefa!"

"What is wrong?"

"The baby!" I panted through clenched teeth, trying desperately to get away from the pain.

He scooped me up into his arms, and in three long strides, we were making our way down the stairs. "Call Sefa! She needs to go to the hospital," he demanded at Dawes as he placed me gently on the sofa. Dawes was kneeling next to Adi who was lying in a similar position to Marshall upstairs. Adi was not unconscious but bound and gagged. His creepy eyes glaring up at me. Dawes' hand was wrapped with a cloth and blood streaked the floor. He'd been cut. Hashim brought me some water and forced me to lie down on my side.

"She was already on her way home. Meet her downstairs," Dawes said. I was weak and losing strength, the exertion I'd used to fight Marshall earlier left me suddenly sleepy. "Marshall?" he asked and Hashim shrugged.

I don't remember much of the details. The pains came in waves, increasing in intensity. Sefa drove while Hashim held me tightly against him. I was admitted through the emergency room and placed in a room on the maternity floor. The medicine to stop the contractions made my heart race and the other medication to help me relax made me edgy and defiant. "Come on, breathe with me like you and Fatma practiced. You need to relax," Sefa said. I tried, really, I did, but it didn't work. She moved slightly so a nurse could inject something into my IV.

"What's that?" I asked.

"Something to help you sleep," the nurse said kindly.

"Here, let me try," Hashim said moving closer to my side and leaning over me.

"Your hair is so long. Where were you? I was so worried." I touched his hair and stroked his beard.

"Kennedy had me, but everything is alright, now. You have nothing to worry about. Dr. Mohamed said you need to relax and rest. Caroline, please, close your eyes." I wanted to see his face; I'd been too long without it. "I will not leave you. I will be here when you wake." I searched his eyes for any hint of deception and then did as he commanded.

"Dawes?" I whispered.

"He is fine. He is more concerned for you than he is for himself. You need to relax and not worry about anyone else right now but yourself and our child," Hashim whispered low into my ear. Hashim's hand on my back was nice and warm, but when he moved it up and placed it on the back of my neck, I sighed. He bent even further and kissed my cheek and the corner of my mouth. Had I not been trying to ward off labor, I would have attacked him. My lips parted as my head leaned back against his hand. I was melting. He smiled and I liked the way his scraggly beard tickled when he whispered into my ear. "Are you relaxed, now?" I nodded.

"I promise to be very still if you keep doing that," I said with a relaxed smile in my voice. He nuzzled my neck and kissed down to my collar bone. I felt a wave of light contraction spread across my belly, but it was pleasant and soothing and almost orgasmic. I moaned in pleasure. The baby kicked hard then and Hashim moved away from me and looked down at my writhing belly. He had felt the kick, too.

"I don't think the baby liked that."

"No, we liked it; we liked it a lot." I took a deep breath and allowed the sedative to take effect.

I don't think I had slept too many hours when I woke hot and uncomfortable. My belly was hard and everything burned between my legs. "It's not working," I moaned.

Hashim was at my side. "Sefa!" he called. She had apparently fallen asleep.

"Oh, no!" I bellowed and bent double with the next contraction. "She's coming too early!" I exclaimed in a panic.

"She?" Hashim asked for clarification. "A girl, then?"

I nodded but only tears fell through the pain. "She won't make it! She's still too little!" I cried. I had to keep her inside me just a little bit longer.

"Caroline, you must relax," Sefa's soothing voice was comforting, but there was an unfamiliar edge to it. "We are doing everything to keep you and your baby completely safe."

Nurses rushed in, and I took a deep breath between the waves that had attacked me. One messed with my IV and the other adjusted the monitor around my belly. Just then another wave erupted over me and I grabbed Hashim's arm and pulled him into me. I needed him close because I thought I might die from the pain that was tearing my body apart. I gasped through the pain; I couldn't catch my breath. "Her name is Abbey, Abbey June," I panted as I held tightly to Hashim's arm. His eyes were wide with surprise. "Promise me, if I don't make it, she'll know Jesus," I panted, bombarded by the next wave that promised to be brutal. He shook his head. "Damn it, Hashim! Promise me or so help me God!"

"You are not dying, Caroline; you are just having a baby!" he argued, logically. Anger laced his words. He was frightened and I could see fear behind his facade.

"Her blood pressure is dropping," I heard a nurse say aloud, but I could already feel myself slipping. I was in so much pain that I thought I might pass out. I heard muttering and things clanging around me. Someone said something about the baby's heartrate. I didn't have time for Hashim's logic; I needed an answer.

"Sefa, Sefa, promise me," I demanded, finding my voice, again.

"I promise; she will know Him," she said, but I couldn't see her face clearly; everything was blurry.

Just then I let out a guttural scream and my water broke, hot and bloody, all over the bed between my legs. The nurses reacted quickly, then, but they were all talking too fast for my comprehension. "We're taking you to surgery, Caroline, the baby is in distress. We need to get her out immediately," Sefa said, her voice sounding professionally distant.

"No!" I screamed and grabbed Hashim's neck. I could feel the pressure of the baby's head between my legs.

"There's no time, Dr. Emir. The baby is here," said the nurse who was examining me. "Call NICU, we need them, immediately."

I opened my eyes then and saw the horror on everyone's faces. They knew this was bad; this was really, really bad. They collapsed the bed and put my feet in the stirrups. Sefa pulled me up into a sitting position and held my hand tightly. "You can do this, Choti Behan."

"When you feel the next contraction, I want you to push," the nurse commanded.

I caught my breath and prayed. *Please God, please don't take my baby,* I begged. *Keep her safe, Lord, please keep us all safe.* Hashim held me the best he could as I bellowed into his chest and panted. The pain was more intense than anything I could have imagined. The next contraction came hard and fast and I felt the instinct to push. I knew that she would be here soon.

Three pushes later and the nurse lifted a bloody, black-haired baby from between my legs. In the time it took to deliver her, several other nurses arrived and two doctors hurried in. I barely caught a glance of my baby before they whisked her away to the other side of the room. I couldn't see her; I was frantic to see her. I wanted to hold her. There were two teams in the room: one to treat me and the other to treat the baby. Sefa had released me almost immediately to be with her niece.

Hashim wiped my brow and forced me to look into his eyes. "Caroline, Caroline, look at me." I blinked and looked at him, but I really wanted to see my baby. He brushed the wisps of hair that clung to my sweaty face.

"I want to see her," I said. He nodded understandingly. I held out my arms like I could will her into them if I reached far enough. Another contraction followed and I delivered the afterbirth. It wasn't as painful as delivering our daughter, but it was not comfortable, either. I held onto Hashim, again, and cried. I was so afraid and felt alone. Although he was there, my insides and my arms were empty. My eyes grew heavy and I blinked back tears. Waves of dizziness washed over me. I tried to see my baby, again, but my vision was blurry. "I don't feel so good," I said as my head rolled back onto the pillow. "Hashim? Hashim?"

CHAPTER 37.5

Fools give full vent to their rage,
but the wise bring calm in the end.

– Proverbs 29:11

I felt her release me as her head lolled. "Caroline! Caroline! Open your eyes!" I demanded. "What is happening?" I asked the nurses and doctors who were working frantically on my wife. I was still holding her hand.

"Sir, please," a small nurse said as she moved in front of me to get to Caroline. She lowered the bed and they began preparing to move her. I heard words like *placental abruption* and *shock*. They were each focused on the necessary tasks. They were ignoring me. Within seconds, they had her ready to transport. Caroline's face was pale and drawn. I stared at her, but I was unable to get to her. They had covered her with a blanket so I no longer saw the blood that covered the bed.

"What is wrong? Caroline? Damn it! Someone, answer me! Where are you taking her?"

"We need to get her to surgery. Step away," the doctor demanded.

As her bed was wheeled through the door, someone handed me Caroline's jewelry: her wedding band, my wedding band, and the necklace she wore around her neck. I stared blankly at the gold in the palm of my hand.

"We will find you as soon as we have an update," another nurse said before she followed the team down the hall.

I looked up at the doctors and nurses who encircled the isolette. They were readying the baby for transport, as well. Sefa caught my eye and walked toward me. She placed her hand over my open palm and closed her fingers around mine.

"Hashim," she said, gently drawing my attention, "they are taking the baby to the NICU. Once she's stabilized, you can see her." I have no idea what she saw in my expression. I understood her words, but I had no idea if that was good or bad.

"Caroline?" I asked, unable to find my voice.

"The baby came too hard and fast; she was hemorrhaging. They are doing all they can. They'll let us know when she's out of surgery." I searched Sefa's eyes. They were willing me to understand, but I could comprehend nothing of what she was saying. "Would you like to see your daughter?" she asked, hesitantly. I could offer her no sign. She took my hand and led me. A nurse moved slightly and I was able to catch a glimpse of the tiny little thing that lay helpless and weak in a clear plastic box. I looked closer to see any detail, but except for a head of dark hair, everything else was covered by tubes and tape and monitors. I sickened at the thought. The nurse moved in front of me, again, and I stepped back and stumbled into the chair where Sefa slept only moments ago. "Do you need me? I'd like to go with them," Sefa said. I nodded. I wanted her to go with them, with the baby.

The room was suddenly empty, no beds, no carts, no equipment. Except for the drops of blood on the floor, there was no evidence that Caroline had even been there. How quickly complete chaos had turned into silence. I placed the chain around my neck, but when I opened my hand and looked at our wedding bands, I noticed for the first time that, like interlocking parts, her band fit inside mine. Had she not made her space in my heart to fit just the same. I replaced my ring and vowed never to remove it again; I held hers between my fingertips, examining the inscription: *Proverbs 31:10-12*

What had the Proverb been? I racked my brain to remember the verse. What was it? Then, the words returned to me: *Who can find a virtuous and capable wife? She is more precious than rubies. Her husband can trust her, and she will greatly enrich his life. She brings him good, not harm, all the days of her life.*

My heart ached and I bowed my head over my hands, over her ring, over the regret. My efforts had been in vain. When it was all said and done, I had saved her from nothing. I was a constant disappointment; I had not been able to give her the assurance that our child would know her god. Caroline had recited my ring's inscription from memory. "It's from the Old Testament," she had said. Ironic that I'd memorized nearly the entire book in Hebrew for fun when I was ten. *Proverbs 18:22. The man who finds a wife finds a treasure, and he receives favor from the Lord.*

In the very moment she felt herself slipping away, Caroline had no thoughts of herself, but for another. She was more concerned for the salvation of our unborn child than for her own. She was unwavering in her faith and was secure in her salvation; of course, she would not be concerned with herself, she was Caroline.

"God, I have no plans to make this a habit, but for Caroline, I ask... for favor." My voice trailed off and I was overcome by the guilt that it was not for Caroline that I was making this request, but for my own selfishness. Everything I did was to indulge my selfish, self-centered nature, but I did not want to lose her. Acknowledgement of past wrongs was hard. Repentance was harder. "I understand and I am humbled," I confessed to no one but God. I sat, head bowed, for a long time.

"Mr. Emir," a female voice interrupted the silence. I looked up. A nurse had come into the room. "Would you please follow me? Dr. Emir requests that you join her in the NICU." I stood and placed Caroline's ring just past the first knuckle of my little finger on my left hand. I followed the nurse to an elevator where she directed me to the correct floor. The elevator opened up into a brightly decorated lobby. There were handprints and footprints lining the walls. A small reception desk sat in the corner of the room near two large doors. "May I help you?" a young woman asked.

"I am Hashim Emir; my sister, Dr. Emir, sent for me."

"Oh, yes, one moment. Please, have a seat." She stood and swiped her badge before she walked through the large doors. I chose to stand. A few moments later, she returned with Sefa.

"Is everything alright? Have you heard about Caroline?"

"No, nothing, yet. It's too soon. Come, I want you see your daughter." She smiled comfortingly and her eyes sparkled with familiar delight.

"I want to see Caroline."

Sefa's face grew serious. "I understand that, but that's not possible, so for the time being, I want you to come with me." I shook my head. I was unsure of my thoughts on the subject. "Come," she demanded, "The doctor wishes to speak with you." I suddenly wanted to fight her. I wanted to deny her. Conflict rose in my chest and my jaw stiffened, but then she gave me a look that dared me to challenge her. She put her hand on my back and gently guided me through the doors.

The room was dimly lit and stiflingly warm. There were clear cases, each containing a tiny little creature. I refused to look directly into any of them. I heard strange beeps and the sounds of air passing through tubes. I considered myself brave and strong, but at that moment, I was weak and fear gripped me. Had it not been for Sefa's hand on me, I would have bolted from the room. I was both repelled and drawn toward the incubator at the far left of the room where Sefa led me.

"Mr. Emir, I am Dr. Morris, head of neonatology." He spoke in a British accent and hesitated like I should be impressed by that. When I said nothing, he continued, "As you know, your daughter was born premature. She will remain with us until she's viable. The nurses here are excellent and will take care of her every need. We are pleased with her birthweight, and although we are giving her some oxygen, she is breathing well and her lungs are clear. Those are good signs; I am very optimistic."

I nodded and looked at Sefa. Her eyes were bright and she was smiling. "Hashim, this is good news."

"She is stable and she is in good hands. You may see her as often as you'd like. You can talk to her and touch her, and when the nurses are ready to help you, you can even hold her. Do you have any questions?" he asked.

I shook my head. "No. Thank you." I did not recognize my own voice. Dr. Morris extended his hand and I shook it without thinking. He turned to Sefa and thanked her as well before he was taken away by a nurse who handed him an electronic tablet and led him toward another infant.

A nurse stepped forward. "Hello, I'm Margaret, I will be tending to your little one. Have you decided on a name? We like to call them by their names as much as possible. Talking to them helps to stimulate their rapidly developing brains."

Without hesitation, I answered, "Her name is Abbey, Abbey June."

"That's beautiful. Would you like to get a closer look?"

Sefa nodded and urged me forward. I leaned over and took a good look at the infant lying there. Little tufts of black hair stuck out from the sides of her pink cap. Thin, black lashes lined her closed eyes and her tiny nose held an even tinier tube. Her skin was tanned but not as dark as mine. Her fingers were long and her tiny little toes were perfect. As I examined her, I exhaled for the first time in hours.

"She's got a strong suck. Look at her go on that hand. We'll offer her a bottle tomorrow. I don't think she'll have any problem with it," Margaret commented.

Abbey stretched and her perfect lips yawned. She was fascinating to behold. Those were Caroline's lips and I was curious to see her eyes, but I knew it was too early to tell. Sefa's arm was around me now. She could sense the overwhelming emotions that threatened to spill out over me. "She's healthy and strong. Caroline did everything right."

I cleared the emotion from my throat the best I could. "There is a word in Estonian that sounds very much like the pronunciation of her name. It means *help me*." I released a tense chuckle. "Ironic, is it not? Her name is a call to aid, yet she is the most helpless thing in the world." Sefa smiled and I shared a meaningful look with my sister. "Thank you, Sefa. I owe you. I had no idea." My struggle for words gripped me. My heart was in my throat, pulsing, throbbing, catching my breath. I could hardly breathe.

"I know, Little Brother. Men rarely do until they see it for themselves."

I stood there for an hour watching Abbey sleep and breathe and found myself counting her heartbeats like each one was precious. Sefa returned with a cup of coffee. "Caroline is out of surgery. She's in recovery. We can see her soon." I sipped on the hot liquid, feeling torn and pulled in two different directions. My mother and my sister were important and significant women in my life. They always had been, but I never, ever, felt a sense of protection over them, even when we were on different continents. They were independent and capable of taking care of themselves. Caroline and Abbey were on different floors in the same hospital, and I felt like I was being stretched across the universe between them.

***

Caroline was pale but breathing easily and resting when I entered the room. She looked peaceful. I pulled a chair closer to the bed and sat watching her. Only moments ago, I had left Abbey resting peacefully as well. I laid my head on the bed next to Caroline and closed my eyes. "Thank you," I muttered and knew God heard me. I fell asleep holding her hand.

"Hashim," Caroline said in a whisper as she squeezed my hand. I lifted my head and saw her eyes were open. "Abbey?" she asked.

I smiled, unable to contain my relief at seeing Caroline's eyes and the joy at the mention of our daughter's name. "She is fine, exactly perfect," I assured her. "She is more beautiful than I ever imagined." That made Caroline smile and tears of relief rolled down her face. I stood and wiped them away. "Today is not a day for tears."

EPILOGUE

Our daughter nurses in her sleep while her father speaks to her in a variety of languages. I warn him that it will only confuse her, but he denies that fact. I have picked up some phrases over time. I like when he sings to her. Well, it sounds like singing to me, but Hashim says they are just the Psalms in Hebrew and complains how the English language butchers the actual beauty of King David's words.

"If she is to know the God of Abraham and His son, then she will know His words in their origin; she will know their true depth," he insists.

We returned to Miami as soon as the consulate finished Abbey's paperwork. She was nearly eight weeks old. It was good timing and I was completely healed by then. Abbey and I spent two weeks in the hospital recovering before they would release us. She made up for lost time, and by her due date, she weighed nearly nine pounds.

Hashim plans to work and teach some locally at the Department of Defense and freelance occasionally, but for now, he works when Abbey and I nap and is completely attentive and absorbed when we're awake. He rarely leaves us and we take nothing for granted. He's still incredibly intense and focused, but he has so much of his father in him that's untapped.

Rana's acceptance of me and the example as a grandfather are marked. He is truly our Abba, our father, Abbey's devoted and indulgent grandpa. Our daughter instantly won Ecrin's heart. My mother-in-law doesn't despise me anymore, but she's still reserved which is her nature, except with Abbey. She's as pliable as butter when it comes to her precious granddaughter. I've grown to love and appreciate Ecrin, and I believe, she's done the same with me.

371

Sefa and Dawes live together in Virginia. They fly down most weekends. Sefa asks him nearly every week when they'll move to Miami to be closer. "When you marry me, I'll move to Miami," he jokes. I don't know who is more stubborn between them. They may live in Virginia forever.

Of course, Nita is amazing and Mizhir, well, he's lost his mind. He walks every morning with Abbey securely in his arms and whispers the secrets of the flowers into her tiny ears, but then I catch his eyes sometimes and I think he may actually be explaining the intricate tuning of engines and the thrill of speed to her.

Hashim doesn't speak of his time at the cabin, and I refuse to press him; I am satisfied with what little he's told me. Kennedy and Marshall are both dead, but he doesn't speak of that either. I know he did everything to protect Abbey and me, and I pray that in time he forgives himself. He's careful and mindful and even more protective than he was before, not in a crazy, creepy way, but in a way that secures me.

Hashim and I had no idea we'd end up here, but I chose to love him and he gave me a child. The best part is that he's chosen to love me in return, and love me, he does. No marriage is perfect because it's a relationship forged by imperfect people. Being forced together and then forced apart permanently altered us. We are determined to get this right. What would Aunt June say? She'd say, "Child, marriage doesn't guarantee you will be together forever; it's only a piece of paper. It takes love, respect, trust, understanding, friendship, and faith to make it last." She would laugh her boisterous laugh, but I could only smile, now. In the beginning, our marriage had just been a piece of paper, an inconvenient necessity, but now it was so much more.

EPILOGUE .5

"Hashim, stop it you're only going to confuse her," Caroline says with a playful smile in her voice.

"I will not confuse her; she needs to know." I kiss Abbey's head as she nurses and then the top of her mother's full breast before finding Caroline's lips.

"Everyone speaks a different language to her," she says between kisses. "I speak English, Nita speaks Spanish, and I have no idea what Mizhir says to her because he's always whispering. Then your mother and father are constantly warring between Turkish and Urdu. I have no idea what her first word will be, and I probably won't understand it when she does start talking."

"Caroline." Oh, how I love to say her name aloud. Instead of continuing my argument, I kiss her instead.

Her calm spirit attracts me even more when she tends to Abbey's needs. I am drawn to their attachment and I want to envelop them both and hold in every minute. We have been back in Miami now for a couple of months. Abbey and Caroline spent two weeks in the hospital recovering from their traumatic birth experience. It has taken me longer than that, and honestly, I am not sure if I am yet recovered. The doctors assured Caroline and me that more children are possible. She hopes to one day give me a son. I am content for now which surprises us both.

"Sing to her," Caroline requests in a whisper as Abbey drifts into sleep. She knows good and well that I am not singing, but I do enjoy the cadence and the rhythm. King David was quite the lyricist. I watch their eyes flutter. Abbey may have my coloring and dark hair, although it is wavy like Caroline's, but she managed to get her mother's light eyes. I can thank Ecrin for that genetic contribution; I can thank my father and mother for many things, their example, especially.

I do not mind indulging Caroline's request; she may have whatever she desires. Selfishly, I find constant comfort in the words. They are easy to remember and picture in my mind. I have no doubt God hears every word, no matter the language. Kennedy and Marshall both died at my hand, and I have made peace with that. God and I are on speaking terms and Caroline is exceedingly grateful.

I love her and I love Abbey, and I want them both to know and hear it often, but the words still get stuck in my throat sometimes. I am much better at expressing it than saying it aloud. One day, perhaps it will roll off my tongue as easily as it does Caroline's.

I wait patiently for my turn, watching and appreciating. When Abbey is content and settled, Caroline turns to me and we focus on one another and reconnect at the end of the day. She is truly my wife, my mate, my responsibility, my beloved. She is my *Sweet Caroline*.

An excerpt from Kelda's next novel:

DAWES

A Companion to Sweet Caroline

MIAMI three years ago

I was on assignment when she arrived. No one expected her; she just showed-up without warning. Apparently, that was her way. The agency I worked for was in the business of keeping assets safe. My current assignment was contracted through the Pentagon. The asset I was assigned was capable of protecting himself, but his handler, Kennedy, thought it best that he be watched and tended to personally. He was doing important work for the government.

We had been at his Miami house for two days. It was a heavily-guarded compound on five acres of prime Florida real estate. Again, I found my services unnecessary. Nevertheless, I did as I was commanded. I was relegated to the guest house and allowed a great deal of leisure. Other than running each morning and occasional errands, I was left to my own devices which included my own training regimen, cleaning weapons, and shooting at the firing range.

My asset's name was Hashim Emir. Very little was mentioned of his family in the preliminary dossier. On paper, they appeared relatively normal. His parents were economists; his older sister was a physician. It listed where they had each been educated, graduate studies, and a brief resume. No photos were included. I wasn't in the habit of presuming anything, but this family was nothing like I had ever encountered before. From the depth of security surrounding this property, they weren't the garden variety economists. They were an intense mixture of intelligence, languages, ethnicities, and cultures. Intense and extreme described them perfectly.

I was invited; no, I was expected to eat dinner in the main house with my asset. The first evening, I met his mother and father. His mother was a beautiful woman with refined features and elegance. She welcomed me to her table, but wasn't interested in me directly. The tension between mother and son was thick, nothing like I had ever experienced. She was beautiful, yet formidable. His father was gentille. He was engaging, and I enjoyed listening to him when he spoke. Unlike his wife, he did not speak anything but English in my presence. He was careful to include me in the conversation.

The second night, I was again summoned to dinner, but this was a completely different evening. We were just being seated at the table, when a new voice trickled down my spine like warm water. It had to be the sister; the likenesses were uncanny. She was vivacious, captivating, electric. Sure, she was beautiful like their mother, but that wasn't the only thing about her that caught my eye. She wooed us all into submission.

She had her father's ability to engage others, but her skills were multiplied like they were on steroids. She spoke English fluently with a hint of slang or was it a twang? I wondered where she'd learned that. She was even more striking than her mother, but softened and easily approachable. Her presence beckoned.

"This is Dawes," Mrs. Emir said, introducing me. "He is here with Hashim. He is staying in the guesthouse."

"Hello, Dawes," she said as she took my hand formally. "I'm Sefa. It's a pleasure to make your acquaintance. So, what brings you to Miami? Do you work with Hashim?" She was to be seated next to me, so I pulled out the chair for her.

"In a manner of speaking, yes," I said, closing the subject. She looked up at me curiously and smiled. *Damn.*

Dinner was delicious. The conversation warmer and more familial the second evening. Sefa brought laughter to this family. She brought a sense of ease. She even made Emir smile which came as a complete surprise. She pressed her mother's buttons pretty easily; that was evident the moment she walked into the room. Their mother was disapproving and judgmental, and yet, at the same time, proud and indulging of her children.

After dinner, I excused myself. I was inside the guesthouse watching a movie when I heard something outside. I removed the pistol from the holster at my side and eased the door open. I heard a splash and saw water moving. No lights were on in the pool; someone was swimming in complete darkness. I cautiously walked toward the pool and peered into the dark. Her head popped up from the shadowy depths and I relaxed.

"It's just me; don't shoot," she said smiling and lifting her hands in surrender. I could see her white teeth and her widened eyes. "Are you always this paranoid?"

"I'm here to look out for your brother. I wouldn't call that paranoia, I'd call it job security."

She giggled and swam to the edge closest to me. "You can put that away. There's no threat," referring to the pistol. "Besides, there are about six guards within ten paces of the house. Security is always heavier at night. I would have guessed they had already briefed you."

"They have." I placed the weapon back into the holster.

"Hmmm. Where are you from?" she asked politely.

"Albany. Albany, New York."

"You don't sound like a New Yorker."

"I'm not from the city; not all New Yorkers have the same accent."

"How long will you be here?" she asked curiously, swimming along the edge of the pool.

"As long as it's necessary."

"So, are you just here to babysit my little brother?"

"Among other things."

"That sounds incredibly boring," she said petulantly and swam backwards toward the center of the pool.

"Part of the job," I said flatly. "Sometimes jobs are boring."

"I know," she sighed, "that's why I like my job immensely. It takes me all over the world, and I rarely have cause to do the same thing twice."

"What do you do?" I asked, although I already knew.

"I'm a pediatrician with World Health, but I work with more than just children." She treaded water and dipped her head back, perfectly at ease. "It's a lovely night; would you care to swim?"

I considered her invitation and looked around the pool. It was indeed a pleasant evening and much warmer than New York or Virginia that time of year. It was late and the house and grounds were quiet. "Do you often swim this late?"

"I'm still a little jet-lagged, so it's not that late for me. I'll settle into Miami time in the next day or two. So, are you going to swim with me, or not?"

"I'm not sure that's a good idea. I'm new here, and I have a feeling it wouldn't be encouraged."

"What, swimming? Exercise is always encouraged." I could see her teeth again when she smiled. Her eyes glimmered like the water. She was teasing and engaging. Her tone and her ease in the water lured me. She made it the most desirable thing in that very moment.

"Okay, I'll swim." I laid my phone and holster carefully on the side of the pool. I pulled off my shirt and dove in. The water was cool and invigorating. I swam a couple of laps and then treaded water in the corner of the pool.

"Want to race?" she asked, playfully. Everything she said sounded fun and enticing. I hadn't spent much time with her brother, but *fun* and *enticing* were two words I would not use to describe him.

I was a decent swimmer and had competed some in high school, but I had a feeling she was the better swimmer. "Alright," I said.

She seemed delighted that I would play along. "We'll start easy. Just one full lap."

"What does the winner get?" I asked.

"To swim with me again tomorrow night." Her eyes danced in the reflection of the water. We moved to the far edge of the pool and took our positions. I flexed my shoulders and rolled them around to loosen them up. "You've swum before."

"Yes, some in high school."

"That will make it all the more interesting." Her eyebrow cocked as though considering me again. "On your mark, get set, go."

We took off and she was a strong swimmer, but thankfully I was able to keep up and not embarrass myself too badly. My height was a noted advantage.

The first race she beat me squarely. "Best two out of three?" I panted. "I need to warm up."

"No, you need to improve your time. I'll race with you again tomorrow night," she said with all the command and benevolence of a queen.

"Is that a request or demand?"

"I never demand anything," she said innocently. "It's ultimately your choosing, but I'd recommend it." She did something with her eyes that she'd done earlier at dinner. It bordered on hypnosis. I blinked hard and shook my head slightly to break the connection. *Damn.* Every cautious fiber in my body prickled and I excused myself from the pool.

"Goodnight, Dr. Emir."

She made no reply and dove back into the depths of the pool.

The next morning, I ran with Emir as was his habit. He said it helped to clear his head. After my brief encounter with his sister, it helped to clear mine as well. Emir returned to his work; I met with the head of security for their property and gained a better understanding of how their operation worked. It was impressive to say the least. I was given a tour of the shooting range and the exercise facility. Again, impressive. I had already been introduced to their gardener and driver, Mizhir. He was a meek, little man, but I recognized former military training. He was incredibly disciplined and intensely humble. He observed everything. I also felt confident he would give his life to protect this family.

The day before, I had been introduced to the household staff and the workings there. Nita, the cook, was a squat Cuban woman who managed the house with three maids. She was a force to be reckoned with. The Emirs were cautious people, but once allowed into their inner circle, the trust ran deep. My job was to protect my asset, but I was surrounded by people who had been protecting Emir for a good portion of his life. They knew him and his habits better. I would observe and learn from them as well.

The second night at dinner with the sister was just as entertaining. Emir was finally relaxed, or at least, relaxed for him. Mr. and Mrs. Emir seemed more accustomed to my presence and for the first time, directed questions toward me. Well, actually the sister asked questions that forced me to engage, and when I didn't expound, it forced Mr. Emir to question me at length. He wanted to know about my background and training. He didn't ask for the specifics of my military service, but he was interested in my deployments, my education, and pursuits. I felt like I was being interviewed for the position I already held. I wondered if Sefa would swim, but I didn't dare mention it at dinner.

Later that night, I put on a pair of swim trunks and decided to improve my time as she'd suggested. I had warmed up and was completing a few laps of butterfly when I heard her dive into the pool next to me.

"I'm glad you're practicing. You don't like to lose, do you?"

"Not if I can help it," I said honestly. I could recognize another competitor. She didn't like to lose, either.

Tonight's race was much closer. I had hope that I would best her sooner than later, but it wouldn't be easy. We swam laps after that and it wasn't long before she was making conversation.

"What is your first name?" she asked.

"Liam."

"Liam Dawes," she repeated. "Are you Irish?"

"You could say that. My mother was a Kelly with a direct line to Dublin. My father's family only arrived two generations ago. They are fiercely proud of our heritage."

"Shamrocks and St. Patrick, Irish stew and cabbage?" she asked playfully.

"Yep, he's my namesake. I was christened Liam Patrick."

"Of course."

"Your English is very different from your brother's," I commented.

She laughed. "I know. My parents sent me to school for a time in the Carolinas."

"Whatever for?" I asked, assuming there were better schools abroad.

"My parents were working for a few years in a part of the world where it would be unsafe for me to live with them. There are many countries that do not welcome young women from the outside. I would have never been allowed to leave the house. It was best they find me a safe place so they could work without distraction. Besides, it was beautiful there and provided me the opportunity to hike and canoe and white-water raft. I enjoy the outdoors, so it was a good fit for me. They also had horseback riding and skiing in the winter."

"With all of that, when did you have time for academics?"

"Academics always came first. It was a small, exclusive girls' school. The student-teacher ratio was two-to-one. It was heavily science and mathematics based which pleased my parents; they intended me for medicine."

I thought briefly about trying to contain this woman, as a girl, in a house in a hostile country. It was probably best her parents settled her in the mountains on the other side of the world. "I guess you don't like being limited very often, do you?"

"Never," she said as she dove under the water away from me.

I looked forward to our evening swims. The third night we tied and the fourth night I finally beat her. She disputed and challenged my victory, but was a relatively good sport when on the fifth night, she couldn't dispute the win. Instead, she smiled, satisfied, swam towards me and kissed me quickly on the mouth. "Congratulations," she announced, "you are a worthy contender. Tomorrow, we will double our efforts and I will test your endurance."

The kiss took me completely by surprise. It was warm and wet and her lips were even more inviting than her smile or her laughter. We had become entirely too familiar with one another. "Goodnight, Dr. Emir," I said and excused myself again as I had the first evening.

ABOUT THE AUTHOR

Kelda shares her south Louisiana home with her husband, their four children and

four wacky dogs. With a passion for education and young people,

both young in age and young at heart,

she has homeschooled her four children through graduation

and has tutored students for over a decade.

In addition, Kelda holds a BA in elementary education and an MA in

counseling. Her fictional writing began in 2016 while facilitating a novel writing

class with her students. This is her second published work of fiction, following

IMPACT.

She self-published two non-fiction works: *Call Their Hearts Home* and

TWPH – Insights into Living with Teens.

When she's not writing, she's watching movies, listening to audiobooks,

knitting, quilting, or crocheting, all the while, playing great music in the

background like a soundtrack. Writing is a compulsion that occurs amid the

chaos of life and dogs and constant interruptions.

She believes life is full of opportunities to love.

Be embraced.

Made in the USA
San Bernardino, CA
01 April 2020

66635145R00236